Deep Stepping Stones

~ § ~

Robert D. Miller

Book Publishers Network
P.O. Box 2256
Bothell • WA • 98041
Ph • 425-483-3040
www.bookpublishersnetwork.com

Copyright © 2010 by Robert D. Miller
Graphic clipart © 2009 Jupiterimages Corporation

All rights reserved. No part of this book may be reproduced, stored in, or introduced into a retrieval system, or transmitted in any form, or by any means (electronic, mechanical, photocopying, recording, or otherwise) without the prior written permission of the publisher.

Author's Note

The characters in *Deep Stepping Stones* as well as the events within the novel are fictitious, and any similarity to real people or events is completely coincidental. In order to give the reader a sense of reality, the names and locations of the cities and towns are factual.

Places, street names, and mine names and locations described about Butte, Montana, are or were real. The facts regarding the mines in Butte are also as accurate as possible.

10 9 8 7 6 5 4 3 2 1

Printed in the United States of America

LCCN 2009914191
ISBN10 1-935359-28-2
ISBN13 978-1-935359-28-9

Editor: Julie Scandora
Cover Designer: Laura Zugzda
Typographer: Stephanie Martindale

Acknowledgement

Deep Stepping Stones would not have been possible if it were not for my wonderful wife, Sukey, and her meticulous reading of each and every chapter draft, making corrections, and giving extremely helpful suggestions. I also owe much to my generous sister-in-law, Joanne, whose proofreading captured many of my errors before the manuscript was sent to the publisher. Without question, a manuscript that is publication-ready could not have been accomplished without the efforts of my editor, Julie. Her questions, suggestions, and meaningful changes helped create a novel which is a good read. Of course, there would be no way of publishing this work without Sheryn at Book Publishers Network. Thank you for your confidence and encouragement! Finally, I owe a dept of gratitude to my family and friends who continuously encouraged me to work on the manuscript and provided helpful suggestions as well. My heart felt thanks and indebtedness goes out to each one. I hope you, the reader, enjoy reading the novel as much as I enjoyed writing it.

CHAPTER ONE

From his cavernous southeast corner office on the eighteenth floor, Peter Zeleniak basked in the warmth of the sun as the new day matured from dawn to daylight. Early rays of the waking brilliance flooded the room. Even though the glass walls reflected most of the solar heat, Zeleniak could feel the soothing warmth. The Federal Bureau of Investigation's Rocky Mountain regional director looked down on the city of Denver, the mile-high metropolis, coming to life.

Spring was just around the corner, and only scattered piles from earlier snowfalls, hiding like thieves in the darkest shadows, still remained as a reminder of the exiting winter. Soon the lawns would come to life, buds on fruiting trees would burst forth, and spring flowers would extend their leafy arms, reaching toward the life-sustaining sun. Suddenly, the door opened and dried up Zeleniak's daydreaming thoughts.

Jessica Michaels, Zeleniak's secretary, stepped briskly through the opening. Graying brown hair gave away her age, mid-fifties, and her no-nonsense attitude. And her simple but professional attire perfectly matched her office demeanor: all business. A navy blue straight-line skirt ended just below the knees, and a stark white blouse showed between the lapels of the matching jacket. Nondescript nylons led to basic shoes, which matched the suit. Ideal footwear for the working office woman, their solid heels lifted her only an inch off the floor.

"Peter," she stated sharply as she walked toward her boss of ten years, "you need to see this. It's a message from our office in Billings." She handed the printed page to Zeleniak and then stepped back out of his personal space, a habit she had acquired early in her secretarial career.

PRIORITY MESSAGE
ATTENTION: Regional Director, Peter Zeleniak
RE: Unknown location of Montana Agents

The succinct statement jumped off the typed page like arrows sent upon Custer at the Battle of the Little Big Horn. Two highly trained agents gone missing? The case they were investigating held little importance beyond the local level. It did not impact national security, nor did it seem to involve a great risk. Why would two agents just vanish into thin air?

Someone had stepped on someone else's turf and looked under the wrong stone. Peter felt the wave of cold as it struck the nape of his neck, as though ice water was being poured down his neck and spine. "This is," he thought to himself, "really bad." His immediate response was to contact his superior in Washington, DC, and request assistance in searching for the missing agents.

Once Miss Michaels had contacted Washington, Zeleniak picked up the phone and relayed the information to his superior, Robert Nickels. Nickels agreed that a team should commence an immediate search before clues grew cold. He assured Zeleniak that within twenty-four hours a team would arrive in Butte, Montana, the last known destination of the two lawmen.

~ § ~

A light snow was falling as Jim Addis glanced out the window of the white and blue Lear jet, anticipating getting back on the ground. At six feet four inches and about 250 pounds, he felt confined in his leather swivel chair on the plane. Far from overweight, the thirty-four-year-old prided himself on his great physical shape and adhering to his exercise regimen, regardless. He worked out every day—lifting weights Monday,

Wednesday, and Friday, followed by running five to seven miles; then running at least ten miles on the "off" days.

As the jet made a slight right turn, seemingly following the mountains, he could see the community of Butte below. A semi-large layout of soccer fields spread out near what appeared to be a school building. He concluded from its size and somewhat small parking lot near the building that the school most likely was an elementary school. Then he was peering into the main part of the city and the larger campus of what he perceived as a college. "Most likely Montana Tech," he thought. He recalled reading about the college in the briefing materials he had received before boarding the plane at Andrews Air Force Base in DC.

The jet was continuing its right turn, and he could make out a large body of water. "Kind of strange location for a lake," Addis muttered. "Why would a city, here in Montana, have that in the middle of it?"

"That would be the lake created when the Berkeley Open Pit mine was closed in 1982 and allowed to fill," the passenger seated next to Addis commented. He turned toward his smaller framed friend with a questioning glance. The companion continued his narrative. "Actually, the water is highly toxic, and being over seven hundred feet deep at its center, it'll take more than a hundred years to render it safe for human use. Every year, flocks of migrating birds land on it for rest only to discover their fatal error too late. Their bodies sometimes are found south of the city because the toxins don't always affect them quickly. However, anything that is left in the water will be dissolved by the acids that the water contains.

"Not exactly the best-liked place to visit by the locals. Seems in the '50s, the Anaconda Mining Company decided that using open pit mining of the mountain was more lucrative than maintaining the entertainment park, called The Columbia Gardens, created by the company for the enjoyment of the local citizens, many of whom worked in the mines. So the roller coaster, plane ride, dance floor, carrousel, and other fun things were torn down, some sold, some mysteriously burned, and the open pit mine was begun."

"Butte," Addis thought, "the 'Richest Hill on Earth.'" Other factoids of information began coming back to mind now. Originally, a gold and silver mining camp, the ethnic groups, including Italian, British, Chinese, German, Irish, and many others, established a community. Mostly a tent city, its population neared a hundred thousand at one time. Naturally, as with most mining towns, prostitution was rather common. Unlike most other cities with such establishments, Butte had its own claim to fame, so to speak. The Dumas Brothel, located in the center of what is called uptown Butte, had been renovated to serve as a national brothel museum. An attempt, recalled Addis, that failed to gain support beyond the city itself. Eventually copper became more desirable than the gold and silver for mining, and by World War II, Butte was producing over 10 percent of the world's copper. Shortly after the war's end, Butte could actually make a legitimate claim as the nation's richest city. Unfortunately, the Anaconda Company could not sustain its prosperity, and as the economy spiraled downward, so did the population to the point that now it hovered around thirty-five thousand.

Another slight right turn and Addis now found himself staring almost face to face with the continental divide running along the eastern edge of the community itself. A large object came into view.

Anticipating his question, Madden offered, "That would be the Lady of the Rockies. She was actually flown up to the mountaintop in pieces by helicopter and, I might add, not without some hair-raising and near fatal flights."

"She looks like she oversees Butte itself," Jim responded.

"And, that is exactly what she does and was intended to do," came Madden's reply.

The pilot announced he was making one last bank for his final approach into the Bert Mooney Airport, approaching from the south-southeast. Addis and Madden fastened their seatbelts snugly and then handed their drink glasses to the lone attendant who walked to their seats from the wet bar area of the craft's luxurious cabin.

The aircraft settled down through the darkness and the gently falling snowflakes as though a shiny white bird gliding to the earth. The city's streetlights could be seen approaching rapidly ahead, and soon the rubber tires met the frozen asphalt of the runway with a slight jar and then continued rolling smoothly as the plane completed its controlled fall from the skies and subsequent return to terra firma. The jet turned off the runway at the first taxiway and taxied past the commercial flight terminal. Jim could see people in the terminal, which gave him reason to believe that a SkyWest commercial flight was not too far behind his aircraft in arriving.

The Lear jet slowed as it approached a hanger, which, until now, had been closed and shrouded in darkness. Only a lonely floodlight from a nearby pole provided illumination of the hangar's entry. With the bureau's jet approaching, the hangar's large doors slowly opened, like a large mouth about to consume its prey, allowing the brilliant halogen white lights from its interior to flood the tarmac. Very slowly, the pilot steered the jet through the door and, when indicated by the ground crew chief, touched the brakes to halt the aircraft's movement. As the whine of the engines gradually softened to stillness, the door on the side of the fuselage by the cockpit door lowered, creating a staircase to the concrete floor of the hanger.

Steve Madden, the senior agent of the two stood just over five feet nine inches and about 180 pounds and, like Addis, Madden also was an avid runner. He quickly released the lap belt and led his partner down the stairs and across the floor of the metal building where a dark blue four-door, Lincoln Towncar with Montana "tax exempt" license plates sat in silence, having arrived before they had landed. The driver remained seated at its wheel. Though smaller than his partner, Madden motioned to the passenger door behind the driver. Addis opened the indicated door, entered, and took a seat as his friend and partner gave a quick thank you to a ground crewman for loading their two suitcases in the trunk. "Ok," Madden said to the driver, and the car began moving out of the hanger and turned toward the guarded gate located next to the hanger. The car picked up speed as it followed the roadway past the parking lot and westward away from the terminal. Harrison Avenue, the main north/south roadway in the community appeared quickly, and the driver slowed and came to a stop. Seeing no traffic, he accelerated onto Harrison, making a right turn and putting uptown in the windshield ahead of them. The car continued its northward progress until the buildings of Butte's business district surrounded it and its passengers. Soon after, it turned into the parking garage of the fabled Finlen Hotel.

"Here we are," the driver offered, bringing the car to a halt. He opened his door and, advancing to the trunk, unloaded the suitcases. By the time Addis and Madden had exited the rear seat area, the bags were already on the pavement, and the driver was closing the trunk.

"You guys won't need me tomorrow since it's a short walk to the Butte-Silver Bow Courthouse up on Granite Street—one block up and three over to the west. The DA's secretary told me they'll have a breakfast set up for you when you get there."

"Not a problem, Al," came Madden's reply. "We'll be there in time for the eight o'clock meeting. Do you know what floor and room we need to report to?"

"The second floor conference room," the driver replied.

With that, the two agents entered the hotel and approached the lobby registration desk. "Jim Addis and Steve Madden," Madden informed the middle-aged man standing behind the counter. The clerk acknowledged their arrival with a friendly smile and hearty hello. He informed them that they were staying in a historic hotel that had been honored with famous guests, such as Charles Lindberg and John F. Kennedy. The décor of the lobby gave every indication that the building had, indeed, seen a great number of historical events during its lifetime.

Thumbing through the box of registration cards, the clerk stopped once for each name and removed the appropriate card. After completing the registration, he handed an electronic key card to each of the men. "Room 454," the clerk uttered as he handed a key card to Steve and then, looking up at Jim, said, "Room 458 for you, sir." He then added, "According to the registration request, we set up room 456, between your rooms, as a workroom for you. We've placed a computer, DVD/tape videotape recording and playback machine as well as a viewing screen in the room. The city offices gave us several different maps, which we also put in there as well. If there is anything else you will require of us, please call the number printed on each of your keys. That's the personal cell phone of the hotel manager; he's taken residence here in the hotel during your stay to accommodate your needs."

"Thank you. That's good for now," replied Madden. Glancing at Addis and seeing no indication of any comment, he continued, "Goodnight. Please give each of us a wake-up call at 5:30 a.m."

As the two walked to their rooms, Madden informed Addis that a dinner reservation had been made earlier for them at an uptown restaurant. Each man placed his belongings in his respective room, returned to the hallway, and then left the hotel, turning west on Broadway for a quick walk to the restaurant in the next block. Upon entering and giving their names to the receptionist, they followed her to a corner table at which two men in casual clothes sat in waiting.

"Steve, good to see you again," the first gentleman greeted them, rising from his chair and extending a hand to Madden.

"Same here, Dan," replied Madden, taking the offered hand in a warm handshake. "Dan, this is my partner, Jim Addis. Jim, Dan O'Reilly, Butte-Silver Bow County district attorney." The two exchanged handshakes and mutual greetings. Dan, turning to the second man at the table, who had now risen, introduced them to Bill Marks, attorney general for the State of Montana.

"I've taken the liberty of ordering a bottle of wine for us," O'Reilly said, gesturing Madden and Addis to the two unoccupied seats at the table.

Addis made a cursory glance about the room. "Interesting atmosphere," he commented aloud. "Not often you find yourself sitting next to a vault for dinner."

Laughing, Marks told the visitors that the Acoma had once been a very active bank in uptown Butte. After closing, it sat for many years without being occupied. "Only about ten years ago did it reopen as the Acoma Restaurant and Lounge. It was more economical and made for better atmosphere to leave the vault in tact."

Addis and Madden took their seats and picked up the menus that had been previously placed in front of them. They could not help but notice before them the huge bowl of steaming hot spaghetti and meatballs, slathered with a thick, rich red sauce, an oval platter filled with sweet hot peppers, carrot sticks, green onions, pickled beets, and several strips of anchovies. A smaller dish containing artichoke dip and a basket of seasoned bread sticks sat nearby. "Doesn't look to me as though we need these," smiled Addis, gesturing to the menu he held.

"Welcome to Butte," O'Reilly replied. "This is our typical restaurant service and hospitality." Pausing for a moment, the local DA added, "I would suggest either a pasty or prime rib. The pasty is a local specialty and is mouth-watering to say the least, and the prime rib here is so juicy and tender you can cut it with your fork."

Madden chuckled and looked at Marks, "Pasties? I've heard of them—what erotic dancers wear—but not anything I'd want to eat."

Marks howled with laughter at the thought of comparing the two. "First of all, one has a short *a* sound, PA-stee, and that one you eat. The other has a long *a*, PAY-stee, and that's the little tassel stuck on the dancer's tits!" The entire group had to join in the laughter at the comparison. Marks then continued his cuisine lesson. "The pasty, I believe, as do a great number of Butte folk, came here from Wales. You begin with a flattened, circular piece of dough. Pile on half of the circle layers of diced meat, usually juicy, tender beef, chopped onion, and thinly sliced potatoes. Add a touch of salt, some pepper, and other seasonings and then fold the other half of the circle over and seal around the edge. Cut a slit in the top to vent it and spoon a little milk in it to keep it moist. Place the pasty in the oven and bake."

"Sounds interesting," Addis chimed in. "Think I might be tempted to try one. How are they served?"

O'Reilly jumped in to answer that inquiry. "Most people eat it with catsup, but some prefer gravy. However, in Wales, the miner would take one to work in his lunchbox. At the coalmine, he'd place it over a natural thermal fault to heat it and just eat it like a sandwich, either as one whole piece or in halves. I like them in half so I can pour catsup into the open end. They make a fantastic meal in a sandwich."

"Some folks add other ingredients to it, like carrots or peas," Marks added. "And some use ground beef instead of diced steak."

O'Reilly stated, "Though I tend to think that's done just to save time. The real McCoy, so to speak, is with chunks of real beef!"

Silence fell over the foursome as they pondered their respective menus. Finally, the waiter, wearing black slacks with a sharply pressed white shirt and black tie, came to the table. "Are we ready to order?" he asked. One by one, the men ordered from the menu. Addis followed through with his earlier implication by ordering the Acoma pasty. Madden decided on prime rib, Marks went for the lasagna, and O'Reilly decided to follow Madden's lead and selected prime rib. The waiter then asked if they were ready for their wine. All nodded in agreement, and he expertly opened the bottle, neatly wrapping a linen napkin around its neck to absorb any dripping from the bottle, and poured a small amount into a glass, which he placed in front of O'Reilly.

The Butte-Silver Bow district attorney lifted the glass and studied it, gently swirling the ruby red liquid. "Great legs," he commented. "Looks like maybe 14 percent." He then lifted the glass to his nose and inhaled its bouquet; finally placing it to his lips, he took a small taste, allowing it to remain in his mouth for a few seconds before swallowing. O'Reilly nodded his approval to the waiter who then poured a half-glass for each of the four and departed from the table to submit the dinner requests for his table guests.

O'Reilly took the bowl of spaghetti, piled a spoonful on his plate, and passed the plate to Madden, who was seated to his left. Each guest did likewise and followed suit with the vegetables and bread sticks. Once each had had an opportunity to enjoy a bite or two, Madden looked across the table at O'Reilly and Marks. Placing his fork on the plate, he took a drink of ice water before speaking.

"I know the two of you were given a very brief memo before we left Washington this afternoon. The reason for our coming here and meeting with you and with your sheriff tomorrow is twofold. First, the FBI has reason to believe that large amounts of drugs are being distributed out of Montana, and we tend to believe that the source is somewhere in or near Butte. The second reason is that about six weeks ago, two special investigators assigned to this case disappeared without any trace."

Bill Marks and Dan O'Reilly had both stopped eating and were listening intently as Addis spoke. O'Reilly was the first to respond. "What makes you think Butte is the responsible area? Just because we're been struggling economically since the mining ended doesn't mean we'd start running drugs. In fact, it makes more sense to me that drugs would be run out of Bozeman, Missoula, Helena, or Great Falls … hell," he exclaimed, "even Kalispell! They're all bigger; most have college age students and more traffic in and out of the area than we do here. I just don't…"

Marks placed a hand on O'Reilly's arm and interrupted, "I understand your concern Steve, but I have to give some credibility to what Dan is saying. Why would you think the focus is here in Butte?"

"Steve's not stating the obvious," cut in Jim Addis. "Butte's in an ideal place for running drugs. You have intersecting interstate highways with I-90 going east and west, connecting Butte to Bozeman and Billings to the east and to Missoula, Spokane, and Seattle to the west. I-15 connects to the north with Helena, Great Falls, and Canada and to the south to Salt Lake City, Las Vegas, and all the way to Mexico."

"By air, you connect through Salt Lake City the same way, and by rail you can ship east or west without much problem," added Steve. "These are all things that the city leaders cited in their attempt to recruit large business to set up shop, like Micron back in the '90s."

Marks and O'Reilly looked at each other and back to their guests. Marks spoke first. "Do you have any hard evidence that you might share with us?"

"Phil Stephens, who was the agent assigned out of the Butte office, and Brad Williams, from the Great Falls office, had been working a lead we received in Washington about possible drug running and even a possible al-Qaeda cell in Montana and had left information with headquarters that they had found some evidence that the drugs were being shipped out of the Butte area. Before they were able to discover anything concrete, they both disappeared," answered Addis. "By disappeared, I mean totally, without any sign, or communication. It's as though they just fell off the face of the earth."

Madden continued, "They checked out of their hotel room in Bozeman one day and never returned. Their rental car, clothes, notebooks—everything, disappeared, and not one trace has been located."

"The bureau's had other agents assigned out of Bozeman looking for them, and after six weeks, they've found nothing with the exception of one possible gas station attendant who thinks he could identify the two on the same day they left Bozeman and hearing them discuss something about Whitehall, Boulder, Butte, and Anaconda while they were getting coffee and filling their car."

Another round of wine was poured as the four pondered the topic of discussion. The waiter arrived with a tray holding the dinners, and the four men sat in silence as he placed the plates before them and each began to savor the entrée ordered. They pushed the talk of their primary mission to the side for the time and spent the next forty-five minutes enjoying the cuisine and wine. After all had finished, the waiter again approached and asked if a dessert was desired. All four declined, and the waiter presented the check to O'Reilly, thanking them for patronizing the restaurant and extending the management's invitation to return in the future.

Marks poured a refill into each of the four coffee cups as the waiter cleared the remaining dishes from the table. After the waiter departed, Addis cleared his throat and began to speak. "We are not sure what, if anything is really happening in Butte itself; however, the indications from Williams and Stephens were more than just suggestive, and that is why we requested meeting with you two and the sheriff tomorrow morning. If you could make sure we have maps of the city and surrounding area, as well as any other information that you might think useful for our meeting, that would be great. Hopefully, we can share and perhaps make sense of what information we collectively have regarding the two agents before they disappeared."

O'Reilly pushed himself back from the table, folded his napkin, and turned to the other three men. "I'm going to call it a night, gentlemen. I think we can resume our discussions tomorrow morning at the courthouse." Looking at Addis and Madden, he added, "You two know how to get up there, right?"

Madden smiled, "Yes, thanks, Dan. We really appreciate the hospitality and the room setup you arranged for us at the Finlen. I checked upon our arrival and know that it's a mere four blocks from there to the courthouse. We know you and your staff have lots going on, and our intent is to stay out of your way as much as possible. However, we also want to be sure that all the channels of communication are open and everyone is kept in the loop during our ongoing investigation."

With that, Madden pushed back from the table, and all four of the men rose. "Well," Addis stated, "looks like we'll all call it a night then." Marks nodded in agreement, and the four walked as a group to the restaurant door. Stepping into the chill of the night air, each of the FBI agents shook the hand of the Montana legal experts and departed eastward toward their hotel as Montana Attorney General Marks and Butte-Silver Bow District Attorney O'Reilly headed in the opposite direction.

Once out of earshot, Addis glanced at Madden. "Well, Steve, what are your thoughts?"

"I'm sure we'll need to keep at least O'Reilly in the loop on a regular basis," replied Madden, continuing, "His reaction was somewhat defensive, but I certainly do understand it. After all, laying the possibility of a huge drug operation as well as the disappearance of two FBI agents on the community of Butte, Montana, is not what one in either position would want to hear."

The two agents arrived at the Finlen Hotel and walked in silence to their rooms. Pausing outside the first door, Madden commented, "Jim, we need to be careful about the discussions in the morning. My understanding from our briefing in Washington was that Joe Kelly, the Butte-Silver Bow sheriff is somewhat offended that his department doesn't have the lead in this and he has the reputation of being bull-headed and rather argumentative when he feels cornered or on the defensive."

Addis nodded in agreement and then, turning to continue to his room, shot back quietly over his shoulder, "We'll put our heads together in Room 456 at 6:15. Rest well. Good night "

"See you in the morning," came the reply, and both men disappeared into their respective rooms for the night.

CHAPTER TWO

At exactly 6:15, Addis opened the door between his room, 458, and Room 456, in which five, six-foot tables had been set up in a "U" configuration. On them lay the assorted maps and hardware that had been requested. Madden, who had entered from Room 454 a good half hour earlier, looked up as his partner joined him and asked, "Did you get your daily run in?" "Yeah, about an hour ago," came Addis's reply. "Got in about three miles, although it is difficult to tell since you're running on the side of a mountain up here," he added, laughing.

"I know what you mean, Jim," Madden said, still sorting out the cords and the respective hardware on the end table. "I got up about four-thirty and ran for maybe thirty minutes. Tried staying on the east-west streets to avoid the hill, but once you cross Montana Avenue, it starts dropping off rather quickly so, no matter which way you run, you eventually have to deal with going uphill. Luckily, the snow stopped early so the streets were pretty good to run on. Once I got showered and dressed, I called Lee and talked with her for a few minutes before the two kids got up to get her day going at full speed."

Addis had started opening the cardboard tubes and pulling out the maps that depicted different areas of the Butte community, spreading them face down as he unrolled each one so that they would begin to flatten out. "How's the weather back in D. C. this morning? Did Lee say?"

Madden chuckled aloud. "Yes, she said it was going to be a beautiful day with blue sky and sunshine and about sixty degrees. Sometimes it's really amazing the weather differences found in this country for the month of April."

Addis grunted in agreement and then posed a question, "How do you want to handle the meeting this morning?"

"Let's review for the sheriff and the narcotics team what we shared last night," his partner replied, not looking up. "I think, once they understand what we know, they might be more inclined to be in a cooperative mood. I think it best to make sure they know we're showing all the cards in our hand."

Addis grunted an affirmative and moved on to unrolling the last of the maps from their confining tubes. "Hopefully," began Madden, "we'll be able to ascertain relatively soon if the theories the guys hold back in DC about a terrorist cell and the drug production and running out of here are related in any way."

"On paper they certainly could be connected," agreed Addis. "The cell needs money to do its work, and drugs are a great way to do it. Besides, as we pointed out last night, like it or not, Butte lies in a very attractive place for exactly that. It has easy routes in and out, no one expects that kind of criminal behavior in this state—or city, and the area has lots of places to hide your behavior. I noticed a lot of cabins on the map of the surrounding countryside."

Each man continued his self-appointed duties until all the hardware had been set up, including the large-format folding screen that stood at the open end of the "U," facing the table that joined the side ones. Madden then glanced at his watch, "Well, what say we start over to the city/county building? We'll be a little ahead of schedule, but I think everything's done here for now. No telling how long our meeting will run. I asked Dan to alert his office staff that if we get to the noon hour, they can order in a lunch for us so we won't need to stop."

"Good idea," Addis replied. With that the two men turned and walked back to their respective rooms, picked up their attaché cases, and rejoined in the hallway for their walk to the scheduled meeting.

Upon entering the second floor conference room in the Butte-Silver Bow Courthouse, they found that Dan O'Reilly had already arrived, had the coffee brewing, and was accepting the check for the variety of doughnuts, rolls, pineapple chunks, peaches in juice, whole apples and oranges, as well as apple, grape, and orange juices, not to mention the condiments for the coffee or tea. Four rectangular tables formed a square in the center of the room, and pitchers of water and drinking glasses were in place.

Observing the two agents entering the room, O'Reilly turned and welcomed them with a bit of Butte colloquialism. "Good morning, youse guys! I hope you found the Finlen comfortable."

"I think we both slept quite well as it was very quiet, and we both got our morning runs in," returned Madden. "Smells as though the coffee's ready; you must have gotten here pretty early," he continued.

"Not really," O'Reilly replied. "Suzy Carter, my admin, took care of that so I didn't need to be that early. In fact, I just walked in a few moments ahead of you."

Addis poured himself a cup of steaming hot coffee, turned, and looked about the room. It was solidly built, looked to be of granite like the rotunda in the entrance to the building. Obviously, very old, the building wore its age well and remained in remarkably good condition. At one end of the room, a stand held several large colored maps, and next to it stood a portable stand with a laptop computer and projector, which was pointed toward a wall-mounted screen. On the opposite end was a large device that appeared to be a whiteboard though it had several control switches and buttons along the left side. "I see you folks have a 3M board," he said to O'Reilly, nodding toward the whiteboard.

"To tell you the truth, it's on loan to us from the Butte Public Schools Administrative Office across the street. The way it gives printouts of what's written on it sure saves time. I figured it'd come in handy for our meeting."

"Good idea, Dan" added Madden. "That should help us to keep on track and still have accurate notes to refer to."

By now the three had all gotten cups of coffee. O'Reilly had added cream and two sugar cubes to his; the agents had both kept theirs black and unsweetened. Bill Marks entered the room, greeted the group, filled a cup, and joined the threesome standing near the tables. "I saw Ken and Jerry getting out of Ken's car as I was coming up the steps out front," Marks reported to O'Reilly. "They should be here momentarily." With that, Madden looked at his watch; its gold hands told him it was seven fifty.

As if on command, Butte-Silver Bow Sheriff Ken O'Billovich entered the room. O'Billovich had been the sheriff in Butte-Silver Bow for the past twelve years, having survived a couple of election scares along the way. For the most part, people liked him. He was friendly but carried some authority with him as well. Standing just over six feet and well over 265 pounds, he presented an image of someone you'd want on your side in a fight. His nose still sported an unnatural bend from a break he incurred playing football for Butte High many years prior, and he showed a well-advanced receding hairline. He wore black trousers and an open-necked white shirt covered by an unbuttoned black jacket with his badge and nametag on the left breast pocket. The left shoulder displayed a cloth patch identifying him with the Butte-Silver Bow Sheriff Department.

"Mornin', gentlemen." He smiled as he advanced to the group. O'Billovich was accompanied by a gray-haired man wearing spectacles that rested just below the large hook at the top of his nose. His pale face further suggested much office work and never any glimpses of the sun. But he did dress the Western part with denim pants, boots, and a plaid shirt under his waist-length zippered jacket that he had since undone. "I want you guys from back East to meet our lead narcotics detective, Lt. Jerry Hocking," said O'Billovich to the two FBI agents.

After a few minutes of pleasantries, O'Reilly suggested they help themselves to the food and drinks his office had provided. Taking their selections to the table, each of the six took a seat and enjoyed a bite or two of the food before the local district attorney addressed them.

"Good morning," greeted O'Reilly as they took their respective seats. "Last night, Steve and Jim met with Bill Marks and me and shared some rather dark thoughts. Rather than my trying to explain to you, I'd like Steve to fill you in."

Madden took a long, slow sip from his cup of orange juice and rose. "What Jim and I were sharing is a possible scenario that involves the community of Butte." He began sifting through information and comments in his mind before continuing. "As you know, there is a lady in northern Montana who has been particularly instrumental in assisting the Homeland Security office and the FBI in identifying some terrorist and al-Qaeda cell operatives. In the information she provided, one of our agents uncovered what he thought was a lead to some illegal drug operations, and there seemed to be a tie to Butte."

A murmur of disbelief escaped from the sheriff and narcotics detective, but no one said anything so the senior federal agent continued.

"The information, little as it was, was passed on to the FBI field agents located here in Butte and in Great Falls. They had the charge to review it and investigate any other leads or information and then send that information back to our bureau. Unfortunately, before they relayed anything to us, Agent Phil Stephens and Agent Brad Williams disappeared."

O'Reilly cleared his throat and looked at Madden, indicating a desire to add his thoughts. With a cynical smirk, he said, "Madden here believes the two agents were investigating drug and terrorist activities that would lead to Butte. I told them I thought they were way out of line last night, but when Uncle Sam wants to point fingers, there isn't much we 'little folk' can do to stop them."

Marks shifted his weight uneasily in his chair but did not comment. Instead he looked toward Madden who had moved to the chart of maps at the open end of the table configuration. Without speaking, Madden flipped through the maps until he found the one he wanted. It was a highway map of central and western Montana showing Gallatin County of which Bozeman is the county seat, Lewis and Clark County, and Silverbow County, with the county seat of Butte being identified.

It also showed interstate highways and secondary highways leading into and out of Butte.

"Stephens and Williams had done some preliminary investigation in Helena, Great Falls, Missoula, and Billings and had just started doing some in Bozeman and Butte. They left Bozeman on March 20 and never returned to their motel. An attendant at a convenience store gas station on North Seventh in Bozeman is evidently the last person to have seen them. The two of them, their car, and whatever notes they may have had all disappeared with no trace since."

Now it was Sheriff O'Billovich who talked. "Yes, Steve, I am very much aware of the missing agents. Bozeman Police had contacted us, as has the FBI, asking us to assist in trying to find them. Like you said, the last identification of the two and their car was on North Seventh in Bozeman, and the attendant saw the car pull out and head north after fueling. His statement to the investigating officer in Bozeman was simple and did not seem to hold anything sinister, however; like you said, they disappeared and no trace has been identified since. But why do you believe Butte is involved? They could have been going to Helena, Great Falls, Missoula, heck, even Spokane or Seattle."

"Of course, you're right," commented Addis, now standing next to Madden. "As Steve said, it's just a hunch they got from their contact and they passed on to the Bureau in a couple of their emails that lead us to believe they were intending on heading this way that morning."

Marks leaned back in his chair and put his hands behind his head. Thoughtfully looking up toward the antique tin ceiling tiles above them, he said, "Last night, Jim and Steve reminded us that Butte is positioned strategically for many operations. You all have been very active in the many attempts to bring large business and industry to the Butte Corridor. You have intersecting interstate highways connecting north, south, east, and west. Further, there's easy access by air, and because the airport is not a large facility, the security is not near what, say, Billings or Great Falls has to have. Finally, there's the rail service that also provides travel in all four directions." Silence fell over the group for a few moments.

Madden finally broke the silence. "In preparing for our trip here, I spent some time looking over some facts about Butte," he began. "We have to remember that just because the seventy-four major mines have been closed for many years, for the most part, there are still over ten thousand miles of mine shafts that exist under the city with some of the vertical shafts dropping down almost a mile—wonderful places in which to make objects disappear. This area holds plenty of places to hide and not be found, in the mountains surrounding the city and beyond as well as in the several quarries both in town and out near Anaconda."

"Ok," inserted the narcotics detective, Jerry Hocking. "This all sounds good, but I still do not see or hear any connection to Butte. Just what is it you suspect, if anything? Why waste taxpayer money, both on your end and here, if you are just digging in the shadows?"

"I presume, Steve," added O'Billovich; "you have some reason for us being here this morning. So far I have to agree with Dan and with Jerry. You guys seem to be on a wild goose chase."

Madden looked to Addis and then cleared his throat again. "Late last week, authorities apprehended a drug dealer in Salt Lake City, and his manufactured drugs contained some paperwork that we identified as parts of the newspaper the *Montana Standard*. Obviously, the drugs had been wrapped, at one time or another, in the Butte paper. So, as you can see, we do have a physical evidence link to Butte."

"Of course we're not stating that the drugs are or were manufactured here," added Addis. "But as you are all aware, we have to follow every lead that appears. That is the lead that brought us to Butte yesterday."

"Let's say you are right, Jim," responded O'Billovich, "What do you want from us?"

"I think where we are," stated Madden, "is that we need you to go back to your staff and review any and all leads and information, regardless of how small or unimportant they may have seemed at the time you received them, that may assist us in finding out, first, where the two agents ended up and where they disappeared, second, what drug traffic can be found and how it might be traced to the origination point."

Looking at his watch, O'Reilly rose and commented that if they were to continue with the meeting, he would ask his assistant to order in lunch.

Before there was any response, Hocking, looking at O'Reilly, began to address the group. "I see no reason to continue here. It's pretty obvious to me that Washington wants us to solve their problem and they don't have a freakin' clue what or where to look, so these two get sent out to dump it in our laps."

Marks glared at Hocking and countered, "I disagree totally, Jerry. I see their point, and I think we owe it to them, and more important, to our own people here in Butte-Silver Bow and the State of Montana to work cooperatively with them." The remainder of the group sat silently as Hocking fidgeted in his seat.

"I think," said Addis, breaking the tense silence, "that we should break into groups of three and do some looking at information you folks already might have as well as exploring potential locations on these maps. We can regroup and share what we come up with, putting it on the white board back there," gesturing toward the opposite end of the room where the electronic board stood.

The members nodded and Madden took the lead. "Jerry, why don't you, Dan, and I form a group to look at the maps up here, and Bill, Ken, and Jim gather at one of the tables and talk about what information Butte has in its possession. Jim has notes from our guys back in DC." After saying that, Steve concluded that maybe a break would be in order and then added, "Let's take twenty minutes to use the facilities, get a snack, juice or coffee before we break into our two groups. We're not on any timetable today."

The groups went over maps, documents, and police and bureau investigative reports for the remainder of the morning before being interrupted by O'Reilly announcing that lunch had arrived.

After consuming a lunch of various cold cuts, breads, vegetables, and fruits and disposing of their paper plates, Madden stepped up to the maps and faced the group. "What my group discussed this morning was that most of the mine shafts, though under water, could be pumped out or sealed off if someone really wanted to do so. The problem would be to discover where that site would be since there are, as mentioned earlier, over ten thousand miles of shafts down there," he said, gesturing toward the floor. "In addition, the Berkeley Pit that was closed in 1982 has now pretty well filled with the water from the surrounding mines. The water is highly acidic, and the water is over seven hundred feet deep. Though it would be difficult, it is clear that if you wanted something to disappear, using that pit would do the trick. Of course," he added, "I'm not sure how you could get something into the pit without being observed as cameras are always providing video of the area to prevent vandalism, among other things."

Madden turned to the maps and, after flipping through a few pages, finally stopped at one showing a closer view of the area of uptown Butte with color shading distinguishing several areas from others. He looked at the map for a few seconds, and then, extending his pocket pen into a pointer, he pointed to a shaded area with the word Centerville. "This," he said, facing the group again, "is where our group thinks some of the greatest possibility exists. The mine is known as the Stewart, or Steward. The shafts of this mine go over four thousand feet down in places and, toward the end of its copper-producing days in the early 1970s, actually had some of its ore being lifted out by the Kelly Mine." Madden paused to allow everyone to focus on his comment and the map.

"So," began Hocking, "you think that because it is a deep mine and sits in an existing residential area of Butte that some gangsters are using the shafts? For what? They are, as you already said, filled with acidic water. It would be a really great trick to access one shaft, seal it off, and pump out the water!" Hocking was obviously agitated with Madden's even hinting of any evil-doings in Butte. "I said it before we broke for lunch and again when we were looking at the maps in our small group session, I think you and the Bureau are crazy!" There was no response to his accusatory statement, and Madden turned to Addis.

"Before Jim talks about his group's discussions, I want you all to be aware that Dan's assistant, Suzy, has joined us and is recording our reports on the white board. When we finish, she'll print out the comments so that each of us has an exact copy when we leave our session later this afternoon." With that, Madden nodded to his junior partner to begin his comments.

"The task for our group, as you are aware, was to review information, recent cases, and possible leads that Ken and his staff have been working on," began Addis. "It is evident that some rather high quality coke and meth has been found in some recent drug-related arrests in Butte and the surrounding area. Tracking the source has been difficult as is usually the case, but Ken feels that there are some indications that most of the stuff is entering the area from Bozeman and Missoula. Common sense tells us that the route of delivery is either from the east or from Spokane and further west." Addis noticed Hocking nodding his agreement at the inflection that the origination of the drugs was most likely not Butte at all. "Unfortunately, Ken indicates that the recent arrests are apparently unrelated though the contraband found in each case appears to be from the same original batch—the makeup and quality are consistent in each case. This, at least, suggests, though there is no hard evidence to support it, that the cases are indeed related and that they represent one supply source rather than multiple sites." Jim paused momentarily as he walked to where Sheriff O'Billovich sat and took a folder the sheriff offered. As he opened the folder, he withdrew several sets of stapled papers and then, pausing before the group, stated, "Knowing that we were going to be meeting today, I had called Ken before we left DC and asked him to prepare some information for us. I appreciate your doing this, Ken." With that he proceeded to distribute a set of the papers to each of the people present. "What you are receiving is a quick glance at the last four arrests made by the Butte-Silver Bow law enforcement this year—what was found in each case and what information was obtained in interrogating the individual as well as other supporting comments and evidence leading to the arrest." At this point, Addis stopped so the members of the group could look through their respective packet, each about twenty pages in length. The contents also described how many people were present, the location where the arrest had been made, and any other information that suggested where the drugs might have come from. None of them identified any specific individual as a seller, and there were no telephone records that might provide a lead.

After pausing for five minutes, Addis brought the group back together. "Obviously, there is some information here that might be part of our puzzle. But Ken and I both feel that we are missing some major pieces. Ken has indicated that each arrest was for minor possession of a narcotic. The amount confiscated was not significant, and therefore, Jerry and his detectives were not able to obtain warrants for home or business searches of the individuals. The four individuals are in their thirties and forties; they are all gainfully employed and had, until their arrest, at least, good reputations in the community and places where they work."

Suzy Carter, finished with recording Madden's and Addis's presentations, remained poised to add more. Making good use of her spare moment, she looked toward her boss. He caught her glance and returned it with a wink. After all, she was not bad looking—about five feet three and maybe 118 dripping wet. She loved to work out, and her firm physique spoke to that. It was pretty well known in the Butte legal circle that O'Reilly and Carter were much more than just employer-employee. Evenings usually found the DA needing to work at the office until midnight, which made getting together with Suzy pretty easy. After all, as he explained to Myrna one time, didn't he need his assistant to research and type his correspondence to keep him ahead of the court battles?

Whether she bought his story remained undisclosed. Their two boys had long since grown and moved on, so Myrna had no real obligations to speak of at the home she and Dan maintained in west Butte. She loved to socialize in her own way, too, and had many times gone out on the town with her lady friends and sometimes with men whom she had befriended through her bowling, golf, and cycling groups. It really would not matter to her if her husband was having an affair; after all, she could find plenty of people to occupy her spare time. She was fit and fairly attractive herself. Just over five feet four, her toned body received many an admiring look from the gentlemen when she and Dan made their requisite public appearances together. She would usually wear spike heels and a sparkly, form-fitting gown with a very low scoop neckline. A long pearl necklace draped around her neck would fall just short of getting lost in her ample and brazenly revealed cleavage. Her long black hair draped down just past her shoulders and left enough of the backless gown uncovered to stir anyone's imagination as she walked by.

O'Billovich carefully laid his papers on the table before him, "As we discussed earlier in our session, I've asked Jerry and the other narcotics officer to go back over each case and dig more deeply. Though these incidents were classified as minor arrests, there seems to be some connection to them, and we will keep exploring them. If we can get something to turn our way, we can get a warrant to get hold of some computers, cell phones, etc. and see what these guys have been doing."

Jerry Hocking sat in silence, staring at the papers lying in front of him. When Addis had handed a set to him, Hocking had flipped through the pages without really reading anything. "Why should I worry about it?" he thought. "After all, I was the arresting officer in all four cases."

The day was quickly coming to an end. A glance at the wall clock showed it was quarter after four. Madden thought for a moment, then motioned Addis to him. "Any reason to keep going here, Jim?" he questioned his younger partner.

Marks, overhearing the question supplied the answer. "Well guys and Ms. Carter, I need to head back to Helena and finish some paperwork in my office before tomorrow so I'm going to head out." With that he stood, collected his papers, and accepted a printed handout from Carter. "I stand ready, as does my staff in Helena, to assist you two fellas in any way I can. Just give me a call or come by the office; it'll always be open to you."

Addis and Madden joined in harmony in their, "Thanks, Bill." Madden added, drive carefully over the pass. Marks nodded and walked out the door, putting on his topcoat he had retrieved from the coat rack by the door of the meeting room.

O'Billovich followed Marks's lead, picking up his materials. He paused upon standing and approached Addis and Madden, extending his hand toward the two FBI agents. "Stay in touch, youse guys," he said. Just as Bill said, "My office is at your disposal, and when possible, I'll allow some of my street patrol to work with you if you need them."

Madden took O'Billovich's hand in a firm handshake and thanked the sheriff for the courtesy. Then it was Addis's turn to shake hands. "Thanks, Ken, we'll let you know, and of course, we will stay in touch."

Hocking stood as his boss was walking by on his way to the door. Without a word, Jerry grabbed his papers and headed toward the door behind him, almost causing a collision as O'Billovich suddenly turned back to call out, "Thanks, Dan, appreciated your luncheon and visit." O'Reilly looked back toward the door from where he stood, facing the two agents, and waved a good-bye. The bulky sheriff then turned back toward the door and exited, following Hocking down the hallway and the curved stone staircase leading to the main floor.

Silence settled in the room with only the agents, the DA, and his administrative assistant still there. Carter had been busy shutting down the white board, storing the erasable markers in the drawer with the eraser, then tidying up the table that lay covered with pieces of broken cookies and some stains from spilled coffee, tea, and other liquid refreshments consumed during the day. Upon completion of her domestic duties, she exited back to her office down the hall, leaving the three men alone.

O'Reilly was the first to speak. "Do you two really think that Butte is involved in something like drugs and terrorism?"

"Well, Dan, who really knows at this juncture?" came the response from Madden. "Jim and I know of the little piece of evidence that we mentioned early on, and there certainly could be some kind of connection between the arrests made here in Butte over the last three months. Other than that, I'm not sure."

The DA looked at Addis with a questioning face. "I have to agree with Steve," Addis replied, acknowledging the unspoken question. "I've been working with some of the Homeland Security folks, and they believe that there is a chance some retaliation might be coming for the undercover work done by Stella Johnson up north. They don't like having their members discovered, setup, and then taken out. It would be a whole lot easier setting up a team in Montana than trying to send one in from elsewhere."

Madden, listening intently to his junior partner, added, "The fact is, Dan, we have no concrete evidence, only a gut feeling of some in DC. That's not enough to ask for more agents out here. So, Jim and I are on the case because, with the drug piece mentioned earlier, the four arrests here that might be connected, and the disappearance of two agents out here, something obviously is going on."

With that, O'Reilly finished collecting his papers, closed the set of maps on the stand, and offered his hand to the agents. "Gentlemen, let me know if you need anything."

"Will do, Dan," replied Madden. Meanwhile, Addis had finished picking up the materials for him and now was collecting those that had been lying in front of Madden.

Taking O'Reilly's hand, Addis thanked the DA for the hospitality of the night before and that day and assured him that he and Madden would be in touch on a regular basis. The three men then walked silently out the door, Addis and Madden turning to the right to head for the staircase and O'Reilly going left toward the office for the Butte-Silver Bow district attorney.

CHAPTER THREE

"What a boring meeting," thought Jeremy Carson, as the junior U.S. senator from Idaho exited the small conference room. Getting back to the hotel room and relaxing with a stiff drink and watching some television was in his plan. Carson had flown to Jackson Hole, Wyoming, for a meeting with the governors and congressional people from Montana, Wyoming, and Idaho. The meeting's purpose was to explore how the three states could develop some kind of coordinated plan to continue a control of the brucellosis disease that seemed always to find its way into the domestic cattle when the buffalo in Yellowstone National Park began meandering outside park boundaries in the spring. Of course, it was not the first time such a meeting had been called. Even back in the late 1990s, the disease was evident. Declaring an open hunting season had helped trim the numbers some, but now the animal activists were at it again, claiming that the hunting was not the answer.

As the delegation had arrived at the resort Monday night for their one-day confab, the activists had gathered in front, yelling derogatory names and chanting "Don't kill the animals." The image of the fifty sign-bearing, finger-pointing, insult-hurling demonstrators came back to Carson's mind now as he turned from the main hallway toward the bank of elevators located at one end of the lobby. "What a bunch of bullshit," he muttered to himself. "And what a waste; just empty talk and a delay on deciding." They had accomplished nothing except setting a date to meet again in the fall.

"But not a total loss," Carson mused. Meeting in Wyoming during spring ski season had its advantages. "Three days of shushing on the slopes will compensate for a few of the hours of droning debates," he thought with satisfaction of his upcoming snow activities before checking out on Saturday. He reached the side of the lobby and stopped in front of the bank of elevators and walked to the far end before pressing the up button. Though there was a stairwell immediately next to where he stood, Jeremy did not consider using them.

As he pressed the elevator button, he noticed two men standing in the corner behind him. "Must be good friends," Carson thought, seeing them talking and laughing as though one had shared some humorous anecdote with the other. But their clothes impressed him more—they seemed out of place in the hotel, not dressed in ski attire, as most of the skiing population normally found there. However, being 8:10 at night, Carson did not give them a second thought. After all, a nice suite with a full bar was waiting for him on the ninth floor.

The door opened, and Carson stepped back to allow a group to come out. Of course, being single and in his mid forties, Carson took note of the ladies who exited. Most were with a male companion. "Probably husbands," he concluded. There were two attractive coeds, who looked to be in their late teens or early twenties tagging along with the rest of the group. "Family spring vacations," mused Carson, stepping into the now empty elevator. He made a slight turn to his left to press the button for his floor and noticed the two men had stepped into the elevator behind him.

Carson prided himself in being observant and now was no exception. The first man on looked to be about thirty-five. He had a medium build, probably weighed about 175, and stood near six feet, the same height as the senator. Carson noticed he wore tennis shoes, which seemed rather odd for Jackson Hole, a pair of blue denim jeans that were somewhere between new and broken in. What struck Carson about the man was his very pale skin color. "This guy sure isn't any skier," wagered Jeremy mentally to himself. The man wore a hip-length jacket of medium weight as one would usually wear in the late fall or early spring in the city, definitely not wear for out in the rugged mountains of Jackson Hole, Wyoming. On his head, the man sported a stocking cap that looked as though it had seen better days and wore it pulled down over the top of his ears and over most of the forehead. Carson's eyes met those of the stranger, and Jeremy felt uneasy as cold black eyes stared back at him. Carson quickly shifted his eyes to the second man who now was pressing a floor button.

The second man was shorter than the first, probably only about five nine but weighed at least two hundred pounds. He was definitely broader with at least a size eighteen and a half neck. Though he sported more appropriate footwear, a pair of Western boots, he did not look the part. He, too, wore denims and topped them off with a blue and black plaid, long-sleeve Pendleton shirt. The top two buttons he had left open and adding to his lack of a jacket, gave Carson the impression that perhaps they had been in the lounge earlier.

As the door closed on the three and the elevator began its ascent, the two men continued their humorous talk, though Carson chose to focus on the drink waiting for him in his room rather than on their dialogue. The elevator slowed and came to a stop on the eighth floor. As the doors opened, the taller man excused himself and after shaking hands with the other, exited. The doors again closed, and the elevator resumed its automated ascent.

The doors opened, and Carson stepped forward, past the man in the elevator with him. He accidently brushed against the man's shoulder as he stepped through the door, and he turned and said, "Excuse me." "Not a problem," came the impersonal reply. The voice was anything but friendly, thought Carson. He shrugged off the cold response and began the walk down the illuminated hall of the pine-walled lodge, arriving at suite 932. Taking out his coded key card, he inserted it into the slot above the door handle. The green light came on, indicating the door was unlocked and could be opened. Jeremy turned the knob and pushed the door inward toward the room.

Suddenly the senator found himself being hurled through the room. As he struck the full-size sofa that stretched across the open room, he went sprawling over it and landed not so gracefully on the glass coffee table, shattering it, before landing in a heap on the floor. He turned to look up and saw both of the men who had been on the elevator. For a split second, he thought he was seeing things. The man who had departed on the lower floor was standing over him and was now pointing a rather deadly looking pistol down at him. "Obviously the dude came up the stairs," thought Carson, steadying himself by resting on his right arm while still lying on the floor. Mentally he did a self-evaluation. "No broken bones, and I don't seem to be cut up," he decided. It was evident that nothing hurt except for the bruised ego and that strong sense of fear that was now becoming rather obvious in his mind.

As Carson was about to open his mouth to ask what was going on, the husky man stepped forward and planted the toe of his Western walking boot squarely in Carson's stomach causing him to contract into a fetal position, gasping for air. The second boot came down hard on Carson's side and he was sure he felt at least one rib crack under the force. Jeremy felt sick. He could not catch his breath, and try as he might, he could not make any sense of what was taking place. He struggled to breathe and gasped, "What the hell…." But before he could finish his question the taller man swung the barrel of the pistol down, connecting with Carson's head just in front of the left temple. Jeremy collapsed to the floor unconscious.

When he finally came to his senses, Carson thought momentarily he was blind. He knew his eyes were open, but he could not see anything. Just before panic set in, he realized he could feel a material against his face. As he thought for a moment, it became clear that some kind of cloth sack covered his head. He tried to reach up to remove it but found that his hands, both behind his back, were tied together and then bound to his feet that were also pulled back behind. He knew he was lying on his left side and must have been for some time as his left shoulder and hip were telling him it was time to relieve the pressure on them. He attempted to roll over but found that something rather large was in the way, causing him to remain on his left side.

"What the hell is going on?" Carson thought to himself. "Surely these thugs can't be animal activists." It seemed that even thinking caused his head to throb more, reminding him of the gun barrel. He could feel something on the left side of his face, and he was pretty sure it was dried blood for as he stretched his mouth to the left the material felt as though it cracked. "Must have been out for some time," thought Jeremy. He tried to get his bearings, but his attempts resulted in very little. The sack over his head was too thick to allow any light to shine through, though he could tell there was available light around him because of the small amount that leaked in under the open end of the sack that sat just under his chin. The light seemed to be that from daylight rather than artificial light so he presumed he had been unconscious through the entire night. Now the question came to his mind, "Where am I?" The floor certainly did not feel like the lush carpet of the suite he had at the resort.

In the absence of any recognizable sounds, Carson tried to provide himself with some rational reason for his situation. He had not received any threats through his senate office, his private phone, or by mail. Sure, all politicians had enemies, but usually they were local folk who were just making a lot of noise, it was never something serious. Carson's legs were aching from being held in an unnatural position for so long, and his shoulders were both nagging him to move, something he simply could not do. A wave of nausea swept over him, and he gagged to keep from vomiting. The pain from his head caused him to feel light-headed, and he passed out again.

When he came to, the bag had been removed from his head, and Carson found himself now sitting in what he deduced to be a wooden chair. He had a blindfold over his eyes, but at least his nose was uncovered. His legs were tied to the legs of the chair, or whatever it was he was tied to, and his arms remained tied behind his back and behind the backrest of the chair. Now, too, he could hear muffled voices.

"You trying to calling Ahmad again?" a husky voice softly asked. Carson thought the voice sounded familiar but couldn't place it.

"As soon as we can get this guy delivered, the better I'll like it," a second voice replied. The young politician didn't recognize this one at all, but it sounded very cold. Then he heard a door open. A cold breeze shot across the room, striking Carson in the face and causing him to realize that wherever he was, it was not any resort hotel. The air, though cold from the early spring, carried a putrid smell, something like oil and garbage. Again the senator could feel his stomach wanting to rebel, but it calmed down again.

"Ahmad will be grateful for the delivery," said the first voice.

Carson heard a phone handset click back on the base, and the first voice said, "He wants the goods brought to him immediately. He'll meet us for the exchange about midnight tonight."

"That gives us plenty of time," chimed in the second of the two voices. This one Carson recalled as being that of the taller of the two men on the elevator. "Let's get ready and get on with it."

The voices went silent, but the hostage could hear the men moving about though not near enough to him to feel their physical presence. The door opened and closed several times, but he could tell someone always remained in the room with him. "Wherever the room is," he thought.

After what seemed to Carson to be about an hour, he detected what he thought was a refrigerator door squeaking open. Then it closed, and he could hear liquid being poured into some kind of metal container. The duct tape was ripped away from his mouth, causing him to cringe. A straw was thrust into his mouth, and he was told to drink. Before he sucked on the straw, Carson inhaled and recognized the aroma of apple juice so he willingly drew the liquid into his parched mouth. It was cold and sweet, and best of all, it was wet. He enjoyed the liquid as it made its way down his throat, well enjoyed as best he could under the circumstances. The juice disappeared rather quickly, and he would have loved some solid food but none seemed to be forthcoming. No one had touched him since the event in the hotel room, and he was thankful for that though he still battled a nagging fear of what more would follow. Nothing made any sense, and reasoning could not calm his terror of what might happen to him. The shooting pain in his ribcage whenever he took a breath reminded him that at least some of the individuals were serious in their work. Time passed, and he could hear the ticking of a clock, ticking away the seconds, the minutes.

"Maybe they're kidnapping me for a ransom," he thought. He had money, and it would not bother him to give some of it up for his freedom. The thought became a verbal question. "What do you want with me?" he asked. No answer. "Is it money you want?" Again silence. "Look," he charged, somewhat louder than his previous queries, "I am a U.S. senator, and I demand to know what is going on." Still no response from the men he knew to be there with him. Just shuffling of feet as the men moved about. As he was about to yell out another question, a sharp, stinging pain hit the back of his neck. Within a short time, he began to feel very light-headed and woozy. It was difficult to hold his head up, and try as he might, his head felt heavier and heavier. The voices were becoming muffled, as though moving off in the distance, and the pain in his ribcage lessened. Soon he drifted into the silence of unconsciousness.

Carson came to in time to hear what sounded like an airplane propeller being powered up and then being brought back to idle speed. Though he was groggy, he could hear voices that seemed to be beyond a wall. He tried moving, but he had no room to move. But it didn't matter; he again found his arms and legs to be bound. Taking notice, he realized he had the hood back on over his head and his mouth again had tape over it so he could not open it.

Cold air struck him as he heard a metal door being slowly opened. Hands reached to him and grabbed him roughly by the legs and under the shoulders, half dragging, and half carrying him before unceremoniously dumping him onto a carpet surface again. The air had felt much colder than before, and the sickening smell was gone, replaced by a clean smell. His ears searched for a recognizable sound but found none, just silence. He tried glancing down the inside of the hood to see if he could tell the time and saw only darkness. "It must be night," thought Carson. "They must have drugged me."

A voice could be heard, distant but close enough to distinguish the words. "Ahmad is happy for the delivery," said a strange voice, thick with a Middle Eastern accent. The senator knew he had not heard it before.

"Thought Ahmad was going to meet us here," said one of the voices Carson could recognize.

Then another voice replied, "Ahhh, he is waiting for the delivery, and we are to transport the cargo to him."

"We're glad to be rid of the baggage," responded a voice, this one from whom the senator thought was the taller man in the hotel room. "We want our cash now, if Ahmad does not mind."

"Here, the money you and your partner were promised is in the bag, and cash is for your pilot," came the first voice.

"Good. Looks like we're done. We'll head back to Twin Falls with our pilot now."

"Good luck," replied the unknown voice.

Carson had been feeling with his hands, and to the best of his knowledge, he was in the back of some kind of large vehicle. This he concluded from the area he was able to move in and the fact that at least two people were also in the vehicle, sitting in front of his location.

From the discussion he had overheard, he was sure he had been flown from Jackson Hole, or somewhere, and was now being handed over to unknown people. He only had heard one name, Ahmad.

Carson heard a door open and close. The sound and the sudden lowering and then rising of the vehicle caused him to believe the driver had just entered. This was confirmed as he heard the motor start up. A second door, on the other side, opened and closed, and again the vehicle moved down and then back up.

"Let's go," the voice Carson had heard minutes before said. The gears engaged, and the vehicle moved on. Though still blindfolded, he thought about trying to count turns, railroad crossings, anything that might be helpful in aiding an escape or rescue, but there was not anything he could really think of. He tried to reason the length of time, but with a sack over his head and not knowing the speed of travel, he had no idea how far the vehicle drove. It was some time, though, before he heard the van's engine slow, felt a sharp turn, followed by a quick rise and fall of the van as though it had gone up and over a rise in the roadway. He felt the vehicle halt momentarily and then slowly move forward for a few seconds before coming to a complete stop. The engine went silent. "Wherever we are," thought Carson, "it's a destination. But is it the final one? Only time will answer that question."

Carson was aware that two doors had opened. Then the door next to him slid open. He felt uncaring hands roughly grab him. The next moment he felt himself being dragged from the vehicle and then dropped. The cold and unforgiving surface he hit convinced Carson that he had hit a concrete floor. The sudden contact with the surface reignited the fire of pain in his side. Though dazed by the intense pain, he could hear what seemed to be a mechanical sound like that of a garage door. Wherever he was, it was in a building. The sound made by the door moving and the slight echoing of the sounds around him gave him the impression that it was metal and of good size. The mechanical sound stopped with a solid, metallic thud. Peering down he saw some light though not very brilliant.

Hands again found his underarms and knees, lifting him from the floor. Carson felt himself roughly carried through a door, followed by the solid bang of it closing. A short walk followed on what sounded like hardwood. Again a pause. Another door opened, and the entourage moved on.

The bound victim knew from the angle of his body as he was being carried, that they were going down stairs. The weight of his own body, pulling down on the hands under his shoulders caused him to breathe very lightly in order to minimize the searing pain in his side. He tried to count the steps as they descended, twelve, thirteen, fourteen? The group paused, and Carson thought he heard a sound similar to metal hinges moving around the holding pins. "What is this," thought the senator, "another door?" The group began moving again down more stairs. The descent was much steeper than before, and Carson thought there were more stairs than they had come down earlier. Carson's feet were dropped to the floor, and he was placed unceremoniously on a chair. He winced in pain from the jolt. A hand pulled the hood from his head, and he had to blink from the brilliant light that was shining directly into his eyes. Before he could aclimate his eyes to the light, however, a cloth band was placed over them and securely tied behind his head. He felt his hands being loosened, and he tried to push his captors away. Unfortunately, being blindfolded and still bound about the feet made him only clumsy, and he quickly fell to the floor. His nose detected a very earthy, moist aroma, certainly strange for a house. "Must be a storage room or something," thought Carson. Before he could give it much more thought, he was yanked rather violently to his feet and slammed back into the chair. His arms were pulled back behind the chair and tied again. Then his feet were untied and retied to each of the front chair legs.

The brilliant light forced a weak ray through the blindfold so Jeremy knew it was still on. Not one voice made a sound, but he could hear feet moving about, a heavy object scraping its way to a new location, and then a door opening. A click and the source of light went away. The door closed, and Carson could detect a metallic click as though a lock had been set. Then, nothing but quiet. No sound, no voices, no walking, nothing at all. Jeremy could swear he could hear the beating of his own frightened heart but was sure it was just his rapid breathing.

Wherever the kidnapped victim was, it was dark and very remote. Having no idea of whether he had still been in Jackson Hole when he was drugged and put on the airplane, no idea of how long the flight was, and no idea of which direction it went, he had no clue to his present position. Or, for that matter, who had ordered his kidnapping and why. He knew he needed to use a restroom but, unable to move and with no one around, he could no longer hold it in, and he urinated on himself. Feeling the warm liquid soaking his suit pants and running down his legs made him shudder in embarrassment, but at least he did feel better.

It seemed for Carson a long time before he sensed the light on again and heard a click and the door opening. He could hear footsteps coming near and then felt a hand on his cheek. This was followed by a quick yank as the tape was removed. Though it was good to have his mouth uncovered at last, the process of removing the tape stung badly.

"Here's some food for ya," a rough voice said. It seemed to be the voice from the airport. "I ain't gonna untie ya so you'll have to open up and let me put it in." Jeremy was not about to argue. He had not had solid food since the evening dinner at Jackson Hole before his final elevator trip to who-knows-where.

He could feel warmth near his lips, and he was prodded to open his mouth, which upon doing, resulted in hot food being put inside. It tasted like meat of some kind. A second bite seemed to be a chunk of potato. Several more bites followed, and then a glass was held to his lips, and the voice told him to drink. He could detect no scent and, upon drinking, not much taste; he knew it was only water, but again, he was feeling thankful. More bites, more drink, and finally the voice spoke again, "That's it." The man left without any further communication, but it seemed only a few minutes until Jeremy heard the door open and close again but this time sensed someone different entering his unknown cell. He felt the person brush against his right side and then felt the presence of another person in the room by footsteps approaching his left side. The memory of urinating on himself made him feel rather conspicuous, but no one said anything.

Hands were now untying his feet, and he was instructed to stand up. Arms on either side of him told him two strong individuals were holding each arm, and any attempt to run or move would result in an immediate and most likely painful response, so he decided to cooperate. A different sound struck his ear, the sound of metal striking metal, like a chain being dragged across the floor. From his earlier fall, Jeremy had already figured the flooring consisted of wood in close contact to the ground, but this sound gave him the belief that the planking must be floating above the substructure. He then realized what the chain was for as some kind of cuff was placed about each of his ankles. An unseen pair of hands then untied his hands and the rattle of the chain was followed by the chain being anchored about each of his wrists in front of him. He lifted his hands to see how much slack he had for his arms to move and, as they reached about face high, he felt a sudden jolt on his wrists and his feet—chains connected his hands to his feet. The blindfold was yanked from his head, and for the first time he thought he might be able to recognize his captors. No such luck. They both wore baggy medical scrubs, and even their feet were covered with medical booties like those surgeons wore in the operating room. A full-head stocking cap with holes for the eyes only completely hid their faces. The caps on each were dark blue or black, Carson was not sure which, and were pulled completely down over the chin, exposing only their necks which he noticed, had no visible marks of any kind. Even though he remained captive and now manacled, a silent thank you crossed Carson's mind. At least now, he thought, he could relieve himself properly, which, after the hours that had passed and the feeding he'd had, he again needed to do.

One of the two strangers spoke, "As long as you cooperate, we will allow you to move around. You can feed yourself when food is brought in, and a bucket's on the table over there," the man gestured to the massive rectangular wood table against a wall. "There's a ladle in it for drinking."

"Don't get any ideas; ya ain't goin' nowhere," the second man added. From the sound of the voice, Carson concluded that the second person must be the one who had fed him earlier.

"Over there," the first man continued, "is a toilet. At least you won't be pissing yourself. And over there," motioning with his arm and pointing behind them, "is a bed."

Carson glanced in the direction of the bathroom and was shocked to see it was simply a wood seat and bench that would be found in an ordinary outdoor privy. "What a classy joint," he muttered. Then his head turned to see the bed and saw a rumpled bare mattress on the floor. "Yup, definitely first class all the way," he added. The two captors chuckled softly.

"You can yell and scream all you want, and no one will hear you," the first captor said. "After a while someone will come to visit you and explain why you're here."

With that, the two captors turned and walked to the door, opened it, and upon closing it after they passed through, made the familiar click as the lock was set. Jeremy was alone but, "At least," he thought, "I have light and can move about a little." With the newly acquired freedom, he immediately shuffled to the bench, dropped his still wet pants, sat, and relieved himself with a great sigh. "Really uptown," he murmured out loud; "they even have toilet paper."

Wondering what time and what day it was, Carson glanced at his left wrist, but his gold Seiko wristwatch was gone, leaving him no reliable way of knowing. By thinking though the events and guessing about his periods of unconsciousness both in the hotel room and again in the airplane, he came to the conclusion that this was probably his third day of captivity. Since the meeting had been on Tuesday, that would make this Friday.

"My staff figured I was skiing through today and I was to check out of the hotel tomorrow," Carson thought. "Shouldn't be too long before someone knows I'm missing, if they don't already. Maybe housekeeping noticed the broken table and that I hadn't been in the bed." The thought of someone reporting him gone and the scene of the broken table made him smile, even if they created just a few weak rays of hope for his rescue.

Only silence accompanied the politician for many hours. He searched the walls and ceiling of his cell. All seemed to be fairly new wood. Even the floor was, as he had guessed earlier, wood planking nailed to cross-members and obviously sitting above whatever the substructure was. With the ability to move, Carson touched the walls. The wood felt damp, and the air smelled musty, like in a cave. "Wherever I am," he said aloud, "I'm underground in some kind of rough-made vault."

Eventually the door again opened. A person dressed as those before entered with a plastic tray holding a microwaved dinner and a plastic fork, knife, and spoon. He placed the tray on the table by the water bucket and, without a word, turned and departed, again locking the door behind.

This was a routine, repeated several more times. Only the type of food differed in the meals, and that provided Jeremy with some idea of time passing by. Usually breakfast would consist of hot mush of some kind mixed with weak milk and some orange or apple juice along with very strong and bitter coffee. Lunches came in the form of cold cut sandwiches and, of course, water from his bucket. Microwaved dinner completed the day's menu with meat and potatoes but rarely a vegetable. Used to dining in quality restaurants with exceptional food, Carson had no love for such cuisine. However, he found that he was hungry at each feeding and quickly devoured every morsel offered to him. Each time the food came, Carson tried to question his captor, but to no avail. No words ever escaped the other's lips; no movements indicated any emotion within. Each visit brought just the audible click as the door was unlocked and opened and the person, always dressed as before, with the tray, setting it on the table, turning, and exiting, leaving Jeremy alone in stark white light and deathly quiet, except for the rattling of the chains as he moved about his new residence. He had been wearing the same clothes since the meeting before his capture, less the suit coat which had been removed somewhere along the course of time. Though normally clean-shaven, his face was covered with heavy stubble, and at times it itched until he would rub it. No toothbrush came with his accommodations, and his teeth felt coated with plaque. Luckily, the water helped a little as he could rub his teeth with a finger and then rinse his mouth, spitting it onto the wood floor where it would seek escape in the cracks between the planks. The odor of urine on his pants slowly disappeared, or maybe he just became accustomed to the stench of his own body.

Chapter Four

Addis and Madden began the walk back to the hotel in silence. After a half block, Addis broke the silence. "Well, that was anything but interesting."

Madden walked a few steps farther before responding. "It went about the way I thought it might, Jim. Like I said before the meeting, people here are very close-knit and they don't easily open up to strangers, especially if they think someone is coming in to tell them what to do." The two walked a few more steps in silence.

"On the bright side, Steve," Addis chimed in, "I think we did get some additional information. Those four drug busts since the first of the year certainly appear to be connected when all the information is laid out together. It would be most unusual that the chemical make-up of the "nose candy" would be the same if not cut by the same process or person. It's just too bad that more investigation didn't go into each one. Almost looks as though law enforcement took the easy out just to get an arrest and conviction."

"I just have a gut feeling of uneasiness about this case," Steve commented. "Not sure what or why, but I just know the drugs and the disappearance of Phil and Brad are connected." Both men again fell silent, hardly noticing that the sun had been out all day, and the light snow from the previous night had melted away, leaving bare and dry sidewalks. As the two reached their hotel, the desk clerk called out to Steve and called him over.

"At two this afternoon, I received a phone call for you, Mr. Madden. It was your office in Washington, and they asked that you call as soon as you came in, regardless of time."

"Thank you," said Madden, acknowledging the message. He turned to rejoin Addis, who was waiting at the elevator, holding the door open to allow his partner to enter.

As the elevator started its rise to their floor, Madden looked at Addis, "That doesn't sound as if the office was just checking in. Something must have happened that they think it's important to share since it's well past six o'clock their time and the offices usually would be closed."

The elevator stopped, the door opened, and both men walked down the short hall toward their rooms. "Let me know what they say, Steve," Addis said as they reached the room assigned to the senior agent. Madden nodded, unlocked his door, and disappeared into his room. The junior agent turned and walked the remaining distance to his room and went inside, placing his briefcase on the bed then, taking off his topcoat, he hung it on the coat rack by the door.

Madden removed his coat, throwing it casually onto the bed, and laid his briefcase next to it. He had a mission in mind, and he immediately sat on the side of the bed, reaching for telephone on the bedside table. He dialed into an outside line and then dialed the area code and phone number he knew by heart. The other end of the call was silent for a few seconds, and then Steve could hear a ringing. After three rings, there was an audible click followed by a recorded voice that he recognized as his secretary, and then he pushed in his personal line code and heard the phone ring again. This time a live voice with a cheerful "Steve Madden's office" answered.

"Hi, Cynthia; Steve here. The hotel desk clerk gave me the message to call in ASAP. What's going on? You don't usually work past five thirty and," he glanced at his watch, "it's almost seven now back there."

Madden could hear some paper being moved about in the silence of the conversation before his secretary began. "Steve, Henry Fields wanted me to share a report that he received from one of the agents in

Wyoming earlier today. He said that the aide to Senator Jeremy Carson called him with a concern about the senator's whereabouts."

It was not completely unusual for people to report missing persons when they had just gone somewhere at the last minute without announcing it to anyone. However, it was highly unusual for an aide to a U.S. senator to make such a call. "Why was he concerned, Cynthia?" prompted Madden.

"The senator had flown out to Jackson Hole for a mini-summit with the folks from Idaho, Wyoming, and Montana. The agenda was to focus on the old problem of brucellosis being spread from buffalo in Yellowstone to the cattle on surrounding ranches. The meetings were held on Tuesday, ending about eight o'clock in the evening."

"Go on," he said.

Cynthia was in her fifties and had worked for the bureau for over twenty years. She often spoke of retiring when she had put in her twenty-five, but she obviously loved her job so Madden doubted she would really give up her work then. At least he hoped not as long as he was there.

"Steve, according to Field's message, Carson was going to stay on until Saturday night so he could get in some spring skiing." Cynthia paused, giving Madden an opportunity to insert a question.

"Why is the aide concerned? Today is Friday so his checkout is tomorrow. He was most likely on the hill."

Madden was sure that his statement was correct, but still he had a feeling that something might have happened to the senator. Cynthia confirmed his feeling when she responded, "Steve, the aide tried calling him both on his cell and through the hotel's desk on Tuesday night after the meeting and again both Wednesday and Thursday before calling our offices this morning."

Madden's investigative mind was clicking through questions, many of which he knew his secretary would not have the answers to so he mentally skipped over those. "Ok, Cynthia, what DO we know?" he asked.

"The senator's car is still at the hotel where the valet parked it. It has not been moved. The aide was able to contact the hotel management this morning. Housekeeping had been in each of the last two days and reports nothing missing. However, as they talked, the management said the cleaner said there were small pieces of glass, like the tables are made of, on the floor where the coffee table was, but she did not find any broken tables in the suite. The bed did not look as if it had been used, or else it had been carefully made."

"What about his clothes and luggage?" posed the agent, attempting to create a mental image of the suite.

"Well, Steve," continued Cynthia's matter-of-fact voice at the other end of the phone, "The senator's suitcase was on the rack and was opened. His ski clothes were hanging in the closet, his ski boots were on the floor there as well." She paused, and Madden could hear paper moving as she reached for another page of notes. "He had checked his skis at the ski lift desk as many of the guests do, and they were still there, never touched by him."

Madden thought of another question and asked, "Cynthia, is there any chance he might have gone with someone else in another vehicle?"

Cynthia, again flipping through her obviously copious notes, quietly studied them for a few moments so that any answer she gave to her boss would be accurate. "The aide told Henry that he was told by management that all of Carson's toiletries were on the side of the bathroom sink and that the towels, washcloths, and terrycloth robe had not been touched since they had been replaced with fresh ones on Tuesday morning after he had left for the meeting."

Madden was mulling over the information that his secretary had given to him. After a silence of just a few seconds, he again began to talk. "Henry did call the hotel and had them seal off the suite, right?"

"Oh, yes, Henry told me that not only did they close the room as he asked them to do, but they also took the initiative to close off the entire floor until it can be examined. The tapes from the different cameras have been set aside for review as well."

Madden knew now what he would need to do. "OK, Cynthia. Tell Henry I have the information, and I'm heading out to the airport for Jackson Hole right now."

There was slight laughter on the other end of the conversation as Cynthia countered, "Steve, Henry knew you would want to handle the investigation so he directed the Bureau plane to come up from Denver and fly you directly to Jackson Hole. The plane should be there any time. When you arrive in Jackson, go to the Rendezvous Mountain Resort, the hotel where Carson was staying. I've already made reservations for you there."

"Thanks, Cynthia," said Madden appreciatively. "That will certainly expedite the travel. Tell Henry thanks as well. I'll talk with him upon my arrival at the hotel. By the way, Cynthia, where is the senator's aide?"

"According to Henry, he was told to be at the hotel to meet you so I am sure he's on a flight from DC to Jackson Hole as we speak."

Madden terminated the call with thanks again to his secretary and appreciation for her remaining in the office until he called for the information. Steve rose from the bed where he had been sitting and quickly walked from his room to Addis's, knocking on the door.

Addis opened the door and stepped aside, inviting his partner to enter the room, which Madden did, walking to the window and taking a seat in one of the two chairs on either side of a small round side table. Addis could see that his partner had something to share, and so he sat without any comment.

"I talked with Cynthia," Madden began. "Seems that the junior senator from Idaho, Jeremy Carson, has disappeared while attending a meeting in Jackson Hole. No traces of him or what may have happened, but I'm flying out shortly to head up the investigation of the scene."

Addis nodded his understanding. "I'll remain here in Butte and do some exploratory follow-up on what we have so far."

Madden nodded briefly and then added, "I don't see my being gone long, but we'll stay in contact. Let's make sure we connect by phone each evening at, say, six o'clock. That should provide time to do our work during the day and still share what we've found."

"OK," replied Jim. "If your plans require you to be gone more than a day or two, let me know. Also, if you need me down there, let me know, and I'll get there as quickly as flights will allow, or I'll drive down."

With that, Madden rose, shook hands with his junior partner, and as he walked to the door, turned his head to say, "Be cool, Jim, and be careful." Then he stepped into the hall, closing the door behind him. He stopped briefly in his own room to call the front desk and requested the desk clerk to obtain a cab for his ride to the airport. Then, gathering his suitcase, he headed down the hall and the elevator. From the hotel, it was a short fifteen-minute drive before the cab reached the private terminal at Bert Mooney Airport out on the flats. After he paid and tipped the cab driver, he entered the building and directly walked over to the receptionist seated behind the counter. "Any information on the flight coming up from Denver?" he asked of her.

The receptionist referred to her computer screen, entered some information, read the display again, and turned back to Madden. "They should be on final approach within the next ten minutes and on the ground in about twenty; there are no flights waiting for take-off clearance so they'll have a direct approach. The pilot indicated that he would taxi over here to pick you up and be ready for immediate departure as the tanks were topped off in Denver before he left."

Madden was forced to smile, knowing that Keith Strong, the senior pilot, was always planning ahead. "Thank you," he said to the receptionist and then walked to a waiting area to await the plane's arrival and the imminent trip to Jackson Hole to begin his investigation into the disappearance of Senator Jeremy Carson.

~ § ~

Addis had entered his room and, while Madden had been conversing with Washington, he had busied himself by reviewing the notes from the day's meetings at the Butte-Silver Bow Courthouse. Though the group had not uncovered a great deal of detailed information, they had found some leads, and he made a note to follow them up in Madden's absence.

Now, in the quiet of his room, Addis took out a notebook and began to write out the agenda he wanted to set for himself.

Re-examine the four arrest cases made since January 1.

Revisit the convenience store clerk in Bozeman about the sighting of Stephens and Williams.

Check with the Bureau for any information about Stella Johnson in Chester, who had assisted in identifying some al-Qaeda operatives.

Visit with local office field rep for Montana Senator Del Smith.

Addis paused in thought for a few moments and then, closing his notebook, decided to get a bite to eat since it was nearing seven o'clock. He put on a pair of grey casual slacks, gray socks, and black shoes, then changed his shirt, removing the dress shirt and tie and replacing it with a burgundy knit three-button pullover and a navy blue v-neck long sleeve sweater. Because of his exercise program, the shirt and sweater fit snuggly on his well-developed upper body. He quickly brushed his hair, which he wore in a "fade" style so it stood up neatly, brushed his teeth, and, grabbing his dark brown, waist-length leather zipper jacket, he walked out of his room. Rather than riding the elevator down, the agent sought the stairs and quickly descended to the main lobby.

The local DA had mentioned a local eatery, Porkchop John's, that would be worth trying so Addis decided to go there. After all, it was close by, and the great weather, crisp and clear, virtually called him outside. He enjoyed the brisk walk from the hotel, going downhill three blocks, turning west, and going one more to the little hole-in-the-wall restaurant. Since he felt the need for some exercise, Addis used the walkup window, ordered a pork chop sandwich, and walked as he ate his sandwich, which, he decided after the first couple of bites, lived up to O'Reilly's recommendation—delicious. Tender pork in a garlic-flavored breading, fried, and covered with caramelized onions, Dijon mustard, pickles, lettuce, and a sprinkling of pepper made it very tasty.

Having no wish to return to his room immediately, he decided to walk some of the streets of the uptown section of town. He found himself walking uphill and soon stood at the foot of a head frame. It looked to be constructed of steel I-beams that were riveted together. The top had a very large metal wheel, which, obviously had been used as a pulley many years ago. Now the large mining frame stood silent like a ghost of the glory days gone by. He slowly walked around the head frame as best he could since a chain-link fence had been set up some years prior, after the mining operation had been shut down.

Madden had shared a tidbit of information with him on the flight in, that when the underground mining ceased, the pumps were simply shut off, and water flooded the tunnels. In a sense, Butte was sitting on a massive cobweb of water-filled tunnels. Sometimes a yard or lot would simply cave-in on itself, leaving a gaping hole many feet deep, and then dump trucks would have to bring in fill to level the sinkhole. So far, no one had been caught in one of those sudden openings, but no one could anticipate exactly where the next one might occur.

Addis changed his walking direction and walked downhill for several blocks. Soon he found himself on Continental Drive. The wide street connected uptown with the southeastern and newer part of the city. As he continued to walk, he noticed another head frame, the Belmont Mine, abandoned. Addis recalled from the information he had read earlier that the city had proposed transforming the mine's mechanical building into a senior center. Pausing to gaze around the area, he noticed a tunnel almost directly across the roadway and found it to be the entrance to the viewing stand overlooking the Berkley Pit. He took advantage of the open gate, walked through the tunnel, and stepped out onto the observation platform. A humongous pit gaped before him, though its true size lay hidden beneath the surface. "Hard to believe the water's over seven hundred feet deep," he thought. Images of the ore trucks going around and around while working their way up to the surface from the depths of the mining operation played vividly in the federal agent's mind. It took over forty-five minutes of driving a continuous curved road to ascend or descend. Pictures he had seen of the pit just prior to its closing showed what looked like very small machines at the bottom. However, he knew that the tires of the ore trucks alone were over seven feet in diameter. He chuckled at the image and how our perception of size depends so dramatically on an object's surroundings.

It was time to start back up the hill so Addis turned and exited the tunnel, returning to Continental Drive and turning back up toward the uptown area. As he strolled rather easily up the quiet streets, Addis allowed his lesson on Butte from Madden to continue. The mountain range north of Butte had many faults in the deep earth, which contributed to fear of earthquakes in the area. Many local theories speculated on what might happen if those fissures should shift. The entire community could sink. But what about the great amount of water held in the Berkeley Pit? Since the pit sits above much of the town, would the southern rim of the pit open and send its toxic contents pouring down upon the lower end, called the flats, destroying all in its path? What about the cracks that were thought to be in the fairly thin wall between the pit and the city's aquifer? If they gave way, then the toxins could contaminate the drinking water.

But when it was all said and done, the people of Butte were known for their spirit and "can do" attitude. Several times in their history, the city had been on the brink of extinction, on its way to becoming another of the mining ghost towns in Montana, but the people always stepped up and revived the city. They were, as Addis knew from reading and visiting with a few locals, a very proud people.

As he stood at the base of the mining head frame, he thought of the thousands of men who had used just such a frame every day as they stepped into the hoist bucket and were lowered hundreds and even thousands of feet into the inner earth to search for and extract ore, such as silver, gold, or some of the more recently sought-after minerals, dumping the earth into ore cars that ran on railroad-type tracks through the horizontal tunnels. When the cars reached a vertical shaft, a bucket was there for the ore to be dumped into and then hoisted to the surface and dumped into waiting train cars to transport the extractions to a refinery. Sometimes they had to go only the twenty or so miles west of Butte to Anaconda to be smelted down. More recently, before the end of the mining in 1982 when the pit closed down, the ore was shipped to far away places like South America for refining at a cheaper price.

As the darkness of night continued to fold in around Addis, the temperature began to descend, causing him to turn up the collar of his leather jacket. "It might be springtime, but at five thousand feet high, the air certainly carries a bite," he thought as he started back to the Finlen Hotel.

Thoughts of the four drug cases came to his mind as Addis walked the distance to the hotel. There had to be a connection with the cases;

he was sure of that. "I need to visit with Hocking, one-on-one on Monday," he thought almost aloud, making sure it was set into his memory. "Maybe Phil and Brad discovered something and were headed up here from Bozeman to continue their investigation. I know folks here don't like the idea, but there didn't seem to be any leads that pointed to Bozeman, Helena, or Missoula," he told himself. "For the sake of those two, we need to find out what happened, and soon."

The young lawman finally reached his hotel, and he appreciated the warmth of its interior as well as the historic trappings and reminders of Butte's past. He had always liked history, and having grown up in Florida, being able to come out to Butte to see its past laid out before him was, in itself, rather special.

Chapter Five

Steve Madden landed at the Jackson Airport and, glancing at his watch, saw it was nearing nine thirty. Once off the aircraft and in possession of his single piece of luggage, he hailed a taxi outside the airport and directed the driver to the Rendezvous Mountain Resort. Situated at the base of three summits, the tallest being Rendezvous Mountain rearing up to an elevation over ten thousand four hundred feet, the resort sat in the fifty-mile long, mountain-lined valley of Jackson Hole. To the right of the resort rose Gondola Summit, almost ninety-one hundred feet, and to its right stood Apres Vous Mountain, just over eighty-four hundred feet. The town itself, called simply Jackson, serves as Teton County's county seat.

Because of the winding valley road, the drive took thirty minutes to reach his destination. Exiting the cab, Madden tipped the driver after paying the fee and carried his bag inside the lobby and across to the reservation desk.

A pert little brunette lady approached from behind the counter and asked if she could be of assistance. Madden introduced himself, and she quickly located the reservation card in his name. "Sir, you will be on the eighth floor in room 832," she said, smiling, handed him the key, and asked if there was anything else he needed.

"No, I think not tonight," he smiled back. As he started to pick up his suitcase, he paused. He had called ahead while onboard the Bureau's aircraft and asked the hotel manager to have ready for him a list of all employees and what days and hours they had worked this past week. The manager had also confirmed with Madden that a master key for the rooms on the ninth floor as well as videotapes of the different areas of the resort would be waiting for him upon his arrival. "Maybe I can get some things done yet tonight," he silently corrected himself. Turning back to the clerk, Madden added, "Would you have the key for me to access rooms on the ninth floor? Also, I would like the videotapes that were set aside for me to take now and a player delivered to my room as soon as possible."

Again the clerk smiled and replied that what he requested would not be a problem. "I'll make sure one of our bellhops brings the player up immediately, sir." She disappeared into the back office and brought out a locked metal strong box. She placed the box and a manila envelope on the counter and said, "Here are the tapes and the other items you requested, Mr. Madden. The manager asked me to assure you that the tapes have been under lock and key since the first contact with him early this morning."

Madden tucked the manila envelope under his arm and picked up the box containing the videotapes, then walked to the elevator. Upon entering his room, he hung his topcoat and suit coat on the clothes rack by the bathroom, then stripped off his tie and carefully placed it on a hanger. He then turned to wash his hands and face. The cool water felt good on his face. It had been a long day, and he wanted to view the videotapes before retiring for the evening. However, first things first; after toweling off his face and hands, he called his office, left a message that he had arrived and again thanked Cynthia for her efforts. He further asked that she fax all of her notes to him at the hotel, knowing that, though it was a weekend, she would check in the morning and follow up. That was just the kind of employee she was. Then he called the local sheriff and arranged to meet with him at eight o'clock the next morning to examine the senator's room and learn what the police might have uncovered so far.

The quiet of Madden's room was interrupted by a knock on the door, followed by a youthful sounding voice, "Bellhop, luggage for Mr. Madden." Steve went to the door, opened it, and was greeted by a young man in black slacks, white shirt with black tie, and a black jacket. "Sir, here's the tape viewer you requested and your suitcase." Madden reached and took the player, and the bellhop stepped in and set the suitcase on the folding rack by the clothes rod. Madden thanked the bellhop and gave him a tip. "Thank you, sir. Have a pleasant evening, Mr. Madden." With that the young man turned and started down the hall.

Madden closed the door and took the player to the dresser that served as the counter for the large television. He connected the cords from the player to the television set. Turning the TV on and setting the channel selector to 3, he turned on the tape player, inserted the first tape, and pulled a chair over in front of the screen. The tape showed many people entering the hotel through the front door. Steve watched intently. Most were carrying ski garb and suitcases and wore ski parkas over their clothes, or at least carried that type of garment.

He could identify the senator coming in and going to the desk, as well as the other members of the conference. Because the camera was positioned in such a way, its viewfinder also captured some of the protesters picketing outside. Once the delegates were all inside, it was pretty obvious that the mingling protesters had had enough and disappeared without any of them entering the building, at least through the lobby's entrance.

The next day's video did not show anything different from the first. The people coming in and going out through the lobby were most assuredly skiers and seemed very relaxed. Madden rewound the tape and viewed it a second time to see if he had missed anything. Satisfied that he had not, he rewound the tape again, ejected it from the player, and placed it off to one side and then picked up the next tape and inserted it into the machine and began to watch the scenes unfold before his eyes.

This tape was, according the identification sticker on the sleeve, of the elevator lobby area. It began with the previous Monday noon and went through Wednesday night. Madden watched intently, looking for something or someone that might run up a warning flag in his mind. Throughout the afternoon of Monday, he only saw people, for the most part, in ski attire coming and going from the elevator. Some carried skis, or snowboards, others just their regular attire without any outer jackets or coats. Finally, about 5:30 p.m., according the running time in the frame of the tape, he saw Senator Carson come into the range of the camera's viewfinder. He noticed Carson was wearing a dark suit and carrying his topcoat. Obviously, the senator had checked in and left his bag at the desk for a bellhop to deliver to his room later rather than carry it up on his own, a practice that most of the resort visitors seemed to follow, as had Madden upon checking in.

Scenes next showed the other members of the meeting group also entering the different elevator doors at different times. It appeared that all of them had had a resort bellhop transfer their luggage to their respective rooms rather than carrying it themselves. The experienced Bureau agent continued to peruse the video and noted the times that each member of the delegation entered the elevator and each time he or she exited. By doing this, Madden had a pretty good handle for how long the dignitary guests spent, presumably, in their room or downstairs. He could later corroborate these times with videos from the respective floors, the lobby views, as well as tapes from the bar and lounge, sauna, pool, exercise room, parking lot and the ski desk area.

As the tape began to get to the end of Tuesday, he focused more closely for this was when Senator Carson's aide suggested the senator might have disappeared, based upon the information that, as Cynthia had relayed to Madden, Carson never answered his cell phone or room phone from Tuesday night on. Madden glanced at the timer in the lower right corner of the display, 7:45 p.m. Nobody was in the area of the elevators. He saw two figures move in from the direction that would be an entrance hallway other than the lobby. The figures were male, one short and one fairly tall. Though exact height could not be discerned very accurately from viewing the tapes, the second man was considerable shorter but much stockier than the other. Neither looked to be a skier, but who knew anymore as they came in all shapes and sizes. Madden studied the figures; both were dressed very casually.

They stopped at the end of the elevator area, and both peered out the floor-to-ceiling windows that faced the ski hill rising up as part of the Teton Range. The taller man was nearer the end wall, and he turned as if laughing and joking with his companion, who had turned to look toward the taller man.

A third figure came into view. This was Senator Carson. Madden watched the video showing Carson pushing the button to call for an elevator. Moments later, the door opened. Carson could be seen beginning to step forward, only to quickly stop, then back away a couple of steps to allow a group of folks to exit. Madden chuckled as the group moved away, Carson's head turning to watch the members of the group journey down the hallway. "He always has had an eye for ladies," mused Madden, knowing the reputation that his Bureau had for the young senator. The two men, Madden noticed, stepped into the elevator behind Carson, still appearing to be carrying on a friendly conversation. No other persons came into the camera viewfinder before the door of the elevator closed and began its ascent. Checking the imposed time on the video frame, Madden noted it read 8:18 p.m.

Madden continued his vigil of the elevator video and saw a group of four, two men and two women, all neatly dressed approach. They were in a party mood for they were laughing and talking. All four entered one of the other three elevators, and the doors closed. The ever-moving digital clock in the lower right corner of the video frame displayed 8:20. No one had come or gone since the group of four. Madden noticed a group of three step up to the elevator control panel and press the call button. The three appeared to be fairly young, most likely late teens to early twenties, Madden thought. All three had on street clothes and medium-weight waist-length jackets. The two taller individuals, both boys, exhibited nothing out of the ordinary, but the third one, a female, glanced about nervously as they waited for the elevator to open for them. The shorter of the two boys obviously was holding something under his jacket as it stuck out in front rather dramatically. Madden started to laugh aloud. "Crazy kids," he heard himself say. "Smuggling beer to their rooms while their parents are out." Finally, after what for the teens—or at least the girl—must have seemed like too many minutes of waiting, the door slid open. The girl couldn't get in to the elevator fast enough, bumping the boy who held the suspected contraband. Madden could see him turn his head toward her and could see the mouth moving, as if scolding her for the near tragedy. The doors slid along their respective track, meeting in the middle, and the kids disappeared from view. Time on the video frame read 8:23 p.m.

Madden's eyes were getting tired from the video, and he did not want to miss anything that might be important so he pushed the pause button on the player, got up, stretched, and went to the bar provided by the hotel. Opening the door of the refrigerator, he extracted a bottle of drinking water and twisted off the cap. Lifting the bottle to his mouth, he took a long drink of the cold water. He then walked to the window and stood there, momentarily looking out at the parking lot below. Not much activity tonight, he thought, though the parking lot was pretty full. Most of the skiers had already checked in during the day and were either out on the town or in the lounge eight stories below. The ones who liked to get that early start on the slopes were probably already in bed. That thought caused Madden to look at his watch. He had spent almost two and a half hours looking at the tapes as the watch told him it was two minutes before midnight.

Madden was glad he had called home and talked to his family as his flight was departing from Butte. Knowing that, by now, all would be fast asleep made him smile. The two children, Audrey, who was seven and in the second grade, and Steven Jr., who had just turned four last month, loved playing with their parents, and the Madden home exuded happiness. When Lee returned from work in the late afternoon and Audrey got home from school, Lee would sit down at the dining room table with her, and they would go over what she did in school that day and work together on any homework Audrey might have. When he came home, loving kisses and hugs flew among them all, and then he would ask Audrey if the homework was done or what she had learned. Typically, little Steven Jr. would get picked up, tossed into the air, and hugged. Then there was usually some happy free time before the parents both exited to the kitchen to prepare the table and the evening meal.

Madden turned off the pleasant thoughts of home and brought his mind back to the present place. He consumed the remaining water in the bottle, placed the empty plastic container in the trashcan by the refrigerator, and returned to his seat in front of the monitor. Clicking the play button, the video's events once again absorbed his attention. The next action at the elevator showed a lone person approach. As he watched, Madden could not distinguish if the individual was a male or female. Dressed in baggy sweats, with the hood of the top pulled up and over the head, the person paused, pushed the call button, stood impatiently for two or three seconds, and then moved off to the exit door, disappearing into the dimly lit stairwell. Madden wrote in his notepad the time on the screen, 8:37 p.m. "I want to know what floor that person goes to," Madden told himself, and added that to the written commentary.

No sooner did he make the note than he saw a second individual, also in what appeared to be a jogging suit appear in front of the elevators. By this time the door of the arriving elevator was open and the individual, whose head also was covered by a hood, stepped inside. As the person turned to push the button for a desired floor, the reflected light of the elevator caught the individual's face and illuminated the inside of the hood. The face looked to be of a man with facial hair. Again, Madden made a note of the time, 8:38 p.m. He now had at least these two to follow on the remaining tapes. "Did they have anything to do with the disappearance of the senator?" Madden questioned himself.

The process of viewing the elevator tape continued, but nothing seemed to capture Madden's attention. He noticed the other dignitaries come and go almost always with at least one or two other people they obviously were in conversation with. Around ten o'clock on the video display, the activity around the elevators picked up markedly. More people were taking the lifts from the main floor, signaling the end of the evening for some of the guests. It seemed to be almost a steady stream from that time on with people ranging in dress from those in classy dresses and suits to couples and singles in jeans, t-shirts, and jackets or no outdoor wear at all. As he watched the flow of humanity use the elevators or the stairs, he was amused by the memory of the three teens and what he presumed was beer that they were smuggling up to the upper floor somewhere. "I wonder if the parents have gone up yet," he chuckled. He could imagine how, after consuming what it was they had hidden under the jacket; they had to get rid of the evidence before any adult appeared. Such behavior reminded him of his collegiate days when spring breaks resulted in far more compromising scenarios than the one he had witnessed earlier on the video.

Madden wanted at least to finish viewing this video before turning in. He glanced at his watch, one forty-five.

Finally when the tape reached midnight of the day's recording, Steve had about run out of energy. It was almost two-thirty, and he reminded himself that he needed to get some sleep since the local sheriff was meeting him at eight o'clock. Unfortunately, he admitted to himself, he wouldn't have time for an early rising early and a run. Though the jog would indeed be invigorating, the sleep would matter more, especially when looking over the senator's assigned room, as well as reviewing the tapes with the sheriff and going over what information law enforcement might have. Observational training already had Madden making mental notes of how he wanted to examine that room and what to look for. He knew he needed to determine the source of the unknown and unexplained glass pieces the housekeeper had found. Madden decided to look at the first couple of hours on the next elevator video series just to make sure there was not some suspicious activity in the early morning hours. After watching for several minutes in fast forward mode, he reached the time stamp on the video of 2:00 a.m. He continued to view the tape but nothing unusual or out of the ordinary occurred as the minutes had turned into hours on the video screen. Very few people had come or gone after the video clock displayed 1:00 a.m. Most of those who did enter the elevators were dressed as though they had been out on the town—nice suits on the men and cocktail dresses or pantsuits on the women. At 2:00 a.m., a pair of men, one with rather long hair and the other with a crew cut, entered the view. Both were wearing Western attire. The long-hair wore jeans and tennis shoes and what appeared to be a denim jacket. He walked in such a manner that Madden believed he probably had spent a good amount of time on the back of a horse. His companion also wore jeans but with Western boots. Though he did not sport a denim jacket, the shirt he wore looked to be a woolen plaid and maybe a Pendleton type, thought Madden. The man carried a dark-colored Western hat in his hand. The two waited for the doors of an elevator to open and then stepped in as the closing doors swallowed them up.

For another six hours on the quickly playing scene, hardly anyone came to or from the elevators, and as light began to bathe the waiting area, housekeepers busied themselves with mopping and buffing the floor and wiping down the walls and windows, erasing any prints left by those who had been there throughout the previous day and evening. The clock readout on the replay, showed 8:00 a.m., Wednesday morning. Madden yawned and decided to stop and get some well-needed shuteye. He turned off the TV and the player, rose from the chair, and went to the bathroom to brush and floss his teeth. Then he washed his face and hands, changed out of his suit pants and dress shirt, which now looked as though it had been worn for several days, discarding the shirt into the plastic laundry courtesy bag provided by the hotel. He put the pants on a pants hanger, draped the suit coat over it, and hung them up. Before sliding into the king-size bed, he removed his socks, throwing them along side the dress shirt, and placed his shoes, long since removed, under the suitcase stand.

Taking off his wristwatch, he carefully set the alarm for 6:30. That would give him all of two hours as the watch informed him that it was nearing 4:15 in the morning.

CHAPTER SIX

A loud, annoying buzzing sounded in Agent Madden's ear. It took a moment before he realized that it was the alarm clock on the table by his bed. After reaching over and terminating the obnoxious screaming, he swung his feet over the side of the bed, stretched, and yawned. To save time, he had purchased a container of strawberry yogurt, a poppyseed bagel, and a small carton of orange juice before coming up to his room the night before. He put the pre-measured coffee filter into the brewing space, poured in the cold water, and turned it on. Then he retrieved the necessary clothing from his suitcase. Knowing the day would be an active one, he selected comfortable clothes, blue slacks, slip-on loafers, black with decorative tassels over the instep, navy blue socks, and a light green, three-button pullover shirt. Next he headed to the shower, turned the handle all the way to hot, and within seconds filled the bathroom with steam. Relishing the hot water beating on his body and awakening him for the day's activity, he stepped in.

Madden exited the shower, toweled himself off, and after wrapping a towel around his waist, he performed that morning ritual of shaving. As he did so, he reflected on how Lee liked to stand in the doorway of their master bath and watch him shave with his safety razor. He always went through the same routine. First he trimmed the sideburns, then the cheeks and the upper lip, followed by the lower lip and chin and then the neck and under the jaw line. Finishing his last stroke, he ran the water in the sink and splashed his face with ice-cold water. It felt so stimulating.

He dressed in the clothes he had set out. Madden took a cup of steaming coffee, walked to the large window that overlooked the parking lot below, and stood, watching the sun slowly make its appearance over the eastern horizon as he enjoyed each mouthful of the hot, black liquid.

Turning from the window after finishing the cup, he returned to the coffee pot and refilled his cup. Taking a seat at the desk and eating his yogurt and bagel which he washed down with the orange juice followed by the coffee, he reviewed the notes he had made the night before while viewing the videos. Glancing at his watch, he saw it was 7:15, forty-five minutes before his meeting with the sheriff. He made sure his notebook was ready. Pencils, pens, measuring tape, and a six-inch rule. The sheriff had indicated he would bring his department photographer with him in case they needed any photos. In addition, the crime scene investigation box he would bring would include special spectrum lights and colored eyewear for viewing specific evidence with the lights, if warranted, necessary swabs with plastic canisters for storing them, latex gloves, fingerprint equipment, and evidence bags and envelopes.

At seven-fifty, a firm knock sounded on Madden's door. Peering through the security-hole, he saw Teton County Sheriff Kyler Mickelson and let him in. Kyler Mickelson stood six feet four and weighed a trimly fit 190 pounds. He was decked out in tan Western boots, dark blue slacks with a gold stripe insert running up the outside of each leg. He was wearing a black jacket with his sheriff's badge pinned to the left breast panel and the sheriff department logo stitched to the right shoulder with an American flag patch stitched to the left shoulder. The waist-length jacket rode slightly high, allowing the handle of his gun to protrude from his right hip. A black leather pouch containing chrome handcuffs was centered on his back, attached to the black leather gun belt. A second pouch on the belt on his left hip held a container that most likely was mace. Mickelson had a dark tan, indicating he disapproved of the idea of a "sit behind the desk" peace officer. Only creases at the corners of his mouth and the corners of his eyes marked his face, suggesting he loved life and shared his enjoyment with others. Eyes of deep blue looked straight at Madden as the two men exchanged introductions and greetings as Madden stepped aside, inviting Mickelson in. Grasping his hand, Madden was not surprised to feel the firm grip of a self-confident man. Mickelson had removed the Western style hat he wore and held it in his left hand, revealing dark brown, medium length hair.

"I've been reviewing videos from some of the resort cameras," stated Madden. "There are a couple of interesting people, though I haven't had the opportunity to check other views from the exterior or other hallways." Mickelson nodded. "I'll continue with that once you and I have gone over the senator's room, as well as any other areas we think might make some difference."

Mickelson was glancing down at the note pad now and said, "Sounds good to me, Agent Madden." Then he continued, "Where do you want to start this morning, sir?"

"Please, Kyler, just call me Steve," Madden said. "I think we can start in Carson's room if you're ready."

"Any time you say," responded Mickelson, starting to walk toward the door. "Dennis Ziegler, our department photog and videographer, is waiting by the elevator, and we can all go up together."

Madden picked up his notebook and, gesturing with his hand, followed the sheriff out the door and to the elevator where they met up with the photographer. The sheriff made the necessary introductions, and the three men stepped into the elevator. Madden entered last, turned, and pushed the button with the numeral nine. The door silently slid closed, and they felt a slight lifting sensation as the elevator made its rapid ascent to the floor above. As the three men walked down the quiet hallway, they discussed a systematic approach to examining the suite at the end of the hall, 932. They decided that before entering the room itself, they would dust both sides of the stairwell door—the handle on the stair side and the crash bar on the interior side, the side exposed to the hall leading to the rooms. Once done with that, they would do the same for the emergency door at the opposite end. Then Madden and Mickelson would be the first to enter while the Ziegler waited out in the hallway. Once the two law officers had taken a cursory look, he would be called in to photograph any potential evidence.

Finished with dusting the common doors, they approached Room 932. As the door to Carson's suite opened, Madden and Mickelson stepped just inside the door, allowing it to close but not quite latch. Their experienced eyes surveyed the room. The walls showed no marks of any kind; the bed, left untouched, still stood as it was that night when the senator entered, completely made up with the exception of a dark blue suit coat lying on top of it. Next to the coat was a closed black briefcase with brass combination latches and a black handle supported by brass anchors.

Mickelson stepped over to the sink and clothes rod area. Ski clothes were hanging neatly on the rods, and ski boots were on the floor immediately beneath them. Everything around the sink appeared to be in its virgin position with the exception of a drinking glass by the sink and a small black leather toiletry bag sitting to the right of the sink. Mickelson donned latex gloves and carefully lifted the glass. Holding it up to the light, he identified marks left by a hand. Setting the glass down, he opened the crime kit and withdrew the brush and dusting powder for fingerprints. Carefully brushing the glass, he found several prints, all seeming to be the same, probably from one person's hand holding it to fill with water and then drink from it. The sheriff then took tape, carefully set it over each of the fingertip prints, and then removed the tape, adhering it to a special card for protection. He wrote an identification number on it, indicating where the prints were found and by whom, placed the evidence card into an evidence envelope, sealed it, and then placed it in the plastic case. Moving on, Mickelson examined the sink and then began taking items from the toiletry bag, carefully looking over each item, stopping to remove any hairs, placing the samples into plastic evidence bags he had removed from the crime scene case. Any latent prints he found he dusted and carefully recorded before they, too, were stored away for the crime lab to analyze and, hopefully, to identify.

As Mickelson worked the sink and clothes area and then the bathroom, Madden began to scour the room for evidence. Carefully working his way in from the entrance door, he examined the walls closely, even with the spectrograph, but nothing showed up. The nightstand revealed only prints on the telephone and the alarm clock/radio, from which, of course, he lifted samples. The suit coat contained a brown leather wallet in the inner left breast pocket. Madden was somewhat surprised to see that the wallet still contained several credit cards, some legislative related identification cards, an Idaho driver's license bearing the headshot type photo of Senator Carson. As he opened the bill partitions, he counted over two hundred dollars. "Obviously this was not a robbery gone bad," he called out to Mickelson.

Upon checking the remainder of the wallet, he found nothing out of the ordinary, nor did he turn up anything else unusual in the clothes pockets. Madden carefully lifted the notepad by the telephone and using a special light held at an angle, found no image of previous writing. The room almost seemed sanitary.

Moving to the windows, Madden carefully examined the glass and metal trim for prints and found none. The same was true of the television. Some prints, looking to be the same as those he and Mickelson had lifted earlier, were also discovered on the handle and door of the suite's wet bar and refrigerator. He used his pen tip carefully to open a leather notebook binder that lay on the round table next to the window and between two armed chairs. He lifted individual pages carefully but noticed only doodling and some notes the senator most likely had taken during the meeting downstairs. The pocket contained several sheets, some additional notes, some "to be done" notes for calls he needed to place, mostly to other senators and to his office. He noted the numbers so he and Mickelson could have those contacted later to see if anyone had actually received the planned calls, but somehow he doubted they would find any affirmative responses since there were no marks next to names and subject annotations that would have indicated the task had been completed. Flipping through a pocket calendar book, Madden found a schedule of legislation that would be coming up for vote on the Senate floor as well as a schedule for several committees on which the senator held a seat, including one for the Committee on Foreign Affairs, a committee on which the agent knew the senator held the position as vice chair—a highly visible and very powerful position and unusual for such a young man but an indication of how much respect his party held for him. Then there was the senator's computer, a fairly new Dell laptop. He carefully placed it in a plastic zip-lock bag and set it aside. That would be sent to Washington for examination.

Madden began focusing on the floor from the door to the center of the room. He looked at the fibers of the close-cut carpet and noted some hardened substance. Taking an evidence bag and tweezers, he carefully removed the material, placed it in a bag, labeled it, and deposited it in the plastic kit. He found several samples, and from each, he took a small part for analysis. As he carefully examined the floor around the sofa, he noticed that the legs of the sofa at one end did not sit in the indented marks it had previously made. "Obviously," thought Madden, "someone moved this end of the sofa for some reason." The rug fibers had been crushed by the leg sliding forward, suggesting that the sofa had not been picked up and moved. Rather, it had been pushed forward, and because the carpet fibers were lying flat, it suggested that the movement had not been a gently gliding motion. "Looks like maybe someone fell into or over this sofa," he called out to Mickelson.

After listening to Madden's description, Mickelson concurred with him. As he was through examining the bathroom and clothes areas, they opened the door so Ziegler could enter with his camera and take photos where samples had been taken, each spot marked by a numbered plastic inverted v-shaped evidence tag. He already saw he had six or seven such areas to photograph.

Mickelson now joined Madden by the sofa and they both crawled very slowly with their eyes focused on the carpet ahead of them and around the sofa itself. After several seconds, Mickelson broke the silence. "Steve, check this out." He pointed to an area about four feet in front of the sofa. "Looks like little pieces of glass." Madden turned and stepped over next to the sheriff.

"I remember the manager saying that when the housekeeper came in to clean, she noticed the glass on the floor but didn't know where it had come from." The pieces sat about twelve inches from a glass coffee table that was positioned in front of the sofa. Each of the law enforcement men picked up select pieces of the glass and studied them carefully. "The glass looks to be the same kind and thickness as that of this table," Mickelson volunteered.

"The strange part," answered Madden, "is that there's not a single nick out of that table. So, if it's the same type of glass, where is the table it came from?"

Mickelson nodded and then added, "Steve, what do you make of this? Looks to me as though there's some blood on the carpet here and maybe even on this little shard of glass," he said, holding up a piece of glass about one-quarter of an inch in size.

Madden carried the investigation case over to Mickelson, set it down, and took out a cotton swab at the end of a long wooden stick. He moistened the stick with a solution from a small squeeze bottle he had lifted out of the kit and then touched the wet tip to the glass piece. "Bingo!" he exclaimed. "Definitely blood. The question is, whose?" He directed Mickelson to save the sample of glass and blood and also to cut out the fibers of the carpet that held a sample as well. Madden stood just beyond where Mickelson had discovered the glass fragments and looked back. The end of the sofa that he had discovered to be forcefully slid forward was in line with the glass pieces and in line with one end of the glass-topped coffee table that stood there. "Kyler, take a look at the sofa," Madden said. "Tell me what you see."

The Jackson Hole sheriff stood, stepped next to Madden, and looked at the sofa. "The left cushion is seated completely on the sofa, but the right one is sticking out this way a little. The back of the cushion seems to be up in the air a bit."

"That's what I see as well, Kyler," said Madden. "The only way it would be like that is if either the front edge was sat upon, lifting the back away from the under cushion, or …"

"Or, the cushion had been displaced for some reason or something," finished Mickelson. "Maybe the senator, or someone, fell over the sofa, landed on at least part of the coffee table and then hit the floor."

Madden smiled, "That's the scene being told to me, Kyler. I think maybe the senator, if that blood sample comes out of the lab as his; either fell over or was shoved over the sofa. We don't know if that occurred during a fight or if he had been overpowered. In any case, we still have a problem."

Mickelson looked at Madden, the floor where they stood, then the table, and finally the sofa. "Steve, from the door to where we are is pretty much a straight line. If the senator had been just coming in, or if he had opened the door to someone, he may have been pushed or forced into the sofa back, going over the top, loosening the cushion before hitting the table. However, if that's the scenario, where the hell is the broken table? There sure isn't any way he or anyone else could hit the table, break off pieces, and leave the table intact. You and I have both looked at it, and there are no pieces broken from it. Just the smeared prints you found on either end of the table legs."

The two men continued to examine the room very carefully, and after three hours, they stood at the door. Madden had placed the suit coat in a large plastic bag, leaving the wallet and all of its contents inside the jacket, noting what he had found specifically. The suitcase, lying open on the chrome and material strapped frame under the coat rack, had been closed and tagged for the lab workers to examine in detail, as well as the ski clothes and boots the two had found upon entering the room.

"I think we've covered just about everything in this room, " Madden said, stepping out into the hallway. "Dennis can finish photographing the evidence locations. Let's you and I take a look at some of the rooms along this floor. We know the floor's been closed and sealed by the management since Wednesday morning when the senator's aide called you and the manager. Maybe we'll get lucky and find something, but as clean as that room was, I wouldn't place any bets on it."

Mickelson had now stepped into the hallway to join Madden, and the two walked away from the room, stopping at the next room, and using the master key provided to him, Madden opened the door. "Do you have any idea what or why anyone would kidnap a U.S. senator?" he asked.

"I've asked my office to visit with his staff back in DC and his field staff in Boise to see if anything jumps out," Madden answered. "Right now, I have no reason to suspect any specific group or individual. Rarely do these guys just disappear, though, and it certainly looks as though something or somebody caused Carson to vanish."

After carefully going through the unoccupied room, the two agreed there was nothing there for evidence. Not one single print, no clothing items, nothing. So, they closed the door and moved on to the next room down the hall. Again, the same result, nothing was out of place, nothing seemed to provide any clues. As they stepped out into the hallway again a short, dark-haired lady, probably in her early thirties, came around the corner from the elevator area and identified herself as Claire Hickey. She said she was the day desk clerk, and in fact, she wore the same dark skirt and jacket, white blouse, and brass nameplate as other female workers of the resort wore. "Mr. Henson asked me to come up and ask you two to join him in his office right away."

Both Madden and Mickelson looked toward each other and shrugged. Mickelson went back to room 932 and informed the photographer that they were going to the manager's office on the second floor where the resort's marketing and private administrative offices were located. He suggested that as soon as he was finished collecting photographic evidence of the room that he, too, should join them. Ziegler indicated that he had only two or three more evidence locations to photograph and would be along in a few minutes. Turning back to Madden and the clerk, Mickelson nodded to Madden, and the trio walked to the elevators and descended to the second floor of the resort.

Claire Hickey led Madden and Mickelson from the elevator to a large door that had a mountain scene with an elk and a bear etched into the glass panel that took up most of the upper half of the massive pine door. The door was one of two, and together they spanned a good eight feet across the roomy hallway. The entire second floor comprised of offices for marketing, sales, human resources, two vice presidents, the manager, and the president of the corporation, not to mention clerical locations for each of the offices and a large mail, sorting, and copy room.

As the three stepped through the doorway, a receptionist immediately looked up from her desk. Recognizing Claire, she smiled and greeted her warmly. Claire spoke to her and introduced both Steve Madden, an FBI agent, and Sheriff Kyler Mickelson before stating that Mr. Henson had requested meeting with them.

"One moment please." The receptionist smiled, picked up her phone, and jabbed at three numbers. "Sonja, Claire Hickey has two law enforcement men who are to see Mr. Henson." There was a short pause and then, "Ok, I'll send them down right away." The receptionist replaced the handset, thanked Claire for bringing the men down, and then stood. "I'll take you back to Mr. Henson's office. Please follow me."

Both Madden and Mickelson thanked the desk clerk for her bringing them to the office, and she slipped out the etched glass doors and retraced her steps to the elevator and then down to the reservation desk. The two lawmen then followed the receptionist down a brightly lit hallway, noticing that both sides of the hall were walled with glass, etched with difference scenes depicting skiing, snowmobiling, hiking, camping, snowshoeing, and fishing along with some scenes of wildlife. Obviously, this resort was doing quite well—or at the very least, putting on a very pretentious image of doing so.

Upon arriving at the far end of the hall, a sign announced that they had arrived at the office of the president of Evergreen Resorts, the company owning the resort. The receptionist opened the door, stepped aside, and gestured the two into the large outer office. A petite blonde with darkly tanned skin and bright blue eyes looked up as they entered. She smiled a wide and very genuine smile, stepped out from behind her desk, and greeted each with a friendly and warm handshake. "Hello, I'm Sonja White, Mr. Henson's administrative assistant. If you will come with me, Mr. Henson has asked that you be shown in to his office immediately."

With that, she turned and led them to the end of her work area, then knocked twice on a large, decorated door, for which the knob was located in the center. She then opened the door and gestured to two men inside. "Mr. Henson, Agent Madden from the Federal Bureau of Investigation and Mr. Mickelson, our Jackson Hole sheriff." With the introductions out of the way, the young lady turned and quickly left the office, quietly closing the door behind her.

Marcus Henson, though graying, had the perfect physique for one at the head of a business catering to the physically active and well-to-do. His deeply tanned, almost leathery skin spoke to much time in the sun; his five fee ten inches and 165 pounds presented a trim and healthy body; and his broad friendly smile displayed sparkling white teeth. Shaking the hands of Madden and Mickelson, his firm grip exuded the self-confidence of one in his position. "Agent Madden, Sheriff Mickelson," he said as he shook their hands, "it's a pleasure to meet you two. However, I wish it were on more positive circumstances, and I do hope that you will honor us with your presence sometime in the future when, shall we say, it will be for recreational purposes?"

Mickelson and Madden both acknowledged Henson's greeting. Madden then spoke. "Mr. Henson, we do apologize for the inconvenience of keeping your rooms off limits. We greatly appreciate the staff's cooperation and willingness to lock down the ninth floor and to provide us with the videos from your cameras. We can assure you that we will release the rooms back to you for use as quickly as possible."

"Not to worry, Agent Madden," Henson replied. "I only hope that the investigation results in something that is positive for you and not something that gives Jackson Hole and, of course, our resort a bit of bad press." With that the corporation president invited the two to take a seat around a circular table. The table was obviously hand carved with deer, elk, moose and bear cut into the top, over which lay a thick piece of tempered safety glass. The table itself seemed to have been cut from a single tree trunk and the base carved to look as though it was actually a trunk growing up from the floor and spreading its branches into a circular and spectacular canopy. As they took their seats, Madden noticed that the chairs were overstuffed leather pieces, very comfortable indeed.

"Mr. Henson," began Agent Madden, "Claire Hickey told us you wished to meet with us."

Henson was standing by his desk. "Yes, that is true. This morning, one of our floor supervisors was sorting out linens and furniture items for the ninth floor and went to one of the storerooms on that floor. When she opened the door to do inventory, she found that the count for the extra and spare coffee tables was off. She informed her supervisor who, knowing what the situation was with 932, came to the HR supervisor who, in turn shared the information with my administrative assistant."

The CEO had now walked over to a third leather chair and taken a seat. "Hotels and resorts are always having some furniture lost or broken, but usually we can account for it by locating the room from which it came. You see, we carefully put a tag on each piece that tells us the number of the room to which that piece is assigned."

Mickelson smiled and nodded. "Yes, we saw the tags on the furniture in 932 and the other rooms as we went through, but of course, without a scanner and the inventory checklist, we have no way of knowing the rooms identified on each tag."

Henson was leaning back in his chair, listening and now leaned forward, placing his spread-out hands on the table. "I think and I hope that maybe we have found something that will assist you in your investigation, gentlemen. I personally accompanied the facilities day manager and the floor supervisor to the equipment storeroom on the ninth floor after the housekeeper met with our HR director. I would like to take the two of you up there and see what you might make of it." Both Madden and Mickelson indicated that they would be happy to do so, and all three men rose, Henson leading the way as they exited the office, walked back to the elevator, and rose to the ninth floor. Once the doors opened, the CEO walked briskly down the hallway, away from room 932. At the end of the hall, Henson took out a key card and handed it to Mickelson who, after donning latex gloves, opened the unmarked door and stepped inside. As he did so, he reached to the wall opposite the door hinges and switched on a bare light bulb that was centered in the room.

Turning to them, Henson said, "This is where we keep the extra pieces. Our floor supervisor, Lucinda Diaz, discovered that a glass coffee table is missing." The mind of Madden quickly analyzed the statement. "So, do you know where that table went, Mr. Henson?"

Henson looked down at the floor before answering. "No, unfortunately, we are not sure what room, if any, the table has gone to. We have checked all the rooms except for those on this floor, and I can tell you that the table, if it is still in the hotel, is in one of the rooms on the ninth floor. Because we did not wish to interfere with your investigation, we stayed away from these rooms. I have with me, however, a small scanner and the inventory list," he said, holding up a small brown three-ring notebook.

Mickelson glanced toward Madden. "We have finished going through 932, Mr. Henson."

Madden nodded and added, "Let's say we walk down there and check that table tag."

The three turned and walked to the opposite end of the ninth floor and stopped at Room 932. Madden took out the master key he still had and unlocked the door to the suite. Stepping in, the CEO took a small electronic scanner from his suit coat pocked, walked to the table, carefully avoiding the plastic evidence tents, and stopped at the end of the coffee table. He reached down and pointed the device at the upper corner of one leg, where, hidden from view, a metallic tag was placed. The device emitted a soft chirp, and he withdrew it. Now he opened his notebook, went to a specific section, flipped through several more pages and, after glancing at the scanner, looked back to the list. He slid his index finger down the list and finally stopped. Looking up from his list, Henson looked at the two, peering over his half-spectacles. "Gentlemen," he began, "this table is not assigned to any room; it is supposed to be in the storage room we were just in. This is the missing table."

The two lawmen looked at each other before speaking. Finally, after several seconds, Madden spoke. "If this table is not the table that was here when the senator occupied this room, where the heck is the table that was supposed to be here, and how did it get removed?"

The three went back to the equipment room where Madden squatted down and looked at the door and jam. "This door has been jimmied at some point," he declared. Pointing to the jam he continued, "Here are the marks from some object that was forcefully pushed into the latch mechanism." Then, turning to the door, he again pointed to the latch area. "These scratches evidently came from the same tool as the marks are alike and match each other. I would guess, from the width of the marks and the sharpness of the cut on one side and not so deep above the parallel mark, that the instrument was a pocketknife." Madden stood and turned to Henson, "Do you know where in the equipment room that table was being stored?"

Henson shook his head and said, "No, I can't tell you exactly where it was, but I know that we encourage each room to be kept the same. Usually the coffee tables, because they are glass topped, are kept against the far wall." Henson pointed to the wall at the far side of the room.

"If what you say applies to this room," Madden continued, "then whoever took the table had to move some of the other furniture. It's obvious that to reach the far side is one thing, but to lift a table off the stack and carry out piece of furniture as awkward as a five- or six-foot coffee table would require moving some of the remaining pieces."

Henson looked at Madden with a smile on his face. "I know that the floor supervisor in charge of this floor is still on the premises. Let me call our HR director and see what we can find out." A short call to the director and Henson clicked off his cell phone. "We should know very soon, gentlemen." Within fifteen minutes, the CEO's phone rang, and he quickly reached for the device. Answering it, he was quiet and then spoke into it, "You are sure of that?" A pause followed by, "Ok. I will let them know. Thank you. And please thank Lucinda for me." He disconnected and turned again to face the lawmen. "Lucinda said she was doing her weekly inventory on Tuesday morning, and all the coffee tables were, as we require them to be, against that far wall. Knowing that the floor was closed down she again counted pieces only yesterday and only in here. When she noticed the difference, she immediately notified her supervisor upon her arrival this morning."

Mickelson and Madden both smiled and looked at each other. "Mr. Henson," Madden said, turning very stern in tone, "it is imperative that nobody comes into this room until further notice. We will want to examine every single piece in here." Extending his hand, he shook Henson's and said, "Thank you very much for letting us know. We will try to release the room as quickly as possible."

CHAPTER SEVEN

The agent and the sheriff entered the elevator with Henson, descended to the second floor administrative office level, and exited where they again met up with their photographer, Dennis Ziegler. After introducing him to the resort manager, Madden asked Ziegler to accompany them back to the ninth floor storage room. After unlocking the door again with the key supplied by Marcus Henson and gently opening it with his hands in latex to prevent damaging present fingerprints or creating new ones, Mickelson directed his staff photographer to shoot some photos of the room as it now stood with all pieces in their present position. As Ziegler clicked off several shots from the floor level and doorway to the ceiling high shots aimed downward, which would reveal a more accurate image of the position for each piece in relation to those around it, Madden was carefully noting where each and every piece was. His eyes were following the path that would lead from the door to the area where the coffee table pieces were stored. The neatness was one thing that struck him. "Every piece in its assigned place," he thought.

It was not until Ziegler had stepped aside to allow the sheriff and the FBI agent to move forward into the room that Madden noticed something that struck him as being out-of-place. As they moved into the room about six feet, the path forked. The path between pieces of dressers and bed frames went straight ahead. The path that led to his right, to the largest area of the room, went about twelve feet, reaching the far wall of the room. On his right stood rows of twin-size mattresses and twin-size box frames, standing on end and placed one against the other all the way to the wall. On his left were two rows of mattresses and matching box frames for both queen- and king-size beds. Stacks of chairs stood beyond, and just past them stood the coffee tables and nightstands, stacked neatly against the far wall. Madden stopped and looked toward Mickelson. "Looks as though someone may have moved a stack of chairs or bedside tables out of the way."

Mickelson looked in the direction of Madden's gesture and nodded in agreement. "The stack of coffee tables appears to be in the corner of the room, with bedside tables stacked next to them and end tables stacked alongside the bedside tables." The tables were stacked in an alternating manner with the bottom unit on its feet, the next one upside down on top of it and then the third unit right side up again. All of the tables stood in neat stacks against the wall.

"You're right, Steve; sure looks like someone moved that stack of bedside tables out away from the wall," Mickelson said, noting slight indentation lines in the carpet that were lined up with the legs of the bottommost bedside table.

"Let's just hope that whoever was involved in the broken table from 932 was the one who came in here and moved them," replied Madden.

Carefully, the two unstacked the bedside tables. As each one was removed from the stack, it was scrutinized for any possible clues and inspected for fingerprints. "Obviously," continued Madden, "we're going to come up with a lot of fingerprints. When I talked with the manager last evening, he informed me that all employees are fingerprinted upon hiring so they'll be able to provide us with a reference for each print we pick up."

"Maybe the pieces are cleaned when brought in here for storage," said Mickelson, handing another table to Madden for examination.

It took considerable time, but after about a couple of hours all the bedside tables, coffee tables, and end tables had been examined and dusted for prints. Having the prints properly identified and tagged for storage and placed in the investigation kit, the two returned to the doorway. The door was installed in such a manner that it opened toward the interior of the room and was set to close automatically. Upon entering the room with the CEO, they had placed a wedge under the door to prevent it from closing. When they reached the door, Madden again opened the kit, withdrew some print revelation dust and applied it to the outside doorknob and around the jamb with the quick swirling motion of the brush. He repeated the process with the exterior panel of the door nearest the latch edge moving upward from the knob. No signs were evident on the door jamb, but as he dusted the door's exterior, prints began to appear, and for each he paused, carefully applied a clear strip of lifting tape over the print, gently pulled it from the surface of the door, and folded the clear backing strip over the recovered print. Then he labeled the strip and handed it to Mickelson for filing in the kit. More prints were located on the interior of the door when they allowed it to close. Finally the two stepped into the hallway to allow Ziegler to gather any additional photos he thought might be helpful before the room was released and employees were again allowed to enter it.

"I noticed," began Mickelson, "that several of the prints we lifted from the end tables and from the door and knob looked much larger than most of the others."

Madden was looking along the ceiling of the hallway from where they stood at one end to where room 932 was located at the other end. "Yes, I saw that too, Kyler. Knowing that fairly small women usually accessed the room suggests that maybe at some point someone, a person with a larger hand, maybe a man, entered and exited that room. The prints on the outside of the door suggest an individual with the larger hand held the door open to allow a table to be carried out." As he continued to study the hallway, he pointed to a camera located above their heads.

"I viewed some of the tapes from cameras last night after I settled in," he said. "Once we're finished here, I'll get back to viewing them. Anything relevant I find in them we can go over when we get together tomorrow."

It was 5:35 when they finally paused in their examination of Room 932 and the ninth floor hallway, storage room, stairwells, and elevators. Ziegler had left a couple of hours prior to return to his office and make some enlarged prints.

"I think that will do it for now," Madden said, stretching his back and arms. "You take the prints and have them sent to the Bureau for any possible identification. Also have your folks run them for any match of employees so we can begin to identify all those we possibly can upfront."

Mickelson nodded his agreement and began to pack up the crime scene investigation kit. As Mickelson was closing the lid, Madden's cell phone rang.

"Agent Madden," he answered as he clicked the button on the Bluetooth earpiece. "Really? When? Where did they find it? Ok, tell them not to let anyone touch it, and we'll come right up." He clicked off. "One of the housekeepers just took some linens to the laundry from her rounds and found a broken coffee table under the stairwell on the tenth floor."

Mickelson stood, stooped over, and lifted the closed kit. "Ok, let's see what it is. You suppose it's the one from 932?"

It took only a few seconds to reach the tenth floor, and a few more to cover the few yards from the end stairwell on which they had run up to the exit stairwell located in the middle of the long hallway. A small Hispanic woman of about thirty-five years of age, dressed in a tan dress with a resort name badge, stood by the doorway, anxiously studying the two men as they approached. "Are you police?" she asked.

"Yes, we are," answered Madden, showing his badge to her. "I am FBI Agent Steve Madden, and this is Sheriff Kyler Mickelson." Mickelson nodded and smiled at the lady.

"I find table under stair here," the housekeeper said in broken English, pointing to the staircase. "Table is broken and should not be here."

Madden stepped through the open doorway and bent over to look under the staircase that led to the eleventh and top floor of the hotel. "Well, well," he said to the sheriff. "Looks like we found our missing table. Hand me a pair of latex, Kyler." After putting the gloves on, he carefully removed the pieces of the table. The table had broken completely in half. The top piece was heavy glass with a wooden shelf under the glass to hold magazines, books, etc. As the pieces were examined, some details of how it broke became evident. The glass top had been snapped and, with the exception of some smaller pieces and chips missing, it was all there. The wood shelf had also been snapped, and the ragged edges extending out and down from the bottom suggested that the breaking force came down on top and caused the splinters to be forced down with the blow.

As had been done most of the day, the two men carefully inspected the entire piece one inch at a time. They paused to lift prints a couple of times and then, noting a blackish red coloring near the broken edge of the glass, they stopped to check what it might be from. The answer was what they had suspected … blood.

"Obviously, someone got cut on this as it broke," Mickelson said, taking a swab of the material; saturating it with liquid, he squirted on the swab from a bottle located in the kit. The sheriff then carefully scraped the remaining material from the glass into a glassine baggie, sealed it, labeled it, and placed it in the box. "One more thing for the lab guys to identify," he said. "We'll check it against known blood types, including the senator's."

Madden again turned to the area beneath the stairwell and partially crawled under the ascending stairs. Mickelson could hear him chuckle aloud and watched with interest as Madden withdrew. In his hand he held a cardboard bottle carrier containing six emptied beer bottles. Holding his prize up, he laughed as he described the scene he had observed on the elevator's video, sharing with the sheriff how anxious the three young people appeared when they entered the elevator. "I wonder," he said, "if they might have any helpful information. I'll see them sometime this evening if they're still here. They had entered the elevator about twenty after eight on Tuesday evening, and if this is their container, more than likely it was placed under here before the table pieces as it was pushed back under the bottom step."

After making sure they had all the evidence from the table they could obtain, the two men each lifted a piece of the table and carried it down to the floor below and placed it in room 932.

"How soon can you have the lab get us results?" asked Madden of the sheriff. "The sooner we can have solid information, the quicker we can begin having other agents work on leads and prints."

"We have a great lab team, Steve," replied Mickelson. "I think we can get most by tomorrow morning. They're lab rats, as we fondly call them, and they'll work all night if need be. They understand the case and know time is of the essence."

The two exchanged good-byes, and Kyler Mickelson headed to his car and began the drive back to the law enforcement office, located in the back of the law enforcement facility that housed both sheriff and police departments for the city of Jackson.

Glancing at his watch, Madden noted it was six thirty, and though he was beginning to feel hunger pangs, he went to his room, washed his hands and face, and changed shirts, putting on a button-front sport shirt. Then he walked to the table by the window, sat in one of the two comfortable chairs, and opened his cell phone. He quickly scrolled down the list of names until he came to that of his partner, Jim Addis. Selecting Addis's name, he depressed the send button and heard the phone ring in his ear. Three rings later, there was an audible click followed by a voice he recognized as his fellow agent.

"Hey, what's up, guy?" came the cheerful voice of Addis. "I got the text message you sent after you arrived there. How's your investigation going?"

Madden chuckled, "We've been doing a lot of crawling around on our hands and knees, Jim. The good side is that we have several pieces of evidence, fingerprints, palm prints, and a blood sample."

There was a moment of silence and then Addis responded. "Blood? From what source, do you know?

"No, not yet, the sheriff here has his lab working on the prints and on the blood. Hopefully, tomorrow we will have some concrete idea. We do know one thing, and that is that Senator Carson is definitely missing, and it looks very much as though there is something going on. I don't believe the guy just left on his own. Nobody here saw him leave after he left the meeting on Tuesday evening and got on the elevator. I looked at the video from the elevator area, the lobby, and several of the floors. Everything pretty much looked normal, just a couple of curious people to check out on the other video sources and have the hotel personnel look at to see if they recognize them."

Addis was quiet, contemplating what his friend and working partner was telling him. "Steve, I think you have a pretty good feel for what happened there. I know your gut feeling rarely leads you astray so, just keep following your instinct, buddy."

Madden thanked him for his confidence and then asked, "How is it going up there? Anything new in the mining city?"

Addis allowed himself to laugh. "Most of the folks have been really cooperative, Steve. Hocking's the only one who still thinks we're trying to make the city of Butte look bad. I've talked with the detectives one-on-one, and I'm convinced more than ever that those four arrests were related. There seems to be a lot of coincidence in contacts, source, date of buy, and date of selling. Attorney General Marks has been most cooperative and even has a couple of his staff boys out checking on some information related to Johnson up in Chester. Seems there've been several threats made against her recently. She kind of laughed them off because she's received so many over the last year and a half. We're checking on the recent ones to rule them out."

"Anything about Stephens or Williams?" inquired Madden.

Addis, hearing the concern in his partner's voice about the missing FBI agents quickly redirected his comments. "Nothing solid right now, Steve. I went back to the convenience store employee in Bozeman. He just recalls seeing the two of them and their car. He thinks it was Williams who was driving and had filled the car with gas before having the kid charge the fuel to his agency credit card and getting back into the car. Then he saw him drive off north on Seventh Avenue."

"I was hoping something might pop up for you in that area," said Madden, obviously disappointed.

Addis quickly responded. "There is one thing, though, Steve," he began. "I had Bozeman police pretty much doing the door-to-door drill all along north Seventh Avenue from the gas station all the way out to the interstate ramps." Addis shuffled some papers in his notebook and then began talking again. "The same was done here in Butte from the exit ramps. One of the business owners thinks that he saw a black Ford, same style and the one our guy had, stop here in Butte at a burger and beer place out on Montana Avenue. The two guys seemed to have met three others and then followed them on up Montana Ave. He remembered them because our guys were in slacks and sport coats with polo shirts, neatly attired, but the other three looked to be in pretty grubby clothes. They sat in a big corner booth. The three guys had been there for about forty-five minutes to an hour before our guys came in. They obviously knew each other from somewhere, but there was not much laughter or joking, according to the manager of the day."

"What kept him so quiet?" asked Madden, frowning at the thought of this guy keeping silent.

"Would you believe none of the Butte detectives thought about stopping there and talking with him? Just figured Phil and Brad had probably gone on to either Helena or Missoula when they scoured the streets looking for the car and found none."

Madden felt his blood pressure rise, "For Christ's sake, Jim!" he loudly exclaimed. "Does someone have to do all the work for them?" Madden's voice softened a bit, and he continued, "So, any other ideas from there?"

Addis smiled at his partner's brief display of frustration. "The boys in blue are working the businesses all the way up Montana to see if there are any others who might have seen them. I guess, from the description of the other vehicle, it was an old, maybe early '60s dark green Chevy pickup. It had a lot of rust spots on the fenders, and the back window was cracked. I think we might make a lead or two from that if we're lucky."

"Ok, Jim," the senior agent replied, "let's stay in touch. I'll call again tomorrow about six and check in. If anything comes up that you need me, I always have my phone on."

"Gotcha, Steve," answered Addis. "You take care, and we'll talk tomorrow."

Madden pressed the button of his Bluetooth, and the conversation ended. Then he went to the room phone and called home to talk with his wife and boys. He always hated being on the road and missing the kids, their giggles and laughter, the aroma of home cooking, the soft and loving voice of Lee. Even more, he missed her in the night, her warm body lying next to him, her clean and soothing fragrance relaxing him into deep sleep. Though he did not share details of ongoing investigations, just the sound of her voice gave him encouragement and lifted his spirits when they might be down. She and the kids were, Steve would freely admit to anyone, the absolute best parts of his entire life; he would do anything for them. In fact, just two years ago, he had volunteered to find a new job in order to stay home and help with the housework and with the kids. Lee had insisted he continue his agency job, citing that he had a "gift" for investigative work. He had a natural instinct for what leads to follow or whom to question or how to bring together supposedly unrelated events. And he always seemed to be led in his work to a successful closing of his cases. The fact was many of his cases did, indeed, look cold at the outset, and somehow, someway, he would find a lead or a key piece of evidence that led to an arrest or to the closing of a case. His reputation was truly bureau wide. Several promotions had been offered, but he had always turned them down because most of them would have required his being relocated or away for extended periods, neither of which he wanted. He was content where he was, and not even the money was going to pry him away.

Chapter Eight

Feeling lifted by his call to his wife and kids and energized by a good three-mile jaunt through the roads and cleared trails around the resort, Madden allowed himself to sit quietly in the elegant Apres Vous Dining Room, the resort's formal dining room, where he enjoyed a dinner of prime rib cooked to perfection, baked potato heaped with a tangy sauce, and tender asparagus, along with a cup of delicious coffee that the young waitress seemed intent on keeping filled to the brim until he finally put a hand over the half-empty cup and declined. After adding an 18 percent tip to the bill, he left and returned to his room.

Again he started the videotape player, turned on the television to use as a monitor, and selected a videotape to insert. This particular tape was, according to the label on its edge, of the ninth floor, recorded on Tuesday. As the tape began, it became clear from the camera angle that the view was from the end of the hallway by Room 932, Senator Carson's room. Madden played the tape in fast-forward until the time stamp displayed 4:35 p.m. and then pushed the play button to return the play back to normal speed. Three people came into view, a female and two males, who turned from the elevator area and walked quickly down the hall away from the camera. Glancing at the time stamp, 5:02 p.m., a smile crossed Madden's face as he recognized the threesome as the youths who had entered the elevator earlier on the elevator tape. He continued studying the tape and soon viewed Senator Carson step around the corner from the elevator area and begin walking toward his room. Interestingly, a second figure came into view also walking toward the camera. Because the angle of the camera was set to view down the hallway, both figures disappeared beneath the viewing range. The senator had arrived at his room, and the second person, short and quite stocky, wearing jeans and Western boots with a long sleeve, plaid shirt, apparently arrived at room 931, which was located across the hall and a few feet further down from 932. The lower corner of the monitor flashed 5:04 p.m.

At 10:23 p.m., according to the tape's digital stamp, two of the youth left the room, one of the males and the female. They walked across the hallway and through the doorway leading to a staircase. As they disappeared through the door, the boy was holding in his hand an object, which, as Madden had concluded earlier, was the container of bottled beer. Further viewing did not show Madden much of interest—many people coming from the elevator area and walking to various rooms in the hallway and a couple who came toward the camera but stopped at a room well before the senator's room and entered, laughing and talking. Finally the tape's time displayed 8:00 a.m., Wednesday, and the tape ended.

Madden then inserted a corresponding tape from the opposite end of the hallway and quickly advanced to 5:04 p.m. Again he witnessed the senator step around the corner from the elevator and begin walking to his room. The smooth flow showing the walking senator suddenly stopped then started again. The next scene that appeared showed the time and date stamp of Tuesday, 5:07 p.m. Madden paused the playback and jotted a quick note of the three-minute time discrepancy before pushing the play button again to resume his viewing. Nothing out of the ordinary occurred as the tape continued to advance through the evening hours. People came and went to the different rooms on the ninth floor. A ray of light seemed to spill out onto the hallway carpet from room 932, and just as it did so, the tape again had a curious jump in time.

Quickly rewinding the tape, Madden again played it back, carefully observing the time stamp on the monitor. Exactly when the tape hit Wednesday, 12:09 a.m., the flash of light seemed to strike the hall carpet immediately outside the door of Senator Carson's room, and then the timer jumped ahead and read Wednesday, 12:50 a.m. Something had happened either to the tape or to the periods of time from 5:04 until 5:07 and 12:09 to 12:50! Perhaps the timer had malfunctioned, or perhaps sections of the security tape had been erased! The evidence was there. Madden was convinced that he was witnessing the span of time during which Senator Carson had been kidnapped. Inserting the video that showed the elevator activity from midnight of Wednesday morning, Madden scanned the entire tape for additional clues or evidence but never saw anything further that appeared abnormal—no senator, no strangers entering his room, no person removing the broken table, nothing that raised any suspicion.

Stopping the tape at 8:00 a.m., Madden ejected the tape and inserted the one he had previously watched—the one recorded from the camera above and just beyond room 932. He slowed the tape to slow motion as it approached 5:00 p.m. and leaned forward in keen study of the screen. At 5:04 p.m., he noticed something different. More light seemed to be shown along the walls and the floor; then the additional light disappeared, and he observed what appeared to be a darker light that moved very quickly off the screen to the right. "Did someone just open the stairwell door and go into the senator's room?" Madden continued to watch, searching for some clue to answer his lingering question. When the digital clock flashed 12:09 a.m., a brighter light again seemed to enter the hallway. He watched intently. No person appeared in the camera's view, but there was that shadowy mysterious movement he had seen earlier. Somehow it seemed larger than before, and rather than moving from left to right, it moved into the view from the right, growing more intense, and then disappeared.

"There has to be something or somebody there!" exclaimed Madden aloud. He stopped the tape, grabbed his room key, and ran out the door and up to the ninth floor by way of the stairwell at the east end of the hall, the end at which he knew he would find Room 932. He paused at the door and looked carefully. There was a light fixture immediately above him as he stood in front of a large, metal-cased door. There was no glass window in the door. Slowly he opened the door and saw what he knew he would. As the door opened, the bright rays of light from the stairwell fixture illuminated the floor directly in front of him and down the hall, beyond the entry to Room 932. As he stepped into the hallway, he studied the effect of the stairway light and noticed his shadow also appeared on the carpet.

Returning to his room, Madden picked up his cell phone and called the cell phone of Sheriff Mickelson. As the answering mode clicked on, he spoke into the phone. "Kyler, Steve Madden here. I've been viewing the tapes and think I've found a significant clue. I found that some footage is missing from the tape by the storage room that would show any activity immediately outside the senator's room. I've also found what I think are the shadow of at least one other person entering his room and a shadow that suggests multiple people, tightly grouped, leaving the senator's room. The shadows I observed leaving 932 coincide with the missing time from the tape. We'll start with those two clues when you get here in the morning. Be here about 7:30 so we can speak with personnel in the security office from multiple shifts. I'll meet you in the Gondola Summit Coffee Shop."

Agent Madden clicked off his phone. It was 9:30, and he knew that sleep would elude him for some time this night. Again, taking the room key and slipping on his dark blue blazer, he took the elevator to the main floor and walked to the check-in desk. Madden introduced himself and inquired if the night manager was available. She was, he was told and then led behind the counter and down a hallway to the office for the "On Duty Manager." Underneath the gold lettering on the window, a nameplate hung by two parallel silver chains. "Martha Young" it read. He stepped inside and approached the desk, behind which sat a lady in a maroon suit with a gold necklace and matching earrings, studiously looking at some communication from undoubtedly her inbox. Upon Madden's approach to the desk, she looked up. Madden held out his right hand as she stood and extended hers. "Hello, Ms. Young," Madden said. "I'm Steve Madden, FBI."

The hand was warm and soft as it took Madden's in a firm grip. Her hazel green eyes met his in a solid connection as she returned his greeting and introduced herself. "I am aware of who you are, Agent Madden," she said, displaying a bright and very genuine smile. "It's a pleasure to put a face with the name. Please do call me Martha."

The night manager gestured to two chairs in front of a large window that looked out over a lit atrium whose glass ceiling, eleven floors above them, brought in natural light to the greenery below. Along all four sides of the atrium on each floor were white metal railings, connecting corner pillars and allowing guests on each of the floors to observe the trees and lush plants below and listen to the large water fountain in the center of the courtyard. A profusion of bright spring colors amid about-to-blossom bushes filled the raised beds on all four sides and bordered a walkway of cream-colored paving stones that circled the center water display and three-story high linden tree.

Madden took one of the chairs, and Young took the other. "Please," said Madden upon sitting, "call me, Steve."

The night manager, looking to Madden to be in her mid to late thirties, held herself with a posture of confidence. Taking her seat, she asked the agent what she could do for him.

"As you know, Senator Jeremy Carson was staying in Room 932. He disappeared on Tuesday night or Wednesday and has not been located since. After reviewing videos of the elevator and ninth floor, I'm convinced that there is something not right about his disappearance." He looked at Young as he spoke and noted she was carefully listening to his comments. She nodded her head without speaking, allowing him to continue.

"There are several people on those videos I want to identify, if possible, by your staff members. In order to do that, I need to print photos from the videotapes. Is your security office able to handle that?"

The manager reflected for a moment on the request and then, smiling, said, "Of course, Steve. I think our chief of security, Randy Yao, can do that. He comes on duty at 8:00 in the morning."

Madden was very glad to hear that as he had been concerned any such printing might have to be taken to a commercial business, meaning more time lost before the identities might be obtained. "I appreciate that, Martha," he said and then added, "I have a couple of additional requests as well, if you don't mind spending a few minutes of your time here."

Martha smiled again. She welcomed the opportunity to visit with someone other than staff during the night shift and responded, "I certainly do not mind," adding, "Might I get something for you? Coffee? Soft drink? Tea?"

Madden was well aware of the amount of coffee he had consumed at dinner and went for a glass of Seven-up instead. Young rose from her chair, quickly, but very gracefully, walked to a small refrigerator in the corner behind her desk and came back with wooden tray upon which sat two glasses filled with crushed ice, a can of Dr. Pepper and a can of Seven-up. She set the tray and its contents down on the small table that stood between the chairs next to the window. Each took a moment to pour the contents from the selected cans into the glass and enjoyed a sip of the cold soft drink. "You were saying you had some additional questions, Steve," invited Martha.

Madden looked at the glass in his hand thoughtfully and then looked up at the manager. "I would like to have a copy of the work schedule for all personnel, starting with last Monday morning and through today."

Somehow, from somewhere, Martha Young had produced a pen and small spiral notebook upon which she quickly wrote his request. Completing the writing, she looked up and said, "That will not be a problem, Steve. We have all the schedules on computer. I can easily get that for you when we finish here."

Agent Madden continued with his next request. "Second, Martha, can you tell me who is in charge of changing the security videotapes?"

The question brought a look of surprise to the woman's face but she did not hesitate in providing an answer. "Whoever is sitting at the video surveillance desk when a tape is scheduled to be changed," she replied. "Normally scheduled changes occur every eight hours, beginning with midnight. Our goal in the next few weeks is to be up and running with an automated system that uses DVD media rather than the tape we now employ. Unfortunately, that's one area we lag in, technologically. Corporate has sent out letters indicating that a total revamp of all security systems for all their resort facilities will be done beginning June 1 of this year and completed by December 31. As of right now, I'm not sure when our facility will be done." She paused, searching Madden's face for a clue and then asked, "Is there a problem with the tapes we gave you?"

Madden thought a moment about her question and, trusting his gut, decided to answer her forthright. "Martha," he began, setting his now half-drained glass on the tray and leaning forward toward her, "I noticed that on one of the tapes, the one from the camera at the east end of the ninth floor, the imprinted time has a block of time missing just a little past five p.m. on Tuesday night and then another span of a longer period just after midnight. That suggests to me that somewhere along the way two blocks of time were either missed or erased from the tape."

A look of astonishment appeared on Young's face as she looked deeply into Madden's face. "I am not sure what to say, Steve," she replied. "There should not be any missing time from a tape. Knowing your job, I am not going to question you. I can accept that what you are telling me is accurate, but I'm not sure if I can explain."

Madden saw the surprise in her face and tried to soften it, "Martha, please don't get me wrong. I am not pointing fingers at anyone. I will, of course, need to visit with the individual who was on duty at the time, and it is important that what I have shared is kept between the two of us until I have had that opportunity."

Young offered a very weak smile, one that said, "Thank you for not accusing me," but also said she understood what the federal officer was saying. "Let me pull up the security office work schedule for that particular block of time and see what we might find."

The two rose as one and walked to the large dark mahogany desk. Madden hesitated, allowing the manager to walk before him, and then he followed her as she went behind the desk, pulled her chair out, and sat down in front of the computer. Young quickly accessed a folder entitled "work schedules" and then a sub-folder marked "security schedule."

She then scrolled down the files until she located the month and date in question. Clicking on the date brought up a spreadsheet displaying the time of day and different people's names. Blocks of cells were filled with different colors, highlighting work schedules for each person. As she scrolled down the time column, she slowed as the highlighted cell hovered over the time of 4:00 p.m., the beginning of the new shift.

Young paused and looked up at Madden, who was standing immediately behind her and intently looking at the screen's display. "Steve, we have eight security personnel, not including our chief, Randy Yao. Each shift involves two people, and they rotate during the tour of time. One is constantly moving inside and around the perimeter of the facility while the other stays at the observation desk where any calls are taken and where monitor displays from all of the cameras can be observed. Rotation is left to the crew, but we require each be given a fifteen minute break during the first four hours and again during the last four with a thirty minute meal break."

Madden nodded in acknowledgement and continued to gaze at the screen. "So, Martha," he asked her in a soft, non-threatening voice, "who was working the evening and night shift on Tuesday?"

A few more motions of the mouse and she stopped the cursor on two names and read them aloud though she was well aware that Madden was already reading them. "The two security employees on the four p.m. to midnight shift were Cary Biffle and Tom Evers. From midnight to eight a.m., Sheila Smith and Mike Thompson were scheduled. The two assigned from eight to four p.m. were John Terrati and Colby Jensen."

Pausing as he read the names and made a note on a pad he had taken from his jacket pocket, Madden then asked, "Can you tell if all four of the evening and morning officers worked as scheduled?"

Young nodded her head. "Yes, I can access the actual time cards from human resources from here." She closed the scheduler file and folder then clicked on the human resources folder. Selecting payroll information, she clicked again and was prompted for a password, which she quickly entered.

Madden watched as the night manager quickly scanned through the list of employees and four times she opened a file under the names of the respective security employees he had entered in his notebook. A few seconds of screen manipulation and a time card facsimile for each of the four was visible on the monitor. Two pairs of eyes studied the forms.

Young's slender right index finger moved to the screen, pointing to Sheila Smith's card. "Steve, it would appear that Sheila called in ill and did not work her shift from midnight to eight." She glanced at the other three time card replicas and again pointed. "Cary Biffle filled in for her. He worked a double shift from four in the afternoon until eight the following morning."

The FBI agent scribbled a few more notes onto the page of his notepad. Clicking his pen to retract the point, he thanked the woman for her assistance. "I really appreciate your doing this tonight, Martha. I'll be speaking to all of the security employees so, if you can print me that schedule as well one of the other resort employees, I can leave you to your work."

As if reading his mind, Young had already sent the request for the work schedule covering the period of time Madden had requested to the printer queue and soon a soft humming sounded as the laser printer began spitting out sheets of paper. Madden stepped back away from her chair, and Young stood up, brushing against him as she turned to the printer, and picked up several sheets of paper. As she stepped past him, Madden detected the sweet fragrance of her cologne. Not too sweet or too strong.

"Here you are, Steve," said Young, handing the papers to him. "Please let me know if you need anything else. Having something like this happen to our facility is not good, but not to know what happened or why is even worse. I only hope and pray that Senator Carson is ok."

"Thank you. You've been most helpful," he replied with a genuine smile. "I'm sure some of the information you've given me will result in a solid lead." He turned and walked to the door, putting his hand on the knob to open it, but stopped and looked back at the woman standing by her chair. "Martha, remember to keep this conversation between the two of us, ok?" Martha Young smiled, nodding in the affirmative. "Have a pleasant evening, Martha," he continued and turned the brass doorknob, pulled the door open, and stepped out into the hallway and across the lobby to the elevator, which would return him to his floor.

Madden was feeling excited as made his way to his room. He quickly opened the door and entered the room. Placing the papers on the counter by the sink, he removed his blazer, carefully hanging it on a wooden hanger on the coat rack. Reclaiming the papers, he walked to the small table that stood between two armchairs, laid them on the table and sat down.

Locating the work schedule for the security personnel, he looked at the times for Cary Biffle. Taking a yellow highlighter from the pens and pencils he had placed on the table much earlier, he highlighted the blocks of twenty-four hour clock times that were marked "2000, 2100, 2200, 2300, 2400, 0100, 0200, 0300, 0400, 0500, 0600, 0700, and 0800." Biffle was the only security person to have been on duty when the corresponding times on the videotape were missing. Madden sat, tapping his finger on the paper, staring at the darkness beyond his window. He heard himself ask aloud, "Did Biffle actually erase the time on the tape? Was he in the observation office when Carson disappeared? Does he know anything about his disappearance?"

Madden stood, walked to the end of the drape, and pulled the cord to close out the night's darkness. His watch told him he had been downstairs for quite some time as its gold hands displayed ten thirty. Feeling exhilarated from the recent chain of events, he kicked off his shoes, changed into his sleeping shorts, and then, sitting back on his bed with his back supported by the padded headboard, he turned on the television. Madden picked up the remote and started clicking through different stations. He considered Jay Leno's *Tonight Show* and then David Letterman and *The Late Show*, but he kept going. After channel surfing for a few minutes, a habit that Lee liked to kid him about, he finally selected a station showing an old black-and-white Western. He really had no interest in the movie, but watching it would help to relax his mind and eventually allow him to fall asleep.

Finally, as the good guy in the white hat rode off to new adventures, Steve Madden turned off the set, laid the remote control on the bedside table, and then walked in his bare feet to the sink to brush his teeth before slipping under the covers for sleep. The digital alarm/radio on the table next to him told him it was midnight. Tomorrow would be an interesting day, one that he looked forward to. He was anxious to find out if any of the prints he and Sheriff Mickelson had lifted would be further clues, and he wondered what would be Biffle's reaction when the two lawmen sat down with him to ask some rather pointed questions about the missing time on that videotape.

CHAPTER NINE

Breaking of dawn found Agent Madden wide-awake. Rising from his bed, he put on his sweats and sneakers, took his room key, and secured it in a zippered pouch held over the instep of a shoe by the laces. He half-jogged down the stairs until he reached a door on the first floor through which he exited the resort. Madden took about fifteen minutes to go through the same pre-run stretching routine he had used for many years and then started a slow gliding run, gradually picking up his tempo as he felt the muscles of his body warming. He felt invigorated jogging the quiet road that led from Rendezvous Mountain Resort to Teton Village, and he thoroughly enjoyed the run. Above him, towered the jagged ridges of the Tetons. Under his every step crunched the roadway. And all around him, he could hear the morning breeze, whispering through the trees, announcing the new day. A day, he thought as he ran, that maybe, just maybe, would bring to light some definitive information regarding Senator Jeremy Carson's disappearance. He lifted his left arm and checked his watch, 5:15. His thoughts wandered off to the East as he thought of Lee. This being Sunday and her work set aside as a legal partner in a small Arlington law firm, specializing in patent and copyright cases, and Audrey's school work finished, Steven Jr. would join them, and the three would probably go to the zoo or a park for a family outing before coming home to make cookies and just enjoy the time together. During the week as Lee headed out for work at 7:30 each morning, Marie, a forty-five-year-old descendant of an Italian bricklayer, who immigrated some thirty years ago, would arrive to look after the children, getting Audrey ready for the school bus and then caring for Steven Jr. until Lee returned around four o'clock. She and her partners had arranged this schedule from the time Audrey was three, and it worked well for everyone, especially the Madden family.

Twenty minutes out and then another twenty back, Madden turned down his pace toward the end, slowing to a walk in the parking lot before repeating his stretching routine. Finishing, he went up the staircase again to the eighth floor, entered his room, and laid his clothes out for the day before heading for a steamy hot shower. It was just six twenty, and he had enough time to relax as he finished his morning routine, plenty of time before he met Sheriff Mickelson in the coffee shop at seven-thirty.

At seven twenty, Madden slipped on a cashmere teal v-neck sweater over his white turtleneck pullover, picked up his notebook, and headed down the hall where he caught the elevator to the lobby.

As he traversed the lobby toward the Gondola Summit Coffee Shop, he saw Kyler Mickelson entering through the main doorway. Their eyes caught one another, and each lifted a hand in greeting before coming together just outside the little rustic restaurant and shaking hands.

Each ordered coffee, black; Madden ordered scrambled eggs with wheat toast and a tall orange juice. Mickelson, who said he had eaten breakfast at his house, just outside Jackson Hole, ordered a cinnamon roll, so that, as he laughingly told Madden, "You won't feel like you're eating alone."

As they ate and drank hot coffee, Madden shared what he had discovered during his tape review and his later meeting with the night manager. He showed Mickelson the work schedule for the days he had requested and the names of Cary Biffle and Sheila Smith with their corresponding scheduled work time and the time card printout of actual time worked. Mickelson quickly concurred with Madden that an interview of the two was a critical next step and the sooner, the better.

Then it was Sheriff Mickelson's turn. He unzipped his dark brown leather notebook that bore a bear's face finely tooled into its cover, lips drawn back, revealing a snarling and very hostile animal. Taking a sheaf of documents from it, Mickelson began his part of their information sharing.

The fingerprints found in Room 932 belonged to the senator, three different resort employees, all current employees of the housekeeping staff, and a bellhop who, the sheriff's office had determined, was responsible for bringing the luggage to the room when the senator checked in the past Monday evening. As for the prints in the stairwell outside the senator's room, all of the useable prints had been of employees.

"What about the prints we obtained from the storage room?" inquired Madden. He almost held his breath, hoping for some good news.

"Actually, most were as we expected them to be," replied Mickelson, "housekeepers or some of the other staff who would normally have access to the room to bring in pieces or move them to other rooms. However …," the sheriff paused to take a long slow sip from his cup, setting it down carefully, "two sets could not be identified as employees. Those were on the side tables that stood right next to the stack of coffee tables, and one of the sets also appeared on the outside panel of the door where it might have been held in the open position while something was taken into or out of the room. The prints were run through our local files, but nothing came up. And, according to the report from the FBI bank, the prints are of unknown persons."

The FBI agent sat for a moment, staring at his cup of coffee and the curls of steam emanating from its open top. He looked up at the sheriff and said, "What about other departments in Wyoming, Montana, Idaho?"

"Copies of the prints were sent to all of those and also Utah, Colorado, Nevada, Oregon, and Washington. As of this morning, we haven't heard from any of them, but I anticipate by noon we'll have something from them. I asked my office to call me immediately when they receive word from any of the states."

"It would appear as though, whomever those prints do belong to, they are not high on any 'watch' list."

"True, and they likely haven't been involved in any major crime, or your office would have had them in their data bank already."

Madden nodded in agreement. On the positive side, if they were dealing with amateurs, then at some point they would have made a mistake, either in the way they carried out the crime or the contacts they made before, during, or after the event itself. Madden felt even more sure of the gut feeling he had that someone on the resort security staff, maybe Biffle, did or knew something, and that is where they needed to focus their next examination.

As the two finished their last cup of java, Madden picked up the tab, went to the cashier stand, paid for their breakfasts in cash, requested a receipt, and then handed a three-dollar tip to the young man who had served them. Mickelson and Madden then walked out of the coffee shop, into the lobby, and stood looking at the atrium through its large open entrance. Water from the fountain splashing into the pool and the cool breeze from the atrium, carrying the fragrance of fresh plant life, enticed one to enter and linger. The two did not, however, take up the unspoken invitation of nature.

"I think," began the FBI agent, "that we need to start with the hotel's security chief. I want to see if some of the faces I noticed in the videotapes can be reproduced without having it sent out. Martha Young, the night manager, told me last night that the chief would be in this morning at eight o'clock." He glanced at his watch; it was 8:25. "She gave me the key for a conference room on this floor and just down the hall from the security office. Not a large room, but it has a table and some chairs. I have a mini-tape recorder with me so we can record our interviews. I suggest we go down and set the room up the way we want and then make a call on our chief."

"Sounds ok by me." Mickelson reminded Madden that he, of course, knew Randy Yao because of their law enforcement connection in Jackson Hole. The two then walked across the lobby that was slowly coming to life with resort guests, most of whom were headed to the restaurant or coffee shop for breakfast before their day of skiing or, in the case of some, checking out to begin a journey home.

Arriving at the designated room, Madden slipped the coded key card into the lock and, after seeing the green light illuminated, pushed the handle down, swinging the door open. The room was about the size of a regular guest room, maybe twenty feet long and fifteen feet across. There was a lavatory and a wet bar so water would be available. In the center of the room stood a dark wooden table with a black inlay for the top. The table looked to be four feet by eight feet and had four chairs, all with wooden arms, two on either of the long sides of the table. The chairs had the same dark wood with black leather seats and black leather cushioned backs. In the center of the table was a tray with ten glasses, a coffee carafe, and a glass pitcher sat next to an ice bucket. Madden looked on the bar and found a twenty-four-cup coffee maker with several pre-filled baskets of coffee. He opened the refrigerator and found that ice had been stored in the freezer compartment and that cans of soft drinks had been graciously placed in the cooling section, along with several plastic bottles of drinking water. On the table next to the tray, a hand-written note addressed to Agent Madden and signed by Martha Young informed him of the services she had provided in the room before leaving at the end of her shift. She further mentioned that any needs he and the sheriff might require in using the room would be filled by the day manager's office or a desk clerk. She further assured them that the resort's restaurant staff had been informed of their location and were on standby for any food service needed, all at the expense of the resort. The note had been written on resort letterhead and was neatly placed on top of four pre-punched letter-sized tablets with a box of more than a dozen freshly sharpened pencils as well as an array of black, blue, and red pens. A wall of the room displayed an aerial view of the resort, parking lots, and surrounding ski hill runs. Another wall held a white board with several different colors of erasable markers and an eraser. In one corner stood a large screen monitor with a videotape player, as well as CD and DVD players. Madden made a mental note to send a special thank-you to Martha for her generous hospitality.

Randy Yao's personnel folder revealed that he had served in the armed forces as a naval law enforcement officer before serving fifteen years with the Denver, Colorado, police department and another fifteen years as chief of security with the governor's office in Cheyenne, Wyoming, before retiring and being named security chief at the Jackson Hole resort three years ago. His military discharge had followed a distinguished career, and many awards followed his work in private life as well. On paper, he came across as a very honorable and outstanding individual who had gained the respect and gratitude of many throughout his professional lifetime.

As Yao entered the room, Madden stood and walked around the table to greet him. Standing well over six feet and carrying somewhere around two hundred fifty pounds, he looked to be in excellent condition. His well-tanned face, hands, and arms suggested he spent a considerable amount of time on the sunny ski slopes or in a tanning booth. Madden motioned him to a seat at one end of the table while Mickelson and he sat opposite each other on the long sides. They briefly chatted about family, traveling, and interests. After ten minutes of social chatter, as Madden called it, they got down to the business at hand. Madden informed the security chief that the conversation they were about to have was going to be recorded as would all interviews he and the sheriff would have with the employees of the resort. Madden reached toward a small black cassette recorder that had been placed in the center of the table and pressed the record switch and began the discussion. He and Mickelson wanted to know first of all if any of the images from the viewed videotapes could be reproduced in printed format. The request was met with "Not a problem" from Yao. He seemed genuinely interested in assisting the two men and, in fact, it was he who had made sure the room in which Carson stayed had been kept sealed, along with the entire ninth floor, until Madden had arrived. He had visited with the local police chief and with one of the deputies at Mickelson's office to let them know he stood ready to assist in any capacity as well as that the areas had been secured from others.

As they continued to talk, Madden shared what he had seen regarding the missing time on the tape and asked what may have caused such a problem.

"I am shocked," replied Yao, "that any time is missing. A recording tape is not terminated until the new replacement tape is inserted and recording on that cassette has begun. Then and only then is the other tape stopped and removed from the recorder. In other words, there is no reason that time should be missing. Especially during the recording period itself."

"What about your personnel?" asked Mickelson.

"Each of the people on my staff has been in place for a minimum of two years. In fact, Sheila Smith is the newest member, coming on board just a little over two years ago today."

Madden withdrew a copy of the actual time worked and a copy of the scheduled work he had shown the sheriff earlier. Now he slid copies of each to both Mickelson and the security chief, along with his notes showing the missing twenty-six minutes of tape. Yao studied the forms intently for several seconds, a frown developing across his face and his mouth showing a tightening of the muscles. "Obviously, you are right about the time stamp," he stated, studying the printout.

Madden watched intently as the chief of security perused the forms and finally asked the obvious question. "I have the tapes from your cameras and want you to see for yourself. Hopefully, knowing your staff, the work schedule as it was originally set, how it actually was done and, seeing the tape, you can give us some feedback." With that, Madden picked up the remote control, aimed it at the television set on the stand near Yao, and pressed the buttons to turn on the monitor and start the video. As he had pre-advanced the tape to 4:58 p.m., it did not take long for the tape's missing block of three minutes from 5:04 to 5:07 to become evident to the three men sitting around the table. After the timing clock had reached 5:10 p.m., Madden fast-forwarded until he saw 11:55 p.m. appear and then slowed the tape to regular speed, revealing the missing forty-one minutes from 12:09 to 12:50.

"I'll be a son-of-a-bitch!" exclaimed the resort's chief of security. "What the hell …?" Yao's voice trailed off as he continued staring at the now-paused screen display. Turning to face Madden and Mickelson, Yao selected his wording carefully. "I have no answer for either of the missing segments of time on the tape. The timer was working correctly because it was functioning properly both before and after each of the questionable periods. There was no break to the tape as that would have been quite obvious on the tape."

Both Mickelson and Madden nodded slowly without speaking. Mickelson, who had written down the times, put down his pencil, picked up his coffee cup and took a long and very deliberate mouthful before swallowing and placing the black ceramic cup with a white silhouette of the resort etched into the side back on the table. "Randy, I know that has to be hard on you. You recommended each of the persons in your department, and I know you did so carefully." A long and thoughtful pause punctuated the room. "I can only come to one conclusion, though, and that is that someone, at some time, erased those particular segments. The question is why was it done at those two times and by whom?"

Agent Madden listened to the sheriff's remarks and then looked toward Yao. "That is the way I see it as well, Randy. I believe, after looking at the tapes several times and coordinating the times with those from other tapes taken by other camera positions on site, that someone or several persons entered Senator Carson's room a little after five o'clock on Tuesday evening, just after the meeting had adjourned, and then removed him from the room sometime between 12:09 and 12:50 a.m. and during that time removed the broken table from Room 932, placed it under the stairwell, and replaced it with a table taken from the ninth floor storage room in an attempt to remove obvious evidence."

Yao sat quietly, fingers folding and unfolding the corner of the work-schedule form. "Sheila had called in sick, and it was I who gave consent for Biffle to work a double shift. He had said he needed the extra cash since his wife, Georgia, just had a miscarriage of their first baby and had to have a hysterectomy. He is the only one of the two who is working, and their medical and living expenses have been hitting them pretty hard. I thought maybe the extra shift would help him out a bit since we pay double for any overtime. That is why HR is so forceful in telling all of our managers not to allow overtime unless absolutely necessary. I do have two local police officers who fill in once in a while when we are short, but that particular time neither was available so overtime fit nicely, especially, as I said, to help the Biffles out."

Yao paused and took a glass from the center tray. Using ice tongs that had been laid beside the ice bucket on the tray, he placed several cubes in it and poured water from a bottle of water that Madden had set before him when he had first taken his seat. After a long drink, he placed the glass on the paper coaster. "I presume that you two are going to talk with Cary, Evers, and Thompson, directly. Do you want me to sit in on the interviews with you?"

Madden considered Yao's offer for a moment before shaking his head. "No, Randy, I don't think so. If you sit in, then it could have a negative impact on your staff. Let Kyler and me do the interviewing. That said, though, it is important that you not share our discussion with any of them. I hope that is ok with you."

"Nope, not a problem at all," replied Yao.

The next couple of hours the three spent the time reviewing the tapes and discussing what had been seen. After viewing, rewinding, and viewing each of the tapes of the ninth floor and the elevator area, the three took a break to use the restroom and stretch their legs. All three felt confident that, clearly, one of three people had played with the tape, and now Madden and Mickelson would have to determine who and why. Yao suggested that since it was ten thirty they might interview Tom Evers, followed by Sheila Smith, both of whom currently were on duty until four that afternoon. Yao explained that pairings for guard rotation was changed weekly so that the same two people did not always work the same shift, nor always work with the same partner. This week's schedule had exchanged Smith and Biffle. Cary Biffle was scheduled to report to duty at four along with Mike Thompson. Madden thought that was an appropriate process to follow. Yao also agreed that any frames from the videotapes Madden thought necessary to capture he would have his security office staff print out.

Both Madden and Mickelson thanked the chief of security and told him they would keep him informed of any progress or new developments in the case. With an exchange of handshakes, Yao left the room, indicating he would have Evers come and meet with the lawmen.

The recorded interview with Tom Evers was pretty much routine—some basic ice-breaking comments to help him feel comfortable as well as to probe his personal life to get a mental image of what kind of person he was followed by questions about his past life and work history. Then the questioning moved into the days in question, last Tuesday and Wednesday. Evers told them that he had spent his time on that Tuesday outdoors until almost seven o'clock, assisting local police and sheriff deputies with crowd control, separating the protesters from the hotel guests. He then had taken the electric golf cart that the security office had use of and patrolled the resort's parking lot. Madden listened to the resort guard and then asked if he had observed any unusual behavior or people who raised any suspicion with him.

"Naw, everything was really quiet. The protesters had moved out quietly, and after they'd left, the police and deputies did too."

"So, there were no people just standing around or looking as though they were waiting for something or someone?" Madden asked.

"Like I said, nobody, except some guests, was even visible. Some were going to dinner, some were putting ski stuff in their cars, and others were standing around, jawing with one another."

"What about while you manned the desk after being outdoors?" inquired Madden.

Again, Evers replied in the negative. "Nothin' that I haven't usually seen any other day of the week. The usual folks coming and going from rooms, dining room, coffee shop, lounge, the atrium, pool. Nothing at all was out of line. I came in, went to the coffee shop for dinner, and then came to the security office about seven when I relieved Biffle for his dinner break." Evers completed his answer by saying that while he finished his time in the security office, there had been no calls, and nothing out of the ordinary had happened.

Mickelson then stepped into the conversation and asked Evers what had been the order of events and time-frame as the shift ended.

"Around eleven-twenty, just before the midnight shift change, Biffle took a twenty- or thirty-minute break, but he was back in the security office just before midnight to relieve me and begin his second shift." Tom reflected on the question for a moment and then added that, as stipulated by the payroll time card, he had clocked out promptly at twelve o'clock midnight. Because the time clock was down the hall in the security office, some thirty feet away, it was most likely and quite reasonable, that Evers had left a few minutes before midnight.

Mickelson glanced toward Madden who nodded; the sheriff rose, shook hands with Evers, and escorted him to the door. Madden, having risen from his chair and now at the door, shook hands as well, thanking him for his candid responses and spoke a genuine "Thank you."

It was now eleven twenty, and within ten minutes there came a knock on the door of the room. Madden, being seated closer to the door, walked over and opened it. A small-framed woman stood in front of him, about five four in height and, probably, Madden estimated, in the neighborhood of 105 to 110 pounds. Dishwater blond hair fell in bangs, just touching the eyebrow line and ending below the earlobe, and tapered down to the back of the head, stopping just short of the neckline. A few longer strands dangled in front of each ear. Deep blue eyes and pursed lips indicated seriousness although he could tell she smiled a great deal because of the little telltale creases at the corners of her mouth.

Introducing herself as Sheila Smith, she offered a rather cool and fairly soft hand to Madden, but shook with a firm grip and met his eyes in an unwavering connection. Though very attractive, she was not, Madden concluded, a weak or timid individual. Stepping aside to allow her entry, he walked her to the chair located at the end of the table. Mickelson had stood to remove the water glass and bottle used previously by Tom Evers and replaced them with fresh ones. He greeted the security officer warmly and pulled the chair out for her to be seated.

"Sheila, would you like something to drink? Coffee, tea, or a soft drink?" Mickelson asked. Sheila Smith sat in the chair and responded that she would love a diet Coke if it were available. Mickelson nodded and walked behind the bar, retrieved a cold can from the refrigerator and set it in front of her on the table. He then slid the tray holding the empty glasses and ice bucket toward her to fill her glass before taking his own seat.

Smith placed several cubes in her glass, poured in some of the Coke, and sat back in the chair, looking at Madden. The FBI agent smiled and informed her that the reason for the meeting was to assist in the investigation of Senator Carson's disappearance from the resort.

"Chief Yao told me you want to ask me some questions." Her eyes never wavered from his, searching for possible clues as to what they wanted of her.

Agent Madden took a drink of water from the glass in front of him, poured more into it, and then swiveled slightly in his chair to face her directly. "Miss Smith," he began, "I want to thank you for coming down to visit with us. I don't think we will be long and," he looked at his watch, "since it's eleven-thirty, you should be able to make the next rotation change of your shift."

"That is not a problem," replied the petite officer. "Tom is covering at the desk so I can answer any questions you two might have." She gave a slight, but genuine smile to Madden and then, turning her head, displayed the smile to Mickelson.

As with Evers, the tape recorder was started, and the questioning began with a request for a brief history leading up to and including her current employment status with the resort. Smith spent several minutes providing a good background of the life she had lived in Denver as a child. The only child of a large retail store manager, she had opted to work for her father while completing an online degree program through Penn State. She had finished her required 120 credits in January of 1994, requiring less than four years to do so. She then obtained a position with the police department of Boulder, Colorado. After working for the detective division she left because of her belief that a major murder case of 1996 was being mishandled. Her supervisor had not allowed her to become involved in the case and seemed to delight in preventing her from any advancement, partially, she believed, because she had a criminology and criminal justice degree and he did not. Returning to Denver, she went to work for a security division of the Denver International Airport, and since she loved the field, she entered an online, two-year graduate program through the University of Cincinnati, rated as one of the top programs. She had completed it in eighteen months.

Upon receiving her master's degree, she worked as a personal security guard for the governor of Colorado, a position, she explained, through which she met her current boss, Randy Yao five years ago. He had contacted her when he took the position as security head for the resort and asked her to be on his staff. His intent, she insisted, was to groom her for taking over the position. Since she loved snow skiing and trail running, she seriously considered his offer. The acceptance was made easy when the package she was offered including lifetime use of the ski hill and trails, an excellent 401K, a fully funded health and long-term care benefit package and hourly pay at fourteen fifty which now had risen to eighteen dollars an hour. Smiling, she acknowledged that for a mere thirty-year-old single woman she was in pretty good financial shape. She was in petty good physical shape as well, filling out even in the nondescript security staff uniform in just the right places.

"Sheila," broke in Sheriff Mickelson, "would you mind telling Steve and me why you did not work your shift as scheduled on Tuesday of this past week?"

"Not at all, Kyler. I began feeling really sick around two in the afternoon of Tuesday. I thought maybe by Tuesday's shift I would be better, but I didn't. So, about five on Tuesday afternoon, I called Randy—Chief Yao—and informed him that I would not be able to make my shift."

"So you did not come in at all on Tuesday, is that correct?"

"Yes, sir. The next time I came in was Wednesday night at midnight."

"What is your relationship with your co-workers?"

"For the most part there is not anything but business."

"Please explain your wording of *for the most part*."

"Because of our shifts, we don't have much opportunity to socialize together. I personally have made the choice not to mix business and pleasure, so what I do in my private time I do away from the other guys. They know that I'm paid more than anyone else and that Randy has brought me in for the purpose of taking over when he leaves in the near future."

"How do the guys react to that knowledge?" Mickelson continued.

"For the most part they are fine with it. None of them has the background and training I have had, and they understand that part. But ...," her voice seemed to trail off as her thoughts picked up another possibility. Pausing for a second or two, she quickly came back to her response. "I can think of only one who ever gave me a hard time, and that was just after I was hired."

"Who might that person be?"

"Mike Thompson seemed a bit ticked that a woman made more than he did since he was the senior person on the staff."

"What did he say and or do to make you feel that way, Sheila?"

"Just some teasing and taunting about being on the chief's favorite list, that maybe I was a *suck up*, or that maybe I had something going with Yao in order to get the job. It lasted only a couple of weeks, and from then on, we've been fine with one another. He does his job, and I do mine. If it were any other way, we wouldn't be able to work together, and Chief doesn't put up with that crap from his employees."

"I know this is not easy, but I need to ask. Did you or are you involved with Yao?"

The jaw muscles of Smith's face tightened, and her eyes, looking directly at Mickelson, narrowed to almost slits as she answered him. "I take that as a personal affront. Randy Yao was good enough to hire me because he knew my family, my education background, and my employment record. That is what led him to hire me. I'm good at my job, and he has told me that if I want to move into a federal position he has some connections that he would contact on my behalf. However, because I love this part of the world and it provides me with everything I need now and even in the future, I would be rather foolish to throw it away, don't you think?"

Mickelson just smiled and repeated that he understood the difficulty of the question but, appealing to her professional side, knew she was aware of the reason for posing it to her. She nodded slightly, offered him a weak smile, and assured him that, yes, she did understand but since this was the first time such a question had been thrown at her it felt a bit threatening.

Madden cleared his throat to change the focus and offered a question. "Did anyone or anything strike you as unusual when you were working on Monday from twelve to eight a.m.?"

The officer thought about his inquiry for a moment and used a slow drink from her glass as an excuse to pause before answering. Then she leaned slightly forward and replied, "As you probably know, Cary and Tom worked the evening shift from eight until midnight, and Mike and I were to have worked the graveyard from midnight to eight in the morning. However, as I had called in ill, Randy replaced me with Cary." Smith paused.

"Please continue."

"I recall on Monday, as I began my shift, Mike had said he would take the first tour on the premises so I was at the desk. Cary usually leaves right after we come on duty, but he said he had some work to finish up at the desk."

"Is that usual? To have unfinished work to do before leaving?

"No, in fact it is highly unusual. We just don't have carryover work. When we finish our shift, we almost always check out right away."

"What time did he finally leave?"

"He was not there long, maybe ten minutes. He left right after he sorted some papers in a folder."

"Sheila, do you know what was in that folder?"

"I have no idea. I'm guessing he sorted them because I could hear them being moved as he went through them. Then he put them all back into the folder and took them with him."

"Did he say anything before he left?"

"No, he just told me, when he said he was staying a few more minutes, to take the main desk seat. He sat in a second chair we have by the door, behind where I was sitting."

"Ok. What were you doing while he was there?"

"Let me think for a moment." Sheila Smith looked off above the opposite end of the conference table as though looking for some image and then spoke. "I followed the same process I always do when I start at the desk. I signed the log that I was on duty, did a scan of the monitors for all the cameras, and then I looked to see if there were any notes left for me, ones that might indicate someone had lost something, things like that. After that I inserted new tapes into the recorders, removing the used ones. I labeled them and placed them in the storage cabinet where they're kept for ten days. Cary left right after I stored the tapes and sat back down."

Sheriff Mickelson had been jotting notes as Smith described the activity from Monday night's shift change. He now put his pencil down and looked at Sheila. "What, if anything, was said as he left, Sheila?"

"Nothing. No—wait, there was something." Smith composed her thoughts before continuing. "He said that he and his wife really appreciated my giving them a gift card for dinner for two at a local nightclub. They've been through so much I just wanted to do something nice for them."

"That was all he said?"

"No, there was something else. He told me that he was leaving a dessert his wife had made in the break room fridge."

"Tell me, Sheila," began Madden, "What was it that he had left for you?"

"It was an old family recipe of custard. I love custard, and she had been so kind to make it and share some with me. I made sure to take it with me when I left at the end of the shift."

"And that was about eight a.m.?"

"Yes. That's when I checked out and went directly home."

"What happened to the custard?

"As soon as I got to my condo, I put it in the refrigerator until I decided to eat it."

"When was that?"

"I'm sorry, I'm not clear as to what you are asking."

"When did you actually eat the custard?"

"I think it was about noon. I slept for about three hours, and when I awoke, I wanted something to eat. When I opened the fridge, I took out the custard because Cary's wife makes such wonderful custard. But I think she must have changed the recipe because it tasted different."

"How so?"

"It seemed to be a little bitter, and usually it's so sweet. Don't get me wrong; it was good, just not quite the same."

"And, you say you began feeling ill about two o'clock?"

"Yes, I know it was two because my mom called at one thirty and we talked for about ten minutes. It was after I hung up and went to get my shopping list and then head out to get groceries. I felt really hot, started to sweat, and my stomach began doing cartwheels. The nausea didn't go away even after I threw up around three; my stomach was cramping, and I felt really weak so then I called in sick and spoke with Chief Yao here at the office about five."

"Sheila, this is really important. Did you eat anything else during the time you left here until you called in sick?

"No. I feel so bad that it happened right after I ate the custard. Georgia made that even though she's just recuperating from major surgery. She would be devastated if she thought it might have made me sick. … So, do you think my getting ill was not coincidence?"

"We cannot be totally sure. We are trying to determine what everyone knows and what they saw or heard. At this point we have drawn no conclusions."

"Why is that so important?

Agent Madden considered her question, fully aware of her strong background in law enforcement, criminology, and terrorism. He was pretty sure her mind was already analyzing the questions and her responses. His gut feeling told him that she had an idea of where the questioning was leading. After all, she knew that the one end of the ninth floor had been secured, all the videos put into a locked box, and Senator Jeremy Carson had mysteriously disappeared without any contact. He decided to give this woman a little more information. "It seems a little more than just coincidence that you receive a food dish you say tasted markedly unlike the same dish you had eaten before from the same source, get sick after eating it, call in to stay home, and then during the time of your absence, two periods of time on a couple of the videos get erased."

"Oh my God!" exclaimed Smith, her eyes opening wide. "Surely you two are not thinking …" She looked to each of the lawmen, both of whom were looking at her. "You're not thinking Cary had anything to do with the senator's disappearance?"

Madden leaned toward her and spoke in a softened tone. "Sheila, we are not sure of anything as of this moment. We have talked with people in HR, with Randy Yao, with Tom Evers, and now with you. We have the office staff for security making some hardcopy prints of different people who appeared on the videotapes. When we get them we will make some additional contacts and see if anyone remembers anything further."

Madden paused to allow his comments to sink in before continuing. "I have shared this with you because I respect your training and background and I feel we can trust you. Sheila, it is vital that you do not speak to anyone about the case and where we are going with it. You do understand, right?"

"Yes, sir," came the quiet reply. "I do understand. I just can't believe that someone, let alone Cary, might do something like that. Is there anything I can do to help?"

"You already have. You can continue to help by not saying anything, just going about your job as usual. If you observe or hear anything, please get back to us immediately. I'm staying here at the hotel, and the desk will always know how to reach me. You can also call me direct on my cell." Madden took a business card from his wallet, wrote his cellular phone number on the back, and handed it to her.

Mickelson nodded and then added his own statement. "You can reach me through my office twenty-four seven as well, Sheila. The resort and all of Jackson Hole does not want the stigma of a kidnapping, for whatever reason, and we will reach the bottom of this. I have another question to pose to you. Have you returned the container, and have you and Cary spoken since last Monday night?"

"I brought the container back when I returned on Wednesday at midnight. I gave it to Cary as he was leaving from his shift."

"Did he say anything when you gave him the container?"

"Only that he was glad to see me back at work and hoped I had gotten over the flu bug and hoped I was feeling better. He knew I was sick since he had filled in for me."

Madden heard something click in his mind and immediately posed a follow-up question. "How did he know you had any flu symptoms?"

Smith again flashed a look of disbelief as she heard the question. It seemed to hit her like a cold towel slapping her in the face. "Christ! I have no idea. I didn't even tell Chief Yao what I had. I just told him I wasn't feeling well and couldn't come in on Tuesday. Oh no! Surely not Cary! Why? Why would he ever do something like that?"

Madden spoke to her common sense as he said, "We are not sure if he did anything yet. But we are going to find out."

With that, Agent Madden rose, thanked the Smith for her assistance, and told her that they would keep her informed. Sheriff Mickelson joined the two as they walked to the door. After shaking hands all around, Mickelson opened the door, thanked her again and allowed her to leave.

After Smith exited, Mickelson closed the door momentarily and turned to his counterpart. "Well, Steve, it looks as though we might have found something. It will be interesting to interview Mr. Biffle."

Madden nodded, smiling. "Yes, won't it be interesting." He looked at his watch, 1:10. "Let's order lunch from the restaurant and see if Yao has the prints done for us. We have until four to see if we can work up some clues before interviewing Thompson and Biffle when they come on board then."

The two ordered lunch and then called the security office. Yao informed them that the prints had been finished and he would personally bring the prints and the tapes to them right away.

Chapter Ten

Lunch from the dining room had satisfied without leaving either Madden or Mickelson feeling overly filled. During their lunch, Yao had entered the room with the promised photos taken from different frames of the videotape.

After receiving the printouts, Mickelson and Madden carried them to the check-in desk in the lobby of the resort. One by one, they talked with the clerks on duty and the bellhops. Finally, a young freckle-faced boy of about nineteen came to the bellhop station from the elevators. As Mickelson showed the photos to him, the boy pointed to three of them and said he remembered them because they were about his age and had been giggling when they came in from the parking lot on Tuesday evening. The taller boy was, said he, carrying what he believed to be a six-pack of beer; trying to conceal it under his winter ski parka.

Madden asked the boy if he knew any others, and he shook his head that he had not seen any of them, but he was positive about the three. Madden went back to the check-in desk. After conferring with his notebook and locating his notation about the three youths captured on the video entering a room, he asked for the names of the party staying in room 925 on Tuesday night.

"That would be the Hendersons," came the answer from the twenty-ish young lad standing at the desk. "They are due to check out tomorrow morning."

"How many in the party?"

Giving another look at the registration card, the boy looked up. "There are three: Dr. Donald and Mrs. Renae Henderson and their son, James."

"Do you know if they were traveling with anyone else?"

"There is a note on the registration card to contact the Vickers in Room 1002; that would be a room with two bedrooms, in case of emergency." The desk clerk volunteered, "There are four in their party—two adults and two kids, a boy and a girl."

Madden then asked when that party was checking out and was informed that they too would be departing Rendezvous Mountain Resort the next morning. He turned to Mickelson. "Might be a good time to see if they're in since we do have some time to kill before our next interview shortly after four o'clock."

Sheriff Mickelson nodded in agreement, and the two rode the elevator to the ninth floor. As the door opened, Madden stepped out and then said, "You might as well go on up to 1002, Kyler. See if the Vicker kids are in. Maybe we can catch them on a break. You have my cell number so you can call me once you know."

Madden walked down the hallway to Room 925, one of only two rooms on the ninth floor that were still being occupied after Yao had secured the other end rooms. Reaching the room, he knocked and waited. No response, so he knocked again. Finally he heard a lock being undone, and the door opened partially, still being held by the chain latch. The face of a young man peered out. His eyes looked blurry, as if he had just awakened, and his head of dark medium-length hair had a desperate need of combing. "Yeah?"

Madden introduced himself and asked if he was speaking with James. The boy rolled his eyes, "I'm Jim," he replied with a rather indignant tone in his voice. "Whaddywan? I haven't done nuthin.'" Quite obviously the boy was not happy to be answering any questions, to a legal officer or not.

Madden told the boy what he had observed on the videotape from Tuesday night and of the hidden treasure he and his two friends had brought up on the elevator and to this room.

"Hey man, don't be hassl'n' me 'bout no beers. I was just with those two. I neva drank none of it." Madden found the kid's attempt at street talk comical; he could tell the youth normally spoke differently and had to work at slurring his words and using poor grammar. His speech sounded nothing like what Madden had experienced when working in rough areas or cities or with street kids. He smiled and mentioned that he had found the bottles under the stairwell across the hall from the room and that they were now with the local sheriff's office having the fingerprints lifted for identification.

"Question, Jim, for you to consider, is whether your folks will appreciate knowing your prints are on at least two of those bottles. You do know that you are under age for alcohol consumption here, right?"

"Okay, mister," Jim answered, a slight look of panic look in his eyes, "whaddya want from me? I don't want no trouble from anyone. 'Specially my old man and old lady."

"When you three came up, did you see or hear anything that got your attention that night, Jim?"

Jim Henderson thought a moment, stirring his already disastrous case of bed hair as he did so. "Well, yeah, guess I did. Sumpin' was going on. There was a loud bang and some loud voices when I was opening the door for me and my friends to come in here."

"Where was the sound coming from?" asked Madden.

The boy nodded his head to his right, in the direction of Room 932. "Down that way," he said. "Sounded like maybe some guys were partying or fighting. There was this loud crash, like glass breaking, then loud voices and a slamming door, stuff like that. That's 'bout all I heard."

"Do you know what time that was, Jim"

"Five sumpin', I guess."

"How do you know the time?"

"Cuz the phone rang when we opened the door. We didn't answer it. It went to the answering machine. It was a message from the old man saying they were gonna be a little late gettin' back from dinner over at the Sequoia Club."

"Just by chance, did you you report the noise to the desk?"

A sheepish look peered out the doorway. "Hey man, we sure didn't wanna get busted for beers up here, and anyway, the noise didn't last long."

Madden thanked the boy, gave him is business card, and told him to call him or the security office downstairs if he remembered anything else. Jim Henderson closed the door, and Madden could hear the latch being set again. He smiled as he thought about a teenage boy on the other side who was saying many "thank yous" to an invisible being for his parents not being in right now.

A soft buzzing sound accompanied by a vibration from the dark blue blazer pocket caught Madden's attention as he began walking toward the elevator. He plunged a hand into the pocket and withdrew his cell phone. "Madden," he answered, flipping open the phone lid.

"Steve, I just left the Vicker room. The mother was in, but the rest of the family is up on the ski hill. She thought they would be back down shortly as they were going to eat lunch together about three." Mickelson waited for Madden to respond to his news.

"Okay, Kyler. Let's see if we can catch them as they come off the hill and turn their skis in to the ski shack storage area. I just finished visiting with the Henderson kid. I'll catch you in the elevator and fill you in as we go over to the ski shack." He clicked his phone closed, and waited for the elevator carrying Kyler Mickelson to descend to his floor. Once inside and with the cubicle again dropping toward the first floor, Madden filled the sheriff in on what he had learned from Jim Henderson.

Exiting the elevator, the two walked briskly across the resort lobby and down the hallway that led to the ski shop where the storage shack was located. They had looked at the photos of the Vicker children long enough to have their images pretty well ingrained in their minds. Now all they had to do was wait and hope to locate them.

It was almost two now, and the family of skiers would most likely be headed in soon if they were actually going to meet with the mother for a late lunch. To most people in the shop, Madden and Mickelson were just shoppers, but they were focusing their watch on the door leading from the ski area to the storage desk at the end of the tony clothing and souvenir shop. After fifteen minutes of milling around, moving hangers, and acting as though they were shopping, Madden spotted three skiers entering the area of the storage desk. One was average height, medium weight, and had graying hair. He would be Derrick Vickers, Madden concluded. His son, Ronald, taller than his dad and with the physique of a good athlete, carried three sets of skis over one shoulder and several ski poles in the other. Theresa, nearing her dad's five feet eight inches or so, had flaming red hair that fell down to the middle of her back. They were all smiles and laughing as they approached the desk to store their skis and poles.

Madden caught Mickelson's eye and nodded toward the threesome. Kyler Mickelson nodded briefly in response, and they casually walked toward the threesome. By the time Mickelson and Madden reached the Vicker party, the ski equipment had been checked, and the three had just begun walking toward the door to the lobby. As they reached the door, the lawmen intercepted them. Madden placed his hand on the door handle, but instead of pulling to open the door, he turned, opened his identification badge holder with his free hand, and introduced himself. "Good afternoon, folks. I am FBI agent Steve Madden and this," gesturing to his partner, "is Jackson Sheriff Kyler Mickelson."

The three family members looked completely surprised but all greeted the peace officers in a kind tone of voice. Mr. Vicker was the one to speak up.

"Is there something we can do for you men?"

Madden informed them that they wanted to visit with the two siblings, which raised the eyebrows of the father and resulted in a questioning glance toward his two children. Madden saw the look and headed off any fear by adding, "We are looking into the disappearance of Senator Jeremy Carson that you most likely have heard about. Though we are sure the kids have no direct knowledge of that, we are checking with anyone who might have seen or heard something that might be helpful in assisting us with our investigation." Derrick Vicker visibly relaxed and sighed a distinguished relief. He had no desire for anyone in his family to toy with the wrong side of the law. As a high-end attorney for several of the larger casinos in Las Vegas, he knew how crime worked, and though he never broke the law, his job always seemed somehow to flirt with the gray area as he, time and time again, had to find ways to keep his clients out of court for a variety of reasons. "What is it you want of them?" he asked.

Mickelson looked at the three and held his arm toward the door. "Let's go over to the lounge area in the lobby and get out of this doorway. We can sit and visit over there." Madden pulled the door open and waved the family through, followed by Mickelson. Madden then stepped through and released the handle, allowing the door to close silently behind them.

Once they had each taken a seat, Madden leaned forward from his leather chair so that he was leaning toward the two teenagers, seated on a leather sofa on the opposite side of a large wooden coffee table which sat on a bearskin rug made from the pelt of a large grizzly. A chair was positioned at the head of the rug as though the bear were about to take a significant bite from the foot of Mr. Vicker, who occupied the chair. Mickelson sat to Madden's left in a leather chair situated between Vicker and Madden.

"When did you and the Henderson family check in?" Madden began.

Mr. Vicker spoke up. "Last Tuesday morning about eleven. We arrived at the airport around ten, and by the time we rounded up the luggage, skis, etc. and were driven up here, it was nearly eleven."

Madden did not speak it, but he knew from looking at the registration card that the time was very close. The card in fact had read 11:15. It was, he thought, close enough for what he had wanted to know.

"That evening I believe," he turned to Derrick Vicker, "you, the missus, and the Hendersons went out for dinner, correct?"

"Yes, that is correct," the elder Vicker replied thoughtfully. "We left about four forty-five for drinks and a dinner reservation at the

Jackson Hole Lodge and Lounge up the road. The reservation was for six o'clock." The man looked at his children and then spoke again.

"We returned around ten thirty or maybe eleven o'clock, went to the Hendersons room, and had a couple of nightcaps before heading up the stairs to our room."

Madden picked up on the time-frame Vicker had just laid out. "What time did you and your wife walk up to your room?"

Again a reflective expression appeared on the face of Derrick Vicker as he mentally rewound his memory back four days. "Well, I am not totally sure," he began, acknowledging his uncertainty of the time, "but I believe it was near eleven-thirty. I guess it might have been as late as eleven forty-five. I know we were in our room before midnight because I looked at the clock before preparing for bed."

Madden had been hoping that maybe, by luck, they would have been either in the Henderson's room or on the stairs around midnight. No luck there. So the parents were not going to be much help. He turned to the two teens sitting quietly across from him. Looking at each of them he posed the question that, though unsure of how their father would react, he had to ask.

"You two went out with the Henderson's son, is that right?"

The two siblings looked at each other, and Ronald spoke up, turning his head back to look at the FBI agent. "Yes, sir. We met Jim in the lobby about three that afternoon. We ate an early dinner in the dining room and then went to his room and watched some movies."

Madden found himself smiling at the vague answer. "Did you go directly to Room 925 after eating?"

Theresa squirmed slightly on the sofa. Her eyes looked down at the table. She reached forward to toy with a copy of *Ski* magazine that lay in front of her. Brother Ronald stared at Madden as if trying to read what he did or did not already know. Finally, Theresa broke the silence. "No, we didn't. Jim wanted to walk to a convenience store just down the road from here. We went up to his room when we got back, around five."

"And, what time was it when you left to walk down to the store?

"I looked at my watch, and it was around four."

Both teens appeared a bit more uncomfortable as the question might possibly be leading to a subject neither wished to disclose to their parents. Though the two young adults did not want to share the activity of the night in question, they also knew that giving false information to these two law enforcement men could be worse.

Ronald leaned forward, physically mirroring his sister's body position, and prepared to speak. He deliberately and slowly placed his hands, palm down on the coffee table and focused on them as though they were going to tell him what to say. Considering his response, he carefully spoke each word of his statement. "Theresa is right. Jim wanted to buy some beer. Since I look older than he does, we went along, and I bought a six-pack of beer. We brought it back here. We were afraid we might get caught since we are all underage, so we came in through one of the entrances off the lower parking lot. Then we took the elevator to the ninth floor. I kept the bottles under my ski parka."

Madden nodded and smiled. "Yes, I know. You were captured on videotape getting on the elevator and then going to Jim's room where, I am guessing, the three of you consumed the beer."

Both nodded and sat with their heads bowed in shame and guilt. Still, neither knew why this federal officer and a local area sheriff were questioning them. The older Vicker, though obviously not happy with the confession he had just listened to, turned to address the two officers. "Ok, gentlemen, my two kids allegedly broke the law and might be guilty of possession by a minor. Not exactly a major infraction. So why the grilling?"

Mickelson continued to finish his writing in the notebook. Madden smiled at Derrick and then looked back at Ronald and Theresa. "As we mentioned, Senator Jeremy Carson had been staying here at the resort and has disappeared. Derrick and Theresa were videotaped on the same floor as the senator's room on the night during which Senator Carson disappeared. We need to know what they saw and what they might have heard. When you left the Henderson room, what time was it?"

"I think it was sometime after ten. I remember we had the TV on, local weather had ended, and the half-hour broadcast was just about half over. It was probably near ten twenty."

"Ronald, what did you do with the empty bottles?"

The boy looked as though he had been caught with his hand in the cookie jar. A slow rising reddening appeared at his neck and moved vertically over his face. He slowly told of leaving Jim's room with Theresa and deciding to go up the stairs to their room, rather than risk the elevator. He had pushed the cardboard container holding all six bottles under the stairs before they went up. Mickelson asked if they had seen anything else under the stairs at the time, and Ronald shook his head indicating a negative reply.

Theresa shook her head and looked up at her father. "Dad, I know we disappointed you. I'm sorry. We just wanted to have some fun, kick back, and relax."

Her father looked at his two children and smiled very faintly. "Theresa, Ronald," he began, "I know that this is not the first time. After all, you are twenty and nineteen years of age. For the two of you to be drinking is one thing, but to buy alcohol for a minor who is only eighteen was pretty foolish. Even though you were in a hotel room and not out running around, it was not smart. I have no idea what James's parents will do, but I do expect that the two of you will talk with his parents and let them know you did the buying." Then turning to the lawmen, he asked if there were any further questions they had for his children.

Sheriff Mickelson opened his leather notebook and took out some photos. Handing them to the brother and sister he asked, "Do either of you recognized any of these people?" The first two of the four photos, taken from the videotapes earlier depicted two men, both in hooded sweatshirts, in separate photos. A second pair of photos showed two other men, one had on a jacket of some kind and a stocking cap while the other wore a shirt that appeared to be plaid and open at the neck. The boy and girl looked at them intently for several seconds. Putting the photos back down on the table the girl was the first to respond.

"Yes, I recognize the photos of these two," pointing to the last two photos. "They were in the lobby when we left to go to the convenience store."

Her brother nodded in agreement. "We almost bumped into them as we went out the door. They were standing nearly in front of the door.

I remember the one in the stocking cap more because he looked kind of mousy, but what really struck me was the look of both in their eyes. Really mean. And they were talking very quietly, like they didn't want anyone to hear them. I took Theresa's arm and pulled her through the door so we wouldn't have to face them."

Further questions about the two or about anyone else who might have raised attention confirmed the description of the loud voices in the hallway. However, like Jim, neither Ronald nor Theresa thought to look out the door or to report it to the front desk as they considered it none of their business. Continuing to question them would be useless. The stories of the two, corroborated by that of James, pretty well set the minds of both Madden and Mickelson. They knew the next piece of the puzzle to unravel would be to figure out who these guys were. They obviously had been on the same floor as the senator and at almost the exact time. The question was *what* were they doing?

Madden and Mickelson both stood and offered their hand to the three Vicker family members. Madden apologized for holding them up and more than likely making them late for the date with their mother. He handed each of them a business card and expressed his appreciation. With that the father and his two children walked away toward the elevator.

Mickelson looked at his watch and said aloud, "Three forty."

Madden picked up his pocket tape recorder that he had used during the morning interviews and the one with the two Vicker kids. He popped out the miniature cassette and inserted a new one. After closing the compartment he carefully labeled the removed cassette and placed it in his shirt pocket under the teal sweater. Then he turned and said they might as well get back to the conference room so they could be prepared for the next two interviews of the day. First they would interview Mike Thompson and then Cary Biffle. But before that, they had to check on some communications.

"Well, pieces are beginning to fall in place now," the agent said as they walked across the immaculately clean tile floor of the hotel lobby toward the lobby desk.

"At least we have some lead to work with," offered Mickelson. "Hopefully, before day's end, we'll have some information from my office about the fingerprints sent to the other states. I'm going to make sure that the copies of the photos we left at the desk were faxed to all the other states as well."

"That's what I need to do as well," countered Madden. "Maybe by now, the senator's computer has been examined back in DC and someone has had a chance to run those photos that I faxed there earlier as well."

As they approached, the desk was almost invisible with all the people standing around it. For the most part, the throng was being patient as the check-in and registration process was being performed. Luggage, ski bags, and boxes were piled onto carpeted carts, and clothes hung above them from the brass rod over the top. Bellhops obligingly followed guests or wrote notes on luggage tickets, listing the room number and name of the respective guest. Skis and poles, along with snowboards, would be taken to the ski shack. The luggage and clothing bags would be brought up to the room for the guest. A movement caught the eye of Madden as they neared the desk. It was the day manager standing near the hallway he had gone down last evening to visit with Martha Young.

Veering off to the left, he went to the man who was beckoning them. A man in his mid-forties, sporting a crew cut and a dark blue suit with light blue shirt and red and blue tie. As they met, the man extended his hand and introduced himself as Andrew Webster, the day manager. After shaking hands, Madden introduced Sheriff Mickelson. Webster then suggested they come with him. They entered the hallway and walked to the day manager's office. It was a duplicate of the office in which he had met Ms. Young the night before. Her office was in fact, just beyond the door they turned in to enter Webster's office.

"I didn't want you two to have to deal with that crowd out there," Webster smiled and continued. "This is a really busy check-in time for us. However, I have something for each of you." He sorted through some papers located in the top basket on his desk, a basket marked "INBOX." Finally, he pulled a large manila envelope and, after looking at the handwritten name on it, handed it to Madden. Then he flipped through several more sheets and pulled a legal size envelope from the stack, handing that to Mickelson. The day manager then stepped from behind his desk and walked to the office door. Going out into the hallway, he gave the two officers privacy to examine the contents of their packages. In chorus, they opened the envelopes handed to them. Madden opened the envelope and pulled out faxes of two typed pages as Mickelson opened his envelop and withdrew a single typed page.

After several moments of silence, Madden placed the papers on top of the envelope and said, "Well, we didn't get anything from the prints. The blood drop sample we found on the broken glass and on the rug in 932 was positively Senator Carson's blood. Furthermore, the glass was the same glass as a piece I sent with it from the broken tabletop we found under the stairwell. There was nothing substantial on the computer that gives us a solid lead. The best the lab folks could come up with was a memo written by Carson. It was written and sent to other members of an anti-terrorism committee that reports to Homeland Security. It mentions an Ahmad Rahman Hassan. The memo states that he was last known to be in Calgary, Alberta, Canada, but that he disappeared from the political radar about two months ago. The concern is that he had voiced opposition to Carson's committee and vowed to end its function. What his political orientation is, nobody really is sure. Nor does it seem that anyone is aware of any threat to any of the members of his committee. The Bureau is still searching its video file for a possible match of our photos."

Mickelson listened to his partner's comments and then gave a rundown on his communiqué. "Utah indicated that one of the sets of prints we sent is identified as a Roger Utter. He was a small-time operator about five years ago around Salt Lake. Never anything real big. Seems he did a couple of small fence jobs for someone, never did find out whom, and finally got busted for using coke. Did some jail time there and was released about sixteen months ago. Since then, he has skipped out on his parole, just last month, and never heard from again. Their offices have tried tracking him through family and friends but haven't found any connection. The only possible contact it seems is that Utter had a friend in Twin Falls, Idaho. The friend's name is Cameron Jefferson. Evidently Jefferson also did a spell for possession a while back but has since stayed straight and recently got off parole. Been running a little antique shop on the east edge of Twin Falls."

"Ok," replied Madden, standing up. "Let's see if the photos we sent shake anything in DC, Utah, or Idaho. In the meantime, since it's five of four, let's get back to the conference room and do our interviews."

CHAPTER ELEVEN

FBI Agent Madden and Teton County Sheriff Mickelson took advantage of the security personnel scheduled shift change to expand their notes each had taken during the Vicker interviews. Though the information the teen siblings and their friend had provided alone was not overwhelming, when coupled with the information Mickelson had received from the authorities in Utah, there was the possibility of a strong lead. The two hoped now that Idaho's authorities would soon respond with more detailed information. What the officers did know was that Roger Utter and Cameron Jefferson had definitely been at the hotel. If the two had taken Carson, who would have hired them to take him and why? There had to be a purpose because the senator's wallet, still containing money and credit cards, was left behind. Ransom did not seem to be the reason as no note or demand had been made. Whatever the reason, some major questions still remained. Madden rose as a knock sounded on the room door, and he strode across the ten-foot distance in no time and turned the knob. Mike Thompson was a good looking, early- to mid-thirties man. He carried an athletic build on his six-foot tall frame and looked as though he could hold his own with almost any one.

Madden greeted the security employee and escorted him to his seat at the end of the table, placed a glass in front of him, and asked if he would like anything in particular.

Thompson smiled and replied that a cup of coffee would be great, and Sheriff Mickelson obliged by bringing one to him immediately. The tray was pulled closer, and Thompson took two sugar cubes and dropped them one by one into the cup and then poured cream until it just appeared on the surface. Setting down the silver-coated vessel, he picked up a teaspoon and slowly stirred, then placed the spoon on the saucer in front of him.

Madden began. "Thank you for coming down to visit with us, Mike. I am sure you know the purpose of our meeting today."

"Yes, Chief Yao said you two wanted to visit with me," began Thompson, after taking a drink from his cup and then placing it on the saucer.

"Our conversation will be recorded," Madden informed Thompson, as he reached to the recorder and turned it on. "First, though," Madden continued, "we would like to know something about you. Where you have been in your life, what major things you might have done, why you work here at the Rendezvous, you know, Mike, the usual background."

The security guard complied with the request. He talked about his being born and reared in Baltimore, that he attended parochial schools through high school graduation. He played football and lacrosse, was named All-State as a defensive cornerback in football his junior and senior years and was offered football scholarships by Boston University and the University of Maryland. After contemplating the offers, his decision had been to attend UM where he played all four years. Though he made the all-conference team his senior year, playing pro ball just was not in his list of goals. He enlisted in the Marine Corps and served four years, the last being in Iraq. When his tour of duty ended, he wanted to see some of the country in which he had grown up. Since he had never been to the West, he drove out and while exploring the Jackson area, he heard of the need for a security guard at the Rendezvous. He was accepted immediately and had been with the resort the last four years.

Continuing his background explanation, Thompson told the officers that he still did not have a desire to move on though he was not positive he wanted to stay there either. When Mickelson prodded him to explain that statement, he said that he liked the resort and most of the people but that he was not sure he wanted to work under some young, know-it-all female when Yao retired in the next couple of years.

Madden smiled and asked, "What is it that bothers you about that possibility?"

"They've wined and dined her till it's sickening. She shows up to work, and they seem always to bowing to her every whim."

"Like what?" interjected Mickelson.

"She gets time off when she wants, they pay her more than the rest of us, and she has perks that none of us get, like free skiing and lodging any time she wants it."

"So," began Madden, drawing lazy circles around the pre-punched holes of his writing pad, "you're saying you are jealous of her and don't care much for her."

"Yeah, you could say that. I mean she's nice enough now, but I just don't think she and I would get along if she were my boss."

"Why do you say that?"

"When she first came on, we were all visiting one day after an in-service that we had to attend. She told us about her being recruited and how great she thought that was. I just told her I didn't think it was fair; it made the rest of us basically peons, and she must think she's really something. I teased her pretty hard for a few days about being such a prima donna. I think it would be difficult for her to be fair toward me now. Besides, there're other things I want to do in life. I'm not married, so I have the freedom to come and go as I want. I am not big into skiing, and I love the water so Jackson and the Rendezvous are not where I want to put down my lifetime roots. I'm thinking that, with a degree in commercial art and design, I want to go out to L.A."

Madden jotted a few brief notes to himself and then looked up at Thompson. "Mike, how do you get along with the rest of the guards, other than Smith?"

"Not a problem with any of the guys. In fact, Tom and I are pretty tight. We hang out when we're both off at the same time. He loves to hike, as do I, so we spend time hiking in the mountains. He has an uncle in Alhambra, just out of L.A. toward San Gabriel. He owns an advertising agency and has indicated that if I come out there he can put me to work. Pay is a hell of a lot better there than here; there are greater possibilities for fun in the sun, as they say. My only hang-up is I know what the prices for rent out there are."

"What about Cary Biffle?"

"Cary is his own guy. I mean he's married and none of the rest of us are. We never hang out with him 'cause he's always going straight home or, if we're off at the same time, his wife always wants him to spend the time with her. Guess that's ok, but the guy just never seems to have his own life."

"You seem to have a pretty good insight into Biffle's life. What can you tell us about him?" asked Madden nonchalantly.

"Cary's been talkin' 'bout getting a second job the last couple of weeks. He's asked me several times if I know anyone who he can get hold of. Said something about paying off a mountain of debt they had. I know his wife just had a miscarriage and had to have some kind of surgery. Guess it was female stuff. All I know is that he needs to make some cash to get the doctors, hospital, car, and house bill folks off their backs."

"What has he been like the last few weeks; since the pressure began?"

"He seems to be more nervous. Like he has a short attention span. He's always preoccupied, which I guess, is natural."

"Anything about last Tuesday night when the two of you worked?"

"What do you mean?

"You and he worked the midnight to eight shift, didn't you? He had just finished working an eight-hour shift and stayed another eight. How was he acting during your shift?"

Mike Thompson thoughtfully considered the statement and question before rendering a response. Finally, after several seconds, he spoke. "When I arrived, he was still in the call desk, where we take calls and watch the monitors, so I decided to see if he wanted to start his shift there. When I came in he was closing a folder and just stepping out into the hallway. He looked surprised I was right there and held up the folder and just said he'd been looking at and sorting bills. When I asked if he wanted to take the tour—do the outside portion—to get some fresh air, he said no. He wanted to stay in the call room for the first part of the shift. So, I got my coat and went out to get the cart for a ride around. Told him I'd talk with him later by radio."

"Did he say anything or do anything that was different?"

"Like what? The guy needs money; Yao was nice to give him a double shift for a few extra bucks. Besides, being inside, he could still do some bill sorting or whatever if he needed to. I wasn't offended. None of us really likes the desk. Just sitting there, usually with not much happening. At least on the tour, we can talk with folks, get fresh air, and stretch our legs. That is by far the better part of any shift."

Mickelson looked at Madden and then to Thompson. "Mike, you are saying he was not unduly nervous or anything that night?"

"No more than he had been the few days before and since. This has been a really hard week on him with all those bills and his wife's recovery. Can't blame the guy for being edgy with all that stuff going down."

"Right. Do you guys, meaning all of you guards, ever share stuff, like food?"

Thompson laughed. "Obviously you don't know who can and can't cook. Cary's wife is darn near a gourmet chef. She makes stuff all the time, and Cary brings samples in for us. Yeah, she does some really great cooking! I do some but eat out mostly. Tom can cook. He learned that from his previous marriage. The wife didn't cook, so he had to do almost all of it. So he brings stuff in at times. As for Sheila, well, she can cook, but she sure is no chef. Occasionally, she brings something in but not often. Mostly it's Cary."

"When was the last time he brought anything in that you know of?"

"Well, let me think." Thompson slowly rubbed his chin. "It must have been last Monday night. Yeah it was. I remember that Cary made such a big deal of the fact that his wife, still recovering from surgery, would make up a dessert for us."

"You said for *us*."

"Yeah, that's right. Cary brought in three plastic containers that each had custard in it. Had them labeled with our names and put them in the fridge for us to take home or eat here."

"Do you have any knowledge of what happened to them?"

"Tom ate his before he left. Probably when he was in here and Cary was doing the tour. His empty container was on the counter in the break room, and he left a note for Cary's wife. I ate mine while I was in here during Sheila's and my shift. Think I ate it about five or six in the morning. It was really good. Like everything else she ever makes."

"And Smith's?"

"Well, she didn't eat it at work. Kept it in the fridge and almost forgot to take it with her when we left after signing out at eight on Monday morning."

"What do you mean by, 'almost'?" quizzed Madden.

"I mean we were headed out the door after clocking out, and Chief Yao brought it to her. He was getting a can of soda from the fridge and saw her name on the container."

As with the other two guards, Smith and Evers, the conversation wound down without much more being shared. Still, the comments about his fellow worker certainly could be used to support doing something for money. On the other hand, Thompson himself had said he wanted to leave the resort in the near future, had no ties or reasons to stay other than the cost of rent in California where he had said he wanted to go.

Madden and Mickelson walked Thompson to the door, and when he had departed, they talked about the interview and the responses the guard had just given them. Madden indicated he would go to Yao's office to confirm the Evers's uncle in California story with Yao and see if anything had ever been said about the possibility of Thompson leaving. Mickelson, while Madden was gone, would call his office to see what, if anything had been received from the out-of-state authorities.

Before the next interview, the officers wanted as much information at their disposal as possible. The outcome of that interview might well be one of the most important that either one had done as a professional lawman.

Chief Yao typed in a few commands into his computer and pulled up the electronic personnel file for Evers. Pointing to the information on the display, he informed Madden, "Here is what you're looking for, Steve."

Madden moved forward and leaned toward the screen to read the page and scanned it from top down. About halfway down the page was a section asking for family contacts if needed. First listed were Evers's parents and right beneath that entry was the name, Richard J. Lawry; relationship: uncle. The home address given was a street in San Gabriel, California, with a business address located in Alhambra. Writing down the information on a page in his pocket notepad, Madden asked if he could use a phone and was shown to a table in a small conference room with a desk phone at one end of it. Sitting down he dialed the home number listed for the uncle. After four rings there was a click and a male voice answered.

Madden introduced himself, assured the uncle that Tom was not in trouble and that no, nothing had happened to him. He then asked Lawry if he knew of a guy named Mike Thompson.

"Mike? Oh yes, of course," replied Lawry. "What about him?"

"Sir, can you tell me if you and he ever talked about him moving out there to L.A.?"

"As a matter of fact, we did. Tom had told me about him about a year and a half ago. This past winter I flew out to do some skiing and actually met Mike. He showed me some of his commercial artwork he had done earlier, and I was highly impressed. He's a very talented artist. Too bad the resorts don't take advantage of him for their advertising."

"Was anything said about him possibly coming out and working for you?"

A brief pause. "We talked about that possibility, yes. I would love to have him work here. However, I cannot compete with some of the major firms and told him, though I wanted to hire him, it probably would not be enough to allow him to stay in a very good neighborhood or a nice apartment or condo."

"What was his reaction?"

"Obviously he was disappointed, and as we talked, I knew that his living standard could not be met easily. After all, he's single and likes to socialize. That is what young people like about the California scene. Without money in the bank to start, it didn't seem feasible for him to move out here."

Madden's mind started to evaluate the man's statements as he wrote. "Anything else you can tell me, sir? When was the last time the two of you talked?"

"The last time we talked was about a month ago. I remember it because I had just taken on a fairly large corporate account. It meant I needed some help right away to get some ad mockups done before a sales and marketing team were to meet. I called to see if Mike was interested in coming out for a week or so."

"And what did he say?"

"Well, sir, he told me that he had some things he had to take care of in the near future and he wouldn't be able to right away. Said maybe by the first of May he might be able to, but that was going to be too late for me."

"Did he indicate what it was he had to take care of?"

"No, he just left it at that, and I didn't figure it was any of my business to pry."

"So, Mr. Lawry, you are saying that you do not have any knowledge of what he had to or was going to do?"

"Yes, Mr. Madden. That's what I am telling you. I have no idea. We ended the conversation with Mike telling me that maybe after the first of the May he might be able to resign his job there at the resort and come out here."

"Would you say that with that statement, knowing what he knows about the money need, that he was going to be able to handle the additional expenses when he arrived there?"

"Seemed to me that that is what he was telling me, Mr. Madden. He knew the cost of apartments and rentals out here as I sent several sources to him when we first started talking about him working here. When he said he might be coming out sometime after the first of May, I assumed that he would have accumulated some kind of funds to cover the early times, until he could locate additional work other than just for me."

"Thank you, Mr. Lawry. You have been really helpful, and I appreciate your candid replies."

"Hope I helped with whatever you are working on."

"If you think of anything else, I'll give you my cell phone number so you can get me directly."

After Madden gave the businessman his telephone number, he again thanked him and ended the conversation. Walking back out of the little room and in to the main front office, he handed the page to Yao, thanked him for his cooperation, and then went back to the room where he found Mickelson enjoying a cold can of cola.

As Madden entered the room, Kyler looked up questioningly. Steve Madden walked to the little refrigerator behind the bar and took out a can of Dr. Pepper, which he opened as he walked to the table. In the silence, he poured the beverage over the ice cubes he had placed in the glass. He then took his seat, picked up the soft drink, and took a long drink, leaning back in his chair. Looking across the table to Mickelson, he shared what he had learned from talking to the uncle of Tom Evers and the relationship Thompson had developed with the man from California. He told of the sudden possibility of Thompson going out there and the unknown of how the money suddenly might have become available to Thompson in order for him to consider the move west.

"Looks like there are now two suspects to consider in figuring out who did the tape editing," commented Mickelson when Madden had finished. "Thompson certainly could have pocketed some serious money in covering up a kidnapping."

Madden looked off in the distance of the room, thinking, and then added, "Yes, we now have at least two to screen carefully. When we chat with Mr. Biffle in a few minutes, hopefully, he'll shed some fresh light on the situation and help determine who it might have been.

And we'll need to crack that person so that we have a positive ID of the kidnapper or kidnappers." Pausing again, Madden looked at the sheriff across from him. "Were you able to learn anything from your conversations, Kyler?"

Mickelson looked across the table and smiled. "Well, my friend, we may have some information at last. One of the detectives working out of Ogden found some people who had been approached in a local bar by Utter. It happened about a month ago. Seems he was looking for someone with a private pilot's license. They weren't sure what the purpose was other than he had said he'd have some cargo to ship and needed it to be flown.

"One of the folks mentioned that he overheard some guy in the bar tell Utter about a guy in Burley, Idaho; wasn't sure of his name but did remember that the guy lived in Burley. I asked my contact to see what he might discover by getting hold of the Burley PD or Sheriff Department. We also got a return call from the police in Twin Falls. They do know of Jefferson, and though he hasn't been in any trouble lately, they acknowledge he's no gem.

"I called them back after hearing from Utah and asked if they could check on any association between Jefferson and anyone in Burley. They were pretty sure they'd have something by tomorrow and possibly tonight. They did say, however, that Jefferson had left his antique store located just out on Poleline Road in the hands of a neighbor. The old man running the store said Jefferson told him he was going to go fishing for a couple of weeks. That was about ten days ago. According to the PD, the guy hasn't heard a word from Jefferson from the moment he drove off in his car. Never even said where he was going fishing or left any contact information."

Madden massaged the information for a few moments then looked back up from the table where his eyes had been focused. He stood and walked to the whiteboard that had been placed in the room for their use. Picking up an erasable marker he wrote as he spoke. "Ok, so here is what we know. We know that we have prints here at the resort for both Utter and Jefferson. We know that Utter was looking for a private pilot in Burley about a month ago and that both he and Jefferson disappeared ten days to two weeks ago."

Mickelson, now sitting on the side of the table added to the list as Madden continued to write. "We have positive IDs of both Utter and Jefferson being here at the Rendezvous last Tuesday evening when the Vicker kids and the Henderson boy went out to buy the beer. According to the Vickers, there was nothing under the stairs when they went up to their room about ten twenty that night. The Henderson kid said he heard a loud sound, like glass breaking and some harsh words a little past five o'clock. That would coincide with the first time the video was edited."

Madden kept the dialogue going. "Kyler, we have fingerprints on the door of the ninth floor storage room from Utter so we know he, at least, was down there, and we know that's the room from which the replacement table came and was put into 932. Plus, we know the blood samples from the carpet and glass were Carson's blood."

Sheriff Mickelson spoke, "Finally, we know the second film editing was done around midnight." Thoughtfully reflecting for a moment, he then added, "I would bet that Carson was taken from his room during that second editing period."

Madden nodded and replaced the marker in the tray at the bottom of the stand. "I would agree with that, Kyler. So, now let us see what Mr. Biffle has to say for himself. It's just now five-thirty. When I was in the security office earlier, I talked with Yao about the need to prevent any compromising of stories between Mike and Cary. Yao indicated he would make sure that Thompson and Biffle did not have an opportunity to visit. He was going to have Biffle come in to see him for some unrelated reason and then would send Thompson outside before walking Biffle down here to introduce him to us."

Mickelson had retaken his seat and copied the notes from the whiteboard onto a page in his notebook. Now he tore the page from the tablet section and carefully placed it face down in the pocket located inside the front cover. Seeing this task accomplished, Madden then applied the eraser to the whiteboard and wiped the board clean so that no trace of the wording remained. The two peacemakers were ready to interview the last of the security guards who had worked the times when Senator Jeremy Carson had mysteriously disappeared. Madden picked up the handset of the phone and dialed the extension of Security Chief Yao.

Chapter Twelve

Senator Carson's investigation of his quarters confirmed his suspicions that his dungeon was below ground. The wooden plank floor beneath his feet felt damp and cool and, coupled with the earthy smell that had greeted him earlier when brought into the room, suggested they were laid over a dirt surface rather than concrete, and the concrete walls had that same damp and chilled feeling of being below ground. .

As for any sounds above him, he heard very few. He thought he had heard the sound of water, as though a faucet were not completely turned off, but it was very faint and distant. The puzzlement came because he thought the sound had been not from above but to one side and below his imprisonment.

Apart from the unanswered questions swirling in his mind, all in all, Carson felt almost comfortable. Although his captors did not speak to him nor to each other if more than one entered his dark room, they treated him politely. They had even provided a small light for him. Carson noticed the fixture was mounted to the cement ceiling and the wiring ran to it by way of a metal conduit. The conduit exited above his door through a hole that had been drilled or cut in the concrete wall.

But those questions really did not bother the Idaho senator. He could deal with his confinement, although to be sure he had had better; but the lack of communication made no sense and constantly attacked him, denying him any peace of mind. Why, he wondered, had they taken him? What did his captors want? Where was he being held? By whom?

As Jeremy contemplated his situation, he heard a key enter the lock in his door. He slowly rolled to a sitting position and faced the door to see who entered. The door opened, and three figures, all in military-type fatigues with black hoods, stepped inside the room. The last figure through the door turned, relocked the door, and placed the key in a pocket located on the side of the fatigue pants. At first, none of the three spoke, but they walked toward Carson and stood so they were looking down on him. The first hooded figure spoke, revealing a deep masculine voice, heavy with a Middle Eastern accent. "You have asked why you were abducted, and you were told that you would receive an answer." Then he turned to one of the others, an individual of average stature. Most likely about five feet ten to six feet tall, average build, and Carson estimated, about 150 to 170 pounds.

Jeremy remained seated as the person took a step toward him. The hooded figure lowered to a squatting position directly in front of the senator. A brief pause of several seconds ensued, as though the person was deciding what to say, and then a voice, also Middle Eastern in accent, cut through the silence. "Mr. Carson, my name is Ahmad Rahman Hassan." Another silence followed, allowing the name to sink into Jeremy's memory.

Carson recalled the correspondence his office had with members of the United States Senate Anti-Terrorism Committee, on which he held the position as vice chair. Carson glared at his captor and spoke in an anything but friendly tone. "So you are the one who had me kidnapped. Obviously you do not know what limitations I have in regard to terrorism. What is it you want from me?"

"We don't want anything from *you*," began the man behind the hood. "I want something from your government. Your committee has been attacking innocent people, and we want it to stop. Your government has falsely arrested and continues to detain our people who in no way have threatened you or your country. You were taken the same way and will not be returned until our requests are met." Another pause during which no one spoke nor moved. Ahmad then continued, "You will appear on videotape that will be delivered to members of your committee and members of the president's inner circle. You will tell them our demands and the consequences if they are not met within our time-frame."

Carson laughed aloud. "You are a lunatic! I won't do any such thing!" With that Carson spat on the floor in front of his captor. Hassan said nothing. Instead, his right hand, which had been at his side, whipped forward with lightning speed, and his doubled-up fist caught Carson fully on the left side of his face, sending him flying across the mattress to his right.

Stars were still sparkling in his brain, and sounds of laughter flooded his ear as he slowly collected himself and raised himself, somewhat unsteadily to a standing position. "You can do to me whatever you wish, but I will not play games with you," he said, trying to put on a tough, "you never hurt me" look. Despite his bravado, Carson figured his words made little impact since he could barely even hold himself upright. The whole side of his head ached as though a train had hit him.

"Oh, I think you will do as we tell you," his captor said with an ice-cold tone. "For if you do not, you will never see the light of day again. You will remain in this room until we determine it is time for you to die, and then your body will be disposed of without anyone able to find it. The waters nearby will take care of any material that is placed in it." The man stood and slowly walked toward the senator, stopping in front of him. Carson could smell his body, heavy with sweat, and he was sure the man had not bathed in some time. The unmistakable body odor reminded him how long it had been since he had showered.

"So you made it out of Canada," said Carson, remembering the FBI memo that had cited Hassan being seen in Calgary before disappearing into the unknown. "Unfortunately, I cannot cause anything to happen for you. I am a junior senator who does not have a chair's power on any committee." The comment was, Carson hoped, convincing to his captors that they were wasting their time holding him. Ahmad Hassan turned to the third member of his group, the one who had locked the door when they had entered. He held out his hand and commanded, "Give me the script." A folded sheet of paper was extracted from the back pocket of the fatigue pants and placed in Hassan's hand. He turned back to Carson and held the paper out to him. "Read this, Carson. This is what you will be saying on the videotape. We will be back in a while to make the video, and I suggest your cooperation."

Carson took the paper and skimmed its contents. It was a very short demand that simply stated that the captors would not negotiate in any way and demanded that, within seven days from receipt of the video, the United States release all prisoners held in Guantanamo and Israel simultaneously release all Palestinian prisoners. Should the seven days go by without fulfilling the demand, Senator Jeremy Carson would be executed by being beheaded and his remains would never be found.

Though Carson felt terror inside, knowing that the US government never negotiates with terrorists, nor did Israel, he played the tough guy again. Taking the paper in his two hands, he made a big gesture of ripping it into two pieces and then, wadding them in his hand, tossed them at the hidden face of the figure who had identified himself as Ahmad. Perhaps he should have saved the "hero" act for some other time. Ahmad stepped directly toward him and delivered a full force blow to Carson's mid-section, bending him over at the waist, gasping for breath. His ribcage reminded him of its tenderness all over again. Before he could stand vertically, a second blow, from Hassan's right knee, caught him on the face. He could hear his nose crack, and the last thing he remembered was falling backward.

When Carson came back to an almost alive state, he put his hand to his face. His head felt as if it had been hit with a sledgehammer. Taking his hand away, he could see it was covered with blood from his nose. By gently palpating its crooked shape with his hand, he could tell the blow had broken it. Slowly he worked his way to a crawling position, and then, using the wall as an aide, he rose to a standing position and walked to the table where the basin of drinking water was located. He then took his handkerchief from his right back pocket, dipped it into the water, and then, very gently, used it to wipe away the blood from his face. He then tore off two pieces of the cool cloth, rolled them into rolls that were about a quarter of an inch in diameter and about an inch in length and painfully placed them in each nostril to stem the blood flow. He slowly made his way back to the mattress and lay down. Never in his entire life had he hurt as he did right now. Again, the agony of his predicament allowed him to drift off in a pain-relieving unconscious state.

The Idaho senator was not sure how long he had been out when he felt something nudging his shoulder. He warily opened his eyes to find a hooded figure standing by him; slowly prodding his should with the toe of a boot. "Get up," the person ordered. Carson recognized immediately the voice of his assailant, Ahmad Hassan. He thought of making a terse remark but had second thoughts as a wave of pain from his face reminded him of the reply he had received earlier for such action. Instead, he slowly raised himself up and stood in front of his captor.

"You do not look very good, Senator," Hassan remarked with an obvious glee in his voice. "Perhaps now you would like to reconsider our demand of you?"

Carson despised this man. He had shown the cruelty his reputation indicated. As much as Jeremy wanted to avoid demonstrations on his body of any more, he was not sure cooperating was going to result in anything positive for himself. "You can do whatever you want, Hassan; I won't do your dirty work for you." Carson tensed in anticipation of another assault, but it did not come. Instead, the captor slowly shook his head.

"Oh my dear, dear Jeremy," he began. "I never thought you would be so defiant. However, it is not a serious miscalculation on my part. Not nearly as it is on your behalf. As of now, you will no longer receive regular food. Your meals will be a serving of rice with a glass of water one time each day. But you will no longer suffer in silence; now you will have … music? Listen." Hassan paused to allow Carson to take note of a high-pitched, annoying squeal—unchanging and never-ending.

Although not loud, the sound, Carson knew all too well, would begin destroying the human mind after a relatively short time.

Hassan, noticing Carson was listening, spoke again. "You know, of course, that within a few days your mind will weaken and you will begin to lose your sense of reality. Therefore, for your interest, I suggest you choose to cooperate." With that, Hassan abruptly turned, walked by the table with the pail of water, and after placing the ladle in the pail, picked it up from the table, replacing it with a piece of paper. "I am leaving the script for you to learn, Mr. Carson. I will be back to see if you are ready to record the message." With that the terrorist cell leader stepped through the door, set down the pail of water, closed the door, and locked it. Senator Carson was alone with only his thoughts and the irritating sound. He walked to the table and picked up the paper. It was exactly the same as the one he had seen earlier. Silently he read it to himself.

I am Idaho Senator Jeremy Carson. I am being held by an al-Qaeda cell and am in good health. This message is for all United States government and military officials. For the sake of world peace, I make the following demands:

All government and military prisoners currently held in captivity at Guantanamo, Cuba, are to be released and allowed to be free no later than midnight seven days from when you receive this tape.

The Palestinian military and governmental prisoners held by the government and military officials of Israel are to be released no later than midnight seven days from when officials receive this tape.

Should the demands I have set forth not be met, I will be executed by beheading.

The thought of the last sentence sent a visible shudder through Carson's body. Knowing that neither Israel nor the United States would ever agree to the demands or to negotiate with terrorists, the young senator found himself struggling with the thoughts rushing through his mind. Even the ache that still existed in his face could not detour his thoughts of the inevitable demise that awaited him.

Chapter Thirteen

Cary Biffle entered the room, accompanied by his supervisor, at five thirty-eight, Chief of Security Randy Yao introduced him to Teton County Sheriff Kyler Mickelson and then to FBI Agent Steve Madden. Yao then excused himself and left the room, closing the door behind him.

Mickelson gestured to the lone seat at the end of the table. "Please, Cary, have a seat." Biffle obligingly did so. When asked if he would like anything to drink, he graciously declined. He sat square to the table, both hands grasping each other on the tabletop. Both Mickelson and Madden took their previous seats, one on either side of the table.

Biffle did not give an especially positive first impression. He wore his hair in a crew cut, which accentuated ears that stuck out too much to be attractive, his nose had an odd bend to it, perhaps from being broken years before, and his face had obvious pockmarks just below the right cheekbone, undoubtedly left over from a bad acne problem when he was younger. Small in stature, perhaps five feet ten inches tall and probably 150 pounds, he looked wiry. His small eyes seemed to burn right through whatever he might look upon. He did not look nice, Madden decided as he studied him, nor did his personality, presented through his facial expression and body language, give the impression he even wanted to be very nice. Madden caught himself wondering what his wife had seen in this guy. But whatever it was, it did not matter. Now it was time to find out what made this guy tick and to unveil whether or not he had been involved in editing the videotapes. Agent Madden made the usual comment that the conversation would be taped and initiated the recording switch. And so the interview began.

As the others had done, Biffle shared parts of his past twenty-eight years. He began by telling of his childhood. He had been born and raised in Nebraska on a farm near Grand Island. His father was not well educated but did okay with the crop of corn they raised each year. But when his mother died, leaving him, the oldest at age twelve, and three younger siblings, he had had to work after school to help make ends meet. Each afternoon following dismissal of the school day, he went to the local newspaper office, folded papers, and then rode his bike as he delivered the evening paper to the nearly two hundred residences on his route. When he arrived home, it was usually after six. His father would have dinner prepared, and he was expected to be there when it was placed on the table. Should he be tardy without a proper excuse, he usually met the business end of a switch as a painful reminder to be prompt.

After dinner, he and his next older sibling, a sister named Rachael, would do the dishes by hand. Afterwards, he would squeeze in time for homework, and finally, about nine o'clock, Cary would crawl into his bed in a room he shared with two brothers and prepare to enter the next day's routine.

By the time he was in high school, Biffle resented his father for not allowing him to participate in athletics. Luckily for him, he told Madden and Mickelson, when he was in his sophomore year, his father married a friendly woman who worked as a legal secretary in a small law firm in Grand Island. With her income added to the family, Cary finally had relief from constant work and had time for sports. The only one he really liked was wrestling. His build and temperament seemed to fit the sport, and he relished the idea of taking his stored up frustrations out on someone else. He learned the maneuvers quickly, and by the time he was a senior, he won the state title for his weight division, 120 pounds.

College was not an option. Though he had excelled in wrestling, he did not attract much attention for collegiate programs, and he could never afford to attend on his own. Besides, as he told the story, he didn't see that college would have offered him anything of value. So, the day after graduation and three days after his eighteenth birthday, he joined the U.S. Navy. Following his basic training, he was assigned ship duty. In 1980, he served aboard the USS *Emory S. Land* and was deployed to the Pacific where the submarine tender provided services to the Indian Ocean Battle Group. He re-upped and, in the summer of 1986, was excited to serve aboard the vessel as it participated in the International Naval Review and Fourth of July Statue of Liberty Rededication. He continued to serve aboard the ship until he left the Navy in 2005.

Biffle related how the size of the ship fascinated him, and more than that, how serving amid a crew of twelve hundred men allowed him some anonymity. He was obviously a loner.

When he left the military, he wandered a bit, never wanting to return home. After all he had had enough of the plains where it got hot in the summer and breathtaking cold in the winter. No sir, not a place he ever wanted to return to.

One day he happened to pick up a magazine in the barbershop in Muncie, Indiana, and spotted an ad for Jackson Hole, Wyoming. Though it had winter to be sure, it was, he thought, a place he could make good money doing something, though what he was not sure. He decided to go there and caught a bus as it was leaving westward. After three days, he arrived in Jackson and started to job hunt. Eventually he spotted a want ad for a security officer for a local resort, and after interviewing with Randy Yao, he had been hired. So, here he was.

Within the first month of work, he had begun frequenting a little bar and grill in the village and met a girl, Tammy, who was a waitress there. They had married in August, and she got pregnant in March. Promptly she began having trouble with the pregnancy, and in early June she had miscarried. The doctors had to perform a complete hysterectomy by removing her ovaries and uterus because of severe tearing and tissue damage. The medical crisis had left the two of them in a serious financial bind since the resort covered only employees and not family members for their first year Since he had not maintained any relationship with his father, he had no desire to ask for help—and little possibility of getting it. And Tammy did not want to ask her folks, neither of whom was able to work because of health issues and who lived on a fixed income in a sub-average apartment near Cheyenne.

Biffle had talked about his past for almost fifteen minutes without any interruption. Finally, hearing enough of his commentary, Madden posed a question to the security guard. "Cary, what kind of friends did you have in school?"

Biffle looked at the agent with an almost irritated look, "Friends? What friends? I stayed to myself. None of the kids in my school were my kind of people. They liked to get together, go to dances, swimming, and stuff like that. I didn't have time for that stuff."

"So, you liked being alone?"

"When you're alone, you're on your own. No one is going to tell you what to do, how to do it, or when. You're your own boss. You answer to no one."

"And that is a good thing, I suppose?"

"Damn right it is! Until I got married, I didn't have to answer to anyone when I wasn't on ship."

Mickelson commented, "So, what happens now that you are married, Cary?"

Biffle rolled his eyes and spoke, "Let me put it this way. If she hadn't gotten pregnant, we wouldn't be in the mess we're in. If she'd been taking the pill like she was supposed to, we wouldn't be in debt like we are. That answer your question?"

"You are pretty deep in debt?" asked Madden.

"You might say that," came the sarcastic reply. "We owe for the surgery, hospital room, anesthesiologist, drugs, the whole bit. The little insurance coverage from here doesn't pay much."

"If you don't mind me asking, Cary, how much do you owe?"

"Guess it's probably somewhere between twenty and twenty-five grand."

Mickelson cut in, "That is a pile of debt, Cary. What are you doing to get out from under it?

"I work odd jobs when I'm off up here. Chief Yao gives me extra shifts when they come up. Sometimes I get off work here and drive down to Jackson where I help do the artwork for a POD printer."

"POD? What is that?"

"That stands for publish on demand. You know, when someone wants to publish a book or something, they can print just the copies they need right then instead of thousands that they have to sell. Saves the person a lot of money. And makes it easier for the small writer to be successful. My boss did that with a book about his life in the hills of West Virginia."

"How did you find that job?"

Biffle, for the first time, allowed himself almost to smile. "It was really funny. About two months ago, I was at the bar after work here, kind of wondering how to make ends meet. This guy was sitting next to me and noticed me reading the want ads. Next thing I know, he's asking me if I'm interested in working part time. Hell, yes, I say to him. Then he asks if I can do computer graphics. Well, I'm not an artist or art geek, but I have pretty good creativity and I do a pretty fair job of graphics using different software. Anyway, he has me go to his little print shop down on Deloney Street. He tells me what he does and then asks if I might be interested in helping with cover design. I said I would like to try. To make a long story short, I went back and did some designing for him. After that he called me up and offered me a job."

"How often do you work for him, Cary?"

"Not regular. I go in and pick up some materials, manuscripts, then take them home, and do some designs."

"How do you like the resort job?"

"It's ok. Pay is ok, and there are some benefits, but they aren't much. I don't like the different schedules and would rather just work a day job. But it is a job. Randy is really a great boss to work for, and the others are cool, too."

"You get along with all the others?"

"Oh yeah. Sheila gave my wife, Tammy, and me a gift card for dinner at one of the really nice restaurants. Mike and Tom are good. We aren't tight but we all get along."

Now it was Madden's turn to ask questions of the suspect. "Cary, you worked a double shift this past Tuesday. Tell us how you spent your time during that period."

Biffle thought for a moment and then shared that he had worked his regular four to midnight shift. He had begun the shift on the desk, gone to the outside duty about seven, right after eating dinner in the coffee shop. He had stayed at the desk so that Evers could grab a dinner when he came in about six-twenty or so. Then he had worked the outside tour until ten o'clock, come in and stopped for a coffee before coming to the desk around ten fifteen. He then had stayed at the desk until the shift ended at midnight.

"What went on as the shift changed?"

"Not much. As you know Sheila was sick and didn't report for work so I was working the shift for her. Mike came in and asked me if I wanted to stay in at the desk or get some fresh air and start outside. Since I was already in the desk room, I said I'd just start inside."

"I want you to think very carefully about the next couple of questions, Cary." Biffle looked at the agent quizzically but nodded in the affirmative.

"During your second shift, what times were you at the desk? I know you started there. How long did you remain at the desk?"

Biffle looked straight at Madden, and it seemed obvious to the FBI agent that he was trying to replay the time in his head before offering a response. Without any looking away, Biffle spoke. "As I said, I started on the desk at midnight. I was getting tired and needed to stretch my legs around two and talked with Mike. He said he was on the backside of the resort and would come inside to relieve me about two thirty."

"And did he?"

"Yes, in fact, it was probably a little before two thirty. I went to the coffee shop, grabbed some coffee. Then I went outside to check the lots, ski lift areas, and shops around the property, and then walked the hallways. I came back in to trade off again around quarter to six and stayed there until shift change at eight in the morning."

"Did you notice anything odd or different during your shift, Cary?"

"No. Everything was pretty normal. Not much happening, being the middle of the week and all."

"So you did not notice anything different?"

"No, nothing." Biffle stopped and then seemed to catch some elusive thought in his memory. "The only thing that was different was that Randy came in during my first shift to see if I was going to be ok with a second straight shift. Once I told him I was fine and working the shift would not be a problem, he left after a few minutes."

"Did that seem strange to you?"

"Well yes and no. Randy cares about his people. That's why he's tried to get me as much work as he can since Tammy's surgery. He's given me an extra shift a couple of times."

"When he gave you the extra shift before, did he check on you then?"

"No, but then I wasn't working a back-to-back shift. It was when I was supposed to have a day off."

"During your shift this past Tuesday, did you change out the surveillance tapes?"

"Of course. Whoever is at the desk changes out the tapes when the time is up."

"Cary," spoke up Sheriff Mickelson, "how much actual viewing of the camera recordings do you do at the desk?"

Cary looked down at the table and fidgeted in his chair slightly. "Not much. I know we should, but it really gets tiring, so usually we only look at it once in a while. When we know there are large crowds or like when VIPs are arriving or departing, we usually watch it more closely. Guess we all pretty much figure that the camera feeds are being recorded so if something does come up we can always review it. Never thought it was any big deal."

"Have you ever edited any of the tapes, Cary?"

Cary looked surprised and shocked at the question and what the underlying meaning might be. "Of course not!"

"You are sure of that?"

"Absolutely! That would be wrong. I might not view the feeds all the time, and sometimes I read a book or something, but I'd never do anything to one of the tapes. Why?"

"What happens to the tapes when you take them out of the recorders?"

"As soon as we take a tape out, we're supposed to put a new one in the recorder so the lost time is as short as possible. Then we put a label on it. The label indicates the date, time range, and which camera view is on that tape. Once it's labeled, it's placed in the tape vault where it's kept for two weeks, then recycled. If a tape is needed for some reason, it's removed from the storage vault and not recorded over."

"Have you ever experienced any recording difficulties?"

"No, not ever. Randy has the equipment cleaned and maintained on a regular basis so it's in really good condition. I understand that by the middle of the summer or early next fall we won't be using tapes any more; we'll record on CDs. That will be good because they take up a whole lot less room."

Madden looked at the security guard. He seemed quite relaxed, certainly not displaying any signs of stress, such as rapid breathing, fidgeting, looking away, licking his lips, or perspiring. "Cary, where is the vault that the tapes are stored in? Is it in the desk room?"

Biffle shook his head before replying. "No. Once we take the tapes out and label them, we put them in a marked metal box on the counter next to the desk. At the end of our shift, whoever is at the desk takes them to the security office, signs off on them, and Randy then puts them in the storage vault."

"Where exactly is that vault?"

"In the little room off Randy's office. The door is just off to the side of his desk."

Mickelson jotted a note, paused long enough to take a drink from his glass of water, then looked at Biffle for a few seconds, as though trying to read his honesty. "Who has access to the storage area where the tapes are kept?"

"Yao controls the tapes," came the reply. "If he's not here and a tape would be needed, the hotel manager has a key and the authority to open the storage vault."

Madden thoughtfully looked at the security guard and then looked to Mickelson. In his mind they had not really resolved the big question of who might have edited the tapes. Biffle, he thought, still had had the opportunity to do so and certainly might have had the motivation with the financial trouble he and his wife were dealing with. Yet, his mind reminded him, there was still another possibility.

"Sheriff," Madden stated, "anything further you would like to ask Mr. Biffle?"

The local lawman glanced at his notes and then, looking at his counterpart, responded in the negative.

"Cary, we're finished here for the time being," Steve Madden said as he stood. Cary pushed his chair back and also got up. Both Mickelson and Madden shook hands with the man as they walked him to the door. Handing him a business card, Madden bid him good-bye with a request that, should anything else come to mind, he should not hesitate to call. He then closed the door and walked back to his chair where he sat for a moment in silence, perusing his notes. "Kyler, I think we need to have one more interview."

The sheriff nodded in agreement and recorded a note in his notebook. "Randy Yao?"

"Yes. However, before we do that, I want more background on him. Can you have your office gather some information? Anything that might help us determine any possible motive. He has a pretty cushy job here at the resort and seems to have a pretty good income."

"I'll call right now," Mickelson replied. The sheriff picked up his cell phone from the table, punched a "quick" call number, and relayed the request for information to the administrative assistant on the other end. After a few moments, he clicked off, setting the phone back on the table. "Should hear something by later this evening or in the morning," he informed the federal agent.

The clock on the sidewall of the room displayed 6:15 p.m. Madden considered the time and the gnawing feeling in his stomach, suggesting that it was time for dinner. "I think we can call it a day," he said. "I need to check in with my partner in Butte and see where his search has taken him. Then take some time to visit with my family since it's 8:15 back there. Let's plan on getting together, say, eight in the morning?"

"Sounds good," Mickelson answered, and both men rose, collected their notes and phones, and then walked to the door. Pausing, Mickelson, turned, held out his hand to Madden, and as they shook hands said, "I have a feeling about this case. I think we're nearing a big break. By morning I should have the information we requested on Yao."

"I have that same feeling, Kyler. Maybe tomorrow will shed some light on what happened and what we're really looking at."

With that, the sheriff turned to his left and continued down the hallway toward a parking lot access where his unmarked car was parked. Madden turned the opposite direction and walked to the elevators to ascend to his room. After entering, he called the restaurant and requested a hot beef sandwich, the house salad, and milk. Then he took a quick shower, put on a pair of blue jeans and a long-sleeve shirt that he left unbuttoned at the collar, pulled on a pair of white athletic socks. Sitting back in the large chair, he took out his cell phone and called home. He spent about ten minutes visiting with his family members before a knock on the door interrupted the call. Opening the door, he was greeted by a room-service worker carrying a tray with the items he had ordered. Madden thanked the male server, handed the young man a tip, and taking the tray, closed the door and set the tray on the table next to the large windows. He had already missed his promised six o'clock call to Addis, but his stomach was telling him it was time to eat. He decided to take care of both at once and call Jim Addis while he ate his dinner.

Chapter Fourteen

Only a hint of the light of day remained, and shadows of the trees painted almost a solid black on the mountainside. The brilliant lights illuminating the parking lot had replaced the sun's light, and with the disappearance of daylight, the temperatures were beginning to plummet as evidenced by the lone individuals scurrying to and from their vehicles, clasping the collars of their coats with a free hand to prevent the cold from entering.

Steve Madden watched for a few minutes and then retrieved his cell phone from the table top, flipped open the cover, and punched the preset number to call Addis. The phone at the other end rang three times, and then Madden heard a friendly, "Hey, there partner! How's the ski bum down in Jackson Hole?"

"Hey, yourself! The skiing's fantastic, Jim. Couldn't have anything better." A hearty laugh followed at both ends, and then, turning to a more serious tone, Madden asked, "Jim, what's going on up in the Mining City?"

"We've been pretty busy, Steve. Actually, we're making good progress, and I expect we'll catch a break soon. First of all, we got replies from our offices in Missoula, Spokane, and Seattle. They had checked with law enforcement and none of the police, sheriff, or highway patrol had any record of the Ford Taurus that Stephens and Hamilton were driving.

"As you know, Sheriff O'Billovich was having his staff try to locate some people who might have seen something. They found a woman who had been at a restaurant when two men in sport coats came in and sat at the counter. She heard them ask several questions about different areas of Butte, Anaconda, and the areas around here, leading her to believe they were outsiders. She told the detectives that they had arrived in a dark, maybe black, Ford Taurus. As the detectives talked with her, she indicated that the two men were approached by two others, kind of scruffy-looking, one in jeans and a fatigue jacket and the other in workpants and a wool shirt. Another person, who had been with the woman, said he saw the four men leave at the same time. He said the guy with the fatigues got into the sedan the two men had been driving, the other guy opened a back door of a black SUV, and the two men with sport coats got in. The strange thing was that it appeared the two did not want to get in, but the guy with the workpants moved his hand while it was in his coat, and they climbed in. The gentleman thought he had seen an arm inside the SUV when the door was open but was not positive. At any rate, the car and the SUV both took off in a direction that seemed to be uptown."

Addis paused for a moment.

"Were you able to pursue their informative statements, Jim?" Madden inquired of his partner.

"Yes, we were. Detectives began interviewing folks around uptown and received a couple of interesting statements. One of the detectives came upon a house on Woolman, in which an elderly man lived who had seen a car matching what agents Phil Stephens and Brad Williams were driving go past his place when he was watching out his window. It was followed by a big black station wagon, which the detective determined was a black SUV with black windows. The guy indicated they caught his attention because they were moving, as he put it, 'too goddam fast for any neighborhood.' He moved to the window to see where they were going and saw taillights from the two cars braking but couldn't see exactly where they went down the street."

Again Agent Addis paused before explaining that the street only went another couple blocks before dead-ending at Wyoming Street. An abandoned mine yard immediately north of the street ran all the way to Wyoming, so the house had to be within the two-block stretch. Addis continued, "We covered all the homes, going door-to-door for information. At the end of the street, an older house on the north side of Woolman has a double garage that has been added onto the west end of the home. The place has had several different owners, and the current residents have not been there long. At any rate, a lady living across the street saw the two vehicles both pull into the garage on Sunday afternoon. The strange thing is, according to the woman, she has seen the SUV go in and out, but there's no other vehicle in the garage. She said that no one ever gets out of the SUV when it enters the garage until the garage door is closed. The lady also reported hearing loud metallic banging the next day, and now it's fairly quiet again. When pressed, she could not recall seeing anyone going in or out of the building, except through the garage."

"All right!" exclaimed Madden over the phone. "Sure sounds like you might be on to something. What's the next step?"

"Actually, Steve, as the detectives were canvassing the neighborhood, they discovered a chrome and black hubcap along the curb. They did some checking with the rental office in Butte, and its description matches the covers that were on the Ford Taurus Phil Stephens had leased in Butte, the one they left Bozeman in the last time they were seen. We're analyzing our information with the plan of getting a search warrant for that property to see if the car is still there. If we can locate the car, or some trace of it, then we'll go into the house."

Jim then inquired of Steve about the progress being made in the disappearance of Senator Jeremy Carson. Steve brought him up to date with his case during the next several minutes. The two federal lawmen ended with some conversation about their own families, their anticipation of completing the cases, and finally, mutual bids of good luck.

~ § ~

Senator Jeremy Carson felt and heard his stomach growl in protest. Two days of one meal a day, each consisting of about a cup of white rice accompanied by gross-looking and bad-tasting lukewarm water left him wanting something substantial. "A steak, baked potato, Caesar salad, green beans with key lime pie for dessert would really hit the spot about now," he said aloud to himself.

Carson had found himself talking aloud quite often since the background sound had started squealing through his confinement area. It was, as he knew, an attempt, albeit not a very effective one, to ignore the irritating noise. On the positive side, his nose had stopped bleeding, and though it still throbbed, his head did feel better and had cleared considerably. As much as he searched his small room, he found no way to escape. The metal cuffs encircling his wrists and ankles, connecting his limbs to heavy links of chain, were the first obstacle to his escape, and he found no way to remove them, short of removing his hands and his feet. Even if he could get out of the metal bracelets, his search of the walls, door, ceiling, and even the floor yielded no way out. He was, in his own evaluation, a prisoner until such time as his captors decided to release him.

The thought of being completely under the control of such criminals made Carson cringe. Knowing there was absolutely no way that government officials, either in Israel or in his own country, would ever agree to the terms of the terrorists' demands gave way to the inevitable. He would never again see sunlight as a free man. He would never see his friends, his office staff, and his family. "These are," he thought, "my final days of life."

In the dimly lit corner of the makeshift cell, the senator sat, beaten physically, mentally, and emotionally. A mere shadow of the man of five days earlier, he wore on his face several days of stubble and dirty skin caked with dried blood and on his weakened frame a bloodstained white/blue sport shirt and wrinkled, soiled, and smelly trousers. He heard the door open and steeled himself for more abuse. "Beaten but not down yet," Carson told himself.

Again three hooded figures entered, and the door closed behind them.

"You are ready for videotaping, yes?" said the front figure, which Carson recognized as the voice of Ahmad Hassan. The three halted in front of the senator, who remained sitting, leaning against the walls forming a corner of his room.

Carson glared at his captors, his eyes full of contempt and dislike. "You bastards won't get anything with your demands! No sane country in this world would even consider releasing prisoners just because you want them to. You might just as well kill me right here, right now!" The young congressman could hardly believe his own ears, hearing his voice say that.

"Is that a refusal to do the taping, Senator?" came a subdued but very firm voice.

"You can take the script, the video camera, and anything else, and cram it where the sun doesn't shine!"

"Very well. We shall see what more isolation time will do." The hooded figure turned, took a couple of steps, then stopped, and turned back. Slowly he retraced his steps back to Carson and then spoke. "I think, perhaps, a little more persuasion might be helpful in your making a final decision whether to do the taping or not."

"Do whatever the hell you want, Hassan! There is no way that I will cooperate with you!" Carson tried to demonstrate a more defiant posture by crossing his arms and drawing his knees up in front of him.

The leader of the group stood silently for a few moments, then nodded his head toward one of the followers who turned, exited through the door, and returned shortly with a wooden chair that had two wooden arms fixed at the side. The chair was placed in the middle of the room. Carson could not help but notice the black belt-like straps attached to the arms, the body, and the legs of the chair. It looked quite ominous. Carson felt the hair on the back of his neck stand up at the sight of the chair, but he had committed his action and could not turn back now. He rolled eyes in an obvious manner and spat out his response. "Like I said before, you can go to hell!"

The leader of the hooded group shook his head slowly from side to side then stretched both his arms out to the sides and then brought them forward, pointing to Carson. The two other hooded figures complied with the unspoken gesture. They stepped forward, one on either side of the senator. Reaching down, they took a firm hold of each arm and very roughly jerked Carson up to a standing position. Then they half-dragged him to the chair, turned him, and slammed him into it. Quickly they tightly strapped both of his upper arms to the chair back followed by strapping the lower left arm against the senator's body. One of the guards then anchored his body to the chair back before tying each leg to the legs of the chair with rope. The two figures stepped back, away from the pinioned man.

"So now what, you son-of-a-bitch?" said the senator, raising the volume of his voice in an attempt to hide his fear. "I am not afraid of you and your bullies. You are all afraid to really stand up for what you believe. You have to hide behind those hoods because you are afraid of being seen. The only thing you are going to get is caught and be killed. Then you can be together with all your other friends and terrorists, rotting in damnation!"

Hassan, still hooded, stepped forward, held out his right hand toward one of the other two. From his back pocket, the silent figure retrieved a long object and handed it to his commander. As he did so, the other quiet figure moved to Carson's right side, took the senator's hand and slammed it down on the wooden arm of the chair then secured it with duct tape. Forcing the hand open, he held it in place so his partner could duct tape Carson's hand so tightly to the chair that Jeremy could not draw his fingers into a fist. Then he looked up and saw Hassan holding the long object in front of him, making clear his intentions. The image had its desired effect, and Carson's stomach immediately convulsed. The head of the ball-peen hammer caught the light and flashed a wicked reflection Carson's way.

"You still refuse to tape for us?" demanded Hassan in an ice-coated voice.

"You know what you can do with your hammer!" yelled Carson.

Carson saw the hammer being raised and the arm of Hassan coming down before he closed his eyes and gritted his teeth, knowing the target was his writing hand.

WHAM!!!!!!

The hammer came down and connected with such force that the entire chair shook. Carson opened his eyes, wondering why he felt no pain. The hammer had not struck his hand; it had struck the chair's arm just beyond the straightened fingertips. The three terrorists all laughed. Carson felt his pants getting wet with urine, released with the fear of the anticipated assault.

"Still refuse, my dear Senator?" smirked Hassan, slowly tapping the hammer against the palm of his left hand.

"Screw you!" came Carson's reply.

Again Hassan raised the hammer and forcefully struck but this time not on wood. A horrid cracking sound came as the metal head connected directly with the index finger of Senator Jeremy Carson's hand, followed immediately by Carson screaming in agony, his head snapping back from the instant, searing pain that started in his right hand sprinted up the arm and slammed into his entire body. He felt sick to his stomach and knew that he was about to vomit.

The ropes around him were released; arms on either side lifted him unceremoniously from the chair and literally tossed him at the mattress on the floor. Somehow, he had no idea how, he rotated his body as it fell through space so that he landed on his left side on the mattress while cradling his right hand and arm with his left. Writhing in pain, he felt his stomach violently empty itself, as he vomited on the mattress. Carson clenched his teeth and held his eyes tightly closed, his body drawn into the fetal position.

Without a sound, all three terrorists turned, one picked up the chair, and then all exited the room, locking the door as they departed. Carson, with broken nose, broken rib, blackened eyes, bruised cheek, and now badly crushed finger, lay on his bed, moaning aloud in pain, wishing that he would die and knowing with fear that his ordeal was not ended, not yet, anyhow.

CHAPTER FIFTEEN

Darkness still covered the mountainsides when Steve Madden arose at six o'clock sharp. With his daily routine so well established, he rarely needed an alarm clock or wake-up call. After putting on his warm-ups, athletic socks, and running shoes, he spent some time stretching and then headed out the door, jogged down the steps and outside where he began his usual half-hour run down the valley highway and back to the hotel. Upon entering the parking lot on his return, Madden slowed to a walk and continued to walk the perimeter of the lot allowing his body gradually to cool. After his pulse had dropped to his normal level, Madden stopped and did a variety of stretching exercises before returning to his room, ascending the stairs two at a time. He turned on the shower until the bathroom filled with steam, then disrobed, and entered the shower stall, soaking up the heat and enjoying the beating spray of the water.

Dressing in a red pullover sport shirt and black slacks, he grabbed his black sport coat from its hanger, slipped it on, slid his wallet and room key into his jacket pocket, and walked to the elevator for the descent to the lobby and coffee shop. As the elevator dropped quickly to the first level, Madden checked his watch, seven forty-five. He had fifteen minutes before Mickelson would arrive for their workday. Madden crossed the lobby, waving to the desk clerk, who called out a morning greeting to him. Entering the coffee shop, he followed the hostess to a booth not too distant from the doorway and took a seat so he could observe the door and catch Mickelson's eye when the sheriff arrived.

He ordered coffee, a small orange juice, and a bowl of oatmeal with brown sugar and raisins. Madden always enjoyed a bowl of hot oatmeal on cold winter mornings. Somehow it always given him a comforting feeling and filled him without making him feel he had eaten too much.

As he was finishing his cereal, he saw Mickelson enter the coffee shop door. He raised his hand, catching the sheriff's eye. Mickelson smiled, nodded toward Madden, and walked over to the booth, sliding into the seat opposite the FBI agent.

"Good morning, Kyler," greeted Madden, holding out his hand.

"Good morning, Steve," replied Mickelson, taking the outstretched hand in a firm handshake. "I have some news to share with you this morning."

"Let's hear it, Kyler."

Mickelson ordered coffee and after it was placed before him, he opened his grizzly-bear-adorned notebook, flipped through a few pages of notes, paused to look over the page he had stopped at, and began to share his findings with his companion. "My office staff spent the past few days doing checks with different agencies throughout the state. It seems our resident chief of security is not so secure in his outside life."

Madden saw the amused look on the sheriff's face, and after taking a long and slow draw from his coffee cup, he nodded as an indication for the sheriff to continue. Mickelson reached to his cup, and after drinking from it, he returned his gaze to the notes before him.

"It would seem that Yao likes to gamble, not just a little but enough so that he is in serious trouble from a couple of known loan sharks, who are also known to be involved in drug trafficking and possibly counterfeiting. One of the narcotics detectives for us contacted a friend with the Laramie PD. His contact informed him that they have been watching Yao for the last few weeks. Yao has taken out a second mortgage on his home because of his debts, and he still is in deep.

According to bank records he is broke and has very little in the way of savings or checking. He has no CDs or other investments that will pull him out of debt." Mickelson paused so Madden could record his own notes on what was being said. Madden looked across the table and asked, "Kyler, you have the names, contact information for all these law enforcement people, right?"

"Of course, Steve," replied Mickelson. "I know that when the time comes these people may be brought forward as witnesses for the prosecution. I know some guys wait and go back to get the information after the initial contact, but I believe in getting it up front. That way, too, if I have any questions, I can go directly to the source."

Sheriff Mickelson returned again to his notes and continued. "My detective contacted our DA and followed up with a check on Yao's local bank account. It shows that he's made regular deposits into his two accounts and withdrawals for different living expenses, such as gas, water, sewer, and insurance. There are also payments made to a third party, named by the undercover agent in Laramie as a go-between for Yao and the loan shark, Lon Belensky. The payments, more than likely, barely make the interest due on the amounts he owes."

"Kyler, based on this information I think a search warrant of both Yao's home and his office here are in order. Can you obtain those ASAP?"

Mickelson nodded in the affirmative and picked up his cell phone. "I'll request the DA obtain one for us and have my deputy run the one for his office out here to us and send a search team to Yao's home. In the meantime, what do you have in mind?"

Madden swirled the coffee in his nearly empty cup, watching the warm, rich brown liquid try to climb the walls of the cup as it went around and around. Setting the cup down, he thought for a moment and finally spoke. "I would like to see if there is any relationship between Roger Utter or Cameron Jefferson and Yao. Of course, we do need to know where they took the senator once they left here with him. Put out an all-points on both of them, and let's see what they have to say. Being guys with rather short track records, they might be willing to spill their guts with a little grilling." The local law enforcement officer finished speaking into his cell phone, disconnected, and then set the phone on the table before responding to the FBI agent.

"Thought you might be headed in that direction, Steve," said Mickelson. "I initiated that process last night, and we're waiting to see if any clues turn up as to their whereabouts."

The two men walked down to the room the resort management had reserved for their interviews. Madden slid his magnetic key into the lock, opening the door, and both entered. Obviously, housekeeping had cleaned up and replenished the refreshments for another full day.

Madden pulled the whiteboard over near to the seats where each had laid down their notebooks. "Let's go back to the senator's arrival, stay, and his disappearance," Madden said, beginning to write. From each speaking out as he had a thought, Madden carefully outlined what had happened, what they knew about the case from beginning to now, who each witness was, what they had seen or heard, and the names of all those who seemed to have become involved in the case. The two men stopped periodically to confirm the accuracy of what Madden had drawn on the board, making slight adjustments as necessary.

Two hours passed before Madden put down his erasable marker, stepped back, and sat in a leather chair adjacent to Mickelson. Pouring a glass of ice water, he slowly drank from it as he looked at the board's tale of a crime. Pieces were beginning to fit together, and a pattern emerged. Fingerprints, videotapes, and witnesses clearly indicated that Roger Utter and Cameron Jefferson had kidnapped of the U.S. senator. Just as clearly, they had to have had inside help to alter the tapes and, in the case of two cameras, actually redirect them away from the senator's room. Only someone with access, knowledge of the crime, and opportunity to make the edits on the video could be the accomplice at the resort. Based upon the information received in the interviews they had conducted only two names surfaced as potential suspects: Cary Biffle and Randy Yao.

"What do you think?" inquired Madden of the sheriff. "Biffle or Yao make sense to you?"

"Well, Steve, the information we initially got pointed to Biffle. He definitely needed money to get out of debt, and he demonstrated some attitude that might lead one to believe he is capable of doing something, especially if it is only altering potential evidence."

"You're right up to that point," agreed Madden. "However, with the information we received at the end of the day yesterday and what you brought in this morning, it certainly appears we almost headed down the wrong road. As I said before, I'm really curious to see what we find in Yao's office and his home. That said, if we come up empty-handed, I think we follow those searches up with searches of Biffle's house."

As Mickelson nodded and began to speak, his cell phone rang. After listening to the caller for a few seconds, he filled Madden in. "That was my office. We have the warrants, and the one for Yao's office is on its way out here with one of my deputies. As soon as we get it, we'll serve it to the management and, if he is in his office, to Yao."

Gathering up his notebook and taking a final long draw of cold water, Madden stepped toward the room's door with Mickelson right behind. By the time the two had stopped at the restroom and walked to the entry lobby of the resort, Mickelson's deputy came through the door, manila envelope in hand. Spotting his boss, the deputy walked directly to him, stopped in front of the two men, and handed the envelope to the sheriff. "Here's the warrant you requested, Kyler," the officer informed his superior. "It allows for a search of the surveillance desk room, the security department's break room, and Randy Yao's office."

Sheriff Mickelson introduced the deputy, Quentin Vannice, to Madden as he withdrew the document from the envelope and perused its contents to be sure of what areas they would have specific authority to explore. He knew that too many criminal cases had had critical evidence disallowed by courts because the overeager search team looked in places that were not specifically covered by the obtained warrant. This warrant was, as his deputy had explained, all in order. He handed the legal document to Madden, and he, too, looked it over thoroughly. Handing the warrant back to the sheriff, he looked at the two law officers and spoke. "Kyler, let's go and see what we might find. Just to cover our own backsides, let's make sure Quentin accompanies us."

"Not a problem, Steve," Mickelson said, looking at Vannice. Once the search warrant had been served on the management of the resort, the law enforcement trio walked briskly to the security office and Mickelson pushed the buzzer button located to the right of the door. Within a minute, a man appearing to be in his mid-thirties and in excellent physical condition opened the door. Brown eyes met the gaze of Steve Madden square on without losing eye-to-eye contact. Dressed in the resort's security guard uniform, he wore his name engraved on a laminated plate, "John Terrati."

Madden reached out his right hand, offering it to the guard. "John, I am Steve Madden, FBI, and this," gesturing to the two men with him, "is Teton County Sheriff Kyler Michelson and Deputy Quentin Vannice."

"John Terrati," the guard replied, releasing Madden's hand and offering his hand to each of the lawmen.

Then, holding the search warrant up to be seen, Sheriff Mickelson told Terrati what it was, what it contained, and that the three lawmen were here to conduct the search. "Who all is working right now, John?" asked Mickelson.

"Colby Jensen and I are on duty right now. Colby's out on the walking patrol, and I'm on the surveillance desk. We're scheduled to trade in another hour."

"Has Chief Yao been in yet today?" asked Madden, beginning to walk down the hall to the surveillance desk area.

"No, but he did call about two hours ago and said he wouldn't be in until mid afternoon and he'd work part of the night shift."

"Has he done that before?" inquired Mickelson.

"A couple of times I know of in the last week or so, but I guess he's done that before according to other guards. At least that's what Sheila Smith and Mike Thompson have told me."

"John, would you just remain outside the door until we have finished the desk room?" It was more of a directive than a question from Sheriff Mickelson, but the security guard understood. He nodded and stepped away from the door to allow the three officers to step inside.

Madden and Mickelson donned latex gloves and began methodically to go through the desk area room. They removed and thoroughly searched each drawer and each shelf—taking all items off and looking at each and every article, book, and note. Finally, Madden lifted the garbage can and dumped it onto the desk. He then began carefully unfolding and looking at each scrap of paper. While the FBI agent and the county sheriff searched the office area, a room that was about twelve feet square, Deputy Vannice stood at the doorway quietly videotaping their search.

Madden unceremoniously dumped the garbage slips back into the refuse container and set it on the floor. "Ok," he said, turning to Mickelson, "Nothing in here so let's move on to Yao's office."

The deputy stepped back away from the door, shutting down the recorder. Mickelson and Madden both walked down the hall. As they did, Sheriff Mickelson turned to the security guard. "John, you can go ahead and go back to your desk. You are not to make any calls until we have finished, ok with you?

Terrati still displayed some surprise at what was happening, but he understood law. "No problem with me, sir."

Reaching the security chief's door, the Teton County deputy began to record again. Madden opened the door and held it open so the video would show where everything was before the search began. Randy Yao's office was slightly smaller than the surveillance desk area, about twelve feet from the door to the facing wall and approximately ten feet between the sidewalls. The sidewall to the right of the door had a window in it that looked out to the break room and the receiving area that was just inside the entry door. A set of three bookshelves, each with only a few books, stood against the far wall. Madden took the shelves and began scouring through the books and the papers that were on the shelves. He had reached the last item, a three-ring binder, which had "Video Log Sheets," printed on the spine. Madden took the notebook down, laying it on the table, which sat along the wall just beneath the lowest shelf. The binder held documentation for every videotape that the security guards labeled and brought to Yao for storing. Madden turned the pages one at a time and was about two-thirds of the way through it when something caught his eye, and he stopped. Picking up the notebook, he turned to Sheriff Mickelson, who had just finished searching the top of the desk. "Kyler, look at this."

Mickelson turned and looked at the page to which Madden was pointing. Like the others, it displayed the date and time each videotape had been turned in and the name of the security guard who had brought the tape in from the surveillance area. In order to prevent any smearing of the entries, pages were inserted into a plastic sleeve in back-to-back fashion with the following day on the reverse side of the clear sleeve. Everything looked normal except for the fact that the sleeve seemed to be thicker than others. The dates shown on the facing page were from July two years ago and the next entry page was, as expected, for the month of August.

"These pages," said Madden, grasping all of the pages from the cover of the notebook to the page in question, "all have only two sheets of paper. This one seems to be thicker and the bulk seems to be in the middle."

Madden popped open the notebook rings and lifted the page out of the notebook. He undid the overlaid hinge on the side with the pre-punched holes and lifted the top-facing sheet, revealing an airline ticket folder. Making sure that the deputy videotaped the folder, Madden then opened the folder and withdrew a document from inside. Looking at it carefully, Madden indicated that the item was a one-way e-ticket from Denver, Colorado, to Miami, Florida, adding, "Date of the ticket is for next week." He handed the ticket to Mickelson, who looked it over and then set it on the table. Meanwhile, Madden had extracted a second document from the folder. "Would you believe this, Kyler? This is a second e-ticket. This one is for the next day and takes a Samuel Withers from Miami to Montreal, Quebec, Canada. Who is Samuel Withers?"

Mickelson looked at the two tickets. "Both reservations were made at the same time, so I'm guessing that the same person made both." Taking the notebook, replacing the sleeve, and placing a bright yellow evidence tag on the page, Madden replaced the page into the notebook. The tickets were placed back inside the airline folder and the folder with the tickets were then placed into a clear plastic zip-lock bag and initialed by Mickelson as evidence. Madden continued carefully to go through the notebook, but the remaining pages contained no more surprises.

Madden then opened the four-drawer filing cabinet and started scrutinizing its contents, starting with the top drawer. Meanwhile Mickelson went back to searching the security chief's desk. He had cleared the drawers on the left side as well as the center drawer and was now going through the top right-hand drawer. To Mickelson, the contents looked to be personal office items. He found a small stapler, staples, hand hole-punch, numerous pencils, pens, marking pens, pins, and tacks, masking tape and scotch tape. In the back of the drawer was a box with unused plastic three-hole sleeves, exactly like those in the notebook Madden had searched. Everything seemed to be in order. Mickelson started to push the top drawer closed, and at the same time, he began to pull the second drawer out. Suddenly he stopped. Had he heard something?

The sheriff returned the drawers to the position before, the top drawer open and the second drawer closed. Again, he began to slowly close the top drawer and open the second drawer. There it was! He heard a distinct though very quiet sound of paper being dragged against something. Mickelson took a pen flashlight from his shirt pocket and leaned down to look along the top of the second drawer. He could see what appeared to be a piece of paper that hanging down from the bottom of the top drawer. The file folders in the second drawer were striking the piece of paper and making the sound Mickelson had heard.

He carefully pulled the top drawer back out and lifted the front. The catch of the drawer was opened, and he withdrew the drawer completely. Sheriff Mickelson proceeded to empty the drawer contents onto the desktop and then turned the drawer over. There was an envelope with the resort's logo affixed on the upper left corner. Nothing else was on the outside surface of the envelope.

Mickelson paused long enough for Vannice to capture the position of the envelope, showing how it had been slid between the wooden center support brace and the bottom section of the drawer. Once removed from the bottom of the drawer, Mickelson opened the envelope in front of the videotape.

Madden had stopped his file cabinet search upon seeing his comrade in law enforcement remove the drawer and then the envelope. "Why would Yao put an envelope under the drawer?" he wondered aloud.

The video camera was watching as Mickelson opened the envelope and took out what a very thin collection of printed papers about the size of checks. Mickelson laid the pieces of paper on the desk and examined them. "Do you see this?" Mickelson asked Madden, pointing to the slips of paper. "They're deposit slips for a newly opened checking account at the National Bank of Miami, Florida." He paused and the two looked at the bank receipts.

"Yes, and see the name of the account holder, Samuel Withers!" responded Madden, pointing to the signature on the slip. "Check it for any latent prints, Kyler."

Mickelson nodded, slipping the receipts back into the envelope and then in turn the envelope was placed in a second plastic zip-lock bag. "As soon as we finish up here I'll have them taken back to the office for prints. Maybe we can get lucky and find Yao's prints on them, along with the tickets."

No other evidence turned up as the two completed their search. The Teton County deputy packed the camera into its case, pulling the shoulder strap over his left arm. Turning to Mickelson, he received the two evidence bags and signed on the form that had been attached to each immediately below his boss's, indicating that the trail of evidence had gone from Sheriff Mickelson to Vannice. The next entry would be by the crime lab personnel when they received the materials to check for latent fingerprints. "I'll get these downtown right away, sir." With that, the deputy turned and immediately departed for the law enforcement offices.

The search had taken just over three hours. It was just after one in the afternoon as the two exited the security office, having told the young guard that it would be in the best interest not to share what had occurred with others. Terrati had understood and, since he had only observed the search in the desk office, he had no knowledge of what had happened in Randy Yao's office. Walking into the hallway, Mickelson turned to Steve Madden. "You know, Steve, you've been the one picking up the tab for my morning coffees. Let me pay you back with lunch at one of my favorite restaurants. It's just up the road, a little place run by an elderly couple during the ski season. They've been operating it for about fifteen years. Food is fantastic and very filling. How about it?"

"Sounds good to me, Kyler," laughed Madden. "My stomach says it is lunch time, and I think we have some time before we get the report back on the prints. In the meantime, we can check and see what might have turned up about Jefferson and Utter."

The two exited the resort and drove off in the sheriff's car the eight miles further up the canyon to a quaint, chalet-looking building. "Most likely missed the main lunch crowd," said Mickelson, as they stepped out of the unmarked patrol car. "Usually the crowd comes in between eleven and one, so I think we'll be in good shape."

The two entered the restaurant and seated themselves in a rear booth. A lady, most likely in her mid to late sixties, approached their table, water glasses and menus in hand. "Hello, Sheriff Mickelson. It's been a long time since we've had the pleasure of serving you."

"Good afternoon, Hazel," Mickelson returned. "Seems I've been kept out of the canyon lately. But not by choice; you and Henry have the best food in the entire canyon."

The restaurant co-owner smiled a sincerely and gently touched Mickelson's shoulder. "Well, I suppose we have to accept that excuse," she teased. "At least you brought someone with you to make up for your absences."

"Yes, Hazel, this is Steve Madden; he's an agent with the Federal Bureau of Investigation out of Washington, DC."

Hazel looked at Madden and smiled. Holding out her hand, she welcomed him to their establishment. "Pleased to have you join us, Agent Madden," she said, taking his offered hand in hers.

"Kyler speaks very highly of the cuisine you have here, Hazel, and I am genuinely looking forward to trying some."

The lady took their orders for iced tea and, after handing the men the menus, she turned to get the drinks. "I'll be back shortly for your orders, gentlemen," she said with a lilt in her voice. After no more than four minutes, she returned with the cold iced teas and a small bowl holding lemon slices. "Are you ready to order?" she asked.

At the recommendation of Mickelson, both officers ordered fish and chips, an entrée, which, according to the sheriff, could not be outdone anywhere. Hazel brought the orders within ten minutes. It took a full-sized round service tray to hold the heaping baskets of fish and overflowing baskets of fries plus the bowls of coleslaw for each.

The food was every bit as good as it had been advertised by Mickelson. As they finished off the last morsel and sat back with their respective drinks, Mickelson pulled out his cell phone. "I'm going to check on some of the questions we were following up on as well as the fingerprints."

Madden nodded an approval and excused himself to use the men's room. When he returned, Mickelson was still on the phone but was jotting notes in his notepad. Madden slid into his seat and patiently waited for Mickelson to disconnect. After another minute, the sheriff thanked the unseen person on the other end of the call and hung up. Looking at his scribbled notes, he smiled.

"Steve, I talked with my detective division captain. He said that Yao was in the military with Roger Utter about fifteen years ago. Yao was Utter's CO."

"That's one of the ties we were searching for, Kyler," Steve commented. "What else have you got?"

"The next thing is interesting, Steve," began Mickelson again. "Seems that one of the Twin Falls PD detectives was doing some asking around in one of the bars—as you know, they don't have a whole lot of those there. He was showing photos of Utter and Jefferson and heard a very interesting comment. An elderly man said he overheard Utter saying he was glad to get back to Twin Falls because it was a lot warmer than Butte, Montana. Utter said it had been twenty below when he flew there from Jackson, Wyoming, with some package. Someone had asked Utter when that was and he said Wednesday night. Said he couldn't wait to get out of that place."

Madden leaned forward, "Are you sure that's what he said, Kyler?"

The sheriff consulted his napkin notes before responding. "Yup. That's what the detective said, Butte, Montana. Because of the APB, the black and white units as well as the detectives are scouring Twin Falls for both him and Jefferson. If they locate them, they'll bring them in at least for questioning and hold them until we make a decision about them."

"I wonder …," said Madden, thinking aloud.

"About what?" prompted Mickelson.

"Just wondering if this case has anything to do with the one Jim Addis is working on in Butte." Madden shrugged as if to bring his mind and focus back to the restaurant table and the discussion with Sheriff Mickelson. "Anything on the bank deposit slips and the e-tickets?"

"Actually, that's the last bit of information for you," chuckled Kyler, "You were gone longer than you thought, right? Anyway, there were multiple sets of prints on both the tickets and the bank slips. Among others, Yao's prints are on them both. Just to confirm, our office sent a photo of Yao to the National Bank of Miami and guess what?"

"Randy Yao is Samuel Withers?" answered Madden with a hopeful and questioning look.

"Right on! There's no question that Randy's planning to make a run for it."

"Let's have him picked up and brought in, Kyler, before he figures out we're on to him and makes his run."

Sheriff Mickelson again opened his phone and called the law enforcement office. He gave the information to the officer on the other end and followed it with a request to obtain an arrest warrant for Randy Yao. "Done," he informed Madden as he hung up. "The warrant will go out shortly, and our officers will begin looking for him."

It was almost three by the time Sheriff Mickelson drove into the resort hotel parking lot. By that time, they had heard on the car radio that a warrant for the arrest of Randy Yao had been issued along with his description, his last known address, and the make, model, and license number of his car. The radio call had also closed with a caution that the suspect might be armed and dangerous.

"Well, I think I need to get back to the office," said Mickelson, "Things could be moving pretty fast in the next few hours."

"I agree, Kyler. I need to check in with my partner in Butte and let him in on the latest information. Let me know if you hear anything about Yao. You have my direct cell number." Madden thanked his counterpart for the lunch, opened the door, and as he closed the door, he wished him a good evening. Steve Madden turned and with a much lighter step, walked swiftly across the parking lot, to the elevators, and up to his room. It had been a good day. A good day indeed!

CHAPTER SIXTEEN

Once in his room, Steve Madden immediately copied all of the facts, evidence, and progress neatly into a larger notebook. As he did so, he had to smile because the case had progressed a great deal this day. Sheriff Kyler Mickelson was, in Madden's opinion, a highly professional, well-trained, and extremely ethical law officer. He had truly enjoyed working with him and felt confident that Mickelson and his competent staff could handle any local work that needed to be done.

Pausing and looking out his room window, Madden considered where the case here seemed to be going. As if a stray thought had suddenly caught his attention, Steve closed his notebook after making his latest entries, picked up his cell phone, and hit the short-cut button to connect with Jim Addis. He did not need to wait long before Addis's voice came on line. "Hi, Jim. I have some information that I need to share with you. We've discovered an interesting twist in our case that will most likely take me back to Butte sooner than I had thought."

"Really?" Addis replied in curiosity. "What would that be?"

"It appears that one of the kidnappers here flew from Jackson to Butte and then returned to Twin Falls, Idaho. I'm going check with the flight room at the local airport to see what, if anything, might be discovered in the flight plan. If, in fact, such a flight was made, it might well suggest that Senator Carson was taken to Butte. Unfortunately, if he was flown to Butte, as of today, we don't know whether he remains there or if Butte was simply one stop in a trail his kidnappers have followed."

"Hopefully, your call to the airport will be productive, Steve," Addis said. "Your case has moved pretty fast in the last twenty-four hours."

"Anything new in your case, Jim?"

"It appears that we've located the house where the SUV is kept. I drove out to it in a rental car and stopped at the house across the street. An elderly couple has lived there for over fifteen years; they told me a little more of what's been going on, though they both adamantly claim that they aren't nosey or snoopy neighbors." Addis laughed as he shared the final words of his statement.

"The lady of the house, who spends most of her time at home, substantiates what we had been told earlier. She says she saw a dark blue or black Ford Taurus and the black SUV both drive into the garage and saw the door close before anyone exited either vehicle. Her husband, who likes to be outdoors, was clearing new snow from their own walk and driveway as well as the next-door neighbor's walkway and says he heard what he thought was someone doing metal work that day. The next day he saw a flatbed truck back up to the garage and lower the back end of the truck bed. He said that he then observed some kind of vehicle, covered by a blue tarplin, pulled up onto the truck's bed. The vehicle was not as tall as an SUV so he assumed it was a sedan of some sort. The truck then left and he has not seen it since.

"Both he and his wife insist that since the two vehicles drove into the garage only the SUV has come and gone, and rarely does anyone get in or out of the vehicle when the garage door is open. The residents who they have seen around the house are Middle Eastern in appearance. The view from their home is somewhat compromised because the couple's home is slightly west of the suspect's home making a view of the entire garage impossible. The couple has only seen the SUV, and they say they do not believe the car is in the garage any longer. Obviously, the car could have left late at night or early in the morning when they were in bed or at some time during the day when neither was in a position to observe such activity."

"So, what do you see as your next move, Jim?" Madden asked. "Certainly does sound as though you're nearing the point of seeking a search warrant."

"Yes, we may. For now, figuring they might have taken the Taurus to a scrap yard, I have Sheriff O'Billovich checking with junk yards here in Butte, Whitehall, Dillon, Anaconda, Deer Lodge, Boulder, and Helena to see if any can tell us what might have been under that tarp. We should hear soon as he has his detectives and street guys looking around. As far as Stephens and Williams, though, we've gotten absolutely nothing more since the few individuals who say they saw two men who appear to have been our guys leaving from the restaurant with the three unknown guys. It's like they walked out of that place, got into the SUV, and disappeared from the face of the earth."

"Ok, Jim, let me know what comes up, and I'll do as well," Madden replied. "I need to talk with Mickelson to see what else he's uncovered. If we reach the point where the case definitely is tracked to Butte, I'll leave him in charge at this end, and I'll fly back up to Butte. Will let you know within the next day what gives. Stay in touch, Jim"

"Stay safe, Steve; talk with you soon."

~ § ~

Within the dim light of his improvised dungeon cell, Senator Jeremy Carson had good reason to feel sorry for himself. Adding to his previous rib, stomach, and head injuries, he now nursed a beaten, swollen, and sore face, swollen eyes, and a brutally crushed finger. Tending to it as best he could, he had torn a piece of wood from the table located along the one end of his room. Using that, he had ripped a strip from his shirt and wrapped the cloth around the wood for padding before he very painfully forced his right index finger into an extended position, placed the improvised splint under the shattered finger, and then wrapped another strip of shirt material around both to anchor the splint to his finger, using his left hand and his teeth to tie an awkward knot for securing the splint in place. His forehead had dripped with perspiration as he had made himself endure the pain of moving the finger. Now that the splint supported it, he found the pain, though not gone, certainly more bearable. The most uncomfortable part of his confinement now was that constant, never-ending, high-pitch sound. At times he felt as if he was losing his mind. If he tried really hard to focus on some memory, it helped to lessen the impact of the sound. Jeremy found that thinking of skiing, hunting, and sailing—all things he truly loved to enjoy—helped in this effort.

Carson was resting, almost comfortably, when he heard a key enter and turn in the door lock. Instinctively, his stomach turned a somersault with the sound, and the thought of what might happen next sent a searing pain through his heart. He eased himself into a sitting position facing the inevitable entry of his foes.

As the three hooded figures entered his room, Carson noticed that one of them carried an elongated canvas bag over the shoulder and, in the other hand, carried a solid, oblong black case. He set both carrying cases on the floor near the door, and the three figures continued to walk toward their prisoner.

"Greetings, Senator Carson," the leader spoke. Carson looked up at the hidden face of Ahmad Hassan but did not respond. Carson became aware that the near unbearable sound had ceased, at least for now.

"You again have an opportunity to cooperate. The question is, are you now ready to videotape our demands?"

Jeremy Carson wanted to do nothing more than to tell his captor what he could do with his demand list and videotape. However, as the thought was moving from his brain to his tongue to be voiced, his index finger and nose intercepted the thought and sent a recollection of pain to his brain for consideration. Carson looked at the floor and contemplated his situation. Finally, he looked at the feet of Hassan and reluctantly, very reluctantly indeed, nodded his head in the affirmative.

"I knew you to be a most intelligent man, Senator. Your cooperation is greatly appreciated." Hassan turned toward his comrades and pointed to the carrying cases that sat on the floor. The two figures silently moved to the cases, opened them, and set up a metal tripod and anchored a camcorder to it. The tripod was set up in the center of the room, facing the wooden wall opposite the door. The figures then retrieved a light stand from just outside the door and set it up next to the camera. When the lights were powered on, the room became extremely bright. Carson closed his eyes and turned his head aside from the intensity of the light in contrast to the previously dimmed room. How long, he wondered, since he'd last seen daylight. And would he ever again?

"Stand up, please, Senator," directed Hassan once all had been set up. He then stepped near the camera, and the two silent figures came to Carson, helped him to stand and escorted him to a place about four feet in front of the illuminated wall. The two then stepped to a place just behind the camera, and Hassan took their place next to Jeremy. He told the congressman to hold out his arms, a command to which he complied immediately, knowing what would follow. Hassan unlocked and removed the wrist bracelets, and Jeremy involuntarily rubbed his wrists with the opposite hand, enjoying the freedom, at least temporarily. "We will hold a copy of the script next to the camera, and you will only need to read it," instructed the terrorist. "However, you must appear sincere as though it is your doing, not mine. Do you understand? If you do not do that, then we will re-record it until you either get it right or I decide you are not willing to cooperate, in which case…" Hassan left the statement open, allowing Carson's brain to finish it with the memory of pain.

"I understand."

Hassan had Carson tuck in his shirt, offered him a warm wet towel to clean his face, and held a small mirror to help him do so. In horror, he had looked at his face and seen reflected the image of a monster. The nose showed a definite bulge at its bridge, and the normally straight line displayed a significant deviation. Black and blue eyes looked out of sunken sockets, and below them, his left cheek exhibited a dark bruise over the cheekbone. The reflected face looked as though coal had been smeared over the jaws and chin due to the fact that the senator had not shaved for days.

Once his face was cleaned up, Hassan reclaimed the washcloth and placed it, along with the mirror on the table along the wall to Carson's right. Then he helped Carson lower himself to his knees so that, he believed, his manacled ankles would not show in the frame of the video. All appeared ready. A red light beamed just below the lens of the camera, and one of the speechless figures produced a sheet of white paper, about sixteen inches wide by twenty-four inches. The paper had the exact text as the typed sheet Jeremy had read earlier.

Being a political figure, one used to making speeches and talks in public, Carson read through the wording to assure himself of the wording, and when Hassan gave the command to speak, Jeremy Carson, United States senator, read into the camera:

I am Idaho Senator Jeremy Carson. I am being held by an al-Qaeda cell and am in good health. This message is for all United States government and military officials. For the sake of world peace, I voluntarily make the following demands:

All government and military prisoners currently held in captivity at Guantanamo, Cuba, are to be released and allowed to be free no later than midnight seven days from when you receive this tape.

The Palestinian military and governmental prisoners held by the government and military officials of Israel are to be released no later than midnight seven days from when officials receive this tape.

Should the demands I have set forth not be met I will be executed by beheading.

Hassan had Jeremy record the message again, and then, as suddenly as they came on, the lights went out, leaving Jeremy temporarily blind. By the time his sight came back, the camera and tripod were separated and being placed in their respective cases. Once the cases were closed, the light stand was folded up and taken out the door. Carson peered out the door as it was opened and thought he saw what appeared to be old wood planking on the floor and what looked to be a bare dirt wall. This made Carson understand the dampish and dirt smell all around him. The observation confirmed in his mind that he was being held in a basement of some building, though where, he still did not know.

After storing the recording equipment and removing the light stand, the two figures came back to Carson, helped him to his feet, and then reconnected his wrists to the chains and locked them in place.

Ahmad Hassan stepped back in front of him and spoke. "Very well done, Senator. You have upheld your part of the process. Now it will be up to your government and that of Israel to fulfill their parts. Should they comply, you will be home shortly after their action. On the other hand, should they refuse; you have seven days from tomorrow to live. Your videotape will be sent electronically and simultaneously to several different governmental agencies in both countries." Hassan turned and walked to the door. Carson remained standing where he had been. Suddenly he stopped and turned back to the senator. "Since you have done as asked, the noise will cease, and we will provide you with good meals from now on."

Carson did not reply, but inside his mind he was jumping up and down with joy. Instead of a reply, he walked over to the table on which a pail of water and a ladle had appeared. He took a scoopful of water and lifted it to his lips. The water tasted so wonderful. He drank the entire ladleful, dipped it back into the pail, and drank a second helping. Then he dipped the ladle into the bucket again and poured its contents into a metallic bowl sitting on the table next to the pail of water. Placing the ladle back into the bucket, he then dipped his hands into the bowl of water with the thought of rinsing his face, but a sharp pain from his right index finger shot through his hand, up his arm, and to his brain. "Damn," exclaimed Carson, withdrawing his right hand from inside the pail. He had not thought that a broken finger could be so sensitive to cold water. Instead of using both hands, Carson used his left hand and clumsily rinsed his face with the cold water; enjoying the refreshing and soothing feeling he derived from its contact with his face. As he walked back to the mattress and lay down, reality hit him. He had no doubt in his mind, no matter how hard he wanted to have it, that neither Israel nor the United States of America would even consider granting the demands of the videotape. Bottom line—he'd bought only seven more days of life, nothing more. Carson knew from his previous search of the room that there was no escape route; the only way out went through that door and up the stairs. At least, Carson allowed himself in consolation, he no longer had to hear that obnoxious noise and put up with white rice and terrible tasting water.

~ § ~

After his call with Jim Addis, Madden looked in his notepad, identified the local airport, and placed a call to the flight plan desk. Once connected, he gave the date of Senator Carson's disappearance and inquired as to any flights that had been logged in. After two or three minutes of patiently waiting, the person at the airport end came back on the line.

"Mr. Madden," the male voice began, "there's an entry in the log for a flight leaving here Tuesday night, arriving at Bert Mooney in Butte at midnight. The same aircraft departed Butte with an anticipated return to Twin Falls, Idaho, at 2:00 a.m. and then terminating its flight in Idaho Falls at 3:00 a.m. I can document that the aircraft did return as scheduled on Wednesday morning. The flight log indicates one pilot, two passengers, and cargo. Both passengers boarded in Idaho Falls and deplaned in Twin Falls." Madden thanked the official for his assistance. Deciding he needed to get some kind of workout, he changed into a pair of swim trunks and put on a white terry robe, provided by the resort, for an early evening swim in the resort's indoor pool. Grabbing his room key, he headed to the door when his cell phone rang. Madden stopped, retraced his steps to the window side table, and clicked the talk key as he lifted it to his ear. "Steve Madden" he answered into the internal microphone.

"Steve, Mickelson here."

"Yes, Kyler," Madden countered. "Anything new?"

"Twin Falls PD apprehended Utter a short time ago and has him in custody. So far they haven't been able to locate Jefferson; however, the person he left in charge of his antique shop says he's due back late tonight or tomorrow. They have the shop under around-the-clock surveillance, and if and when he shows up, they'll pick him up as well."

"That's great, Kyler."

"The other item is about Yao. Remember that his office said he was coming in at three today, which is when you and I returned from lunch? Well, he seems to have disappeared, at least for now. After taking the evidence to the office for processing the prints, Deputy Vannice went back out to the Rendezvous, and as of right now, Yao has not appeared. I also have a local PD unit watching Yao's home, and he hasn't been there either. An unmarked surveillance unit is camped out and watching for him. Other units are on alert as are the bus station, cab service operators, and the airport. Though we haven't established roadblocks, we do have patrol cars located along the highways in and out of Jackson. If he's still in the city, we'll get him. One of my detectives is checking all the hotels and motels to see if he's registered in any of them."

"Ok, Kyler," Madden said. The FBI agent then shared the information he had just obtained from the flight office personnel in Jackson. "Without a doubt those two passengers were Utter and Jefferson, and the listed cargo was probably one U.S. Senator Jeremy Carson, though I don't know how they concealed the body. If we can get Utter or Jefferson to talk, we might discover more detail. Guess that's it for now, Kyler. I'm off to the pool for some exercise. Then I'll catch some dinner, but I'll keep my cell with me, so call if you get Yao."

"Gotcha. Talk with you soon, Steve."

Madden put the cell phone in his robe pocket and, after picking up his room key, headed to the pool to work off his energy.

CHAPTER SEVENTEEN

Fifty laps of the Olympic-size pool later, Madden hoisted himself onto the pool deck, dried off with one of the lush towels provided for the resort guests, and slipped into his robe. As he strolled back to the elevator and ascended to his floor, Madden felt somehow even more energized than before his swim. He had experienced this renewed energy many times after long runs, but this time he felt a greater charge than usual, which he knew came from the case of the missing senator starting take a huge turn in favor of the good guys. The walk down the hall from elevator to room seemed to take no time at all, and soon Madden was in his hot shower. Once dried off and dressed in jeans and a t-shirt, he considered dinner: dine in his room or go out to the restaurant or coffee shop? Reminding himself that Kyler Mickelson might call and it would be advantageous to have access to all of his notes, he decided to order room service.

After placing his order, he called home on the room phone, leaving free his cell phone, in the event either Addis or Mickelson tried to contact him. As the telephone in Arlington, Virginia, rang, Steve glanced at his watch—6:35 p.m.; that meant 8:35 back home.

"Hello," came a friendly female voice.

"Hi, gorgeous lady," replied Madden, smiling at the thought of Lee.

"So tell me, are you about to head back home?" questioned his wife.

"Actually, not yet, but I have a really good feeling it won't be a whole lot longer," answered Steve. He knew that Lee understood the demand of his job, but she also had heard this explanation before, and he complimented himself in silence, she knew he usually was right.

"Things are going well in Wyoming, dear?"

"We got some really great breaks in the case during the last forty-eight hours, Lee. If we can locate our chief accomplice suspect here and get some answers, I might be able to fly back up to Butte and rejoin Jim. The strange part is that our case is turning to Butte from here."

"Do you think there might be a connection between your case of the missing senator and the missing agents, Steve?"

"I see no reason for that connection right now, Lee, but I admit that it's been rolling around in my brain the last few hours. It would be weird but certainly not the first time Jim and I started out on separate cases only to find we're actually working the same case but from different events."

"How are the local officials working for you?" asked Lee, knowing that sometimes-local law enforcement does not relish feds coming in and being involved in a case.

"Kyler Mickelson has been a fantastic asset, Lee. He has tremendous ethics and outstanding investigative skills. Not to mention his deputies really seem to like and respect him."

"I'm very happy for you, hon."

"How are Audrey and Steven?"

"They'll be sorry they missed your call. But they're still doing really well. Audrey's making good on her goal of reading twice the number of library books assigned by her teacher, and she's just floating on cloud nine. Stevie is Stevie—just as active as when you left, if not more so. The day-care workers tell me each time I see them that he keeps them running all day. I have to say, Steve, both of our kids are really doing us proud."

"I'd have to agree, Lee."

The conversation continued with other small talk about weather and Lee's work, and after thirty minutes on the phone, Madden suggested they end the call as his dinner was at the door.

Agent Madden rose, walked to the door, and opened it to receive his dinner. After devouring every tasty bite of the spaghetti, he made himself comfortable by stretching out on the bed, turning on the television, and lying back against the two pillows he had piled up against the wooden headboard. He clicked the remote several times until he located a sports channel that was telecasting a game between the Denver Nuggets and Utah Jazz. Madden did not really follow professional basketball—he was much more into baseball—but watching the game would take his mind off the case and allow him to mentally relax for a while. Before long he was asleep.

Madden awoke to the ringing of his cellular phone on the nightstand next to him. It startled him and he abruptly sat up, knocking the remote from his lap to the floor. He realized it was dark and looked at the illuminated bedside clock. The digital numbers showed nine twenty. Now fully awake, Madden answered his phone.

"Steve, Mickelson here."

"Kyler, I wasn't sure if you'd get back to me this evening or not. What gives?"

"You might want to drive down here. We have Yao in custody. Found him in a rented car trying to drive out of town. Just to add a little more to his probable guilt, he looks a little different from when we last saw him—longer hair and a moustache. Seems he actually did make it in to his office. John Terrati was out on lot patrol, and Colby didn't know we'd been there so he never suspected anything. Yao must have walked in with his disguise to get by our deputy and then removed it before entering his office. And when he discovered that the airline tickets and bank slips were missing, he probably figured what had happened so he fled, and figuring someone would be looking for him, he went to the Teton Car Rental with disguise and Samuel Withers ID and rented a car. Then he headed out of town."

Hearing the news of the arrest, Madden jumped off the bed, slipping on a pair of blue socks as he cradled the phone between his ear and shoulder. Next he slipped on a pair of shoes and grabbed his room key.

"Is Deputy Vannice still on the premises?" he asked Mickelson.

"Yes, in fact I radioed him that I was calling you and to be prepared to drive you down here."

"Thanks, Kyler. I'm heading out the door right now and will be there in a few minutes."

Throwing his jacket over his arm, Steve flew out the door and nearly jogged to the elevator. It seemed an eternity before the door opened and Madden had to catch himself and allow a young couple to step out of the wood-lined cage before he entered and descended to the lobby floor. As the door opened on the first floor, Madden stepped quickly through the small groups of people standing around the lobby and headed out the resort's main door to the parking lot. A white patrol car pulled up in front of him before he could step off the curb. He recognized Mickelson's deputy at the wheel. The front passenger window slid down, and Madden heard the deputy ask, "Care for a lift, sir?"

Madden slid into the front seat of the unmarked car, and as soon as he had snapped on the seatbelt, the car picked up speed, crossing the parking lot and heading to the highway. At the same time, Deputy Vannice initiated the emergency lights, and the red and blue lights began flashing through the front grill and out the back window, giving them a fast, smooth trip to the law enforcement building. Meanwhile, Madden began formulating questions in his mind.

The county deputy maneuvered the car to the main door and stopped to allow his passenger to exit. "Good luck, Steve."

"Thank you. Let's hope we get Yao to spill some information for us." Madden got out, took the steps leading to the door two at a time, and walked briskly to the desk officer. He paused, showed his credentials, and introduced himself.

"Go right in, sir," said the desk officer as she reached under the counter for the button to unlock the door to Madden's left. "Sheriff Mickelson is waiting for you in his office. Go to the back of the office and to the right; his office is the first door on the left." He nodded his head in the direction of the desk officer as a thank you and headed for the sheriff's office. Before he got there, Kyler Mickelson stepped around the corner and greeted him. Mickelson had shed his official uniform and was dressed in black denim jeans, Western boots, and a light blue denim Western style shirt.

"Hi, Steve," the youthful sheriff said cheerfully.

"Hello, Kyler. You sure know how to interrupt a guy's catnap," Madden joked.

"Let's go into the interview room. I'll have Yao brought down from upstairs."

The two entered the interview room, Madden looked around. Two doors allowed access to the room. On the side from which he and Mickelson had entered was a heavy wooden door, not much different than any door one might find in an office setting. Directly across the room was another door, constructed of heavy metal with a small reinforced window. Looking at the handle, Madden recognized the usual key-access-only style. This door, as he knew from many years of interviewing suspects, led to the area of the law enforcement building containing the individual holding cells.

Mickelson stepped to the table and placed a cassette tape recorder in the center of the table then plugged two mics into it and placed them so one was facing the single chair and the other facing the two chairs. Glancing around the room, he found it appropriately sterile. The fewer items around, the less chance of having a potential weapon available. A stainless steel table in the center of the room stood with all four legs bolted directly into the floor. On the side of the room from which Madden and Mickelson had entered there were two chairs, molded plastic with fabric cushions on the backs and the seats of both. They would provide enough comfort for sitting during an extended period of interrogations. Madden's eyes moved to the other side of the table and the metal chair located at the middle of the table. Though it also had padding on both the back and the seat, it lacked the cushioning quality of the other two. And, like the table, bolts secured it to the floor

Further study of the room revealed two one-way mirrors, a large one located in the wall at the end of the room directly to the right of the two chairs and another located immediately behind them. These two mirrors allowed observers to watch the suspect during interrogations. The microphones would allow all verbal communication to be heard by unseen personnel as well as to be recorded for later transcription. Madden heard a metallic sound of a key being inserted in the lock of the metal door, and an audible click announced the release of the latch. The door opened, and in walked none other than Randy Yao, chief of security for the Rendezvous Mountain Resort. He looked rather humbled as he entered, hands cuffed behind his back, and saw both Madden and Mickelson present. The accompanying guard walked Yao to the isolated chair, instructed him to sit, then unlocked the handcuffs from his right hand, placed his left hand on the table, and locked the handcuff through a metal loop that had been fixed to the side of the table, out of sight from those sitting across the table. The guard then stepped back to the door and stood vigilantly watching the prisoner.

"Let me first remind you of the Miranda rights that were given to you when you were arrested," began Mickelson. "Anything you say here to us can and will be used against you in court but you do have the right to have an attorney present when we question you. Do you understand that right?"

"Yeah," came a husky, soft voice from Yao, without lifting his head.

"Well, Randy, you almost had us fooled," began Mickelson. "Unfortunately, the fact that you receive the surveillance tapes and store them led us to begin to wonder how the editing occurred."

Yao sat dejectedly staring at the table surface.

"Randy," interjected Madden, "we found, as you well know, your e-tickets from Denver to Miami and from Miami to Montreal. We also found your bank deposit slips, which pretty well show you were paid to edit those tapes and redirect the hallway cameras so Utter and Jefferson would not be observed going to or from the senator's room on Tuesday night."

"It will make things a lot easier on you if you cooperate with us, Randy," Mickelson added. "Helping kidnap a U.S. senator is going to earn you an awful lot of time inside. Your help, before something happens to the senator, might sway a judge to be a little more lenient in determining your sentence."

The two officers let a long pause hang in the air to allow the reality of their words to sink in. Then Madden leaned forward, both arms folded on the table.

"Randy, we know that the senator has been taken over State lines, which makes your problem even more difficult; you are looking at the rest of your active life in prison, at the very least."

They allowed another pregnant pause for effect as well as to allow Yao to respond. Slowly, the head of the dejected man lifted from his gaze from the table to the two lawmen sitting across from him, and then Randy Yao looked down as he drew little imaginary circles on the table with his right hand, thinking about his predicament. Finally, he stopped his invisible artwork and looked up again and spoke. "I know you have figured it out," he started. "I had so much debt I had no way out. No options left." With encouragement from Madden, Yao continued to talk about seeking a loan shark. "The problem with the loaner," Yao started again, "was that my debt just kept getting bigger. Late in December, his goons paid me a visit and made it clear that if I didn't pay up things were going to happen. They left little doubt about their seriousness. The next day, a guy called me at work and told me he knew that there was going to be a big meeting at the Rendezvous and that Senator Carson would be attending. I was told that if I would only edit the tapes as instructed and make sure the cameras that showed the door of the senator's room were positioned so movement in and out of the room could not be observed I could earn some money. I asked what the payoff was, and he told me it would be, in his words, 'worth your while.' I pressed him for what was going to happen, and he just said it was not for me to know. He said if I just did my job it would give me a new start in life. When I asked what that meant, he told me I would be contacted shortly with instructions and if I did my job I would receive an envelope with the front money. Then he said I would hear from him soon. In the meantime, I would be watched so not to talk to anyone. As I said, I was in way over my head, so I agreed."

"How did the envelope arrive, Randy?" Madden queried.

"I received a page from the front desk the next afternoon that a man was there to see me about our surveillance system. When I went out to the desk, I saw Roger Utter who had been under my command during my last year in the military. He stepped toward me and took me out of the lobby and back toward my office before handing me an envelope. He said that I should deposit it immediately so it wouldn't be lying around for eyes to see.

"A check made out to Samuel Withers was in it. Twenty-five thousand dollars. I thought for sure they'd made a mistake, but then I looked behind the check and found an ID card and a photo driver's license for the State of Florida with my photo on it, but the name was Samuel Withers. Utter told me that I'd get a new social security card with a second check once the senator was gone from the resort. I didn't know the plan. I swear to God, if I'd known that was going to happen, I would never have gotten involved. But, I needed the money."

"When did the second check arrive, Randy?" asked Madden.

"The day after the senator disappeared, a special delivery envelope was brought to my office, and I signed for it. When I opened it, there was a check made out for twenty thousand dollars with a new social security card clipped to it, just like the guy had told me."

"Randy," interrupted Madden, "do you still have the envelope and the two cards?"

"Yeah, I have the license and the social security card in an envelope that I stuck up under the dashboard of my car. I shredded both of the envelopes, and I already checked the checks and the cards for prints, just in case I needed to flip on these guys. There were no prints on either card, and the checks were both clean as well."

Madden nodded, disappointed because he had hoped someone somewhere might have slipped up and left a print on something. However, his experience had told him that such a fishing expedition usually ended up with an empty net, but it was always worth a try. "Go on, Randy," he told the soon-to-be former chief of security.

"Three days after I got the check, the guy called, told me the name of the bank in Miami where I needed to deposit the checks."

This time Mickelson raised a question. "What date were you told to deposit the checks?"

"The first check deposit was on a Monday, the day Senator Carson was arriving. I flew to Miami on Sunday under the pretext of looking at a new security surveillance system. Once there, I used my fake identities to open the account and made the initial deposit as soon as the bank opened. As soon I finished, I took the next flight back to Denver, connected with a commuter back to Jackson, and came in to work. The second check was delivered on Wednesday morning, and I deposited that one by electronic deposit from a local bank office, one I didn't bank with and had never been in. I went in and used my other identity to send the money. I was told it would go into my account in Florida immediately; however, until the bank in Florida could substantiate the availability of funds from the paying account, the money would not be available for me to spend."

"So, the new surveillance system that some of your guards mentioned in our interviews is not real, just a hoax," commented Mickelson.

"Sadly, yes, that is true," replied Yao. "I really want a new system, but we have too much invested in this system now. Maybe in a year or two we could seriously consider it, but they're really expensive."

"The only problem, Randy, is that you won't be making those decisions about the security system any longer," threw in Madden. Randy Yao, having lived a good and honest life for the most part, was now reflecting on what his future life held in store. The thought of living in a small concrete cubicle of a prison cell with barred windows, being told when and what he would eat and when he would be allowed to go outside made him physically shudder as if a sudden chill had invaded his spine. No one spoke for several seconds. Madden finally broke the painful silence and asked, "Please tell us what you know of the actual night on which Carson was abducted."

"I knew the guards were pretty lax about observing the tapes as they were actually recording, and I built on that by talking to them or giving them things that they needed to do, which detracted them from likely watching the monitors at the specified times. Then, after the tapes were signed over to me, I closed my door and went to the times I had been told to look at and edited as I was told to do."

"How did you know what times to look for and what tapes to edit?" asked Mickelson, trying to uncover some identity of the person or persons behind the kidnapping.

"Guess it would have been maybe one or two in the morning on Wednesday that I got a call on my cell phone. I have no idea how or who got my number, but the called told me what I needed to do."

"Is the calling number still in your phone?" asked Madden.

"There was no number, no name. I even tried to have it traced through my cell provider since they know who I am, but they couldn't identify who made the call or where it came from. They told me that more than likely it was from a disposable phone."

"Ok, Randy," said Madden, "what do you know of the kidnapping, and who was involved?"

"I knew only one of the guys on the tape—Utter. I can't tell you anything about the other one. No names were ever given to me, only two phone calls in my office, one on my cell phone, and two envelopes. That is the total communication I received. I'm sorry for what I did." Yao took a deep breath, exhaling very slowly, and then continued. "I know I've destroyed my life. I'd do anything to turn back the clock, but I know I can't. I only wish I could help you find the senator, but I have no clue where he was taken, or even why."

The interview went on for another half hour or so without any more information coming to light. Finally, Madden looked toward Mickelson, and the sheriff recognized the signal that the interrogation, at least for this night, was over. Mickelson looked at Yao and said, "Randy, what you have participated in is, as you know, a felony, and you will be held accountable for your actions. In the immediate future, you will be held in custody until you are arraigned and bail might be established. I suggest that you get your attorney involved as soon as possible. Once you do, we'll provide your attorney with a copy of the tape as well as a transcribed copy of the recording from this interview. Thank you for your comments and honesty. If you think of anything else, please let your guards know, and they will arrange to have you speak with Mr. Madden or myself."

With that, the two law enforcement officials stood, an unspoken signal to the guard to attend to the prisoner. He stepped forward and, after unlocking the handcuff from the table anchor and having Yao place both arms behind his back, secured the loose cuff to the right wrist once more and led Randy Yao back to his jail cell.

Mickelson disconnected the microphones from the portable tape recorder, picked up the two mics and the recorder, and then opened the door behind where he and Madden had been seated. Stepping into the hallway, the two men silently walked together the few steps to the door with pebbled blue glass and the gold leaf stenciled title of SHERIFF on it. Mickelson opened the door and allowed his companion to enter before him. The approximately sixteen-foot-square room allowed for adequate and comfortable seating. Several photos of wildlife, captured by a local professional photographer and gifted to the likeable sheriff, hung on the walls. Carrying on the hunter's theme in the room, the solid oak desk had intricately hand-carved panels on the end piece, each of a grizzly bear poised with its right front paw lifted and teeth barred in an obvious challenging attitude. A tanned leather protector lay on top with items neatly organized upon it, and the sheriff's comfortable, light tan leather chair sat in front of it. Two four-drawer file cabinets along one wall matched the oak of the desk and its brass hardware. Inside the door and immediately before one reached the desk stood an oval oak table with a sculpted skirting that wrapped around just below the tabletop displaying a hand-tooled mountain and forest scene. Two captain-style chairs matching the appearance of the sheriff's chair sat on either side of the oval table, and two matching chairs sat in front of and facing the desk. Along the wall behind the oval table was an oak trimmed wet bar with built in refrigerator and small sink. A small but usable coffee urn was located on the counter next to the sink.

"Nice décor," commented Madden as he entered.

"Thanks," said the sheriff, accepting the compliment. "But I can't take any credit; it was all here when I was elected four years ago." Mickelson gestured to Madden to have a seat at the table. Then he placed the recording equipment on his desk, and before he took his place in the seat opposite the federal officer, indicated he was getting a diet cola for himself and asked if he could get his guest anything. Madden accepted the offer and decided on a diet cola as well.

Both men took long drinks from their respective containers before either spoke. Finally, Madden, setting his container down on the table, said, "I had hoped that Yao might have more information for us. But, over the many years I've sat in on similar interviews, I've rarely found any to add more information. The boss of any such operation is usually very careful in covering identities. That said, I don't think it was a waste of time by any stretch of the imagination."

"I agree, Steve," countered Mickelson. "If nothing else, Yao confirmed what we had theorized about his involvement. Knowing the definite link between Yao and Utter solidifies the theory. I think solving cases is kind of like crossing a steam that has no bridge. You carefully step from one stone to another, and before you know it, you have crossed and accomplished your objective."

"Good analogy, Kyler. That's precisely how you solve a mystery, taking one step at a time, always looking for the next clue, or the next stone in the stream, and keep building on what you have."

The oak grandfather clock that stood in one of the far corners of the office indicated almost ten thirty. It had been a long day but certainly one worthwhile. Madden finished his cold drink and started to push his chair back in preparation to leave when the phone rang. Mickelson held up his hand in a sign of stop and stepped around the table to his desk. He picked up and greeted the caller, most likely his receptionist, with a very cheerful "Mickelson." He listened attentively, nodding, and winked at Madden just before thanking the caller and hanging up. Madden had risen to a standing position and waited by the chair he had occupied.

"That was my receptionist. She said that Twin Falls PD just called about three minutes ago to report that Jefferson has still not shown at his shop or his apartment located about a mile away. However, they are maintaining surveillance and will call both of us on our cell phones should anything come down."

"That's good. We can hope he shows and hasn't been tipped off by anyone in the chain. Guess I'll head back up to the Rendezvous if I can bum a ride, if Quentin is still on duty and available."

"I'll run you back up, Steve. It's not that far and certainly not out of the way."

The two officials walked through the main office, down the stairs to the enclosed parking, and entered the sheriff's unmarked vehicle. Stopping only to be acknowledged by the guard at the entry gate of the garage, they made the journey back up the canyon in only fifteen minutes, thanks to very limited traffic.

Arriving at the resort, Madden thanked the sheriff for the lift and then as he began to open the door, he suggested that since both he and Mickelson were now off duty he might join him inside for a nightcap. "It's been a pretty long day, Kyler; I'd enjoy just sitting back in the lounge and decompressing over a drink or two."

Mickelson accepted the invitation, and after parking the car, the two entered the Apres Vous Lounge and secured two chairs and a small cocktail table next to a stone fireplace that had an opening large enough that a grown man could easily stand in it. The bright flames licking at the large logs and the crackling of the sap made the atmosphere very inviting. After taking their seats, a cocktail waitress walked over to them and asked for their order. Madden ordered a brandy, and Mickelson ordered a soda water since he would need to drive back to town. Deliberately avoiding talking "shop" with one another, they focused on small talk of personal interests. As each was finishing his third drink over a period of an hour and a half, they concluded it was time to call it an evening. Madden paid for the drinks and walked with Mickelson to the lobby door where they parted company with the understanding that they would be in touch by phone the next morning.

Choosing to take the stairs instead of the elevator, Madden took his time walking up to his floor, then down the quiet hallway to his room. After entering, he prepared for bed, slipped under the covers, and then clicked on the television and mindlessly watched the end of a late talk show. He was just convincing himself to turn off the light and television for sleep when his cell phone began to vibrate. Reaching for it, he glanced at the time; it was one fifteen.

After Madden's greeting, the caller on the other end identified herself as a Sergeant Holly Poitress with the Twin Falls Police Department. Madden acknowledged her identity.

"Mr. Madden, I'm calling to inform you that a subject of interest to you has been apprehended in the last fifteen minutes, a Cameron Jefferson."

"That's good news, Sergeant," Madden said.

"Both Mr. Jefferson and Roger Utter are in our custody, and we are holding them pending instructions from you and Sheriff Mickelson of Teton County there in Wyoming."

"I appreciate your cooperation, and I'll be flying up to Twin Falls sometime today and would like to meet with your chief to inform him of our case and to interrogate both Utter and Jefferson. Has Sheriff Mickelson been notified?"

"Yes, sir, one of our other night staff is calling Sheriff Mickelson as we speak. We will hold them and have them here for your arrival, sir. Just report to the front desk when you arrive, and you will be admitted to Chief Morris' office."

"Thank you again for your call, Sergeant."

"You are welcome, sir; good night."

The call ended and Madden placed a call to the cell phone of Sheriff Mickelson.

"Hi, Kyler, Steve Madden. I presume you received the call from Twin Falls regarding Jefferson?"

"Yes, Steve. Just hung up a few seconds ago. What are your plans? I'm sure you're going to fly up there ASAP. Do you want or need me to go?"

"You have enough on your plate here, Kyler. Why don't I fly up sometime this morning, as soon as I can get our department aircraft to come up here from Denver, and I'll make sure you get both a copy of the interrogations and a typed copy of the transcripts."

"That works fine with me, Steve. No question that my plate is full here. Besides, this is really your case, not mine. However, I do appreciate being kept in the loop as it will help keep the story intact. If I don't talk with you before you leave, have a safe flight, Steve. Have enjoyed working with you and look forward to our paths crossing again sometime in the future."

"I'm sure they will cross again, Kyler. Keep up the great work; you are one of those rare local officers who is not only highly skilled but also highly ethical. Someday you might want to consider applying for the Bureau; you'd be a great addition."

"Thank you, Steve."

"Talk with you later, Kyler."

Madden then called the Denver Bureau office and, after giving the agent in charge a briefing, he asked to have a Bureau aircraft fly up to Jackson and transport him to Twin Falls, Idaho. The officer checked the aircraft and pilot schedules and confirmed that the craft was available and, weather permitting, could be in Jackson about noon.

Madden thanked the agent and hung up. Then he called the front desk, using the room telephone, and informed them of his upcoming departure, requesting a ride with the resort shuttle to make his connection at noon. That confirmed, he turned off the table lamp and lay down to sleep, it was now 2:10 a.m.

CHAPTER EIGHTEEN

It was 2:28 when the Bureau's jet touched down and taxied to a private hanger in Twin Falls. Steve Madden had called ahead while waiting for his departure and had been informed that a detective from the local police department would be at the airport to drive him to the police department. As the door dropped out and down, forming the stairway from the cabin, Madden descended quickly, looking for someone who looked conspicuous. Off to his right he spotted a gray colored sedan. A middle-aged man with a bald head was leaning against the driver's door, left leg casually crossed over the right and his arms folded across his chest.

As Madden walked up to the car, the man stepped forward and extended his right hand. "Greg Thorson, Twin Falls PD. Let me help you with your luggage, sir."

"Thanks, Greg. Steve Madden," he replied, stepping back to allow the detective to stow his luggage in the trunk.

Madden walked around to the passenger side and entered the car as the detective slid in behind the steering wheel. Thorson started the engine and slowly exited the tarmac. The car moved over the parking lot and then through the exit gate to the airport. Picking up speed, Thorson moved onto the highway that would lead them into the town of Twin Falls.

"So you're here to interrogate our two guys?" began Thorson.

"Yes, I have a meeting with your chief when we arrive at the station, and then we'll get some interviews set up. Were you involved in picking up either of them?

"Yeah, I picked up Jefferson early this morning. He sure looked petrified when we collared him. I thought he was going to run for a moment, but he must have thought better of it. As it turned out, there was nothing to it. No resistance."

"I really appreciate the cooperation from your office, Greg. I know that Sheriff Mickelson in Jackson is most appreciative as well. Through the efforts of your staff, we've been able to make some excellent progress in our case over the last couple of days."

"Not a problem with us, Steve. Usually it's pretty quiet around here. The interstate was built north of the town so we don't get a whole lot of folks going through and staying over. Our biggest draw is the falls themselves, and let's face it, in the winter that's not going to be much of an attraction." Thorson looked over at his riding partner and chuckled.

"I suppose that would be true, Greg."

Small talk filled the rest of the short trip, and before long, the car pulled up in front of a one-story brick building. Scanning the front, Madden noticed on the cornerstone the date of 1945 cut into the surface. All the windows of the building had metal bars over them, giving the impression, in Madden's mind, of a very old, maybe even outdated jailhouse. But as he reminded himself, you can't judge a book by it cover, and the same adage applied to law enforcement structures. It is a matter of what happens inside that counts.

Thorson popped the trunk, withdrew Madden's luggage, and led him up the sidewalk to the five concrete steps leading up to the oak framed doors. Grabbing the brass handle of the left hand door, Thorson pulled it open. Madden stepped through the double door, crossed over a rubber mat, and then pushed one of the double doors open, entering the building's main hallway.

Old, indeed, but the building wore its age well. The small one-inch octagon-shaped tiles of the floor, alternating black and white, gave the attention to detail rarely seen in modern buildings anymore. Above, long, black metal rods held opaque white glass lighting fixtures suspended from the high ceiling. The fixtures reminded Madden of the ones he had seen in his schools as a youth. Walking down the hall, he could not help but notice the building was trimmed in dark oak and had been well cared for.

About halfway down the hall, an oak sign projected out from the wall about eight feet above the floor. The routered lettering, which had been painted white, read, "Police Department." Immediately below the sign was an open door. Thorson, walking next to Madden, gestured at the door for him to go in.

A long counter, oak faced with a smooth black top on their left extended the full length of the room, with the exception of a swinging gate about mid-point. Approaching a uniformed officer standing at the counter, Madden introduced himself.

"Yes, sir," the officer snapped politely. "If you will go through the gate here and walk over to the back right corner, you will find Chief Morris's office. He just came in, so he is expecting you."

"Thank you, Lieutenant," Madden said, noticing the insignia of rank on the police officer's shoulder.

Thorson handed Madden his bag, stated he had another appointment, and wished him well. With that, Thorson disappeared, walking back the way the two had entered.

Madden stepped through the gate and walked among the grey metal desks making his way to the back corner where he spotted a door that was ajar. As he approached, he read "Chief" on the door window, pebbled to prevent observation through it. Knocking on the open door, he waited to be called in.

"Come in!" barked a male voice from within.

Madden stepped into the office. Oak wainscoting to about four feet above the floor gave way to light blue walls to the high ceiling. In contrast to the extensive wood in the building, two gray metal file cabinets sat unceremoniously in the corner by a window, which framed an older man sitting at an even older oak desk. Age betrayed by his grayish hair, he wore spectacles and a police issue uniform—a grayish blue, long-sleeve shirt with a black tie. Atop the shoulders, epaulets, one on each shoulder and pined in the center with a silver star, indicated, Madden assumed, the rank of chief of police. The man looked up, smiled, and removed his glasses as he stood, extending his right hand.

"Agent Steve Madden, I presume," greeted the chief. "I'm Ken Morris. Welcome to Twin Falls."

"Thank you, sir," Madden replied, noting that the chief was not the best example of physical fitness as a significant paunch protruded above the chief's black slacks, held in place by a wide black belt with a black leather holster on the right side and a handcuff pouch, also black leather, on the left side.

"Please, have a seat, Steve."

Madden took his place in one of three chairs sitting in front of the chief's desk. The chairs were identical, oak with a rounded back, supported in place with oak spindles spaced about every two inches.

"What can you tell me about Roger Utter or Cameron Jefferson, Chief?"

"Please, Steve, call me Ken. Jefferson's been living here in Twin Falls for the last couple of years on a pretty regular basis. He started working part time for Edna Smithson at the antique shop out on the east end of town. When she got so she had to live in an assisted living facility in Pocatello, he bought the shop from her and has been running it ever since. He had a run in with the law a while back, but he's been keeping his nose clean. While on probation he never failed to meet with his officer and made an effort to stay in touch. I have to tell you that I was somewhat surprised when an arrest warrant was requested on him."

"What else can you tell me about him, Ken?"

The police chief lifted a file folder on his desk and handed it to Madden for his examination. "One thing that is not in that folder, Steve, is the fact that when Thorson and another of our officers arrested him, Jefferson led them to a paper bag hidden in the wall of a display case near the cash register that contained several thousand dollars in unmarked bills. We have it in the evidence vault.

"His record shows that he has some pretty good skills when it comes to defending himself. He was a black belt in karate and, as a man in his early twenties, was a finalist in the U.S. Olympic trials for boxing."

Madden continued to peruse the file folder's contents. He stopped after a couple of pages and pulled a sheet out of the folder. "A private pilot's license?" He raised his eyebrows as he glanced at the police leader seated across from him.

"Yes. Cameron still flies small craft now and again. In fact, he's part owner in a small craft that's usually kept in Boise. Once in a while, he brings it in here but not often."

"When is the last time you know of him flying?"

"Gosh, Steve, I don't know. He told folks he was going fishing some days ago, but his plane, as far as I know, was still in Boise."

Madden began wondering about the flight log he had been given by the airport personnel in Jackson. He had been told the flight was based out of Idaho Falls, nowhere near Boise. So, what was the connection? Where did the third pilot come from?

"What about Utter?" Madden asked, closing the file folder and laying it in his lap."

"Ah yes, Roger Utter. He's one bad dude, Steve. I met him down at the antique shop once about two months ago. Short, probably only five eight, and pockmarked face. He seemed rather rude and, I would have to say, very crude. He swore a lot, and it actually embarrassed Jefferson, I think. It wasn't long before you guys had the warrant issued that we connected this guy with the guy who had skipped out on his parole. There is no question that, regardless what happens with your case, that fella is headed back to the joint somewhere."

"I think I would like to visit with Jefferson first, Ken, if that would be ok?"

Picking up his phone, the chief pushed a series of four numbers and waited for the call to connect. "Gary, Ken here. Our FBI guest wants to interview Jefferson. Can you set up the recorder in room one and have Sarah stand by to type up the transcript of the session?" A pause and then, "Ok, great; thanks, Gary."

Hanging up the phone, Morris turned back to Madden and told him how to get to the interview room located on the second floor. "When you finish with Jefferson, Steve, just let Gary know and he'll arrange to have you do the same with Utter."

Both men stood and mutually extended their right hands. "Thank you, Ken," Madden said. "Hope to talk with you soon."

"Same here, Steve. Good luck."

Madden exited the chief's office, leaving his suitcase behind at the request of the chief. He found the stairs and went up to the second floor. Checking in with the officer, he was led down a hall to a room with a sign, "Interview Room 1," over the door. Madden opened the door and entered. He was thinking of his questions when the door opened again, and a rather tall and slender man in an orange jumpsuit with his hands handcuffed behind his back entered, accompanied by a uniformed guard. The prisoner was led to a chair and told to be seated. Steve took a seat on the opposite side of the table.

"Mr. Jefferson, I am Steve Madden with the Federal Bureau of Investigation."

The prisoner looked at Madden with little or no expression on his face. Madden deduced that the recording of the session would be handled outside the room itself as there was no recorder visible.

"We obtained your fingerprints from a coffee table as well as broken pieces of another table at the Rendezvous Mountain Resort in Jackson, Wyoming. We also have identified you on several videotapes from that resort during the time Senator Jeremy Carson from Idaho was abducted. The chief of security for the resort has been arrested and has admitted his part in the abduction. I have decided to visit with you first, Cameron, and next I will interview Roger Utter. So this is your opportunity to set the record straight. If you cooperate there may be some credit granted when it comes to your trial."

Madden decided not to feed any more information to Jefferson so anything the prisoner might say could be compared to what Madden knew. Jefferson squirmed slightly in his chair. He looked down at the floor and the top of the table between them. Finally, he cleared his throat to speak.

"If I tell you everything I know, can we work a deal?"

"Cameron, I cannot make any promises. Our interview is being recorded, and your comments here will be given to the legal staff as arraignments and trials are set and held. I can tell you that I will be willing to put in a good word, if we are able to get the senator back. You have to remember you participated in a kidnapping over state lines, which makes it a federal offense."

"I understand," said Jefferson. "I am not the bad guy here; Roger is."

"How so, Cameron?" Madden asked.

"I was running the antique shop here in Twin Falls and minding my own business. I was actually enjoying living here. Had my private pilot license and was part owner in a small plane we keep in Boise. One day Roger walks into my shop. Just walks in like we'd seen each other yesterday, but it'd been years. He starts talking about how the world has been unfair to him, and then he starts in on me and what a crappy life I actually have here. Reminds me that I told him how badly I wanted to live in Virginia and raise horses. I tried telling him that that was the old me and that I had a good life. After a couple of meetings, he said he wanted me to take him up in the plane. I agreed, and we drove down to Boise, checked out the plane, and took it up. When we were flying around, he pulled out a map from his jacket and showed me where Jackson was in Teton County, Wyoming. He told me he wanted to see it from the air. It wasn't really that far so we flew down so he could see it. Said something about him having to go down there to transport some cargo for a friend."

Madden had been taking notes on a pad of paper, and as Jefferson stopped, he looked at the prisoner. "Go ahead, Cameron; what happened from that fly-over?"

Jefferson licked his lips and continued. "We circled the Teton area, and then I began to turn back west to head home. As we made the approach to Idaho, Utter told me to take him over Idaho Falls. I tried telling him that wasn't where we needed to go, that we were headed to Boise. He got kind of angry and said to fly him to Idaho Falls. Well, sir, it wasn't worth a fight in the air, so I did. We flew over Idaho Falls, and then I immediately returned for Boise. He didn't say anything until we were in the car on our way back to Twin Falls. And then he said he had a business acquaintance that would pay "handsomely"—yeah, that was his word—if I would help him move his cargo from Jackson to another location. He wanted me to line up an airplane that would have a good luggage compartment and hold at least two passengers. He also said it would require night flying, and the pilot would need to be instrument rated. I asked what kind of cargo, and he said that was none of my business. Then he said I'd know when I needed to know.

"We got back to Twin Falls and went to a local bar. We sat in a booth, and he pulled out an envelope and slid it across the table to me. Told me to look in it. I picked it up and opened it. It was filled with money. Now I'm not telling you it was just bills, these were big bills! I saw three digits on every one of them, and the envelope was, as I said, stuffed full. There were thousands of dollars in that envelope. I pushed it back to him without saying anything, and he picked it up and pushed it into his inside jacket pocket. Then he told me that that was just a small part of what I could expect if I helped him."

Jefferson paused and closed his eyes, letting out a long slow breath, as though he could see that packet of money in his mind. Or, maybe wishing he'd never seen it in the first place. But he continued. "Oh, it was tempting. Oh, man, yes. Well, my greed must have overcome all the good in me sitting right there. I remembered how nice it was when I did have money back as a younger man. That's what got me into trouble before, and I learned my lesson—or thought I had. Maybe I'm just not cut out to go straight. I don't know. I just have to accept what I did and take my consequences. I know I did wrong. I know I can't undo what I did—oh, how I wish I could. What a mess. I'm really sorry. The only thing I can do to try and make it right is this. I knew that before you and I ever met today."

"You are doing the right thing, Cameron. Keep going."

"Let me think. After that night at the bar, Utter left for a day or two, and I thought maybe that was it. Don't I wish! But he came back two days later, and this time he wasn't so friendly. He flat out told me that I was to work with him, and if I didn't, then he'd make sure some of the things I'm not so proud of from my past would be made known in town. You have to understand, Mr. Madden, this is a small town; everybody knows everyone and everything about them. Some of those things from my past get out, and man, my life here is over. I have everything in the plane and the shop; I'd be ruined, and with my record, I'd never get a clean start anywhere, so I agreed if he told me what we were to do.

"He told me I'd be paid fifty thousand dollars to help him. Fifty thousand dollars! Man, that would be a good start to a new life. Then he said that his boss would make sure I got a small horse place in Virginia. That is just exactly what I had always dreamed of! I didn't even think about what we were going to do. Yeah, money talked, and I was stupid.

"Utter called me one night and said to contact a pilot and get things set up for the following Tuesday. We were to drive to Idaho Falls and join the pilot, then fly to Jackson. The plane was to stay there, and then we'd bring our cargo to the plane and fly from Jackson to Butte. After we off loaded the cargo, we'd fly back to Twin Falls, and the pilot was return to Idaho Falls. I called a guy I know, Henry Butler, who's a good pilot. Spent a lot of years as a bush pilot in Alaska. He needed some cash and said he could make the run without any problem. I told him that he could not and did not want to know what the cargo was. Just sit in the plane and look straight ahead; that's what Roger told me to tell him.

"We got down to Jackson and rented a van; then we drove out to the resort. That day we just kind of walked around. Roger was casing the place for what, I didn't know. In the afternoon, I saw something going on out front—a crowd protesting something, but we didn't care. Then we drove off and sat in a little bar, playing cards, killing time until about ten or so. Then we went back to the resort and sat in the parking lot, talking about the things we used to do together, the good times we had, until Utter said it was time to move. I asked what we were doing, and he told me that we were going to kidnap a U.S. senator. I told him he was nuts! He just laughed and pointed a pistol at me, told me it was a little late to get honest in my life. What was I gonna do? He told me what we would do and how. I knew I was too far into it to back out, and Utter just told me to pretend we were good pals out for a fun evening and to laugh it up. We got to the elevators and waited for Carson to appear. When he did, Utter nodded toward the elevator, and we got on, laughing and talking like we were the buddies of old. Next thing I know we're beating up that poor guy, tying him up, stuffing him into one of those long canvas bags that zip closed, and hauling him down the stairs to the van.

"Once we were in the van, I said something about the cameras in the halls and stairs. Utter just laughed. He told me that the cameras had been moved, and the videos would all be erased so there wasn't any way to trace us. No prints either. We had gloves, but I guess I took them off when we finished with the senator. Only we weren't done because of the tables. Just goes to show you we aren't the great criminals Utter thought we were."

Madden continued to write and paused to ask Jefferson if he needed anything. The prisoner said a glass of water would be good, and Madden nodded to the guard who tapped on the one-way mirror located on the wall facing Jefferson. Within seconds, the door opened, and a female officer stepped inside the room with two tall Styrofoam cups of water. She held the cup to Jefferson's lips so he could drink and when he nodded that he had had enough, she put the cup on the table and stepped back through the door, closing it behind her. "You're doing great, Cameron; please continue," Madden encouraged.

Jefferson nodded in the affirmative. "Yes, sir. I'm trying to give you everything I know. We drove out to a junkyard west of Jackson, someone Utter knew."

Madden interrupted the prisoner, "Do you know the name of the guy?"

"No, there wasn't anybody around. No one. We drove up to the gate, Utter got out and opened it, I drove the van into the yard and waited for him to close the gate behind us. Then we drove to this shack. It was filthy. We took the senator in, put him in a chair with a blindfold over his eyes. We were there for a while. Utter made a telephone call, and when he hung up, he said it was time to leave.

"Utter took a syringe from a bag he was carrying and stuck it into the senator's neck. When he was unconscious, we put him in the van and drove to a private hanger at the airport where Butler had the plane waiting for us. Just as I had told him, Butler was in the pilot's seat looking straight ahead. We approached from the rear of the plane and put Carson into the storage compartment; then Utter drove the van off to the side of the hanger. I climbed into the passenger seat behind the pilot, and Utter got in behind the co-pilot seat when he came back from dumping the van. There was no co-pilot, of course, so that seat was empty. Then we flew to Butte. I'm not sure what time we landed, but it was really late, somewhere about midnight. We taxied to a private hanger there. No lights except on the plane. A SUV pulled up. I think it was a black or midnight blue GMC Tahoe. Two guys got out. One of the guys mentioned Ahmad, but I'm not exactly sure who that is. I only know that Utter had mentioned the name before. They took the senator and put him in their SUV, one of them gave Utter a black bag, and they dove off. All that happened in back of the plane so the pilot couldn't see what was going on.

"Utter and I climbed back aboard, and we took off to Twin Falls where we got off and the pilot went on to his home field in Idaho Falls. Utter and I drove back to my place and he said it would be good to disappear for a few days. He opened the black bag and took out a wad of cash that was bundled. He put it into a paper bag and handed it to me, saying it was my share. I stuffed the bag in a hidden spot in a wall in my shop. I don't even know how much is there. I never looked in it and wish I'd never gotten it. I just took my truck and went fishing for a couple of days after arranging to have the shop covered. That's about it, sir."

Madden nodded. "Cameron, I thank you for your honesty and assistance. You've been a great help. I only hope that we can locate Carson before it's too late."

Madden nodded to the guard and stood. The guard moved to Jefferson, helped him to his feet and led him from the room. Madden followed out of the room and paused, watching the figure in the orange jumpsuit walk forlornly down the hall toward his cell. He turned and recognized the attractive brunette sitting at a chair operating a stenograph as the one who had brought the water in. "You must be Sarah," deduced Madden from the chief's comment on the phone in his office.

"Yes, sir," the officer smiled. "I'll have a typed transcript for you by tomorrow morning as well as a CD of the tape," she nodded toward the wall on which a tape recorder was slowly turning the reels that had recorded the conversations in the interview room. "Is there anything else, sir?"

"I appreciate your help, Sarah. I'm going to get a cola and a sandwich. Then I'm coming come back, and we'll do an interview with Utter. Is there anything I can get you?"

"No, thank you, sir. I've already had my lunch break and have some water right here. Thank you for your kindness, however. I'll see you when you get back."

With that, Madden walked down the stairs, stopping by the chief's office for his suitcase, and walked to the front desk. While there, he took a few minutes to brief the chief about the interview he had just completed and suggested locating a pilot named Henry Butler out of Idaho Falls might be worthwhile. Then, after notifying the officer at the front desk of his intentions, Madden went outside and walked about two blocks to a hotel that he had seen as he and Thorson had approached the police department building. He went to the registration desk, obtained a room overlooking the main street from the second floor, and took his belongings to the room. He paused at the window looking out onto the street below. Twin Falls was, as Ken Morris had said, a very quiet place this time of year. Turning away from the window, Madden exited the hotel and found a little café two doors further down the street. He went in and ordered a Monte Cristo sandwich to go, selected a can of ice-cold soda, and paid the cashier. With lunch in hand, he walked back to the police station, up the stairs, and to the interview room. Finding no one around, not even Sarah, he entered the room, left the door open, and sat at the table to enjoy his lunch before the next interview. Madden had barely finished his sandwich and popped open his soda when Sarah stepped into the room.

"Agent Madden!" Her voice sounded urgent, and Madden turned quickly in his chair. "You need to go to Chief Morris's office right away, sir." The female officer stepped back as Madden rose and quickly strode through the door to the chief's office to find a very serious-faced chief.

"Steve, we just received word about Senator Carson." The chief then handed a typed sheet to the agent. Madden looked at it, and his mind started to go into overdrive as he read the notice. It was from the FBI headquarters in Washington, DC, issued by the director of the Bureau. The notice stated that the FBI, the White House, and key congressmen had electronically received a video that Senator Jeremy Carson had recorded for Ahmad Hassan and his terrorist sleeper cell. Slowly Madden reread the demands that the video listed. Looking up, he let out a slow breath. Another stepping stone in the stream had just become visible, and it was a slippery rock for sure. He knew now that the kidnapping of the senator had just taken a much more serious tone. But at least he apparently was still alive. He looked at the chief of police. Morris pointed to an open cabinet on the wall behind the chair in which Madden had been seated earlier. The open wooden doors revealed a television screen. Morris picked up a remote control, pushed a button, and played the video of Senator Carson making his plea for the demands. Madden noted the senator's face, showing clear evidence of severe beatings. Obviously, the senator had not given in easily to his captors, nor could they count on his receiving fair treatment even after the taping. Madden recalled the private discussions he had heard in the circles of the Democratic Party in DC. Highly intelligent and personable and especially popular with the younger voters, Carson was viewed as an up-and-coming national star and a possible presidential candidate for his party.

Madden used the chief's telephone to call his superior and learned that a letter accompanying the video stated that the governments of the United States and Israel had forty-eight hours to make a decision before the video and the demands would be made available worldwide through the Internet. Forty-eight hours until international publicity; seven days until the execution of the senator. Madden's conversation with his boss focused on obtaining as much information on Ahmad

Hassan and his whereabouts as well as any known recent activity. Suddenly time became a whole lot more precious.

"Steve, I know you're going to interview Utter next. Following that you'll most likely want to head off to Butte. I'll have a car pick you up at your hotel in the morning and drive you to the airfield. I'm told your pilot and aircraft have returned and will be waiting when you arrive out there. The officer who picks you up will have the materials you need from your interviews. We have a search warrant for Jefferson's apartment and his store, and we'll exercise that tomorrow."

"Thank you, Ken. That's great. I have a room at the hotel just down the street and can be ready to leave at seven in the morning, if Sarah can have the transcriptions completed and the CDs made by then. I have a favor. Could you send copies of the transcripts and the CDs to Sheriff Kyler Mickelson in Jackson for me? Also, please make a dub of this video and send it to him with the other materials. That would be most helpful."

"Not a problem, Steve," the chief assured the agent.

Madden turned and exited the office with another thank you and almost sprinted up the stairs. He noticed Sarah at her stenograph, transcribing from a recorder.

"Are you ready for Mr. Utter, sir?" asked Sarah.

"Yes, let's do it, Sarah. I have a hunch this'll be shorter than the first one so I don't think you'll need to worry about water for this guy."

Madden entered the room and stood at the far end, facing the door, waiting for the next prisoner to be brought in. He heard a door closing in the distance, and footsteps growing louder. Roger Utter entered with his escorting guard keeping one hand on the prisoner's handcuffed hands and the other on the right shoulder. Dressed also in an orange jumpsuit, Utter carried an obvious defiance over his whole body. The guard pushed Utter into the chair and extracted a second set of cuffs. Reaching behind the prisoner, the officer placed one wrist link around the cable connecting the cuffs on Utter's wrists and snapped the other cuff around the back of the chair on which the prisoner sat. Madden slowly walked to his seat across from Utter, sat down, and opened his notebook to begin the interview.

"Mr. Utter," Madden began, "I have interviewed both Randy Yao, the chief of security at the Rendezvous Resort in Jackson, Wyoming, and Cameron Jefferson, your partner in the kidnapping of U.S. Senator Jeremy Carson. In addition to the kidnapping, Mr. Utter, I am aware that you skipped out on your probation just over a month ago. No matter how you might want to look at it, you are going to be spending a very long time in prison. I would like you to share with me your perspective of the kidnapping."

Utter sat still and did not move. His eyes stared straight ahead, directly at Madden, without blinking for several seconds. Madden met the stare and did not look away, recognizing Utter's play at control. Finally, Utter blinked and dropped his gaze to the tabletop in front of him. Several more seconds passed in silence. Madden settled in to wait and let the silence weigh on the prisoner.

Utter shuffled his feet on the floor and began to speak. His perspective collaborated what Madden had learned from Jefferson earlier, which meant he would not need to spend additional time backtracking their stories to identify which was closer to the factual information. As Utter drew to a close, Madden leaned forward and asked, "Who contacted you in the first place?"

"Not saying."

"Mr. Utter, you're going down for this kidnapping. Do you really want to be the only fall guy? You know the others, when apprehended, will not be so nice to you. Why should you and Jefferson be the only ones doing time? You might as well take your accomplices down with you, too."

"Yeah, I guess so," admitted the prisoner after several seconds. "When I was still in Utah and reporting to my PO, I got a call from a guy I knew in the joint. Aaron Donatelle. We'd talked before about the war in Iraq and thought it was stupid. A real waste. He said he was in a group trying to help out the prisoners in Guantanamo. Donatelle told me if I helped his group I'd be in line for some sweet cash. Hell, you do time, you don't get no good paying jobs."

"So, what did Donatelle say you would have to do?"

"He said he'd bring me some information if I'd work with the group. Shit. No job. No smell of anything that would pay good money so I said ok. Three days later, I met him in Salt Lake City at a bar just off the strip downtown. We had some brews and then he pulls an envelope out of his coat. He opened it and slid a photo across the table to me, some guy in a suit, and told me it's a senator from Idaho by the name of Carson. He said the guy's on some terrorism committee and they're responsible for a lot of the stuff in Guantanamo. He told me that he'd have everything lined up so I'd just have to get a guy to help me get the senator. I asked him how much was in it for me, and he wrote something on the envelope: one hundred thousand dollars." Utter leaned back his head and laughed. "Shit! One hundred thousand dollars! Man, can you imagine what a hundred grand would do for me?"

Madden nodded, not necessarily in agreement but to encourage Utter to continue. "That is a lot of cash, Mr. Utter. Please, go on."

Biting on his upper lip slightly, Utter thought through the timeframe of events. "He said he'd give me fifty grand more for my "assistant." Then I asked what I had to do, and he told me I only had to bring the senator to him. Seemed pretty easy. He said they'd take care of the hotel's cameras. No one'd see us. I asked where we had to take the guy, and he said Butte. No way I wanted to drive someone that far when I knew feds and cops would be swarming the highways looking for the guy. I told him that, and he just laughed and said I was being stupid. He said fly him. That was even more stupid I said. Who the hell was going to fly the plane? He pulled out a piece of paper and handed it to me. Cameron Jefferson's name, address, and phone number were on it. I knew him but I couldn't see him flying no goddam plane with those kinda goods. I looked at Donatelle, and he was laughing at me. Must've thought I was pretty dumb, I guess. I said Jefferson wouldn't fly him even though I knew he did fly sometimes. Donatelle just laughed again and said he was sure Jefferson could find someone who would be an innocent pilot to deliver a cargo for him.

"I asked who was in Donatelle's group, and he mentioned Ahmad. He said he'd lived in Afghanistan and fought in Pakistan. He said the group would use the senator to make sure the U.S. would quit mistreating the prisoners in Guantanamo and would release the prisoners being held there."

"So you agreed and set up the deal with Jefferson?" pitched in Madden.

"Yeah. We got the senator, took him to a junkyard where I knew the owner was out of town, and called my contact."

"Do you have that number still?" asked Madden.

"Naw. They gave me a disposable phone with that number already in it. Then we went to the airport, threw him into the cargo of a plane, and flew to Butte. Donatelle and one of his group met us and took the guy. Donatelle gave me a bag with the money for Jefferson and me. Then he gave me money to pay the pilot. We came back here, and I gave the money to Jefferson. He said he was going fishing for a while so I was getting ready to disappear when I got nabbed because of a damned taillight out."

Unfortunately, as Madden realized, the disposable phone had been destroyed and discarded with no way to retrieve that pre-programmed number. More questions and answers did not shed any additional useful light on the matter, and Madden gathered his notes and thanked Utter for his information. After the prisoner exited down the hall, Madden stopped at the desk where Officer Sarah was sitting. She had finished the stenograph entries. She looked up and smiled. "All through, Steve?"

"Yes, Sarah, and it was helpful."

"Good, I'm glad. The CD from the first interview is already cut, and as Chief Morris instructed, I made a second copy to go to the Jackson sheriff's office. I'll have both transcripts ready before you leave in the morning along with the CDs."

"I really appreciate your work, Sarah. I know it means your putting in a lot of overtime. Thank you."

"You're welcome. Good luck with your case, Steve. If I can help in any way, let me know." Sarah smiled, stood, and reached out her hand.

Taking her hand in a thank you, Madden expressed again his gratitude. Then he went down the stairs, thanked Chief Morris for his cooperation, and walked to his hotel room. After putting his notebook in his room, he decided to go for a walk around town to stretch his legs and think through the happenings of the day. A half hour later, he walked back into his room. He changed clothes and, after dinner at a local steakhouse, retired to his room and watched some television before turning out the light and drifting off into a deep sleep.

At eight o'clock sharp, a patrol car pulled up in front of the hotel, and Steve rose from his seat in the lobby, waved good-bye to the desk clerk, and walked to the car. As he sat in the passenger seat, the uniformed officer behind the wheel introduced himself as Luke Atkinson. The two shook hands as Madden countered by introducing himself. Atkinson picked up a large manila envelope on the seat and handed it to Madden. "This is your copy of the interview CDs and the typed manuscripts. Sarah said you'd be expecting them."

Steve Madden took a few seconds to look inside the envelope and confirmed that there were two CDs and two sets of manuscripts, one for each interview he had conducted the previous day. He withdrew a note written in a very feminine script that read, "Steve— I have sent duplicates of both CDs and manuscripts to Sheriff Kyler Mickelson in Jackson, Wyoming. If you need any further assistance, please let me know. A pleasure to work with you. Sincerely, Sarah Pintella."

Madden replaced the note into the envelope and tucked it into a pouch on the side of his bag which now lay on the seat between Atkinson and himself. As he finished his storing, the car was pulling through the gate at the Twin Falls airfield and moving toward the private aircraft side of the tarmac. Directly ahead with engines idling stood the Bureau's regional jet aircraft, waiting for his arrival. Another stepping stone crossed in the stream, he thought as the car came to a halt. Kyler Michelson certainly had a way of describing the process in solving crime.

"Thanks, Luke, for the ride. Take care."

The officer waved and did a U turn to exit the airfield. Madden, taking bag in hand, jogged up the exposed steps of the jet aircraft. As soon as he was inside the cabin, an attendant pushed a button and the staircase once again took on the role as exterior door. The jet began its roll to the end of the runway and then lifted off into the bright blue, cloudless winter sky over Twin Falls and began its journey to the Mining City.

CHAPTER NINETEEN

Madden placed a call to Jim Addis as the aircraft soared above the thin layer of clouds speeding toward Butte. "Hey, Jim. I'm sure you received the memo and video from DC earlier today."

"Yeah, I did, Steve. What the heck's going on, anyway?"

"I finished interrogating the two suspected kidnappers, and their stories pretty much match. What I find interesting is that the contact for one of the two was in Butte. I'm on my way up there as we speak. Can you call contact O'Reilly and O'Billovich? See if they know the name Aaron Donatelle. Sounds like he's a member of a terrorist sleeper cell that may have located in Butte."

"Wow! I don't mean to question you, Steve, but are you sure of that?"

"I'm pretty sure. Donatelle made the contact with the major kidnapper, Roger Utter, and from what Utter says, Donatelle's group wanted Carson to influence the government's treatment of the prisoners at Guantanamo. The leader's a guy named Ahmad. It would seem very possible that the Ahmad Hassan last known to be in Canada has moved his operations into the U.S. His known history would certainly make him a primary suspect."

"The last part does, Steve. "That might well be Ahmad Rahman Hassan, and our reports list him as a leader of a sleeper cell."

"Affirmative. That is the only name I keep coming up with. At any rate, see if anything in Butte might indicate their presence. Why would the kidnappers fly Carson to Butte in the middle of the night? Well, "middle of the night" makes sense. But why Butte? And where in Butte?"

"There's an awful lot of land around here, Steve, as you know. There have got to be thousands of isolated cabins out there, not to mention abandoned mine openings. That said, I'll contact the DA and the sheriff and see if they can come up with anything. I'll also contact Bill Marks in Helena and have him check on a statewide basis for you. What's your TOA, Steve?"

Madden looked at his watch; it was eight twenty-five. "We're about ten minutes out of Twin Falls so I think we can be on the ground at Bert Mooney by nine thirty, depending on winds, traffic, and so on. Can you arrange to meet me there?"

"For sure! I'll be there with the car. Look forward to having you back here, guy. I'd say I missed you, but that'd be too mushy for you."

Madden heard a belly laugh from his friend and partner. "Yeah, right. See you in about an hour." Madden disconnected and then called his office in DC. He heard the phone ring twice and then a woman's voice answered, "Federal Bureau of Investigation, Agent Madden's office. Sandy speaking"

"Sandy," began Madden, recognizing the voice of Sandy Manion, one of the secretaries in the pool, "Steve Madden. I received the video and the memo that were sent to me in Twin Falls yesterday. I finished my suspect interviews and am headed toward Butte right now. I'm hoping to have some information on the whereabouts of Senator Carson by tomorrow morning."

"I'll make sure the director gets your message, Mr. Madden. Anything else?"

"No, that's it for now, Sandy. Say hi for me to the staff. Hopefully, Jim and I will be headed back there in a few days. Both of our cases seem to be headed toward that proverbial light at the end of the tunnel."

"Okay, have a good flight and you and Jim stay safe."

"Will do. Bye, Sandy." Madden hung up and sat back in his swivel seat, turning to look out to the mountains below, glistening from the sun reflecting off the snowy peaks. Nature at its best in untouched beauty.

Agent Madden had just finished a cup of coffee and picked up a magazine when the attendant came forward from the rear of the cabin and informed the lone passenger that the pilot was beginning the descent into Butte and that Agent Addis awaited Madden at the airport. He thanked the attendant and gave him his ceramic coffee mug. Then he went back to window gazing as the plane descended into the valley holding the city of Butte.

He felt a slight bump as the rubber tires made their initial contact with the ice-cold asphalt on the runway, then lift off the surface a few inches and come back down. This time the tires were spinning at nearly the same speed the jet was traveling so the next contact with the runway was much smoother, and the pilot gently brought the white bird to taxi speed, turned off the runway, and taxied to the hanger area just beyond the Butte/Silver Bow Flight School building and fuel center. Approaching a large white hanger, the jet slowed to a stop, engines whining as they were shut down. The door once again became stairs, and Madden unbuckled his seatbelt, took his luggage from the storage closet by the stairway, and trotted down the steps, looking for the designated car and Jim Addis. Addis was standing by a white Dodge Durango that he had rented and started walking toward Madden as he descended the steps.

"Hiya, Steve," called out Addis, reaching his partner and taking his bag. "Good to see you."

"Good to be back here as well," said Madden. The two agents walked to the SUV, its tailgate open. Addis laid his partner's suitcase on the deck and closed the rear gate. Both climbed in, and Addis began driving toward the main terminal parking area. Madden pointed to the terminal and asked his partner to pull into a parking place near the front door. The two men exited the vehicle and as they were walking in, Madden apprised Addis of the reason for stopping. They entered the terminal and, after locating a directory, went to the security office and entered. Madden introduced himself and Addis to the administrative assistant sitting at the front desk. He then asked to speak with the officer in charge. The middle-aged woman escorted them to a conference room at the back of the security office suite and told them to be seated and that Officer Wagner would joint them shortly.

A tall, balding man, appearing to be in his late fifties, wearing a light gray uniform shirt with the Bert Mooney Airport Security patch on one shoulder and an American Flag patch displayed on the opposite shoulder, came in.

"Darrell Wagner, security chief," the man said as he approached the two seated agents. Both men rose and shook hands, introducing themselves one at a time.

"What can I do for the FBI?" Wagner inquired of the two. Madden then gave him a brief history of the case, highlighting the senator's abduction and the likelihood he had been flown into Butte on a private aircraft. As luck would have it, the chief had been on duty both the Tuesday night Senator Carson was taken captive and the night following. Madden requested a copy of the surveillance videos for the Wednesday night, matched with the arrival time of the private aircraft from Jackson, Wyoming. "That might give us the vehicle identity and maybe a license plate number." Madden also requested copies of the video taken that night for the parking lot entry and exit and the hanger areas as well. Unfortunately, according to Wagner, they made no surveillance recordings of the hanger areas because non-commercial flights rarely arrive or depart during the nighttime hours. "Whatever you can get me would be most appreciated," said Madden. "Can the copies be delivered to me at the Finlen where we're set up?"

"That would not be a problem," answered Wagner. "We'll have copies to you this afternoon. It is just a matter of contacting the flight desk to ascertain the exact arrival of the flight and then run through the videos, selecting a time-frame a couple of hours before and a couple of hours following that arrival time. I'll make sure you have views from the camera over the terminal lobby doors as well as from the camera that's positioned above the only gate your suspects could enter and exit through. That should give you a good view of the vehicle, from the front, side, and rear." Madden shook hands with the security officer, and then he and Addis returned to the Durango.

Addis followed the same route from the airport to the Finlen Hotel in uptown Butte that the two had taken upon their first arrival in the Mining City and informed his partner during the drive that he had been able to obtain the same room for Madden that he had occupied prior to departing for Wyoming. Driving into the underground parking garage, the two exited and entered the hotel lobby where they took the elevator to the fourth floor and headed for the rooms that were reserved for them. Pausing outside Madden's door, the first of the three rooms, they agreed to meet in Room 456 in fifteen minutes.

In 456, Madden quickly spread out maps that showed the cities of Jackson, Wyoming; Idaho Falls and Twin Falls, Idaho; and one with the states of Idaho, Montana, and Wyoming. Next to the larger area map, he laid a street map of Butte. The two then retraced the steps of both of the missing agents, Williams and Stephens, and the trail taken by Utter and Jefferson in their abduction of Senator Carson. Somehow, although they had no tangible reason for their belief, both federal agents felt that more than coincidence played into both trails ending in Butte.

Addis pointed to the city map of Butte and showed Madden where the suspected house in which the black SUV had been parked and into which the black Ford Taurus that the missing FBI agents had been driving had entered, never again to be seen. Pointing at the dot representing the residence, Addis said, "This is the house on Woolman. Just behind it," he moved his index finger just up from the dot on the map, "is abandoned mine land. Specifically, it is the mine yard of the Stewart, sometimes called Steward, Mine. From what I've learned, the mine was one of the most successful copper and silver mines for almost a century. It was one of the deepest in Butte, reaching a depth of over forty-four hundred feet. But, interestingly, the mineshafts served more than the Stewart Mine; near the three-thousand-foot level, the shaft of the Stewart connected to a horizontal shaft of the nearby Kelley Mine. The Kelley had a more powerful lift engine, and the cars, called skips, in the Kelley were larger than those in the Stewart and, therefore, held more ore." Addis paused and let his index finger slowly move from the mark that indicated the head frame of the Stewart Mine back to the residence on Woolman.

"Steve, this whole area here," Addis tapped the area around the location of the residence, "is honeycombed with horizontal and vertical mine shafts. Almost all of them are now filled with water. Water, which I am told, is loaded with copper, arsenic, cadmium, and zinc, among other things, making it highly toxic to people and animals. Contact can cause severe chemical burns. Eventually, the toxins eat away whatever falls into it; anything—metal, wood, fabric, even human flesh and bones—that falls in disappears forever. The same thing happens with the Canada geese that inadvertently land in the Berkeley open pit mine. The birds that land there are usually found somewhere south of the city, killed by the contact with the toxic water. It would be a great way to get rid of items that could be handled easily. The only requirement would be to have access to a shaft. With active operations terminated within all these shafts, the pumps shut down, and the shafts completely filled with that same toxic water, no one will ever enter these shafts again, Steve." Addis's voice trailed off as the dark thought again crossed his mind—had the two missing FBI agents met their final destiny in such a place?

Addis finished his part of the discussion and then turned to his partner and asked him to review the missing senator case. Madden mulled Addis's comments over in his mind and then took the conversation to the map of Idaho, Montana, and Wyoming. "Senator Carson was in Jackson for a meeting and went missing Tuesday night after the last session ended. Latent fingerprints in a storage room and on some pieces of broken glass from a table that had been in the senator's room led us to two smalltime operators, Roger Utter and Cameron Jefferson. Interviews with the security staff led to Randy Yao, the chief of hotel security, as the one who edited the tapes. Utter and Jefferson identified the pilot as a Henry Butler of Idaho Falls, and the PD in Twin Falls is checking him out right now.

"Then there is the name of Aaron Donatelle who was the contact for Utter and, according to Utter, was or is a member of a group that is protesting the treatment of prisoners in Guantanamo. During the time I was in Twin Falls I saw the video that Carson had done for the group. I think you saw the same video as it came out from Washington." Addis nodded.

"Up until I saw the video, I was thinking maybe this kidnapping was similar to the Iranian kidnappings at the end of Jimmy Carter's presidency. No reason or demand was ever made, and when Ronald Reagan took office, the kidnapped victims were released. That all changed with the video, as you know. Utter's comments and his mentioning of Donatelle and of someone named Ahmad prompted me to have you contact law enforcement up here. Hopefully, we'll hear from those folks soon, as well as a report on Henry Butler."

Madden then referred to a large map of the Bert Mooney Airport and indicated the main entry gate through which suspects would have to drive in order to go over to the hanger area located to the south of the main terminal area. Drawing his finger from the hanger area, through the main terminal parking area, and out the exit road to Harrison Avenue, Madden theorized that cameras above the terminal building and at the gate of the parking area should give some opportunity to identify the vehicle and obtain a license number from either the front or rear plate.

The two discussed their cases for a while longer and were interrupted by a knock on the door. Opening it, Addis was greeted by the bellhop from the hotel. Holding out a plastic case, the young man explained, "This came for Mr. Madden. It's from the security office at the airport." Addis accepted the case, reached into his pocket, withdrew a couple of bills, which he handed to the bellhop as a tip, and thanked him for the delivery. The case contained two DVDs; one was labeled "Terminal Camera," and the second "Exit Gate Camera." Each DVD was labeled with the captured time from 10:00 p.m. until 2:00 a.m.

Madden placed one into the tray of a DVD player, pushed the button to close the tray, and turned on the television on the top of the same stand on which the DVD player was sitting. After waiting a few seconds the video began, displaying the main parking lot at Bert Mooney Airport. Madden picked up the remote and depressed the fast forward button. As the minutes flew by quickly, many cars, vans, hotel shuttles, and small buses came and went. Occasionally, a car or truck drove toward the flight school and fueling area. At 11:38, according to the imbedded clock on the screen, a dark SUV entered through the main entrance gate. Madden paused the playback and pushed the zoom button, zeroing in on the front license plate. There wasn't one! "Maybe the back plate will show when they leave," Madden said, starting the play again. The vehicle turned to its right slightly and drove toward the hanger area. Its dark tinted windows revealed nothing inside. The two agents continued to view the scene on the monitor in front of them. At precisely 12:52 a.m., the dark SUV once again came into view, this time from the camera's left. Crossing the main lot, its driver turned west and drove the vehicle down the road toward Harrison Avenue. Again Madden paused the video, pressed the zoom button until the license plate area came into a close-up view.

"Damn it!" exclaimed Madden. "They took both plates off the vehicle. The only thing we get is knowing it is a dark-colored newer model GMC Tahoe with limo-black window tinting on all windows but the windshield." Obviously, the senior agent was not pleased. He pushed play once more, and the vehicle began moving away from the terminal and finally out of sight as it turned right to head toward the uptown area of Butte.

Madden pressed the eject button, removed the DVD, and replaced it with the second disk. Repeating the process, Madden slowed the play mode, and both men watched intently as the vehicles paraded in and then left the airport property. At 11:38 p.m., the dark-colored SUV entered view from under the gate camera's view and turned right, going south to the hanger area. That was a good sign as the time stamp on both videos were synchronized. The vehicle reappeared at 12:52, approaching the terminal parking from the camera's right, the south, and slowly moved toward the exit gate. The camera's position aimed down at the vehicles passing from the lot toward Harrison Avenue. As the dark SUV approached, a flash of light from one of the parking lot tower poles entered the windshield at an angle that highlighted, for a very brief instant, the face of the passenger in the front seat.

Madden pressed the pause button on the remote, and slowly backing up the playback, he stopped the frame when he could see the lighted face inside the SUV. "Well, well," he exclaimed, "maybe, if we're lucky, we'll get this guy's face!" He then connected a laptop computer to the machine and typed a series of keys, entering a command. The computer screen blinked, and the screen shot from the DVD appeared. A few more commands, and the image was enlarged and enhanced to be more identifiable. Madden then saved the image to his hard drive and followed that by sending the image to the computer's printer. The agent repeated the same process to print out a photo of the SUV. He handed the images to Addis and sent an electronic copy of the image to Butte/Silver Bow Sheriff Ken O'Billovich with a request to have his officers take the photos and see if anyone could identify the person. Madden then exited the program on his laptop, ejected the DVD, and turned off the player and the television set.

"I think, Jim, that you and I should visit your elderly couple on Woolman."

Woolman was only about ten blocks from the hotel, and it did not take long to make the trip in the Durango. Approaching the door of the couple's house, Addis knocked and waited. After several moments, the door opened. Addis introduced himself and then introduced Madden. Producing the image from Madden's printer he asked if the man was someone they recognized. The elderly gentleman couldn't say, he thought the man looked familiar but wasn't sure. When Madden asked who he thought it might be, the man told him that he thought the man might live in the house down the street. Then a second image of the SUV was shown, and he nodded that it looked like the one he had seen driving on his street.

Addis thanked the man, and he and Madden drove back to their hotel. Along the way, Madden called the office of Ken Morris in Twin Falls.

"Chief Morris," the voice answered.

"Ken, Steve Madden here. Just calling to see if you were able to gain anything on Butler, the pilot."

"As a matter of fact we did get something back from the Idaho Falls PD, Steve. According to an interview with Henry Butler, the officer indicated that they are convinced he had no knowledge of the kidnapping, that he was only a contracted pilot to carry freight from Jackson to Butte for the two men. The police over there don't think he had anything to do with the kidnapping or knew what his cargo was."

"Ok, thanks, Ken. I'm not surprised after talking with Jefferson and Utter."

The conversation ended, and the two arrived at the Finlen and parked the rental car. As they entered the lobby, the desk clerk waved them over and handed Madden a special overnight delivery envelope.

Once in Room 456, Madden opened the envelope, noting it had come from his D.C. office. Withdrawing some typed sheets, he summarized the contents. "Our office has done the background checking we'd requested, Jim." He then read directly from the printed page. "Name: Ahmad Rahman Hassan. Last known location: Calgary, Alberta, Canada." Madden paused and then continued, referring back to the delivered pages as he needed. "This has to be the same as the Ahmad mentioned by Utter. The information cites his being raised in Michigan by both parents who had emigrated from Iraq in the mid-1970's. Ahmad received his college education at the University of Michigan. Following his graduation in 1995, he went overseas to work as a construction foreman in Pakistan, where he became a member of a political activist group. From the time his construction job ended in 1999 until now, he periodically appeared only to disappear without any trace. Many of his contacts are known to be involved in al-Quaeda. It is believed that he has been a member of a group that swore to bring the United States to its knees politically and to drive all Americans out of Iraq, Afghanistan, and Pakistan. The message with the analysis says that Hassan more than likely has become an al-Quaeda cell leader and that is most likely why he's staying 'under the radar' of the government and military."

"Jim, I think that's who has Carson. It would be a huge coincidence that someone with the same first name of Ahmad had kidnapped a U.S. senator to pressure the government to release prisoners in Guantanamo and it not be Hassan."

"I think that makes sense, Steve. We know from what DC says that Hassan is a likely leader of a terrorist sleeper cell, and the demands that Carson states on the tape would fall in line with his purpose."

"Jim, do you suppose the place on Woolman, where you think Williams and Stephens might have been taken, is the same place where Carson was taken?"

"The evidence and the information from the couple who live up there certainly suggests it."

Madden looked for names of any other people who were either known or thought to associate with Hassan. His half-hour search of government files came up with nothing. Finally, he exited the connection with the Bureau's computer, logged off the computer, and closed the cover to the laptop. It was just after six o'clock.

Turning to Addis he said, "Let's go get something to eat and relax. Tomorrow maybe we can get some information for O'Billovich." Addis agreed and the two went to their respective rooms to clean up and meet for dinner. At seven-ten, Addis knocked on the door of his partner. Madden opened the door, room key in hand and stepped out into the hall. The two walked to the rental car and then drove down the hill from the uptown area to a small restaurant called The Lamplighter.

"I recommended this place," began Addis, "for its prime rib. Simply super. I came here one time with Dan O'Reilly while you were in Jackson. It's run by a couple, and they take great pride in everything about the place."

The two entered the restaurant and, since the tables were all in use, took a seat in the lounge area, ordered a couple of drinks and relaxed. They gave in to small talk to ease the stress and tension from working their cases. Forty-five minutes later, a young waitress approached and said their table was ready. They followed her into the dining room and were seated. The usual "Butte starters" were brought: sweet potato salad, spaghetti, and a relish tray accompanying a tossed salad. Addis and Madden looked over the menu and both settled on prime rib, queen cut. When the platter arrived, it held a baked potato with all the trimmings and a huge cut of meat with three ribs. The lawmen, though hungry, could not make much of a dent in the volume of food before them. They eventually finished their respective dinners, leaving most of the "starter" items behind and even declining a dessert. Drinking a cup of coffee, they enjoyed ribbing each other and talking of well-deserved vacations that remained, unfortunately, very much in the future. About nine-thirty, they arrived back at their rooms; they chatted for a few minutes and then bid each other good evening.

"Tomorrow," said Madden, "let's contact O'Billovich and O'Reilly and see if they got any info on the car Williams and Stephens were driving or an ID on the photo we sent them."

"I agree with that," replied Addis. "The statements from Jefferson and Utter during your interviews connect them with Donatalle and Ahmad. Going from that info to what we just received from DC gives us another point, and the flight data that matches the arrival and departure of the SUV is another stepping stone. If that vehicle's actually the same one I've been tracking, it's going to be really interesting. You said Utter was into the drug circles, and even Jefferson had been nailed for using once. Then the chief of security at the resort got connected with known drug kingpins who we've identified as having probable suspects in running, supplying, and selling drugs into Canada. Here in Montana, we know that Stephens and Williams were investigating the possible running of drugs from the south through Butte and on up north into Canada, so that piece seems to fit. The other day I was speaking with the narcotics division chief in Missoula, and he told me that a major drug bust in Seattle and Everett, Washington, identified the trafficking as being carried north and south along Interstate 5 and east on Interstate 90."

"There's a pretty good chance that the two cases are related, Jim. Guess tomorrow we'll see if we can fit more pieces into the puzzle. Or, as Kyler Mickelson would say, take one more stepping stone over the stream."

With that, the two entered their own rooms for the night, agreeing to meet at six for a joint morning run.

Madden decided it was too late to call home and instead popped open his computer, as he had every day, and sent Lee a message, ending with, "I love you, Lee. Hope to be home soon!" After getting ready for bed, he turned out the light and drifted off to a sound sleep

CHAPTER TWENTY

The two agents arrived in the lobby within seconds of each other, both dressed and ready for their run in the brisk winter air of Butte along a route they had mapped out earlier that morning. Heading out, they ran west on Broadway to Montana Avenue and then turned right, heading uphill for about one-half mile to a short street, Ruby, that cut back to the east. The street dead-ended at a cyclone style fence that marked an abandoned mine yard. Taking another right turn, the runners began to descend, now following Main Street. As they continued to run, they came to Woolman Street and took a left, again heading in an easterly direction.

About a hundred yards after turning onto Woolman, they ran past the vacated mine yard punctuated by a tall metal frame that had a large pulley-looking wheel on a platform just below the top of the rusting I-beam construction. Addis pointed at the object and informed his companion that it was the Stewart Mine head frame. Madden nodded, and they continued to run east, reaching the dead-end of Woolman. There on their left was the house where the elderly couple had said they thought the black SUV had gone. Although the house appeared to be an older home, it was obvious that a doublewide garage had been added to the west end of the home.

As when the two had run past the head frame, Addis nodded toward the house. Madden glanced at it as he ran past, making note of the location of the front entrance, located about a third of the way between the garage and the east end of the house It had two large windows, one on either side of the door, and a smaller one toward the east end. Madden also made a mental note of the fact that a mine yard extended along the back of the property as well as in a much larger fenced-off area just to the northeast of the house. The larger area he remembered from the map Addis belonged to the Mountain Consolidated Mine. The head frame rose over 120 feet into the brisk morning sky and had a construction similar to the Stewart with I-beams riveted together with batten plates that were in turn set on footings of poured concrete. The mine had a hoist, installed in the late 1920s, that could haul up several miners at a time from over a mile beneath the surface of the earth.

The runners continued their run around the corner onto Arizona Street and then south to the main east-west street in uptown Butte, Park Street. Turning east, they followed Park as it paralleled the fence line surrounding the famous Berkeley Pit. Rather than following Park all the way down, they exited back to the west again, turning onto Mercury Street that led them back into the business district to Main Street. Turning up Main Street, they arrived at Broadway and, turning east, were soon back at the Finlen Hotel. Once they had turned onto Park, they had picked up the pace considerably, running at a five-and-a-half-minute-per-mile pace. They slowed to a walk a block from the hotel, and upon reaching the hotel, they stepped into the parking garage entry and did their post-run stretching routine. Then they walked up the stairs to the fourth floor and down the hall to their rooms.

"How about breakfast at the Gold Rush Casino?" Addis asked Madden.

"Sounds good to me, Jim. See you in about thirty minutes."

After walking to the twenty-four-hour casino and restaurant and having a hearty breakfast, the two returned to the hotel and entered Room 456. Addis said he would call Sheriff O'Billovich to check on the junkyards in the Butte area, and Madden said he would contact the county district attorney, Dan O'Reilly.

Madden completed his call with the DA and looked over the notes he had jotted down during the conversation. Addis was still writing as he listened to the person on the other end of his call. Finally, after thanking the person, he hung up, added a few more notes, and then turned in his chair, notepad in hand, to face Madden.

"What did the sheriff's office have to say, Jim?"

"Might have found something in Anaconda. According to the owner of a scrap yard there, a guy brought in a flatbed truck with a car body on it that he wanted cash for. The scrap guy said the guy claimed falling rocks had destroyed the car when it was parked at a private mining claim site. The body had been destroyed beyond repair, but the interior seemed okay, and the engine looked to be in extremely good shape. The scrap yard owner didn't buy the guy's story, but he said he'd resell the engine and what parts he could. The other parts were beat up, dented, had metal tears in the sheets of metal. He's already removed the wheels, engine, sterring wheel, seats, radio, and other usable parts and was going to crush the rest of the car, but he has agreed to hold off until we examine it." "Anything on the photo yet?"

"The sheriff said that his staff is continuing to go door-to-door with the photo today. He thought that businesses might be a good place, like grocery stores, drug stores, hardware stores, and lumberyards. He'll call as soon as they get a hit."

"Good. I talked with O'Reilly. He's touched base with the state's AG and indicated that Marks had told him Johnson has received threats against her life as well as her family for uncovering the identity of terrorists. The threats seemed to have begun about two weeks ago and have been pretty steady in the form of untraceable e-mail messages and telephone calls made from disposable and untraceable cell phones. That's about it. Nothing on Ahmad Hassan, although Marks did tell O'Reilly that they'd received at least one report that he'd come over the border and was somewhere in northern Montana. For that reason, they're monitoring the area around Johnson's house, and they've put up a blockade just outside the drive to her country home.

"But that car—doesn't it seem a bit odd that those metal parts weren't dropped down one of those shafts?"

"I wondered the same thing, Steve. But how would they explain to neighbors that a vehicle that came there disappeared without being driven off? In any case, given the report from the junkyard in Anaconda, I think we need to drive out there and check what pieces we can."

"I'm with you, Jim. Let's go."

The two picked up their overcoats, went down the stairs to the parking garage, and hopped in the Dodge Durango, Addis again at the wheel. Using the built-in GPS, he followed the directions to the junkyard in Anaconda.

Forty-five minutes later, Addis drove through a chain link gate and into a lot filled with car parts and sorted by fenders, tires, rims, doors, and just about any other part one might need. Stopping at the office of the junkyard, both men exited their vehicle. An overweight man with a gray beard extending to his chest and graying hair on top pulled back into a ponytail stepped out of the office shack to greet them. "Can I help you gentlemen?" he asked.

"I'm Steve Madden, FBI, and this is my partner, Jim Addis." Both agents flipped their wallets to exhibit their gold badges and photo identification cards.

"Chris Jenkins," the man returned after looking at the identifications. "I presume you are not here to buy some used parts?" The statement was more of a question than a simple statement.

"We are following up a contact one of the detectives from the Butte/Silver Bow sheriff's office had with you yesterday. Do you recall that officer being here?"

"Yes, sir, I do."

"Then you are aware of what we want to see. You had mentioned that some of the parts were in pretty good shape and good enough for resale. Please show us those parts."

Jenkins complied and, after picking up a clipboard and looking through the list of parts that were handwritten onto the sheets of paper, led the agents to several different areas of the yard. Each time he identified a part as being from the flatbed truck, the agents would carefully inspect it, looking for anything that might help with their investigation of the missing agents. After two hours of looking, moving, and examining, and in some cases photographing, the agents returned to the office area with the owner.

"Ok, Mr. Jenkins, that takes care of the parts you wanted to set aside for sale. You also indicated some of the pieces were not fit for recycling as useable parts so they were being crushed for sale as metal scrap and recycling. Is that right?"

"Yes, sir."

"Would you please take us to the remaining parts?"

The owner led the two agents to another part of the junkyard with a crushing machine and, beside it, a rather large pile of parts. Jenkins pointed to the pile and said, "Here's what's left from the flatbed truck."

"Thank you, Mr. Jenkins. We'll take it from here. If we need anything from you, we'll come and get you."

Jenkins shrugged, "Ok," he said and turned to walk toward his office.

Removing each piece and carefully examining took hours of tedious and painstaking work, to say the least. Around mid-afternoon, Madden called Addis over to where he was kneeling, bending over a badly bent and torn piece of metal covered with foam and a black fabric. "Jim, I think this is part of the dashboard!"

Addis came over, kneeling down to look where Madden was pointing with his pen. Taking out a pocket flashlight, he directed it at a piece of metal or plastic that had some kind of embossed letting on it. "Steve, this is the VIN number! Or, at least part of it." Addis read off what numbers and letters he could read and Madden wrote them down, repeating each for accuracy. Madden then took a roll of bright red tape from his pocket and placed it on the part, numbering it and then recording it in his notebook. He stepped back, took a photo of the pile of parts, and then again kneeling, took additional photos of the part, showing the partial VIN number.

The two then resumed their search. Another hour passed with nothing significant showing up. After searching for another thirty minutes Madden again called his partner over. "What do you make of this, Jim?" Madden was pointing at a piece of material caught between two pieces of metal. Addis looked at the fabric.

"It can't be fabric from the upholstery," he stated. "The upholstery was grey and black, and this piece is blue, and on top of that it looks satiny, definitely not a fabric you'd find in vehicle upholstery. Let's see if we can get it free and have it run through the lab in Butte." Madden nodded and together they tried lifting, sliding or moving pieces around it but it was not going to release the entire piece of fabric. Having been able to free up a little more of the fabric, Addis took out a small pocketknife and cut the fabric as close to the metal as possible. Then he placed the piece of fabric in a zip-lock evidence bag after recording the location of the piece on film.

By five o'clock, the two agents had not recovered any other evidence and, after thanking the junkyard owner for his cooperation, instructed him to not crush or get rid of any part from the flatbed truck until told the pieces were released by authorities. Jenkins agreed to comply.

The two drove back to Butte and stopped by the sheriff's office. They dropped off the fabric piece and requested the office to run a DNA test on it, sending the results to the FBI headquarters in Washington, DC. Then they gave the partial vehicle identification number to the officer and asked that a search be done as well as contacting the rental office in Bozeman for comparison to the vehicle that was rented to the missing FBI agents.

Back at the hotel, Addis suggested that they dine at the Bronx Lounge restaurant, a long-time favorite among Butte residents and less than a block from the hotel. Madden eagerly agreed to try a new local favorite, and off they went to experience another memorable dinner.

Taking their time with a couple of pre-dinner drinks and house-special hors-d'oeuvres, they got serious with a stomach packing dinner. Each pushed the caloric envelope a bit more than either would normally do with a dish of spumoni ice cream. Feeling filled from the meal and satisfied with the progress on their cases, the two lingered a little longer over an after dinner drink.

A leisurely walk took them around several of the uptown blocks and businesses, and they paused to look through the open door into the fabled M & M Café, which had stood in the exact place since 1890. Known for allowing illegal card playing and serving delicious fried steaks, the wooden bar had indentations worn deep from the number of arms that had rested on it while enjoying food and drink. They casually meandered past other buildings, many of which had stood since the late 1800s. The perfect complement to a filling meal, the enjoyable walk kept them outside until almost nine thirty. As they entered the lobby of the Finlen, the desk clerk hailed them and waved them over to the registration desk.

"Mr. Addis, Mr. Madden, I hope you had a good dinner." Both of the men nodded that they had indeed. The clerk continued, "While you were out I took a call for you." He turned and removed a folded piece of paper from a mailbox slot. The clerk turned back to the federal men and handed the message toward Addis. Jim unfolded the note and read it, and then he handed it to Madden, who read the message, which had been called in by an officer at the sheriff's office. The note read:

The partial VIN number you asked to have run through DMV matches the same series on the Ford Taurus rented in Butte to Phil Stephens. Though not a 100 percent match due to missing digits, it is likely that the auto parts located in Anaconda junkyard are that of the missing vehicle. Contact Sheriff O'Billovich with further instructions.

Madden folded the note and handed it to Addis. Their eyes met in a non-verbal confirmation of the foreboding implication. Phil Stephens and Brad Williams, the missing FBI agents, had indeed arrived in the Mining City. Two questions remained: Where were they and what happened to them?

Answers would have to wait until morning.

~ § ~

It seemed as though six o'clock came awfully fast to Madden. He rolled out of bed, called Addis, and then dressed in his running gear. The two ran for forty-five minutes before re-entering the hotel and stretching. They showered and dressed before meeting in the lobby at eight o'clock. Following a quick breakfast, they walked over to the sheriff's office and requested to see the sheriff. O'Billovich came out of his office and greeted the two, waving his arm to invite them to join him. As they walked to his office, O'Billovich asked his administrative assistant to bring each of his guests a cup of coffee.

Two cups of steaming black coffee arrived shortly, and the three men sipped from their ceramic mugs. Madden was the first to speak. "We know that in all likelihood the parts of vehicle we inventoried at the yard in Anaconda are parts of the rented car that Stephens and Williams drove. The sample of fabric that we brought in could add to that likelihood. Have you heard anything on the DNA?"

"Actually we have," returned O'Billovich. "I was going to call you guys just as you walked in here." The sheriff reached over to a note pad on his desk. "It's a preliminary finding, but according to the lab, the DNA on that scrap of material matches that of Brad Williams. The lab analysis concluded that the fabric is rayon and is from a dress shirt. We are waiting on confirmation as the lab here and the lab you boys have back East confer. If they concur, then it's pretty much a sure thing."

Madden and Addis went back to sipping their coffee and staring at the shimmering and steamy contents. Both of the agents shared the same thoughts, "What happened? Why?" and maybe the most important one of all, "Where are they now?"

Madden had one other question. "Ken, were your guys able to get any ID on the photo we sent over the other day?"

O'Billovich smiled and reached for another slip of the note pad. "Jerry Hocking, you remember him? He's my narc detective. Anyway, Jerry said one of his men came up with two people in the water department who recognized the person. They say without a doubt it is Raul Alkaheem. Alkaheem is, according to further search, a man in his mid-twenties, a student in mining technology at Montana Tech. I called the registrar's office late yesterday afternoon and was told that he's an honor student. At any rate, the guy bought a house at 565 East Woolman Street from Wayne Sullivan. Sullivan works for Pacific Power and Light. One of our guys is over at the Power Company's office to see how long Alkaheem has owned it and anything Sullivan may know about him. ."

The three visited for the better part of an hour before the agents got up to leave. As they made their way to the main door of the office, the administrative assistant, having transferred a call to the sheriff, called out to the agents to come back. They turned, somewhat surprised, and walked back to the sheriff's office where he was still on the phone. They waited patiently until he disconnected. Turning in his chair, O'Billovich said, "That was Jerry's guy who went to see Sullivan. Sullivan tells him that in addition to Raul Alkaheem, he knows that Alkaheem's cousin also lives there. The cousin's name is Anwar Ramana. Not sure what the cousin does. Sullivan didn't think he attended Montana Tech but wasn't sure about Butte Vo-Tech. Sullivan also said that he has been told by his former neighbors that at least two other men are seen coming and going on a somewhat regular basis. The neighbors are not too happy with the people Sullivan sold the house to from the sounds of it. When asked where the guys came from, he knew Alkaheem came to Butte from Iraq about four years ago. As for the cousin, Ramana, he thought he came from the Middle East somewhere but wasn't sure. Should be something in the immigration files on both of them, though."

"Thanks, Chief," Addis said. "This is a tremendous help. As you know, 565 East Woolman is where we think the car that Williams and Stephens were driving had been taken to and then from. I think we're getting close to a search warrant for that place."

"Let me know when you want it, and we'll get O'Reilly to obtain one for us."

The agents left and walked back to the hotel. They went back into the workroom, and Madden called the Immigration Office in Washington. After giving the names of the two young men, Raul Alkaheem and Anwar Ramana, to the clerk who had picked up, he was informed she would call back within fifteen minutes.

True to her word, she returned his call in fourteen minutes, saying she had some information regarding the two men he had inquired about. With that she began sharing the information displayed on her screen.

"Agent Madden, as you know because of terrorist activity and since prior to 9/11/2001, we keep historical records of immigrants to this country, in particular, immigrants from the Middle East. Our records show that Alkaheem lived in Iraq from birth, and during the U.S. military action, his father and a brother were both killed in fighting near Baghdad where they worked as stone masons. In interviews before he was allowed to enter the U.S., he indicated that he was extremely bitter and wanted to find a way to help his country once peace was obtained. For that reason he came to the United States and went to Butte, Montana, to enroll in the minerals and mining program at Montana Tech. It is one of the best in the country, and being a small school, it would be to his advantage." Madden typed the information into his laptop as the clerk gave it to him. Pausing, he asked about the man's cousin, Ramana.

"Yes, sir. According to our records he is Alkaheem's cousin. He was born in Pakistan, and his family moved to the United States in 1989 when Anwar was seven years of age. He is a naturalized citizen, and so we have kept in-depth records on him. Due to the recent terrorist alerts, we did conduct some investigation to identify any possible links to terrorists. So far none have been identified save one, that of a working partner in one of his businesses, doing drywall work for home and business construction in North Dakota and then in Great Falls, Montana."

"You said you have the business associate's name?"

"Yes, sir, one moment and I will get that for you." A pause of several seconds and then the bombshell of the day came through the cell phone. "Agent Madden, the associate's name is Aaron Donatelle."

"Are you certain of that name, Aaron Donatelle?"

"Yes, sir that is what our records indicate. Is there anything else I can help you with?"

"No, ma'am. That will be everything for right now. Thank you for your assistance."

Madden closed his cell phone, set it down on the table, and turned to Addis, who had been eavesdropping while his partner was on the phone. "So, Jim, the net grows tighter. Donatelle is the contact between Utter and the group leader who goes by the first name of Ahmad. I wonder…" A long pause followed as he rolled some ideas around in his mind. "I wonder if that is Ahmad Hassan." Is the terrorist sleeper cell here in Butte? They would be in the main thoroughfare for drug running to and from the West Coast as well as from Alberta, Canada south. It's out of the way, so activity wouldn't draw a lot of attention. It's almost a perfect setup for the cell, if it's here."

Addis leaned forward in his seat. "What's your call, boss?"

Madden thoughtfully rolled a pencil in his fingers, all the while looking at the map of the city. "I think … instead of waiting for a search warrant … I think we have enough to raid the residence. I don't know if our guys are there or if Senator Carson is there, but I think we have to go on the assumption that all three are there. Carson doesn't have a great deal of time left, if the kidnappers are going to follow through on their promise, and I don't think there's any question that they are deadly serious about the demands and their promise."

Addis offered, "I'll call O'Reilly's office and then O'Billovich to set up the raid."

"In the meantime I'll call DC and notify them of what we're up to. Let's have O'Billovich and his Tactical Response Team leaders meet us here, and we can go over the plan. In the meantime, Jim, let's see if we can get a blueprint of the house from city/county offices."

Addis nodded as he dialed the sheriff's office, making arrangements for the raid, and next called the DA and notified O'Reilly. Then he asked to be transferred to the city/county office that handled building permits, gave the address of the suspect residence, and asked to have the blueprint for the residence made available to them. Assured that it would not be a problem, Addis indicated he would pick up the copy within the hour. Hanging up, he told Madden he was going to the courthouse for the blueprint, and Madden nodded that he understood.

Madden continued to review the cases with his office in Washington, DC, describing what evidence they had and that they were planning a raid on the residence. They would be using local Butte/Silver Bow TRT members and would work cooperatively with the local sheriff and the district attorney. Having concluded his call, Madden walked over to the city map of Butte to look at the houses and areas around the targeted residence. They could not risk tipping off the suspected terrorists by evacuating the nearby homes, but they also could not place the neighboring residents in danger. The raid would have to take place quickly in order to minimize any injury or death to law officers and the terrorists' captives as well as the surrounding residents.

As Madden was evaluating the neighborhood around 565 East Woolman, Addis reappeared with the blueprint and related material for the residence. He unrolled the blueprint and both of the FBI agents stood at the table studying it. The house plan displayed a three-bedroom, one-story residence with a parking slab at the west end of the house. An approved building permit notice had been stapled to the blueprint, granting permission to the owner, Wayne Sullivan, to enclose the slab with an attached double-wide garage, extending from the front to the back of the house. To the left of the center of the house, the front door opened into the living room, which had a large window looking south, toward the street. A coat closet was indicated to the immediate left just past the entry door. Beyond the closet, the wall extended a few feet before ending; turning left would place one in the dining room. It, too, had a window that looked out at Woolman Street in front of the house. The dining room led into the kitchen, occupying the northwest corner of the original building.

A window over the kitchen sink on the north side of the house looked out into the backyard and the empty mineyard beyond the fence line. Madden traced a pathway through those areas with his finger. On the south end of the kitchen next to the west wall, a doorway led down a few stairs into an area that extended toward the front of the house. The area was a laundry room and was parallel to the dining room. The laundry room had two additional doors located within it. One went west and was most likely the original entry from outdoors on the side of the house. Now it served to connect the garage with the house. The second door within the laundry room was at the foot of the short stairway to the kitchen. Going through that door would lead one down a flight of stairs into the unimproved basement. In the garage, there was an additional doorway. Located at the back or north end, it opened onto the property's backyard. According to the floor plan, the basement had never been finished and was only concrete walls with a partial concrete slab on which the gas-fired heating source and gas water tank were installed.

One of the driving factors in getting rid of the house was the fact that there was a significant level of radon gas, most likely due to the deposits in the ground beneath. No family with children would seriously consider purchasing the building, and when Alkaheem was interested, Sullivan jumped at the opportunity to get it sold.

Addis had followed his partner's tracing finger, and now he traced a new path from the front entrance. Moving across the living room from the front door toward the back of the house, one would go through an opening. A wall blocked any movement to the left, and a person would have no alternative but to turn to the right into a hallway that extended to the east wall of the house. There were four doorways along the hall. Three on the left, or back of the house, and one on the right. The first door on the left as one proceeded down the hall opened into the main bathroom. Beyond that each of the next two doors opened into bedrooms. The bathroom and first bedroom each had smaller windows looking into the backyard. The second bedroom, because it was on the northeast corner of the building, had two windows. One window looked into the backyard and the other window looked east, toward the Continental Divide mountain range that formed the eastern border of the Butte/Silver Bow valley.

The one door shown on the right side of the hallway, toward the front of the house, allowed entry to the master bedroom. The master bedroom, located east of the living room, had a window that looked out beyond the end of the house and a second that provided a view of the street. A small bathroom was connected to the master bedroom, as was a walk-in closet that was accessible from either the bathroom or the master bedroom.

FLOOR PLAN FOR 565 EAST WOOLMAN

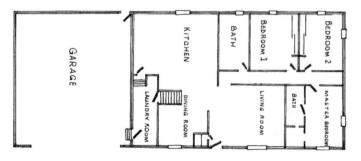

The two agents offered ideas for setting up the raid and had come to an agreement when someone knocked at the door. Madden walked over and let in O'Billovich and Jimmy McCarthy. The sheriff introduced McCarthy to the two agents as his TRT commander. O'Billovich looked at Madden and said, "This is your baby, Steve. Our guys will follow your lead. You just tell us what you want, what you need, and we'll do it." McCarthy nodded in agreement with his boss's commitment to the federal officers.

Addis discussed the street, the neighborhood, and the location of the house to be raided. He spoke of the importance that the team remained hidden until given the "go" command by Steve Madden. He pointed to the exit door from the garage leading out to the backyard and to the rear windows of the two bedrooms along the back of the house. Pointing at these potential exits, he emphasized the importance of not allowing any of the suspects to get over the cyclone fencing that separated the yard from the abandoned mineyard beyond. In the end, Addis committed a squad of officers to enter the mine yard from the east and to move undetected to a position behind the house. At that point, they would use the underbrush and bushes for concealment and cut the cyclone chain line, allowing them to sneak through and prevent a rear escape route.

Then Madden took a turn. He pinned the blueprint onto the top frame of the white board so all could see. Going through each room, he showed where the windows and doors were located and then to the individual closets, places armed suspects could be lying in wait for the Tactical Response Team members as they rushed through. Drawing their attention to the basement, he noted that though the blueprint did not show individual rooms, they had to be prepared for their existence since many people remodeled basements without filing for building permits or submitting plans to the local community offices.

As for the frontal attack, Madden recommended that the team try a two level approach. First he, Madden, would go to the door under some false pretense and attempt to gain entry into the house for the purpose of getting a first-hand evaluation of the layout and the number of suspects inside and, just as important, where they were located.

During his phony evaluation, he would be wearing a monitor so that the commander, McCarthy, O'Billovich, and Addis would be able to hear his descriptions as he talked to himself. After his exit, he would evaluate the attack plan and make changes if needed.

Initially, the majority of the team members would wait in two unmarked vans, one parked on Woolman before the suspect's house and the other around the corner from Woolman, on Arizona. The vehicles would arrive at different times so as not to arouse suspicion. Madden would arrive in a work van, concealing several more members. When given the "go" command, the members would rush at two points, the garage door and the main entry door. Two smaller assault teams would go wide, one left and the other right. One of the two squads would cover the windows on the east end and the back of the house. The other team, going left or around the west end of the house, would cover the walk-through door from the garage to the backyard and would enter when it was opened by Madden.

O'Billovich inquired what cover Madden would use to enter the house. After some discussion, they settled on a Pacific Power and Light uniform. The advantage was that his name would not need to be sewn onto the shirt; rather, he would only need a simple photo ID badge that could be made up easily. In addition, he could use an actual PP&L work van, which made the ruse more believable.

The lawmen discussed timing, and Madden, looking at his watch, said, "It's 3:48 right now. Can we have our guys ready, say, at 7:00 p.m.? That puts most people in their homes and not coming or going on the streets. Let's have the utility people power off the streetlight on the corner. The remaining light will be almost gone, giving our guys the advantage of cover. The disadvantage, as I see it, is that we'll be going from the darker areas outdoors into light if they have the lights on, but in this case, I think, the advantage of surprise outweighs that negative."

O'Billovich looked at McCarthy and asked for his opinion. The TRT team commander thought for a moment and then nodded and agreed with Madden's plan. "I think it's doable, Ken. I like the plan and having that much time to prepare; getting onsite will be pretty simple. I'll make sure each of my squad commanders has an earpiece and mic for communication. In about an hour, I'll send a van and have the driver, in plain clothes, walk to a neighbor's house, gain entry, and remain inside to insure the residents' safety. About half an hour later, between five thirty and six, a second van will do the same, the driver going to a different neighbor's home. Around six thirty, a third vehicle will drive into the abandoned mine yard from the west entry gate, locking it behind them. The vehicle will advance to the head frame, and two officers will appear to work at the base of the structure. Meanwhile a squad of four officers will move forward, slowly and under cover, until they reach the point directly behind the house. They'll cut the chain link to allow them access when the time comes. The remaining assault team will be in Madden's van awaiting his "go" command."

Addis and Madden looked at their counterparts. No one had anything else to question or offer. Madden spoke, "Ok, let's do this and get it right. Lives depend upon us."

O'Billovich stood and told Madden he would have a PP&L van brought to the hotel parking lot and left, and he would make arrangements with Wayne Sullivan for the corner streetlight to be shut down. Asked for a photo to use on the ID badge, Madden produced one from his notebook and gave it to the sheriff. "You'll find your new ID on the uniform coat pocket," O'Billovich said.

With that the local lawmen left. Madden and Addis retreated to their respective rooms to change. They each would need their side arms and their vests that protected their chest and abdominal area from firearm penetration. Madden took a few minutes to call his wife, Lee, spoke quietly with her and then visited with his children, each of whom was very excited to visit with Daddy. Then having Lee back on the phone, Madden assured her that he would be home within forty-eight hours. After he hung up, Steve again went over his scenario and double-checked his equipment and firearm. He knew he kept his sidearm in its optimal operating condition, and out of nervous habit, he looked it over again, making sure it was loaded and action ready. He knew that two doors down, his partner, though younger, was highly trained and was going through the same ritual with his equipment. Convinced he was ready, he went out of his room, down the hall, and knocked on Addis's door.

When his junior partner opened the door, Madden asked if he would like to join him for a brief walk and catch a light meal. Addis agreed, and the two left the hotel.

It was five-thirty when they returned to their rooms and collected their equipment, their flak jackets, and weapons hidden in duffle bags. As they entered the Pacific Power and Light vehicle, Addis moved to one of the two bench seats that had been placed along either side of the enclosed back of the van. Madden reached over to the passenger seat and picked up a gray shirt with blue piping and the appropriate lettering over the left-hand breast pocket. Having slipped on the shirt, he then put on the matching gray jacket with the same lettering in the same spot and his ID badge pinned to the right side. Next, he adjusted the band on a dark blue baseball cap with the company's logo on the front but put it back on the seat. Then Madden looked over a clipboard with all the correct paperwork, familiarizing himself with it for his ruse. Finally, he retrieved an official-looking gadget that flashed a red or green light, depending upon which hidden button Madden pressed under the handle. Pressing the red-light button also produced a beeping sound. Madden smiled, appreciating the bit of humor in such a serious adventure.

Starting the van's engine, Madden backed out of the parking space and slowly drove around the loop of the parking garage. As he reached the farthermost end of the garage, he stopped to allow the back door of the van to open and eight fully armed commandoes quickly and quietly entered and took seats on the two benches. Jerry McCarthy entered last and pulled the door closed behind him. "All set, Steve," McCarthy indicated. Madden, without looking back, began to drive the van to its destination. As the van advanced through the streets toward 565 East Woolman, Addis quickly emptied his duffle bag and prepared himself by donning his vest, gun and holster, handcuffs, and cap. He also reached between his feet and unpacked Madden's duffle bag so his partner would be able to get ready for the assault in short order.

The van pulled up in front of the target at 5:55 p.m. Madden picked up the clipboard and his electronic gadget. Before exiting, he reached under his jacket and pressed a button on a thin cord that ran under his shirt. "Jerry, Jim, do you two copy?" Both lawmen replied affirmative out loud so Madden could hear them. Since he had no ear bud through which to hear any reply, he did not check with O'Billovich. He was wired for one-way communication only, for the sole purpose of allowing his fellow assault leaders to hear what he found in the house—provided he got in.

Madden took a deep breath and let it out very slowly, calming his nerves and slowing his breathing rate. Then he stepped out into the darkening daylight and walked up to the front door of 565 East Woolman. He rang the doorbell, and the door opened. A Middle Eastern gentleman Madden instantly recognized as Anwar Ramana from the images received through Immigration stood before him. Madden introduced himself as Phil Green from Pacific Power and Light, a company, he reminded the man, that also provided natural gas. He then spun a story about complaints of insufficient gas being supplied in the neighborhood and he was checking each house so that a natural gas explosion would be avoided.

The ruse worked, and Anwar stepped aside, letting Madden in. He then said he needed to check each room to make sure there was no gas leaking in any of them as gas lines ran under the flooring to the furnace and hot water tank located in the basement. He slowly walked around the living room, holding the gadget so it pointed to the wall. Periodically he would depress the green light button. "Everything looks good in the living room, sir. No leak is evident in here. Let's check the other rooms." To Addis and the other members of the assault team, who heard the comment, it carried a message that no one was in the room except for the one who had admitted Madden.

Next, the two men went to the master bedroom and repeated the staged examination with the same result. The same occurred in the two remaining bedrooms and the main bathroom. Madden then followed Anwar to the dining room and then to the kitchen, pretending to test the air in each of the rooms. "So far, so good," Madden informed the resident. "Nice layout of the house, sir. It must be really quiet with nothing behind the house." The comment relaxed Ramana, and he thanked him for his compliment and added that nights were especially quiet with no neighbors or streets there.

Checking the laundry room, Madden again pressed the green light button, as he had for every other room to indicate there was not a gas problem. He asked about the garage and Anwar opened it. "This is impressive," commented Madden as he stepped into the garage. "You could put at least two full-sized vehicles in here as large as it is." He walked around the garage's inside perimeter. "Really good looking door here," he said, knocking on it with his hand as if admiring it though he really was checking it for accessibility from outside by the assault team. "Is this aluminum that's insulated?" he asked Anwar. Anwar nodded that it was a thick door to keep the cold out and, as Madden thought, to keep sound in.

Motioning to the exit door at the back of the garage, he asked if that was an exit. He was told that it was a door to the backyard. Without knowing it, Anwar was participating in the description of his own security for the waiting assault teams. When the two stepped back into the kitchen, Madden stepped toward a closed door, the one which, according to blueprints, was to the basement. He reached for the knob to enter but found it locked. He turned to Anwar and asked him to unlock it so he could check the room. Anwar told him it went to a dirt basement, they never used it, and he did not have the key. He said that his cousin and roommate, Raul, had the key but he was gone for the moment. In Madden's mind, as well as in the minds of McCarthy, Addis, and O'Billovich, it was a very strong indicator that if the missing agents and Senator Carson were being held in the house, it was through that door.

Walking back to the front door, Madden shook hands with Anwar, and thanked him for his cooperation. He stopped long enough to falsify a report form, scribbled his phony initials at the bottom, and after obtaining Anwar's signature acknowledging the house had been checked except for the basement, tore off the carbon copy, which he handed to Anwar, closed his metal clipboard with built in storage box, and turned and walked down the steps to his waiting van. He climbed into the van, started the engine, and drove around the corner, out of sight of the house on East Woolman, giving the appearance he was moving on to another house. He stopped and changed his shirt and jacket, replacing them with his flak jacket, gun and holster, and dark blue cap with FBI in gold on the crown. The time was 6:32. Twenty-eight minutes to assault time. Everyone in the van sat quietly. Each member of the team was mentally reviewing the procedure for the upcoming attack. One question crept into Madden's brain and that was the location of the dark-colored SUV. Since it was not in the garage, and Anwar had indicated Raul was gone, the question was, where was it and when would it return. The minutes ticked away—now 6:58 and time to get ready to move.

Chapter Twenty-one

Madden contemplated the upcoming conflict. The more he thought of it, the more concerned he became over the whereabouts of the SUV. It would not be good if all of the assault team were to be inside when it arrived and the occupants of the vehicle were armed.

Steve depressed the button on the two-way radio that was clipped to the top of the right shoulder of his vest. "Sheriff, do you copy?"

An audible click, "Back at ya, Steve," came the husky voice.

"You heard as I did the walk-through, Ken? I didn't see anyone else, but as you know I didn't get to go to the basement. I'm concerned that the SUV is not there and that at least Raul is gone. That leaves Donatelle and Hassan unaccounted for."

"How do you want to handle it, Steve?"

"Let's cool our heels for a while and see if the vehicle arrives. The darker it is, the easier not to be observed in approaching the house."

"That is a copy, Steve. I'll notify my guys here; have McCarthy tell his squad leaders."

"Will do, Ken. I'll get back to you in a few. Over and out."

Another forty minutes passed with no movement. All the while, Madden was studying the floor plan that was firmly etched into his mind's eye. He looked at a Toyota 4Runner that was parked across the street. Suddenly it came to him. He clicked his two-way again. "Madden here."

"Go ahead, Steve."

"I want to review some our assault plan with you. We know the windows of the SUV all around are limo-black tint, right? As the vehicle begins to enter the garage, the door will be going up. Even with the interior light on, it'll be next to impossible for the driver to see anything immediately behind him. I'll take one of the guys in here with me now, and we'll set up by the hedge that's along the left of the driveway. When the vehicle goes past and the door opens, the driver's attention will be on the doorway and entering the garage. The two of us will circle behind the SUV as it goes by and hug the tailgate, entering the garage at the same time. Most likely the door will close before anyone exits the vehicle, and when they do, we'll stick them with the Tasers. As that door closes, Jerry will give the "go" command for the rest of the team to move. Once we have the personnel from the SUV under control, we'll open the walk-in garage door. That'll allow an easy access for the team attacking the west end of the house."

"Sounds good," came the reply from the sheriff. "Jerry and Jim, okay with that?"

Madden glanced at the two seated on the benches immediately behind him. Both gave a thumb's up signal, indicating their approval. "They both are go, chief."

"Copy that, Steve. Good luck. Out."

Madden spoke to the TRT leader. "Jerry, who goes with me?"

Without any hesitation, McCarthy pointed to the young man seated next to Addis on the other side of the van. "Vic's your man, Steve."

The young man in his early thirties looked at Madden and nodded.

"MacCormick's been battle tested many times with the Los Angeles S.W.A.T., and I have no reservations. He's excellent with firearms and carries a black belt in martial arts."

"Ok, that's great. Vic, let's get into position by the hedge."

"Yes, sir!" the officer responded, rising from his seat and heading for the back door of the van. MacCormick stepped out onto the street and as he observed Madden step out of the driver's door, he began a run across the street, joining Madden as they made their hasty way to the hedge. Once there, they took only seconds to conceal themselves within the hedge, in a position from which they could easily step out onto the driveway and get behind the vehicle.

Madden, clicked his radio button and said softly, "Birds are in the bush. Wait for McCarthy's signal."

McCarthy responded, "Numbers one and two ready," indicating him and Addis, respectively. The sheriff then replied, "Copy that. We await the "go."

Minutes seem to crawl, and Madden knew that the longer the team's members had to wait, the tenser they might become. The Tactical Response Team, waiting for the command to go, reacted much the same as an athletic team before the big game. Despite extensive training and practice and preparation for the confrontation, the teams knew each situation carried potential surprises. Having no way to identify the unknowns caused the tension to mount, which could interfere with the need for a balanced reaction to those events.

Madden, looking west along Woolman Street, saw a pair of headlights turn toward them. He gently tapped MacCormick's arm and the man nodded, shifting his feet in preparation of moving out fast. Then he clicked his radio, "Stand by. Vehicle approaching." No answer or reply was necessary. Madden knew that every man was being alerted and making their own final preparations, mentally as well as physically.

Watching the approaching vehicle, Madden's heart rate increased with each turn of the vehicle's wheels. Was it the SUV? The headlights grew larger as the vehicle drew closer. Then a flashing light on the lower right of the front. The vehicle turned to the right into a driveway three houses down. Madden clicked radio, "Wrong vehicle." He needed no more comment but knew everyone shared his disappointment. Again, like the athletic teams, law enforcement, as well as the military, looked forward to the battle for which they had prepared and hated the letdown in delayed action.

Several more minutes passed, and a new set of lights headed their way. "Stand by; another vehicle." Again, Madden tapped the shoulder of his comrade crouched beside him.

The vehicle grew closer. As it passed the street lamp just down the block, Madden studied the approaching vehicle. It was an SUV, and it was very dark, maybe dark blue or black. He clicked his radio. "This is it!" he spoke softly into his mic.

Madden's body tensed, ready for action. The SUV slowed and began to swing left into the driveway. The garage door opener hummed as the door began slowly to rise. A band of bright light flashed along the bottom edge, indicating the interior light of the garage had come on. As the vehicle rolled past the two crouching figures, Madden tapped MacCormick's shoulder. "Go," he whispered. Two crouching sillouettes stepped out from the hedge onto the concrete driveway, and two running steps later, they were both centered behind the large vehicle, continuing to crouch low to avoid the interior rearview mirror. The black SUV slowed and then came to a stop with them right behind, now in the garage. The humming repeated, bringing a rumbling sound as the double-wide, insulated aluminum door began dropping to the floor, shutting out the darkness of night behind it.

Madden, on the driver's side, pointed to the right side of the vehicle, indicating that his companion should go that way and handle anyone exiting on that side, implying he would take the driver's side. Both men withdrew Taser guns from their belted holsters. Slowly they moved to their respective sides of the Tahoe. The engines stopped, and Madden heard the door open, which meant the outside rearview mirror would no longer reveal him on the side. The vehicle lowered and then rose, indicating that the driver had exited from his seat. Madden stepped out beyond the side, turning and aiming his Taser simultaneously. He quickly squeezed the trigger, and the head of the tagging unit found its mark, sending a powerful and incapacitating surge of electricity into the victim, instantly making his immobile body drop to the concrete floor.

As he stepped quickly toward his subdued victim, Madden's trained eye swept the interior of the SUV for any remaining passengers. None present. Madden forcibly rolled the suspect over onto his stomach, pulled out his handcuffs, and snapped them onto the man's wrists. He then placed a strip of tape over the man's mouth to prevent him from yelling out any warning. At the same time Madden had stepped around the side, MacCormick had done the same on his side of the Tahoe. Seeing a person exiting the front door, the officer fired his Taser, striking the passenger on the back of the right shoulder, immobilizing him immediately. MacCormick ran forward, rolled the man over, and quickly applied the handcuffs to the wrists behind the man's back, and like Madden, placed a strip of tape over the secured suspect's mouth.

Madden called out to his partner, "All clear here," letting the young officer know that he was in control of his suspect.

"All clear here, sir," the officer replied.

MacCormick sprinted to the garage door and opened it. Immediately, members of the assault team stepped through. Preparing for the house entry, Madden and MacCormick led the small squad to the door to the laundry room, each with his side arm at the ready. As the small band reached the closed door, Madden grabbed the doorknob, opened it, and stepped through, turning toward the left. No one there. MacCormick went up the two steps, reached for the door to the kitchen, and opened it for his team as he stepped back down to clear the way. Two officers sprang through the door; the first looked right, the second stepped into the kitchen beyond the first officer. MacCormick ran back up the steps, followed by Madden and two other officers, one carrying a battering ram. As they approached the steps, Madden heard "pop, pop, pop," the unmistakable sound of rapid small-arms fire. MacCormick, entering the kitchen, dropped to his stomach, took quick aim, and squeezed three shots in rapid succession in the direction of the dining room. There was a loud crash and then silence. Unfortunately, the second officer of the assault team coming through the door from the laundry room and into the kitchen had found the armed Anwar Ramana the hard way. He lay on the floor, blood oozing from a wound in his upper right arm.

MacCormick raced over to the downed officer and determined that he was not critically or mortally wounded. Next MacCormick went to the assailant. He knew his fire had killed the suspect as his second shot had struck where the nose met the forehead. The officer took the victim's handgun and tucked it into his waistband. He then checked for any other weapons on the body and found none. MacCormick then proceeded through the living room where he met up with the assault unit coming through the front door of the house. Madden joined them and went to the entry of the hallway to secure the bedrooms.

Madden held up four fingers and pointed to his right, a reminder that there were four rooms along the hallway they were about to enter. Two officers quickly moved down the hallway, staying to the right side. Simultaneously, Madden and MacCormick quickly covered the distance on the left and secured the bathroom and then the two bedrooms along the back of the house. The other officers covered the master bedroom and its bathroom as well as walk-in closet. No suspects were found in any of the rooms. They had effectively swept the living area, incurring only two minor gunshot wounds to their team plus the dead terrorist. Re-entering the kitchen, Madden found himself standing next to Addis, who had come in through the front door at the end of the assault group. Turning to his partner, Madden spoke. "Ok, so much for the the main floor; now let's take out that basement door and see what's down there."

O'Billovich and McCarthy joined the agents. McCarthy turned and called one of his subordinates. "Mike, bring the ram! Let's take out that basement door."

A hulking form of a man stepped into the laundry room, carrying a metal battering ram. Quickly he moved to the side of the door, drew the ram back, and in one hard thrust, splintered the doorjamb. Three officers stepped through the broken door, only to be greeted by automatic fire from down the stairwell. The impact of the bullets threw the officers backward, leaving significant holes in their Kevlar vests. More fire and one of the officers let out a yell, grabbing instinctively for his left leg. The bullet had ripped through the flesh and muscle and shattered the femur. The assault officer's foot hung at a strange angle as two other fellow officers, standing immediately behind those making the initial entry, grabbed the man by the shoulders and dragged him back up into the safety of the kitchen, away from the gunfire.

Lying on his back as a result of the initial impact, one of the two remaining officers first through the door pointed his automatic rifle down the stairs and squeezed the trigger. Five shots flew downward. Then the basement shooter fired again, striking the vest of another officer trying to get out of the way. By now, Madden and Addis had arrived, and as the fire burst ceased, Madden stepped into the doorway and fired at the figure crouching at the bottom of the stairs. Just enough light from upstairs illuminated the darkened stairwell so that Madden could make out the crouching figure. Aiming and firing at the same time, his bullets found flesh and bone, and then all went silent. Madden slowly descended, taking the steps one at a time, never moving his eyes from the motionless figure, and keeping his gun aimed on the suspect while also being aware of any movement elsewhere in the basement. The figure remained still. Madden reached the man who was covered in blood from Madden's shots. All three had created mortal wounds, one in the head, one dead center in the chest, penetrating the heart, and the third penetrating the larynx and trachea. Madden kicked the automatic rifle away from the victim and rolled the body over. The face, unmistakable despite the blood, of Raul Alkaheem stared back at him in the coldness of death.

The basement was exactly as the assault team had pictured, with no walls creating rooms and only a portion of the floor covered in concrete, and then some—folding tables holding plastic packages stood against one wall. To a trained eye it was obvious what the multiple packages contained—a variety of drugs, likely prepared for distribution throughout Montana, the Pacific Northwest, and probably into Canada. "Sheriff, your narcotics division will have fun processing all of this stuff," commented Madden to the sheriff.

The other side of the basement held several sleeping cots and folding chairs. Madden tapped Addis on the shoulder and pointed directly straight across the basement from the stairwell. Many piles of earth, each about three or four feet in height, lined the east wall from the back all the way to the front of the house. Someone had been doing some serious digging somewhere nearby. As their eyes scanned the mounds of dirt, it struck them. At the base of the dirt was a layer of wood. At first it appeared to be just that, just a layer of wood planks. However, as the two agents approached, it they noticed hinges along one edge and a hasp with a padlock on the opposite side, nearest the stairwell. "I'll be," said Madden aloud. "It's a trap door. There must be another level under us!"

The officer with the bolt cutter appeared, and with a quick snap, the padlock was rendered useless. Several police officers aimed their firearms at the soon-to-be exposed entrance beneath the door. Madden reached down and quickly yanked the door open. A second and very steep stairwell of wooden steps greeted them. The team, led by Madden and Addis, descended to the bottom of the steps. The walls were dirt from the top all the way down the stairwell. At the bottom, they found an area of about five feet square on which to stand. On either side of the stairway landing was a heavy wooden door. Trying to open either one failed; they were both locked.

Again the battering ram was brought forward, and after Madden pointed to the door that went toward the back of the house, the officer holding the ram swung it hard and hit the door just above the door knob and latch. The door trembled but did not open. At second and then a third strike and the door released its lock and opened.

A thick rank waft of air escaped the room and greeted the men in the stairwell. Madden and now Addis and O'Billovich stepped through the doorway, and all three instinctively held their breath as the strong smell of stagnant air struck their nostrils. Through the very dim light, the officers studied the room, entirely of dirt covered over by wooden planks and, Addis guessed, about twelve by sixteen feet. At the end, two additional doors faced them. Forcing one of them open, the law officers found a closet-size room, no more than three feet by six feet, holding an emaciated man in tattered, filthy clothes. He was sitting in a corner, knees drawn up to the chest, arms around the legs. His face was unshaved, and he showed the telltale signs of imprisonment in such poor living conditions.

Madden reached to the prisoner. "I'm Steve Madden, FBI. What is your name?" The person's head looked up. A smile began to appear and quickly stretched the width of his face.

"I'm Phil Stephens, FBI," a weakened voice uttered. "Sure is good to see you, Agent Madden. Just about had given up on getting out of this hellhole."

Madden leaned down and placed his hands under the man's arm to assist him to a standing position. Slowly and carefully, Madden led the man to his freedom. "Jim, get the other." Madden nodded to the other cubicle.

Jim forced open the second of the doors, and as in the first, a bedraggled man sat on the floor. Helping him to his feet, Addis introduced himself, "Jim Addis, FBI. I presume you are Brad Williams?" The man smiled as he began to stand and nodded in the affirmative. "Good to see you Agent Williams," Addis added as he gently drew the man up and helped him exit his small cell. Open sores covered the bodies of both agents. Dehydrated and weak from lack of adequate food and fresh air, the men would need immediate medical attention. Officers of the assault team helped Williams and Stephens up the stairs and to a waiting ambulance for a quick trip to St. James Hospital for several weeks of recuperation.

Once the two missing agents had been taken upstairs, Madden had the battering-ram assault member approach the door on the other side of the staircase. This one, too, composed of very hard and apparently thick wood, needed several blows of the battering ram to force the door open enough to spring the latch and be pushed completely open.

As the assault team stormed inside, weapons drawn in readiness, they stopped short. An overhead light; one single bulb of no more than 25watts, emitted a faint light. The men strained to see in the dimness and then heard a rattling of chains from the back and darker end of the room. Madden cautiously moved forward. As he reached a point about three-quarters of the way across the room, his eyes could make out a figure sitting on what looked to be a mattress. Drawing closer he saw a face that he recognized, not from any personal contact but from a video he had watched a few days ago in Twin Falls, Idaho: Senator Jeremy Carson, junior senator from the State of Idaho. As Madden introduced himself to the senator, he noticed as in the film, the senator's badly swollen face barely revealing two slits of eyes, definite dark circles beneath both of them, and a nose unnaturally crooked. As the man stood to welcome his rescuers, Madden's eyes were drawn to the bandaged finger. Carson, seeing the gaze of the FBI agent, gamely smiled and told him what had happened when he refused to cooperate with his captors in making the videotape.

Calling for the bolt cutter, Madden walked the senator to a location under the light bulb. Though not the Royal Hilton, the lodging for the senator had several amenities over that of the two agents—room to move, a mattress, a bucket half full of water with a ladle, and, luxury of luxuries, a towel.

The requested bolt cutter came forward, and within seconds, the four metal bracelets fell from the wrists and ankles. Two of the Butte/Silver Bow police officers gingerly walked the senator up the two flights of stairs and out to an ambulance. Carson gladly accepted the ride, finally allowing himself to release the fear that he might not live much longer. Emergency Medical Technicians immediately began treating him for the cuts on his face, arms, and hands, and an air splint was placed over the shattered hand to provide support.

Agent Madden accompanied the senator to the ambulance, and as Carson was laid onto the gurney, he placed a comforting hand on the shoulder of the now freed hostage. "We will give you the night for treatment and rest, Senator. Agent Addis and I will be in to go over the details of your kidnapping and detention in the morning."

The very relieved and thankful man responded in a raspy voice, "Thank you, Steve, for what you and the others have done." Carson flashed a weak smile and lifted his left hand in a wave of appreciation as the attendants slid the gurney into the back of the ambulance and closed the doors.

Sheriff O'Billovich and his narcotics division chief, Hocking, remained in the basement to supervise the photographing and chronicling of the residence, including the main floor to show the exact location of Alkaheem's body, the stairwell to show the location of the body of the other dead kidnapper, followed by all the drugs and equipment used to separate, measure, and weigh the drugs and for repackaging for distribution. Photos were then taken of the hand-dug detention area, starting with the piles of dirt in the basement and the trap door, then moving down the steps to each of the holding areas and the individual cells occupied by the FBI agents and then the side of the crude prison that had held the senator. Each physical item had to be tagged and recorded in the evidence book before packing and transportation could be completed.

Other police officers placed the bodies of Raul Alkaheem and Anwar Ramana in black zipper body bags after photos had been obtained and then carried them to an unmarked van to transport them to the city/county morgue, located in the basement of the hospital, for the required autopsies.

Madden and Addis returned to the garage to examine the two handcuffed men who had arrived in the black SUV. The driver was identified as Ahmad Rahman Hassan, and the passenger was found to be Aaron Donatelle. The agents conducted a brief interrogation before walking the prisoners to a police cruiser, placing them in the rear seat, and speeding them off to the local jail. Meanwhile, a flatbed truck with a tilting bed backed on the drive and pulled the SUV, its transmission disengaged, up the inclined bed. The truck bed was then lowered and the SUV secured before being transported to the local impound garage for thorough examination and for use as evidence, if necessary.

Once the drugs and bodies of had been removed, the property was secured with new locks. The well-known yellow and black "CRIME SCENE—DO NOT ENTER" tape that had been stretched around the house and driveway once the house was secured was removed and official "DO NOT ENTER" notices were affixed to all entrances of the house and garage. O'Billovich assigned one of his local policemen, on a rotating basis, to remain with a patrol car to ensure security of the property until notified by the Butte/Silver Bow District Attorney's office that all evidence needed for the pending trials had been collected.

Able to relax with the knowledge that his direct involvement was no longer crucial, Madden walked to the north end of the now empty garage. Turning his back to the wooden counter that had been built along the wall, he jumped up and sat on it. After removing his Kevlar vest, he took his flip-phone from his pocket, opened it, and after highlighting the name of his superior officer, pressed "talk." When the desired voice answered at the other end, Madden gave a brief summary of the events, making a point of the fact that both of the missing federal agents had been rescued successfully and with recuperation would be "physically okay," as he put it. Then he explained the captivity of Senator Carson, informing the bureau's division chief that he would be ok and would be held at St. James Community Hospital for a day or two before being flown either to his home in Idaho or back to DC. A police guard would be assigned for security purposes at his hospital room's door. Madden finished his call with a comment that he and Agent Addis would complete the necessary written reports upon their return to the Washington office, after debriefing agents Phil Stevens and Brad Williams and Senator Carson and interrogating Donatelle and Hassan.

As his partner closed his flip-phone, Addis approached. Madden slid off the wood counter, and the two lawmen shared a friendly embrace and a "well done." "The medics say both of the officers will be ok, Steve," Addis reported. Then he offered, "Jerry Hocking thinks the street value of the confiscated drugs to be around one and a half million." Madden's friend and junior partner paused and then continued. "Williams and Stevens certainly were on the right track when they came here in their interstate drug investigation. Williams told me they were sure the drug routes were going through Butte and that the drugs, once arriving here, were then distributed east and west as well as north to Canada. They were about to call in the local narcotics guys when Alkaheem and Donatelle nabbed them."

Madden smiled and nodded his approval. "The raid went well, Jim. Now that everything here is under control, let's get out of here. I could use a steaming hot shower, some of that filling Butte food, and a relaxing drink."

Addis chuckled, "Have to say you are right on there, boss." The two bid the remaining police officers goodnight and walked to the van that had been loaned to them by the local power company.

"Think Sullivan would mind if we borrow his van one more time to ride back to the Finlen?" laughed Madden.

EPILOGUE

Over the next two days, the federal agents completed their interrogation of Hassan and Donatelle, and debriefed the field agents, Williams and Stevens, as well as Senator Carson. They had met with the local district attorney and briefed him on the case, assisted by the popular sheriff, Ken O'Billovich, and Narcotics Division Chief Jerry McCarthy, who had led the Butte/Silver Bow TRT assault team. Now finished with their duties in Butte, they would board the Bureau's jet in the morning and be whisked back to their homes on the East Coast. Both looked forward to returning to DC, but Madden, especially, longed to join his loving wife and wonderful children once more.

During the time Addis and Madden were finishing their investigation, the local authorities had returned to the crime scene and had gone over every inch of the residence. The local detectives found, just to right of the senator's privy, a moveable partition that could be opened by moving two pieces of the wood wall planking, revealing a "death" hole. Ten feet below the floor's surface, the emptiness gave way to water that dropped eleven hundred feet. It was the remnant of a mineshaft, now filled with the toxic water; anything dropped into it would eventually vanish without a trace.

Addis and Madden sat in a comfortable booth at Lydia's Restaurant, its old leaded glass windows lending a welcoming ambiance. They enjoyed the fantastic cuisine, but most of all this night, they relished each other's company and bathed in the satisfaction of two cases successfully brought to a close. For now, the two ate and laughed and reflected on how much good filled their lives. Loathe to end their dinner too soon, they took the waitress's suggestion and ordered an after-dinner drink. Picking up the goblets, they gently clinked glasses, and with a smile, toasted each other, "To finding the final stepping stone and crossing the stream."